Liz Eeles writes heartwarming and uplifting women's fiction about family secrets and relationships, and romantic comedies full of love and laughs. A former journalist, Liz wrote fiction in her spare time and thought becoming a published author was probably just a pipe dream – until she was shortlisted in two national novel writing competitions. That gave her the encouragement (and the kick in the pants) she needed to carry on writing and make her dream come true. Liz was brought up in Gloucestershire, but now lives on the Sussex coast with her family and can't imagine ever moving away from the sea.

ALSO BY LIZ EELES

Heaven's Cove series
A Letter to the Last House Before the Sea
The Girl at the Last House Before the Sea
The Key to the Last House Before the Sea
The Path to the Last House Before the Sea
The Sisters at the Last House Before the Sea
The Diary at the Last House Before the Sea

The Cosy Kettle series
New Starts and Cherry Tarts at the Cosy Kettle
A Summer Escape and Strawberry Cake at the Cosy Kettle
A Christmas Wish and a Cranberry Kiss at the Cosy Kettle

Salt Bay series
Annie's Holiday by the Sea
Annie's Christmas by the Sea
Annie's Summer by the Sea

Secrets
at the
Last House
Before
the Sea

LIZ EELES

bookouture

BOOKOUTURE

First published in 2021 by Bookouture, an imprint of Storyfire Ltd.
This paperback edition published in 2025

1

A CIP catalogue record for this book
is available from the British Library.

PB ISBN 978-1-83618-136-1
EB ISBN 978-1-83888-742-1

Printed and bound in Great Britain by
Clays Ltd, Elcograf S.p.A.

Papers used by Bookouture are from well-managed forests
and other responsible sources.

Bookouture
An imprint of Storyfire Ltd.
Carmelite House
50 Victoria Embankment
London EC4Y 0DZ

An Hachette UK Company

The authorised representative in the EEA is Hachette Ireland
8 Castlecourt Centre
Dublin 15 D15 XTP3
Ireland
(email: info@hbgi.ie)

www.hachette.co.uk
www.bookouture.com

For Ivor Frederick Eeles, the best dad a girl could have.
We miss you.

Prologue

My darling Saffy,

You are in my heart for as long as the world turns. Before you, my life was empty and cold, and your love has brought me more happiness than I deserve. The thought of our wedding day, and spending the rest of my life with you, fills me with joy.
Know that you are always loved.

J

Chapter One

Rosie turned the corner, into the salt-laced wind, and pushed up the collar of her jacket. She'd forgotten quite how chilly the English coast could be in early spring. Despite the grey clouds piling up over the sea, tourists on the quayside, with mottled bare legs, were still licking ice creams, grimly determined to enjoy their holidays before the rain set in.

Yes, Devon was just as she remembered it: dreary, damp and depressing. If only she was still in Spain, and she'd never got that phone call.

Seagulls screeched mournfully overhead as Rosie imagined herself under the tree in her Andalusian garden: her skin hot on the sun lounger, glimpses of azure sky through the palm fronds and bright splashes of Moorish tiles on her apartment wall.

Colours in southern Spain were vivid and vibrant, not muted and soft like here in Heaven's Cove. She stared at the moss-green waves breaking against the harbour wall and darkening the pale stone. Like the ebb and flow of the tides, nothing here ever seemed to change. It was the *same old, same old* year after year. Narrow lanes clogged with tourists, barn dances in the village hall, cholesterol-boosting cream teas for sale. Though after this week's shocking news, she didn't suppose anything would be quite the same for her ever again.

'Oi, watch out, Lily, or you'll run that lady over.'

Rosie gathered her thoughts and side-stepped swiftly to avoid a girl on a pink bicycle with stabilisers. The dark-haired child wobbled past her on the pavement, scraping along the side of Rosie's battered suitcase.

'I'm so sorry. She got the bike for her birthday but hasn't got the hang of steering yet.' The short, curvy woman chasing after the youngster stopped suddenly and buried her hands deep into the pockets of her grey hoodie. 'Um, aren't you…?'

She trailed off as Rosie scoured her memory for the woman's name. It began with a V, she was sure of it. Veronica? Violet? No, Vanessa, that was it. Though she was known as Nessa at school and nicknamed The Loch Nessa Monster – not because she was scary but because, like the fabled creature, she was rarely seen. Nessa was a serial truant. And now a mother, it seemed.

Rosie huddled further into her jacket as dark spots of rain began to splatter on the cobbled pavement. 'I'm Rosie. We were at school together. I think you were in the year below me.'

'Ah, that's it.' Nessa nodded, her tone suggesting she already knew exactly who Rosie was. 'I haven't seen you around here in a while.'

'I've been living abroad for the last few years.'

'Yeah, I can tell. You didn't get that tan in Heaven's Cove.' Nessa shifted from foot to foot and ran a hand along her shiny, brown ponytail. 'I was really sorry to hear what happened to your mum, by the way. It was such a shame. Hey, Lily, stay there and wait for Mummy, please.'

Such a shame. Rosie blinked behind her sunglasses, the knot in her chest tightening. 'Thank you. It was a huge shock.'

'It must have been. I guess that's why you're here.'

'I needed to come back for a week or two. I've already been to the funeral home in Exeter. There's a lot to be sorted out.'

'I can imagine. Your mum's death was a shock to all of us, coming out of the blue like that. And it doesn't seem right that her home is empty now. It looks kind of sad.'

For the first time since arriving in the village, Rosie allowed herself to glance up at Driftwood House. Her family home, perched high on the cliffs above Heaven's Cove, did look rather lonely with its blank windows reflecting the steely sky.

She looked away quickly. Crying in front of someone from school wouldn't do. News of her distress would spread around the village like wildfire and then a stream of people would come to the house, offering condolences and veiled disapproval that she had, to all intents and purposes, abandoned her mother.

Why hadn't she come back to Heaven's Cove last month when she'd had a few days off work? Instead, she'd spent the time decorating her apartment and drinking sangria in the sunshine with friends.

Rosie pushed her fingernails into the palm of her hand, willing herself to stay in control for a while longer. 'It's really sad,' she agreed, unsure if she was referring to her mother's death, or the fact that the house now stood alone and empty.

Nessa nodded and ruffled Lily's hair. The girl had given up waiting and wobbled back along the narrow pavement. 'So will you be staying in Heaven's Cove for long?'

'I certainly hope not.'

The words were out before Rosie could stop them and Nessa's face fell. 'I dare say Devon is a bit boring after all your travels. Which amazing place are you living in at the moment, then?'

'I've been in Andalusia for the last eighteen months, in southern Spain.'

'Yes, I know where Andalusia is,' replied Nessa, with an almost imperceptible eye-roll. 'What do you do there, then, in exotic, faraway Andalusia?'

It was hard to tell if she was being sarcastic or was truly interested in her life.

'This and that.' Rosie shrugged, keen to bring the conversation to a close. 'I'm working part-time in a B&B and the rest of the time for a property company, mostly flogging apartments with sea views.'

'That sounds wonderful.'

Rosie nodded, though showing hot, sweaty people around tiny flats was less wonderful than Nessa seemed to imagine. Especially when the promised 'sea view' turned out to involve leaning over the side of a balcony on tiptoe, to catch a glimpse of the sparkling ocean. She'd grown used to potential buyers' excitement turning to disappointment but it made her feel uncomfortable nonetheless.

Nessa was still staring at her. 'Um, what are you up to these days?' asked Rosie, taking off her sunglasses and wiping spots of rain from the lenses.

'Oh, nothing as exciting. I'm working part-time in Shelley's hardware store and bringing up this little one, of course.' She smiled down at Lily, before pulling a tissue from her pocket and scrubbing at the dark stain around the child's mouth. 'Birthday chocolate! She doesn't usually eat sweets. I'm not the kind of mother who fills her kids full of sugar to shut them up, in spite of what some people think. Single parents get a bad press, specially round here where everyone has an opinion.' Nessa's cheeks flushed. 'Sorry. I don't mean to get on my soapbox but this place does my head in sometimes.'

Rosie smiled, her facial expressions on autopilot. 'I know what you mean. But I'm sure you're doing a brilliant job. I admire anyone who's bringing up kids.'

'Really?' When Nessa grinned, the crease between her eyebrows disappeared.

'Really. How old is your daughter?'

'She was four two days ago.'

'Is she your only one?'

'Yeah, thank goodness. One's quite enough for me.'

When Rosie nodded, too wrung out for more small talk, Nessa glanced at her watch. 'Look, I'd better be getting on but it was good to see you again. And I am so sorry about your mum. I know what it's like.'

A vague memory surfaced in Rosie's mind, of Nessa's mother passing away years ago after an illness. She'd wondered at the time if Nessa was truanting from school to look after her. And now both of them were motherless.

'Nothing feels real at the moment. I keep thinking it's all a mistake, a really horrible mistake, and I haven't even cried yet. Is that wrong?'

Rosie hadn't meant to blurt that out, but Nessa seemed unfazed. 'Nah, I reckon that's totally normal. It's the shock of it all. I didn't cry for ages and then I couldn't stop.' She hesitated for a moment, lost in a memory, before grabbing Lily's hand. 'Look, losing a parent is rubbish but you'll get through it. Honest. And if you need anything, just look me up in Shelley's. I seem to spend most of my life there.'

'Thanks. I appreciate that.'

With a nod, Nessa scurried off with her daughter, and Rosie picked up her suitcase. That might have been her life if she'd stayed in Heaven's Cove. She could be bringing up young children and working part-time selling rubber rings to tourists. Would that have been so bad? At least she'd have been close when her mum needed her, and her mum would have so loved being a gran.

An image of her mother lifting up a child and laughing flitted into her mind. She wasn't sure if it was a memory or a might-have-been, and the knot in her chest tightened until it was hard to breathe.

'Just. Stop. Thinking!' she said out loud. A middle-aged man in baggy shorts glanced at her nervously and ushered his family away from the crazy lady.

This wouldn't do. Rosie gulped down the deepest breath she could manage and focused on the brightly painted fishing boats bobbing at the quay. She took in the gentle slap of waves against stone and the scent of the briny air, and gradually her torturous thoughts began to slow.

Everything was so familiar here, even after being away for so long. And at least her first encounter with someone from her past had gone smoothly. She'd been worried that habitual feelings of not belonging in this tight-knit community would come flooding back. Her face had never seemed to fit around here. But Nessa had been pretty decent, actually, so maybe returning to Heaven's Cove and facing her old school friends and neighbours wouldn't be as bad as she feared.

Buoyed up by this thought, Rosie ducked into one of the narrow lanes that led away from the sea and walked past a row of whitewashed cottages. She'd certainly imagined the villagers being less welcoming during her journey back to England: a three-hour flight from Málaga that seemed to last forever. The plane had been full of happy holidaymakers coming back from trips away, their high spirits contrasting sharply with her grief and guilt.

'Maybe it'll be OK being back in Heaven's Cove,' murmured Rosie, ignoring the fact that she was talking to herself again. 'It's going to be all right.'

But when a barrel-shaped woman stepped out of the fishmonger's with a parcel wrapped in newspaper, Rosie's brief flash of positivity did a nosedive. There were two people she was desperately hoping to avoid during her stay. One of them was Katrina Crawley, who'd been a right cow to her at school and never missed a chance to put her down. The other was Belinda Kellscroft, who was now homing in on her like a heat-seeking missile. It was ages since they'd last met and Belinda knew very little about Rosie's life now, but that wouldn't stop her from commenting. Belinda commented on everything and everyone at length, whether she was well informed or not.

Rosie put her head down and picked up speed but it was too late. Belinda stopped directly in front of her, parcel tucked into her bag, hands on her hips and the gold rings on her fingers glinting in the watery sunlight peeping through cloud.

'Rose Merchant, as I live and breathe. So you finally made it home.'

She pursed her lips, no more words needed because her sour expression said it all: *Such a shame you only came back after your mother's death.*

Rosie tensed, noticing the extra grey in the tight perm that curled around Belinda's lined face. She'd had the same hairstyle for as long as Rosie could remember.

'I've only just arrived. I got the first flight I could after… after I heard the news. A doctor called me from the hospital.'

Though it hadn't been Rosie who'd taken the call. She'd been too busy cooking paella and drinking wine in the kitchen of her sunny apartment to answer her ringing phone. Matt had answered it instead, which upset Rosie hugely – not only was she a thousand miles away when her mother had a stroke, she hadn't even been the first to know that something was wrong. What kind of daughter was she?

Belinda sniffed as though she knew exactly what kind of daughter Rosie was. 'I'm very sorry for your loss. Poor, poor Sofia to be taken so soon. Tell me, when were you last back in Heaven's Cove?'

'I'm not sure. It must be about three years.'

'Such a long time.'

'I guess so, but Mum regularly came out to visit me, wherever I was.'

The newspaper around Belinda's parcel crackled when she folded her arms, crushing her bag against her chest. 'Sofia showed off her holiday photos to everyone in the village. She lived for those visits.'

'And we Skyped a lot when she was over here. All the time, really.'

Sorrow washed over Rosie as it hit her there would be no more internet calls, no more picking up Mum from foreign airports, no more sending her pics of hot and dusty Spain on WhatsApp. It still didn't seem real.

'Hmm, well, I suppose that was better than nothing. And it's good you're back now. I dare say there will be a lot to sort out up at the house.'

'I expect so. That's where I'm going now.'

'Right.' Belinda's sharp features softened. 'If you need any help, don't forget that we're all here and watching over you.'

She was only trying to be nice. Rosie knew that, but the back of her neck still prickled. She always felt claustrophobic in Heaven's Cove with its tiny, cobbled streets that were jammed with tourists in the summer months. Even the cove itself had a hemmed-in feel, with its crescent of bright sand curbed by cliffs at either end. But it was the constant feeling of being watched that had got to her as a teenager.

She couldn't put a foot out of line without someone – usually Belinda – reporting back to her mum. Whether it was sitting with her legs dangling over the cliff edge, jumping off rocks into the cool sea, or skipping out of school at lunchtime to buy chips, the gossips of Heaven's Cove made sure that her mother heard about every minor transgression.

'Thank you, Belinda,' said Rosie, her throat tightening. 'But I'm sure I'll be fine.'

'You'll be jetting back to Greece or Italy, or wherever it is you're living now, before you know it. Everything done and dusted and Heaven's Cove forgotten forever.'

Rosie nodded, not trusting herself to speak, as Belinda launched into one of her infamous gossip-fests. 'Did your mother keep you up to date with village news while you were away? Did you hear that Phyllis Collins has moved to Exeter to live with her awful niece, Serena near the quay has taken up with a chartered accountant, and Simon in the old coastguard's cottage has decided he's gay?'

Rosie nodded again, although it was the first she'd heard of any of it – unlike Belinda, her mum didn't revel in passing on village gossip. She was also sure that Simon hadn't simply 'decided' to be gay, as Belinda had so succinctly put it.

'And we've just carried out repairs on the village hall roof because the old one was leaking like a sieve. I ended up chairing the fundraising committee, of course. If you want a good job done around here, do it yourself.' Her laugh juddered through Rosie like nails down a blackboard. Belinda was mostly well meaning, but she was hard to cope with on a day like today.

Rosie stepped into the road and moved around her. 'Sorry not to stop and chat but I'd better get to Driftwood House.'

'Oh yes, of course. As I say, we're all very sorry about your mother. Sofia was an unusual woman – a bit of a hippy, really. But she was one of us and we'll miss her. Look after yourself, my dear.'

A hippy? That was probably fair enough. Her mum was never happier than when walking barefoot over the cliffs, with wild flowers threaded into her long hair. Rosie batted away the painful memory and walked along the lane, dragging her suitcase over the cobbles and feeling Belinda's eyes on her back until she turned the corner.

Chapter Two

At the edge of the village, where the lane became a rutted track, Rosie picked up her suitcase and started climbing up and up the steep path. It was wide enough for a car, though few drivers risked their suspension. That was why her mum had driven an ancient midnight-blue Mini.

There's no point in shelling out on a fancy car, Rosie. It'll only get wrecked by the potholes or the salt spray when a storm's blowing in.

Rosie spotted the rusty car when she reached the end of the track. It was parked on the grass at an odd angle, as though the driver had leaped out, keen to get on with her day. That was Mum all over, always full of ideas and enthusiasms and never still. It was hard to take in that such a big personality could be snuffed out by such a tiny blood clot. It just didn't seem possible.

Abandoning her suitcase, Rosie walked to the edge of the cliff and looked back at the house which faced the green-grey sea.

From the village, the house looked the same as it had for decades, with its bumpy whitewashed walls and dark tiled roof – too big to be described as a cottage, too small to be described as grand.

But up close, Rosie could see that ocean winds and rain had taken their toll in the three years since she'd last been home. The bottom of the wooden front door was swollen as though it might burst, and paint on the walls had bubbled into huge blisters. Driftwood House looked sad, as if in mourning for her mother.

Images suddenly cascaded through Rosie's mind: her mum laughing during her last trip to Spain; the look on her face when Rosie said she wasn't ever planning on coming home for good; her body at the funeral home. 'I'm so sorry, Mum, if I let you down,' whispered Rosie. But her words were whipped away by the wind and carried out over the white-tipped waves towards France.

Rosie unlocked the front door and used her shoulder to shove the bloated timber across the hall tiles. The last time she'd been home, the house was filled with the smell of freshly baked biscuits and caramelised sugar. Mum was always on a mission to feed her up. But today only a musty aroma of damp and dust greeted her when she dragged her suitcase into the house and pushed the door closed behind her.

'OK, I'm back, so what happens now?' Was talking to herself a normal symptom of grief? Matt had googled 'grief' on his phone while she was desperately trying to book a flight, but she couldn't remember what he'd said about it. He hadn't been terribly helpful, actually.

'When will you be back, Rosie? I need you,' were his final words as she shoved her suitcase into the taxi. As though she was letting him down by going back to England.

Rosie gave her head a shake to dislodge the memory and started walking around the house, almost expecting her mum to leap out from behind a door and give her a hug.

See, love, it was *all a big mistake after all. Of course I'm not dead. Now get yourself unpacked and we'll have a walk to Sorrell Head before tea.*

But there was no Mum, no mistake – just an empty house that had become shabby and worn since she was last here. Rosie noticed damp patches on the walls and windows rattling in the sea breeze as she moved from room to room like a ghost. When did Driftwood House start to fall apart?

After going back to the kitchen and making herself a cup of Earl Grey, she sat in the silent conservatory and gazed at the view. Built on the back of the house, this room lacked a sea vista. But the view was magnificent, nonetheless, overlooking acres of rural Devon that stretched in a soft green swathe towards Dartmoor in the west. People would pay, thought Rosie, to enjoy such an amazing panorama while sheltered from blustery clifftop winds.

This was where she would play as a child when the weather was too poor for a walk. And when the sun finally came out, she'd sit here and watch her mother gardening. The tiny kitchen garden, with its pots of herbs and tubs of potato plants, was her mother's sanctuary from the stresses of life, and was created in the months after Rosie's father left. He'd moved to Milton Keynes when she was ten, and lived there with a succession of girlfriends until he died of cancer eight years ago. Their relationship had suffered after he left, but they'd still loved each other.

Rosie picked up the framed photo of her mum and dad in the windowsill and brushed her finger across their faces. She'd insisted on having a photo of her dad in the house after their divorce and her mum had never put it away, even after Rosie moved out. Maybe she'd still loved him too, just a little bit.

That reminded her. Pulling her mobile phone from her bag, Rosie checked for calls from Matt but there hadn't been any. She had missed a text, however, that had arrived unnoticed in all the flurry of airports and funeral homes and train journeys. *Glad you're there safe. Missing you already. Hope being home isn't too tedious. I'll call you. M x.* It was the sort of message you'd send if your girlfriend had been summoned home for a family birthday, rather than a family bereavement.

If only he could have got time off work too and come back with her for the funeral. Matt wasn't always the most empathetic of boyfriends, but he was loving and full of fun. The two of them had hit it off immediately when he'd joined the property agency she worked for a few months ago.

Sighing, Rosie put away her phone, then climbed the stairs to her mother's bedroom, with its lilac walls and heavy cream curtains she'd loved to hide behind as a child. A thin layer of dust had settled on the dressing table and she wiped it away with her hand before sitting on the bed. What had her mother been reading? Rosie tilted her head to read the title of a book splayed open on the duvet. *Myths and Legends of Old Devon.* That was just the sort of book her mum loved, with fantastical stories and ancient secrets. Rosie could imagine her reading it on the clifftop, all bohemian in a long dress with her blonde hair tied back with a scarf. Belinda's gossip was often founded on half-truth and rumour, but she was right about one thing – Sofia was a bit of a hippy.

Leaving the book where it was, Rosie climbed fully clothed under the covers and breathed in a familiar smell of lavender. Mum swore by herbal remedies to help her nod off when the weather-blown house creaked and groaned. She must have been so lonely here, all on her own.

At last, the tight knot inside Rosie began to unravel and she cried great heaving sobs that echoed through the empty rooms. Tears soaked into the pillow as she begged, 'Please come back,' even though she knew that was impossible. It was just her now. Just her and Driftwood House.

Chapter Three

Liam Satterley carefully picked his way up the track that had been turned into a mudslide by the latest downpour, and turned up his collar against the persistent drizzle. He hoped this wasn't going to be a wasted journey, but there were signs that she'd arrived. A light was on in one of the bedrooms at Driftwood House, and Claude in the village reckoned he'd caught a glimpse of her this afternoon.

'Blondish hair, tanned face, big suitcase,' was Claude's description. A man of few words, he could usually be found in the pub when he wasn't at sea. But big, bearded Claude was rarely wrong, so Liam had decided to take a chance and deliver the letter, even though it was inconvenient. It was a busy time on the farm and he was behind with so many tasks. Fenella, one of his prize ewes, wasn't herself, and might need a visit from the vet. That could prove expensive and money was in short supply right now.

But the letter in his pocket might be urgent – he suspected from the envelope that it might even mean trouble. And though he didn't like to admit it, he was curious to see peculiar Rosie Merchant again.

He'd been on a course at the agricultural college the last time she'd made it home, ages ago. Although, thinking back to how she'd once described him at school, that was probably just as well. *Full of himself and tedious.* Ouch. It had rankled at the time, when his mate Kieran passed on what he'd overheard. And it still did now, to be honest. He'd always had a way with women but Rosie was apparently immune to his charms. Not that he'd been interested in her, with her long plait and funny glasses that made her look like an owl. Plus, she always had her head in a book.

He pushed the letter further into the pocket of his wax jacket and cursed himself for not wearing his bigger boots. Although it was spring, as a farmer he should understand the vagaries of Devon weather and have chosen more appropriate footwear. Billy, trotting along beside him, had a glistening wet coat and looked totally fed up with this unexpected walk.

'Hey, boy, come here.' When Liam whistled softly, the black and white border collie slithered closer to his side. 'This won't take long, thank goodness, and then we can go home. OK? Good boy.'

Billy leaned into his master's pat, smearing mud across the tall man's faded jeans.

At the top of the cliff, the two of them made for the back door of Driftwood House, which faced away from the sea. It was more sheltered here and clumps of spring squill lined the path, their violet-blue petals deceptively delicate.

How had Sofia described these flowers? 'Hardy little buggers'; that was it. More hardy, it turned out, than she was in the end.

'Are you ready, boy?' asked Liam, his voice suddenly gruff with emotion. Honestly, he was getting soft as he slid into his thirties. Sofia Merchant was a nice enough woman, but she kept herself to herself so he hadn't really known her. Just as he'd never really known her daughter with the striking, russet-brown eyes who'd escaped from Heaven's Cove as soon as she could.

Liam placed the carrier bag of provisions his mum had insisted he bring with him on the ground and knocked on the back door. There was no light on in the kitchen or in the ramshackle conservatory with its salt-streaked panes of glass, some of them chipped by small stones swept from the beach by the relentless wind.

When no one came to the door, he knocked again, but the house remained silent as rain drizzled down the kitchen window. Perhaps Claude had mistaken a tourist for Rosie, and Sofia had left the bedroom light on when she was last home. This miserable wet walk had been for nothing. He knocked again for luck, more loudly this time, as Billy waited with his ears pricked.

What a total waste of time! Liam had already turned to go when the back door was wrenched open, and there was Rosie Merchant, looking dreadful.

Chapter Four

'Yes? Can I help you?' Rosie knew she sounded unwelcoming but she was too exhausted to care. Her mother was dead, her childhood home appeared to be falling down, and the last thing she needed was a nosy villager turning up to tell her what a rubbish daughter she'd been.

Plus, she must look a sight. She glanced at herself in the mirror propped up on the kitchen dresser. Her sun-streaked hair was all over the place and even a golden tan couldn't disguise the bags under her swollen eyes. Was it shallow to care what she looked like in the circumstances? Belinda would certainly think so.

'Sorry to disturb you,' said the man on the doorstep. He brushed a hand through his dripping wet fringe. 'And I'm so sorry about your mum. This arrived for Sofia and I thought it might be urgent.' He delved into the pocket of his jacket and pulled out a large white envelope which he thrust towards her.

'Thanks.'

Rosie took the letter and turned it over in her hands. There was a return address stamped high on the back of the envelope: *Sent on behalf of: Mr Charles Epping, Esq, High Tor House, Granite's Edge, near Kellsteignton, Dartmoor.*

That was strange. Charles Epping, rich local landowner and absentee landlord, was infamous in Heaven's Cove for both his irritable temper and his total lack of interest in the village. Why was a well-known Dartmoor recluse, and possibly the most disliked man in Devon, sending a letter to – she turned the envelope over – *The Family of Mrs S. Merchant*?

Rosie slipped her finger under the flap of the envelope. 'How come this letter came to you?'

'The local postman, Pat.' The man shrugged. 'That's his real name. Anyway, Pat can't make it up the cliff to deliver post to Driftwood House any more. He reckons the potholes play havoc with his sciatica. So he'd started leaving Sofia's post at my place and I've been nipping up to deliver it a few times a week.'

'That's kind of you.'

'Not really. I live at Meadowsweet Farm so it's not far, and Billy can do with the exercise. He's not as young as he used to be.'

Billy. That was a nice name for a dog. Rosie looked up from the letter she'd pulled from the envelope and studied the man properly for the first time. Young, thick black hair, a scattering of stubble across his square jaw. She knew him, she realised, though they'd hardly ever spoken. He wasn't the sort of man to bother with her. Yet here he was, on her doorstep. What a strange, surreal day this was turning out to be.

'It's Liam, isn't it?' she asked, brushing hair from her eyes.

'That's right.' He stepped closer, out of the gloom cast by the stone porch. 'It's been a long time. I'm surprised you recognised me.'

Rosie raised an eyebrow at that because Liam had the kind of face it was hard to forget. Back in school, he'd been the good-looking golden boy who was popular with students and teachers alike. And he knew it. He'd had a confident swagger that both infuriated and intrigued Rosie, who could only dream of such self-belief. He was a clever boy with the world at his feet. But the tragedy, in Rosie's eyes, was that he didn't want to leave Heaven's Cove because he was earmarked to take over the family farm.

He hadn't looked like a farmer when they were teenagers. He'd been tall and slim with pale skin and a thick sweep of dark hair that flopped across his forehead. To her fury back then, his handsome face had made her heart beat faster, though at school he'd never looked twice at her – the weird girl who didn't fit in.

But he looked like a farmer now, in his boots and wax jacket, with broad shoulders and colour in his cheeks that brought out the cornflower blue of his eyes. He bent down and picked up a dripping carrier bag.

'You might as well have this, too.'

Rosie peeked into the bag that Liam handed over. Muddy potatoes and dark-green spinach leaves were inside, with a clingfilm-wrapped chicken breast balanced on the top. Liam Satterley, Heaven's Cove heart-throb, was bringing her food, though he'd never had a reputation for being kind.

'That's really… well, I mean, it's good of you,' she stammered, annoyed with herself for sounding rattled and even more annoyed for caring.

He shrugged again. 'My mother insisted I bring them.'

'That's good of her, then. Are they from your farm?'

'The veg is. Not the chicken, though. That came from Tesco.'

His words were deadpan but Rosie almost chuckled before catching herself. The bereaved didn't laugh, did they? To be honest, she really had no idea how she should be behaving right now. Bereavement was like a foreign country and she was lost without a map.

'Anyway.' Liam gave her a straight look before pulling up the collar of his jacket. 'I'll leave you in peace to read your letter. And I am sorry about Sofia. It's a shame you weren't here when it happened.'

'Meaning what?'

That came out more sharply than Rosie had intended, and Liam frowned before shaking his head.

'Meaning nothing more than I'm sorry you didn't get a chance to see your mother before she was taken ill. Come on, Billy. I think it's time to go.'

He leaned over to grab his dog's collar but the animal, having none of it, bolted past Rosie into the kitchen.

'Billy, come back!'

The dog blinked at his master but didn't move. Liam might be a hit with the ladies but he was absolutely rubbish with animals. Rosie moved towards Billy with a sigh but caught her breath when the animal tensed. Surely he wouldn't…

Liam had noticed too and yelled, 'Billy, don't you dare!' But it was too late. Mud flew in all directions as the dog shook himself, vigorously.

It would be funny, thought Rosie, watching wet earth splatter everywhere, if this were a television sitcom. She would laugh and Liam would apologise and, while cleaning up the mess together, their hands would touch and they would share an awkward moment of sexual tension.

Rosie bit down hard on her bottom lip. Why was she having such an inappropriate thought about a full-of-himself old school acquaintance when her mother was dead? Grief was making her mad.

Still on the doorstep, Liam shifted from foot to foot. 'Billy never normally misbehaves like that. Can I…?'

When he hesitated, irritation shuddered through Rosie. Did he need permission to cross the threshold, like a vampire? The Liam Satterley of old would have laughed and marched in to take charge. But standing in shadow on the doorstep, with a glowering grey sky above him, he seemed unsure of himself.

Rosie stepped aside. 'You'd better come in and sort out your dog.'

Liam brushed past, his wet boots slapping on the tiles, and grabbed the dog's collar but Billy had his own thoughts on the matter. He plonked his backside down on the floor, resisting all efforts to make him stand up. Uttering a string of swear words under his breath, Liam pushed the animal across the tiles and into the garden before wheeling around on the kitchen doorstep, his cheeks flushed.

Comedy gold, thought Rosie, before another wave of guilt washed over her. She steadied herself against the kitchen counter, almost knocking over a yellow jug that her mum had picked up at Heaven's Cove Market. Chuffed with her bargain, she'd FaceTimed Rosie specifically to show it off. Rosie picked up the jug and ran her fingers gently across the china.

'Sorry about all that,' said Liam, not meeting her eye. 'Have you got a cloth?'

'Don't worry about it,' said Rosie, wearily, but she passed him a cloth when Liam held out his hand and watched while he started mopping up the splashes. He was making a good job of it. Much better than Matt would have managed. In Spain, the kitchen was Rosie's domain, purely because Matt always made such a mess when he cooked a meal, and was pretty slapdash when cleaning up afterwards. She'd started to wonder if he did it on purpose so he could sit and sip wine while she got hot and bothered over the cooking.

As she daydreamed, the letter she was holding suddenly slipped from her fingers and fell onto the muddy tiles. Scooping it up and unfolding the stiff, cream paper, Rosie read the words embossed in silver at the top: *Clarence & Buck Solicitors.*

Why were solicitors sending a letter on behalf of Charles Epping to Driftwood House? She scanned through it quickly and then read it again, more slowly. There had to be some mistake.

'Are you all right?' Liam had come to stand beside her, the muddy cloth in his hand and his breath warm on her cheek.

'I just can't believe this.' She waved the letter, as though the words might slide from the paper. 'He wants the house.'

'Who wants the house?'

'Charles Epping. He says the house belongs to him and he wants it back now that Mum… now she's…' She couldn't say the word because saying it out loud would make it real. Liam took the letter from her shaking hands and started reading aloud:

'*To the family of Sofia Merchant. I am writing, on behalf of my client Mr Charles Epping, to inform you that, following the regrettable death of Mrs Sofia Merchant, Driftwood House has reverted to his ownership. Mr Epping appreciates that this is a difficult time and is therefore willing to grant a stay of one month before the house must be vacated. I have enclosed documentation regarding the arrangement with Mrs Merchant. Mr Epping sends his condolences on your loss. Yours faithfully, Ellis Buck.'*

'The house is Mum's,' Rosie whispered.

Liam pulled a wad of paper from the envelope and twisted his mouth as he started flicking through the pages.

After a few moments, he frowned. 'Not according to this. Is that your mum's signature?'

Rosie tried to focus on the yellowing paper that Liam was showing her. Someone had signed it in black ink and, though the spidery squiggle was almost indecipherable, it looked familiar. 'I think so. Mum's handwriting is always terrible. But it looks like her signature.'

'In which case…' He flicked through the pages. 'I'm a farmer, not a lawyer, but this seems to be a legal agreement that says she can stay in the house until her death, and then it reverts to the Epping family.'

'Can he do that?'

Liam wrinkled his nose. 'When it comes to the Eppings, they can do anything they want. Look' – he moved closer until Rosie was aware of his arm brushing against hers – 'Jackson in the village is a solicitor. He's semi-retired but he knew your mum and he'd probably look through this as a favour. Did your mum tell you she owned this house?'

'Yes,' said Rosie, trying desperately to remember such a conversation. 'Well, no, not in so many words, but she'd lived here since before I was born and she always talked about the house as if it was hers. When I was growing up, I thought she and Dad were paying a mortgage, not rent.'

Rosie sat down and drummed her legs against the stool. She used to sit here and watch her mum baking, knowing she'd be allowed to lick the bowl after the cakes went into the oven. Mum loved baking in this kitchen. She loved this house.

Liam pulled out another stool and sat in front of her, his hands on his knees. Raindrops on his jacket ran down the waxed fabric and dripped onto the tiles. 'I know it's early days and your mum has only just… but were you planning to live here?'

He glanced at the back door as a squall of rain hit the kitchen window and Billy started to whine.

'No, not long term. I'll be going back to Spain as soon as I can.'

'Of course.' His mouth lifted in one corner. 'So I suppose you were planning to sell the house.'

'No, definitely not.'

Did he think she was worried about the money? Maybe the whole village saw her as an opportunistic gold-digger who'd come back purely to claim her inheritance. Rosie swallowed. 'I could never sell Driftwood House. I haven't had time to consider things properly. Everything's such a muddle, but I suppose I'd have rented the house out.'

'Why, when you're hardly ever here?'

So he did blame her, just as Belinda did, for not being around enough. Rosie's cheeks grew hot and her stomach churned with guilt and irritation. Why were people around here so swift to judge? All she'd wanted was an adventure – a chance to see a world outside Heaven's Cove. A world that people like Belinda and Liam hardly knew existed.

'Living somewhere other than Heaven's Cove isn't a crime,' she told him.

'I never said it was. But why keep the house on when you're in Spain?'

That was a fair enough question, but Rosie hadn't quite got her head around the answer. It didn't make sense but, instinctively, she recoiled at the thought of losing Driftwood House. This dilapidated place, battered by sea winds and fierce winter storms, was her safety net. A place where she was always wanted and loved, however much she screwed up.

'My mum loved Driftwood House,' said Rosie, her voice shaky. 'It's full of memories and I thought it would always be here for me to come back to one day. If I wanted to. That's all.'

When Liam stood up and took a step towards her, she thought for one alarming moment that he was going to hug her. But of course he wasn't. People like Liam Satterley didn't hug unglamorous women with eye bags and bed hair.

He set down the documents on the oak kitchen table.

'I'm sorry,' he said stiffly.

'Perhaps Mr Epping will change his mind if I write to him and say I'd like to take over the house and make sure the rent is covered.'

'You could try that. Or you could just go back to Spain.' He frowned as a gust of wind slammed more rain against the window and Billy's whining reached a new high. 'I'd better be going because I'm busy tonight. Will you be all right here on your own?'

'Yeah,' said Rosie, her voice sounding strangely flat, as though it didn't belong to her at all. 'Thank you for bringing the letter and the food.'

'That's all right. And I'm sure things will look up.'

Things will look up – such an anodyne phrase that meant exactly nothing. Rosie merely nodded as he opened the back door and disappeared into the grey, wet afternoon.

She already regretted telling golden boy Liam Satterley her business. He'd be sinking pints in The Smugglers Haunt this evening and telling everyone that Driftwood House belonged to the Eppings.

I'm sure things will look up. Had Liam really said that to a woman who'd just lost her mother and now faced the loss of her family home?

He groaned as he slid his way down the sodden track, with Billy by his side. He used to be a smooth talker, someone who said exactly the right thing at the right time, even when he didn't mean a word of it. But there was something about Rosie Merchant – there always had been – that unsettled him.

And seeing her so upset had thrown him even more. He winced, remembering how fragile and lost she'd seemed when speaking of her memories at Driftwood House. He'd never been a touchy-feely person but he'd almost hugged her then. Though thank goodness he'd seen sense and backed off, because she was virtually a stranger.

They'd been aware of each other at school of course but unlike him she'd never been a part of the alpha crowd. Rosie had been a loner, out of step with his group of friends, and determined more than anything to get away from Heaven's Cove. That had never been an option for him.

Liam trudged on through the relentless rain, wondering if Rosie would really go to the effort of writing to Charles Epping. Whatever she did, it wouldn't make the slightest difference. Charles Epping owned half the village, including some of his farm, and was the kind of absentee landlord who didn't give a damn. He'd just upped the rent on the fields at Meadowsweet Farm and was bleeding the business dry.

The same shiver of anxiety that kept Liam awake at night rippled through him, and he stopped to catch his breath. Keeping the farm afloat, for his parents as much as for himself, weighed heavily on him these days.

'Hold on, boy. Let's rest a minute.'

Billy stopped immediately and flopped down by his master's feet. Liam bent and scratched behind the dog's ears. 'Typical! Why weren't you so obedient in Rosie's kitchen, rather than splattering the place with mud? She can add *hopeless with dogs* to her poor opinion of me now.'

Oh, well. What did it matter what strange Rosie Merchant thought of him when she'd be back in Spain for good before long? He straightened up, noticing that Heaven's Cove far below him was starting to close down early. The rain had chased away the tourists and lights were shining in cottage windows even though it wasn't yet five o'clock.

'Let's get home, Billy, and have our tea,' he said, picking up his pace when he reached the gentler lower slopes of the cliff.

His thoughts turned again briefly to Rosie, as he pictured her cooking the potatoes and chicken he'd brought. Though, having seen the state of her, he doubted that she'd bother. Just as he hadn't bothered with cooking or looking after himself after his life had imploded last year. She'd probably sit in the kitchen, lost in memories as the sky turned black, before dragging herself to bed.

Maybe, pondered Liam, Charles Epping was doing Rosie a favour by severing her ties with Heaven's Cove completely. It meant she could escape back to Spain after her mother's funeral and leave the village behind forever, if that was what she wanted.

'Devon in the rain, or wall-to-wall sunshine in southern Spain. It's a hard choice, Billy,' said Liam, feeling water dribble from his collar down his neck. But Billy was gambolling ahead and no longer listening.

Chapter Five

Rosie pulled her cardigan more tightly across her shoulders and shivered as she made her way down to the village. Her tanned wrists, golden against the soft cream wool, were pitted with goosebumps.

It would be nudging twenty-four degrees centigrade in Spain today. Rosie had checked her weather app that morning, as a cold wind whistled through the eaves of Driftwood House. She pictured her tiny garden, vibrant in the sunshine, and a heat haze over the rugged, russet mountains that rose up behind her apartment.

Here in Heaven's Cove, the village was pretty in springtime with its whitewashed cottages and window boxes coming into bloom. The sky was a delicate china-blue and the sun was shining. But it held no real warmth and the chill wind was a shock to the system.

Where on earth was Jackson Porter's office? The local solicitor's rather antiquated website said it was here, in the cobbled High Street. Rosie peered at door numbers until she spotted a brass plaque etched with his name. It was attached to the front of a small cottage, with latticed windows and a dark thatched roof.

The pretty house had once belonged to the Carvers, whose son Brendan was a couple of years above her in primary school.

Mrs Carver worked part-time in the local bakery but was always at the school gate in good time to pick up her son. Unlike her mum, who used to rush up at the last minute, hands covered in paint or lumps of clay.

Those were the days when Sofia spent every spare minute creating bowls and flower pots in her tiny studio at the back of Driftwood House. Later, she moved on to painting Devon landscapes with thick brush strokes, before taking up tie-dyeing plain T-shirts – selling the vibrant clothing she created at the monthly market. Then she became passionate about ecology and spent most weekends tramping the wilds of Dartmoor.

Rosie smiled. Her mother was a woman of enthusiasms who threw herself heart and soul into everything. As a child, she'd longed for a 'normal' mum who didn't stand out, but her embarrassment had faded over the years, as her urge to escape and see the world had grown. *You get your adventurous spirit from me, Rosie Posie.* She could hear her mum's voice as though she was standing right here, in Mr Porter's cottage garden overflowing with golden daffodils. They were among her mum's favourite flowers.

With a slight shake of the head, Rosie pushed open the shiny black door and went inside.

A middle-aged woman with metal-rimmed glasses and short, blonde hair glanced up from her computer when the door thudded shut. 'Can I help you?' she asked, her tone implying she wasn't keen to be of any assistance whatsoever.

'I was hoping to see Jackson, if he can spare a few minutes.' Rosie instantly regretted being so informal when the woman's smile froze. 'I mean I'd like to see Mr—'

'Do you have an appointment?' the woman demanded, pushing her chin into her white polo-neck jumper. She started flicking through a diary on her desk while Rosie wondered if Mr Porter had hired a Rottweiler receptionist on purpose. Her stubby fingers were poking out of fingerless gloves and she raised an eyebrow when she spotted Rosie staring at them. 'The heating's not working again and this old building never seems to get warm.' She suddenly frowned. 'I can't see an appointment in his diary.'

'I don't have one, I'm afraid. But I was hoping to nab him, just for a minute or two, for some quick advice.'

'I'm afraid that won't be possible,' said the woman, closing the diary with a snap.

'Liam Satterley recommended him to me.'

'Liam did?' The woman almost purred, though Liam was surely young enough to be her son. He obviously hadn't lost his allure with the opposite sex. 'It's most irregular but if you wait here I'll see if Mr Porter can spare a few minutes. What's your name?'

'Rose. Rosie Merchant.'

A spark of interest glinted in the woman's small eyes, which were the colour of conkers. '*The* Rosie Merchant? Well, you're quite the local celebrity. You were the sole topic of conversation in the post office this morning.' She grinned, as though that was a good thing. 'I hear you're planning to ship all of your mother's furniture to Spain.'

'That's not my plan,' sighed Rosie, realising that the Heaven's Cove rumour mill was already in full flow. But was it common knowledge yet that Charles Epping owned Driftwood House?

Rosie bit back the urge to ask what else had been said about her. It was probably best that she didn't know.

Getting to her feet, the woman looked at Rosie with a kinder expression. 'I didn't really know your mother because I've only been working here for a couple of months, but I'm very sorry for your loss.'

Tears prickled Rosie's eyes at this unexpected sympathy and she blinked them away. 'Thank you. It's my mum I need to see Jackson – Mr Porter – about, actually.'

'Take a seat and I'll ask him. Do you need a cup of tea?'

Tea, the British answer to everything from disappointment and grief to crashing guilt. When Rosie politely declined, the woman knocked on the closed door behind her desk and bustled inside.

There were muffled voices as Rosie paced what must once have been the main living room of the cottage. A red-brick fireplace on one wall was almost obscured by a large filing cabinet and printer, and the ceiling was criss-crossed with white-painted beams.

Old photos of Heaven's Cove lined the walls: black and white scenes of times and people long gone. Rosie focused on the photo nearest to her, trying to imprint every detail on her mind to distract her from the gnawing ache inside. A child with bright eyes was standing next to a horse and cart in Moor Lane, staring straight into the camera. There was a hint of mischief in the tilt of his chin and Rosie wondered what became of him. Did he spend his life as one of Heaven's Cove's most popular residents, like Liam, or did he, like her, always feel like an outsider?

'Miss Merchant?' Rosie spun around. 'Mr Porter can spare a few minutes to see you.'

The woman held open the door and let Rosie into the office behind her. A stout man with a flushed complexion was standing behind a large oak desk, and gestured for Rosie to take a seat in front of him.

'Miss Merchant, it's good to meet you at last. I've heard so much about you from your mother and you're a hot topic of conversation in the village.' He held out his hand and engulfed hers in a vigorous handshake. 'Though, of course, I'm sorry that we meet under such tragic circumstances. Sofia was a marvellous woman.'

'Did you know my mum well?' asked Rosie, extricating her hand and sitting on the hard-backed chair opposite his desk.

'I knew her very well, many years ago. But I left Devon as a young man and only returned to my roots a short while ago. Sofia and I had only recently renewed our acquaintance, and then this happened. I'm so sorry. I'll miss her terribly.'

Rosie was surprised to see Jackson's eyes fill with tears. She'd been expecting him to be distant and professional, a bit of a cold fish. But he had a heart and it seemed that a part of it belonged to her mother. Perhaps local people's affection for Sofia had made up for her own daughter's lack of care.

'Here you go.' Jackson opened the top drawer of his desk and took out a small box of tissues, which he slid across to her.

'Thanks,' sniffed Rosie, who hadn't been aware that tears were trickling down her cheeks. She dabbed at her face and took a deep breath before rummaging in her handbag and pulling out the paperwork she'd received from Charles Epping.

'It's a bit of an imposition but I was hoping you could do me a favour. This has arrived, about Driftwood House, and I'd be grateful if you could give me your opinion on it. I'll pay for your time, of course.'

'No need. Anything for Sofia,' said Jackson, pushing the glasses perched on top of his head down onto the bridge of his nose. 'Let's see what we have here.'

'I'd be grateful if you could keep this confidential,' said Rosie, hanging on to the paperwork. 'It may be that people know already but I'd like to keep it quiet if possible.'

'Of course,' said Jackson, looking at Rosie over the top of his specs. 'Anything said in this office remains confidential. Let me have a look at what you've brought in.'

He scanned through the letter in seconds, while Rosie tapped her foot anxiously against the leg of her chair. Then, with just the slightest raise of a bushy grey eyebrow, he began to read the lease.

Rosie stared at him as he turned the pages, willing him to say it was not worth the paper it was written on; that of course the house had belonged to her mum all along, and Charles Epping was merely trying his luck. But Jackson sucked in air through his teeth as he read on and whistled softly when he got to the end of the document.

'Well, well.' He sat back in his creaky leather chair and folded his arms. 'That appears rather cut and dried, I'm afraid. Sofia was a tenant at Driftwood House and the tenancy reverts to the owner, the Epping family, at the time of her death. You haven't lived in the house for some time, I believe?'

'Not for a few years.'

'Hmm. And I'm assuming that Sofia didn't leave a will.'

'Not as far as I'm aware. She wasn't a will-making kind of person, really.'

'Hardly surprising. Those of us sliding into middle-age rarely feel compelled to set our affairs in order. We can't quite believe in our own mortality.'

'Mum was always optimistic and full of hope. She'd never have believed that she might…'

'No, of course not. But are you quite sure that there's no will or other paperwork about this arrangement?'

'I haven't come across a will and I'm sure she'd have mentioned making one, although…'

Rosie trailed off. She was equally sure that her mother would have mentioned, at some point over the last twenty-nine years, that their house belonged to someone else, but she never had.

Jackson sniffed. 'We could question this lease but, knowing what I do about Charles Epping and his family, I have to warn you that it would be expensive, and with next to no chance of success. Though it wouldn't do any harm to scour Driftwood House for any other relevant paperwork your mother might have left.' He breathed out slowly through pursed lips. 'So Charles Epping is the legal owner of Driftwood House. Whoever'd have thought it?'

Not me. Rosie screwed her tissue into a ball and pushed it into her pocket. 'If you were friends, I'm surprised Mum never mentioned anything about it.'

'She never said a dicky bird. But I left Heaven's Cove rather abruptly shortly before she moved into Driftwood House and married your father.' Jackson shifted in his chair, the leather creaking. 'So what about you, Miss Merchant?'

'Please call me Rosie.'

Jackson smiled. 'Rosie, then. What are your plans?'

'I don't know. First of all, there's the funeral to finalise.' Rosie closed her eyes for a moment to steady herself. 'And then I'll go back to Spain. I've been living abroad for some time.'

'So I understand. I've always loved travelling and have taken quite an interest in your adventures since becoming reacquainted with your mother. You're living near Málaga, I believe.'

'That's right. I work part-time for a property agency and the rest of the time for a B&B near the beach.'

'Marvellous. Which job do you prefer?'

'The B&B, definitely. I've met all kinds of people through it and I enjoy helping them to have a brilliant holiday. It's hot work when you're changing beds at the height of summer, but it's fun.'

'I visited the area a few years ago and thought it was beautiful, but I almost melted in the heat.'

Rosie winced, imagining the relentless sun on Jackson's florid skin. 'A lot of visitors find the heat quite draining.'

'Well, I almost fried.' When he grinned, dimples appeared in his cheeks and he looked like a cheeky little boy, in spite of his unruly thatch of grey hair. His grin disappeared as he walked round from behind his desk and took hold of Rosie's hand. 'But now is not the time for levity. If there's anything I can do to help while you're here, please don't hesitate to contact me.'

'Thank you. You've been very kind,' said Rosie, getting to her feet and smoothing down her lemon linen dress that was far too thin for the Devon climate.

'Not at all. I'm keen to help in any way that I can. Just give me a call.' He fished in the pocket of his suit jacket hanging on a wooden coat rack and handed over a business card. Then he stared into Rosie's eyes so intently, she began to feel uncomfortable. 'Your mother was very dear to me, Rosie.'

'Thank you, that's very kind.' Rosie looked away and swung her bag onto her shoulder. 'I'd better leave you to get on with your work.'

'Of course.' Jackson strode to the door and opened it wide. 'I hope to see you again soon.'

The receptionist didn't glance up from her computer when Rosie walked past her and out into the fresh air. Jackson had been nothing but kind from the moment she'd entered his office, but Rosie felt smothered and couldn't wait to escape.

Some fresh sea air would clear her head. Rosie started wandering down to the quay and soon spotted a group of people sitting at a table outside Becker's Bakery. She winced when she recognised Belinda and Liam: the two of them together was not only an unlikely pairing, it was also a worrying combination. Liam had read the letter from Epping's solicitor so knew all about the house's ownership, and Belinda would love to be in the loop so she could tell the world and his wife. It was too late to veer into a side street without it being totally obvious so Rosie kept on walking, with her head held high.

The two of them, sitting next to a man she recognised from school, glanced up from their coffees and pastries and watched while she approached. It was very much like walking into a party while the in-crowd viewed you with curious disdain, thought Rosie, as Belinda folded her arms across her ample bosom. But there was nothing for it but to brave out the next few minutes.

Chapter Six

Rosie was nervous, thought Liam, watching her stride towards them. She was trying hard to hide it and doing a pretty good job, but the tight set of her jaw gave her away.

A year ago, he'd never have noticed it. Before Deanna, he'd been far too busy with his charmed, carefree life to pick up on subtle body language. Then he'd been too absorbed in planning a life with the one woman to finally win his heart. But when it all went horribly pear-shaped, smashing his heart, his eyes had been opened to other people's pain.

He didn't like it. Recognising sorrow or fear in the set of a mouth or the tilt of a head was draining and he sometimes longed to be the oblivious man he once was. His friends were expecting him to bounce back and be the Liam of old, and he'd tried. He really had. But he couldn't escape the fact that he'd changed.

Alex nudged him hard in the ribs. 'Is that Weirdo Rosie walking towards us? Bloody hell, she's improved. I wouldn't have touched her with a barge pole a few years back but now… what d'ya reckon?'

Liam winced at the cruel nickname some of the boys had used for Rosie at school. He reckoned she was looking much better than the last time he'd seen her, though her eyes were still smudged underneath with dark shadows.

'I wouldn't kick her out of bed,' he laughed, because that was what Alex expected him to say. Although the truth was that no one had shared his bed for a long time.

'For goodness' sake, have some decorum,' hissed Belinda, who'd shamelessly gatecrashed his coffee with Alex, intent on talking to them both about the monthly village market. She'd just taken over as head of the market's organising team – the woman had a power complex – and was champing at the bit to make changes.

'Sorry, Mrs Kellscroft,' said Alex contritely, rolling his eyes at Liam, who pretended not to notice.

'Good morning, Rosie, my dear,' boomed Belinda, looking her over from head to toe. Rosie gave a self-conscious smile and tucked her fair, shoulder-length hair behind her ears. 'How are you managing up there in that lonely house? It must be utterly dreadful being there on your own with only the memory of your poor mother for company.'

Liam winced. It was a good job Belinda had never decided on counselling as a vocation. But Rosie replied calmly, 'I'm managing, thank you.'

She was shivering in her pretty dress and cardigan and Liam had a sudden urge to take off his jacket and drape it around her shoulders. But she wouldn't want that, and Alex would totally take the mick. *Treat 'em mean and keep 'em keen* was his friend's mantra, and he didn't even say it ironically. Had Liam ever been so crass? He rather feared he had been, before Deanna brought him down a peg or two.

He glanced past Rosie to the top of the church tower, just visible above the tall beech trees that lined Bakehouse Lane. It would soon be exactly a year to the day since Deanna had left him in such a public fashion, a fact that had been disrupting his sleep as much as Charles Epping's latest rent rise. He hoped that no one in Heaven's Cove was aware of the upcoming anniversary so it could pass unnoticed. But people around here had long memories, and Belinda especially appeared to possess a photographic recall of local tragedy and humiliation.

When he sighed, Rosie glanced at him but she'd looked away before he could rearrange his features into a smile.

'We're having a meeting to see if these two young men would like to help organise Heaven's Cove Market in the future,' said Belinda, which was news to Liam.

'I fear we're about to be press-ganged,' said Alex, treating Rosie to his best flirtatious smile. Though he'd probably agree to Belinda's request in a flash, realised Liam, because Coral was also a part of the organising team. Coral, mid-fifties, stout and married, wasn't Alex's type. But her daughter, Ella, most definitely was.

'We've got so many plans,' said Belinda, 'For a start, we're going to rebrand the market and I've asked Charles Epping and his wife to perform a grand re-opening ceremony – cut a ribbon or something. Though I don't suppose they will, even though they owe a great deal to Heaven's Cove. A good number of people here have paid them rent over the years, including your own mother, it seems, Rosie.'

'That's right,' said Rosie levelly. Liam hoped that only he noticed the telltale tightening of her jaw muscles.

'We all assumed that Driftwood House belonged to your mother.'

'Well, now you know it doesn't.'

Rosie gave Liam a hard stare. She obviously suspected him of gossiping about her business, as though he didn't have more important things to keep him occupied these days. When Liam glared back, annoyed at being cast as the villain for no good reason, she held his gaze for a moment before looking towards the sea.

Belinda shook her head. 'I must admit it came as quite a shock to find out the truth.'

'Tell me about it.' Rosie bit her lower lip as though the words had tumbled out without her permission.

'You did know that the Epping family owned Driftwood House, didn't you, dear?' Belinda's eyes were shining at the prospect of more juicy gossip.

'Of course I did,' said Rosie brightly. 'Mum told me everything. We were really close.'

She looked again at Liam, but this time her gaze held a plea rather than an accusation. When he gave her a tight nod, her shoulders dropped under her cream cardi. He would keep her secret, even if she thought he'd already partly blabbed.

'Well, I suppose you were close emotionally, even if rarely geographically,' said Belinda, with a small laugh.

Pain flickered in Rosie's big brown eyes and she clasped her arms around her waist, like she was giving herself a hug. 'It's good to see you but I'd better be getting on.'

'Of course, dear. I expect you've got a lot to organise, what with moving your mother's belongings out of Driftwood House, and then there's the funeral next week. It's on Wednesday afternoon, I believe.'

'That's right, and I'm on my way to see Reverend Hill about that now so I'd better hurry. Good luck with the market.'

Without looking at Liam again, she scurried off, and Belinda's talk turned back to the market. Even Alex, relishing the chance of getting closer to Ella, was getting bored and they'd just managed to bring the conversation to a close when Alex's very pointy elbow landed in Liam's ribs once more.

'Look who's gracing us with her presence now. We're like babe magnets this morning, mate.'

Liam was pretty sure no one referred to themselves as 'babe magnets' any more. But he followed Alex's head tilt and groaned. Katrina Crawley had just come into view and was walking purposefully towards them. She looked magnificent, with her slim hips swinging and her long dark hair streaming behind her.

Any man would be tempted by Katrina. He should be tempted, especially as she'd made it very clear that, in spite of having a long-term boyfriend, she wouldn't kick *him* out of bed. And sometimes he did imagine taking her in his arms and kissing that knowing smile from her beautiful face. It would be so much better than the adolescent fumbles they'd shared as seventeen-year-olds. But his imaginings always stopped at the bedroom door these days, as though Deanna had slammed it shut in their faces.

Basically, he'd changed from an over-sexed Jack the Lad into a boring, celibate farmer with few prospects. And Rosie Merchant, once a total nerd, now had an aura of the exotic about her, and must consider him dull, plodding and provincial. What a turnaround.

'Well, hello there,' said Katrina in her breathy voice as she reached the small group. 'How lovely to see you all. Who was that woman you were talking to?'

'Rosie Merchant,' said Belinda. 'She's finally made it home, just in time for her mother's funeral.'

'Poor, poor Rosie. I heard she was back in the village. She was always a strange one.'

Katrina sidled up so close to Liam he could smell the heady floral perfume she was wearing. She sank onto the chair next to him and leaned across the table. 'So what are you three up to? Anything I can help with?'

'We're talking about rebranding the monthly market,' said Belinda, frowning at Katrina's cleavage.

'Rebranding? Heavens, that sounds exciting.'

'It's long overdue. You know me. I don't like to speak ill of people but the organising team has been coasting rather for the last couple of years without proper leadership and the whole thing needs a shake-up. Why don't you join us, Katrina? You'd be ideal with your marketing experience.'

'I'd absolutely love to but I'm afraid I just don't have the time, Belinda. Running my own business is all-consuming. It's twenty-four-seven with no holidays and I have to force myself to take time out occasionally. Talking of which…' When she turned to Liam and clasped his arm, a shiver went through him. 'Are you going to the dance in the village hall next month? It'll be fun.'

'I'm going,' Alex assured her, but when Katrina continued staring into Liam's eyes, her mouth pulled into a pretty pout,

Liam made a decision. He'd be an idiot to pass up on the chance of some fun after the year he'd had.

'Yeah, I'll probably be there, depending on how the lambing's going.'

'Well, just make sure you are, or I'll come and hunt you down in your lambing shed. I can stretch out on the hay and keep you company while you're doing all the work.'

Belinda narrowed her eyes at that but Katrina had already got to her feet and was tugging down the hem of her very short dress. Her legs seemed to go on forever.

'Take it easy, boys,' she said huskily. 'Bye, Belinda.'

'You've still got it, mate,' said Alex, sotto voce, as Belinda tutted quietly and started clearing their cups from the table.

'Did you ever doubt it?'

Liam watched Katrina's pert figure disappearing into the distance. Only a fool would turn down Katrina and the truth was, he was getting lonely. Once the anniversary was over, maybe it was time to stop mooching about and get his life back on track. His parents would be glad to see him having fun, even though they'd never really approved of his hectic love life pre-Deanna.

'And I can't get over how much little mouse Rosie has changed,' said Alex, breaking into his thoughts. 'Though she was shooting you daggers. What have you done to upset her? Oh, tell me you didn't sleep with her years ago and break her heart.'

'I didn't sleep with her and I definitely didn't break her heart. I'm pretty sure I'm not her type.' Alex's smile faltered at Liam's serious expression. 'Hard though that is to believe when I'm a total babe magnet,' he added, for Alex's benefit.

That did the trick. 'You and me both,' said Alex, with a wide grin. 'Pint in The Smugglers on Saturday before trying out that new night club in town? It'll do you good.'

Maybe he was right. Liam was tired of being sad, and tired of the anxiety that dogged him. He never used to be a worrier but, these days, he worried about everything: the farm, his mum's worsening arthritis, his dad's increasing forgetfulness. But most of all, in the early hours, he worried that Deanna had been his last chance of a meaningful relationship and he would be alone forever.

'So Saturday. Pub, pint, club?' tried Alex again.

Liam nodded. 'Yeah, why not.'

Chapter Seven

Rosie's breath caught in her throat as she took in the flowers piled up on her mother's grave. She'd seen them at the funeral yesterday, but the afternoon had passed in a blur of shaking hands with people she knew and others she didn't, making small talk afterwards in the pub while people ate chicken mayonnaise sandwiches, and trying not to cry.

Actually, that last bit had been easier than she'd imagined. She'd cried so much since arriving in Heaven's Cove over a week ago, she didn't seem to have many tears left. This morning she felt bone dry, as though her soul had been wrung out. Grief had desiccated her even more than the scorching Spanish sun. But the pretty flowers on the dark earth still brought her up short.

She started leafing through the cards attached to the blooms. *Gone far too soon but never forgotten – love from the girls at Becker's Bakery; Rest in peace – Belinda and Jim; Heaven's Cove's finest! We'll miss you, dear Sofia – Fran, Paul and the boys x*

Her mother had been well loved in this village. That was a comfort. She hadn't been totally alone while her daughter was off gallivanting overseas.

The church tower was still in shadow but the sun, rising over the cliff, had reached the edge of the ancient building and beams of light were making the reddish stone glow. It was beautifully

peaceful here, and the weathered gravestones around her were
strangely comforting, reminding her she wasn't the only person
to be weighed down by grief. People had mourned over the
centuries in this picture-perfect village, and survived.

Glancing down, a flash of blue caught her eye and there,
behind the pile of wreaths and bouquets, was a simple spray
of white lilies interspersed with blue iris, the flower her mum
had loved above all others. She hadn't noticed those yesterday.
She was sure they hadn't been there.

Rosie picked up the flowers and breathed in their aroma.
They were tied with twine, and the words on the small card
attached were written with the thick, black strokes of a fountain
pen. *Rest in peace, Saffy. Never forgotten. J.*

It wasn't the anonymous 'J' that caught her attention. It was
her mother's pet name, Saffy, used only by the people who had
loved her mum the most – Rosie's grandparents, and her father
when she was little. They were all gone now, but someone still
living – the mysterious J – was on intimate enough terms with
her mother to use the endearment.

Rosie turned the card over, looking for clues, but it was blank.
Her mum had rarely dated since her dad left years ago, or so Rosie
thought. She'd certainly never said there was anyone significant
in her life – but then she'd never said anything about the situation with Driftwood House, either. Rosie carefully placed the
flowers back where they'd been but kept the card in her hand.

'Did you have any other secrets, Mum?' she asked softly. But
there was no answer, just the gentle whoosh of the sea breeze
rustling the leaves of the trees edging the graveyard.

Rosie closed her eyes and turned her face towards the sky. Life was so carefree in Spain, so easy. She missed Matt, and her friends there who'd been texting her to ask how she was. She also missed the baked smell of hot earth, the relentless chirrup of cicadas, and the anticipation on the faces of visitors arriving at the homely B&B that overlooked the beach. Here, she was surrounded by complications and secrets that threatened to overwhelm her.

The sound of someone approaching interrupted her thoughts and when she opened her eyes, her heart sank. Liam had just come through the lych gate at the boundary of the churchyard, with Billy jumping at his heels. He hesitated when he saw her before walking over.

'I didn't realise you'd be here so early or I'd have come later.'

'I won't be in the churchyard much longer,' replied Rosie, stung by the irritated tone in his voice.

'Whatever. I'm heading into the church anyway.'

'I didn't think you…' She shook her head.

'You didn't think what?'

'It doesn't matter.'

'Tell me.'

'OK. I didn't take you for a church-goer.'

'Why not?'

Because your reputation suggests you've always been far too busy drinking and socialising.

Rosie took a deep breath. 'No reason. I just didn't.'

Liam stepped further into the shadow cast by the squat church tower. 'I'm not particularly religious but I felt like coming today, if that's all right with you?'

Why was he being such an arse? Rosie suddenly remembered how he could turn on the charm at school when it suited, but didn't bother with the people he figured weren't worth his time. Which, presumably, was her right now.

She stuffed the mysterious card from J into her jeans pocket and swung her bag onto her shoulder. 'I'll leave you to it, then.'

Rosie started to walk away but he stepped into her path and ran a hand across his face. 'Look, I didn't get a chance to speak to you at the funeral yesterday. How are you doing?'

'Fine.' That sounded too blunt and she didn't want to stoop to his level. Rosie took a deep breath and tried again. 'I'm all right, thank you. I'm sad, but glad that the funeral is over.'

'I'm sure.'

When he stooped to let Billy off his lead, Rosie studied him more closely. He was as good-looking as ever. More so, now that the slight gawkiness of youth had gone. But the bristly golden haze of brashness and self-confidence that always surrounded him seemed tarnished today. Beneath his irritation and general arseyness, she realised, he was sad, like her.

'Are *you* all right?' she asked.

When Liam glanced up and caught her eye, Rosie looked away quickly. He stood up and stretched his long legs. 'Why would you ask that? I thought you of all people wouldn't listen to gossip.'

Rosie tensed. He really was being impossible this morning. 'What gossip? I was only trying to be nice. And I'd appreciate it if you didn't gossip about *my* business, actually.'

'I didn't.'

'So how did Belinda find out that Driftwood House belongs to Charles Epping?'

'I heard her telling Claude that she knows someone who knows someone who works for the Eppings.'

'So it wasn't you?'

'Not guilty.'

'Right.' Rosie winced. 'Sorry.'

When Liam stayed silent, Rosie attempted to get their conversation back onto a more even keel. 'I went to see Jackson Porter, like you suggested.'

'That's good.'

'He reckons there's nothing I can do and the house will revert to Charles Epping.'

'That's not surprising.'

'So I've started packing up Mum's stuff.'

'Hmm.'

This was hopeless. Liam had one eye on Billy, who was rooting round the oldest headstones in the corner of the churchyard, and was totally distracted. Rosie idly wondered what the 'gossip' was about him that he was being so uppity about, but he clearly didn't want to talk about it, or anything else for that matter. She tightened the laces on her trainers.

'I'm going to walk up to Sorrell Head so I'd better get on.'

A flicker of relief passed across Liam's face. 'OK, I'll see you around. Billy, come here, boy!'

Billy raised his head at his master's sharp tone and ambled over to meet him at the church door. Once the two of them had disappeared inside, Rosie pulled the card signed by J from her pocket and flattened it out. It should be with the beautiful lily and iris bouquet. She took a photo of it before placing it back on the flowers.

The sea breeze whispering through the trees sounded like voices as she left the churchyard.

*

Rosie had reached the edge of the village, where the land started to rise steeply, when a man in long shorts, a bright Hawaiian shirt and a green spotted neckerchief waved at her.

'Hello, it's Rosie, isn't it?' he called, locking a grey Corsa parked close to the hedge and crossing the lane to join her. 'I'm Jerry Wilson, a friend of your mum's. I wanted to say how sorry I am about what happened.'

'Thank you.'

'How are you doing?'

'I'm doing OK, thanks.'

'Your mum was so full of life. It's hard to take in what's happened.' His grey-streaked ponytail swished from side to side when he shook his head.

'It was a terrible shock. What did you say your name was?'

'Jerry. Jerry Wilson.'

'Jerry with a J, or a G?'

'With a J. Why?'

'I just wondered.'

Rosie took a good look at Jerry with a J. Tall, good-looking in a grizzled kind of way, eccentric dress sense, paint splodges on his arms that hinted at artistic talent – just her mother's type. Might he be the mysterious J?

'Were you at the funeral yesterday? I don't remember seeing you but it was all a bit of a blur.'

'That's understandable. It's such an emotional time. I was at the service, right at the back because the church was so packed. But I couldn't go to the wake, I'm afraid, because I had to get back to work.'

'That's OK. Mum would have been touched you could make the service. Had you known each other long?'

'A while. I live in Upper Selderfield but I'm often in Heaven's Cove and your mum and I would meet up when we could.'

'Were you close friends?'

'Um…' Jerry puffed air through his lips. 'I guess we were quite close.'

'So you knew her pretty well?' Rosie knew she was asking too many questions, but couldn't help herself.

'I suppose I did,' said Jerry, looking puzzled.

'How did you first meet?'

'I can't remember exactly. I think it was at a literary talk at Selderfield Library. Your mum was a great fan of poetry.'

'She was. Saffy always had her head in a book.'

'Saffy?'

Jerry's only reaction to Mum's pet name was confusion. He looked totally bemused now actually, probably because she was giving him the third degree. Rosie abandoned the subterfuge and got straight to the point: 'I hope you don't mind me asking but did you bring a lily and iris bouquet to the funeral?'

'I didn't. Should I have? I didn't bring flowers at all. I gave a donation in your mum's memory to a literacy charity instead.'

'Oh, that's really nice.'

'I thought Sofia would approve.'

'She would. That's just the sort of thing she'd like.'

When tears sprang into Rosie's eyes, Jerry put his big paw of a hand on her arm and squeezed. 'Are you sure you're all right? Losing a parent is so hard.'

'I'm coping, but thank you.'

'Good.' He smiled. 'I assume you'll be leaving Heaven's Cove soon, what with Driftwood House not being in the family any more.'

'You heard about that?'

'I did, in the pub last night. I didn't realise the house belonged to the Eppings. That was a surprise, and they never miss a trick to make money, but building a hotel is a new one, even for them. I guess the cliffs are an ideal spot, thanks to that amazing view, and as they say, it's all about location, location, location.'

Rosie frowned. 'Do you mean they're planning to build a hotel near Driftwood House?'

'Ah, you haven't heard that bit.' Jerry started shifting from foot to foot. 'Perhaps. I don't know for sure and it would be a shame if the house…' He stopped and shrugged. 'Who can tell what a man like Charles Epping has in mind?'

The truth of it suddenly hit Rosie like a sledgehammer. 'Does he want to build a hotel actually where the house is? Is that why he's so keen to get Driftwood House back? He intends to knock it down and put a hotel in its place?'

'Maybe. That's what people are saying. Look, I shouldn't have mentioned anything. It's only a rumour.'

'Who did you hear it from?'

'Belinda. She said she knows a man who knows a man—'

'—who works for Charles Epping?'

'That's it. Apparently, he overheard Epping talking about it on the phone and saying the house would be demolished. But please don't upset yourself because he might be wrong.'

Rosie nodded, but only to make Jerry feel better about being the bearer of bad news.

Belinda's source had been spot on about Driftwood House belonging to the Eppings so chances were he was right about their hotel plan. It made sense – a small boutique hotel overlooking the ocean would be a huge tourist attraction. Guests would pay good money to wake up to that view every morning, and she'd even suggested to her mum a few times that Driftwood would make a fabulous guesthouse.

'Anyway, enough of the Eppings and their expanding property empire,' said Jerry, stepping to one side as a car trundled along the lane and turned right towards Exeter. 'Are you heading for Driftwood House now?'

'Not yet. I thought I'd walk to Sorrell Head first.'

'Perfect morning for it.' Jerry smiled. 'And when will you go back to Spain?'

'Soon. I haven't booked a flight yet.'

'Well, Rosie, it was very good to properly meet you after all this time. Your mum spoke about you often. She was very proud of you.'

'Thanks,' gulped Rosie, desperate for lovely, kind Jerry to stop talking. She needed to think through what she'd just found out. Her mind was filled with images of a wrecking ball pounding Driftwood House to dust.

Jerry frowned. 'I am sorry to give you such sad news about what might happen to the house, when you're still mourning your mother.'

'It's fine,' Rosie assured him. 'At the end of the day, Driftwood House is just bricks and mortar. That's all.'

Did she sound convincing? Presumably so, because Jerry's face relaxed into an expression of relief, similar to Liam's in the churchyard when she'd told him she was going.

Rosie stood for a moment, watching Jerry wander off towards the village, her mind whirling with emotion.

The thought of Driftwood House, the only proper home she'd ever known, being knocked down, stone by stone, was almost too much to bear. First, her mother gone and next, her mother's beloved home. The Eppings would build their hotel, time would move on, and one day soon it would be as if Sofia Merchant had never existed at all.

Chapter Eight

Rosie climbed higher and higher, her legs aching and her lungs feeling as though they might burst.

She'd chosen the steepest path to Sorrell Head and was glad no one was around to cast judgement on her fitness. Or rather, lack of it. Good grief! She stopped and bent forward with her hands on her thighs. Sleeping in late on precious days off and drinking with work colleagues in the sunshine had made her soft.

A walk to the highest point of the cliffs would toughen her up a little and give her time to think. And she couldn't face going back to Driftwood House for a while, anyway – not now she knew the house was under threat. Losing her family home to the Eppings had hit her hard, but knowing that this precious link to her mother would likely be smashed into rubble… Biting down hard on her lower lip, she pulled in deep breaths of fresh salty air to steady herself and ease what felt like panic grabbing at her throat. She wasn't normally a panicky person but now everything felt overwhelming.

She started climbing again, her feet slipping on the stony path. Out here, she felt close to her mum, who loved tramping across the cliffs, with a scarf tied around her hair and the ends flying in the breeze. The two of them would often walk to Sorrell

Head, a jagged peak which stretched out into the sea. The red sandstone had been worn away by the pounding waves and Rosie supposed that, one day, it would succumb and the cliff would fall into the sea.

Five minutes later, she was standing close to the cliff edge. Being up so high made Rosie's stomach flip – it always had, even as a child hanging on to her mother's hand for dear life. But she walked as far as she dared to the end of the land.

Further along the coastline, tucked in by the beach, Heaven's Cove was waking up. Shopkeepers were putting out sandwich boards and people were busy on the quay, preparing to take today's influx of tourists on pleasure trips around the bay. Some would end up feeling queasy, because the water was scattered with white-topped waves today.

The curve of sand was empty except for a couple of dog walkers. Their pets ran in and out of the sea, which had turned from moss-green first thing this morning to a sparkling blue, mirroring the cloudless sky. It was going to be a beautiful spring day and she could almost imagine herself in Spain were it not for the chilly wind blowing through her hair.

Pushing her fringe from her eyes, she sat down heavily on the ground, leaned back on her elbows and stared up at the seagulls wheeling overhead. Her mum wouldn't be pleased that she was lying on damp grass. No lolling about after a rain shower or heavy dew – that was one of the very few rules she laid down. *Think of the grass stains, Rosie!* But she'd be heartbroken at the thought of Driftwood House being flattened to make way for a hotel.

Would Charles Epping really be so heartless? Definitely, if all she'd heard of him was true. The Eppings were rarely seen in Heaven's Cove but their reputation for ice-cold, business-based decisions was common knowledge. And their indecent haste to claim back Driftwood House was testament to that.

Rosie didn't usually bear grudges but right now she thoroughly disliked Charles Epping and his haughty wife. And she wasn't too keen on Liam Satterley either, who'd been so irritable and dismissive in the graveyard this morning. Though the sadness coming off him in waves bothered her. Despite the mild hostility that seemed to permeate their encounters, this shared sadness made the two of them almost kindred spirits right now.

The shrill ring of her phone interrupted her thoughts and startled the gull nearby which was eyeing her up as a potential source of food. Walkers were regularly dive-bombed by scavenging seagulls trying to snatch their sandwiches.

'Hello?'

'Babe, it's me, checking up on you. How's life in boring old Heaven's Cove?'

Matt's deep voice was a soothing balm on her troubled thoughts. He'd called her after the funeral yesterday, but they'd only had a brief chat because he was working late.

'Life is… challenging. I've just been to the churchyard to look at the funeral flowers.'

'Is that a good idea? It'll only upset you.'

'I'm upset already so it doesn't make much difference.'

'I guess. Hold on a minute.' Matt's voice became muffled while he spoke to someone in the office. As his conversation continued, Rosie's attention drifted to the waves lapping the shore far below. She'd spent some happy times on that beach, swimming in the cold sea before drying off on the sand.

'Are you still there, babe? Sorry about that. Carmen needed a bit of guidance. She's taken over some of your work while you're away and is doing a great job. She sends her love.'

'That's kind. Tell her thank you.'

'I will. Did I tell you that she closed a great sale this week? Those apartments with limited views – she managed to offload a couple of them.'

'The ones with ridiculously small second bedrooms?'

'That's the ones. She guaranteed to the buyers that you could get a double bed in there, though I don't suppose you can.'

'So she lied, basically.'

'She was economical with the truth, Rosie,' laughed Matt. 'There's a difference.'

Not one that Rosie could see, but she'd had this argument with Matt before and couldn't face rehashing it right now.

'I had some surprising news today,' she told him. 'It looks like the Eppings hope to knock down Driftwood House and build a hotel in its place.'

'Wow.' She heard him catch his breath.

'I know. That's how I felt.'

He whistled down the line. 'That is one hell of a good idea. The house is past it, from what you've said, but the views are great, right? It sounds like the perfect place for a bijou hotel that charges the earth.'

OK, that really wasn't how she felt.

'I'm quite upset, actually,' she said quietly.

'Aw, of course you are, but you have to approach it from a business point of view, rather than emotional overload.'

'Do I?'

'You know it makes sense. Mind you, anyone with half a brain holidays abroad these days, but I guess some people prefer a staycation.'

'Loads of tourists visit Heaven's Cove every year. It's a jewel in Devon's crown.'

That was taken directly from a tourist brochure Rosie had come across while searching the hall cupboard for a will. She hadn't found one.

Matt sniffed. 'Jewel or not, it's still Devon we're talking about, not the Costa del Sol.'

'Devon has its own unique charm.'

'If you insist. But what a crying shame you don't actually own the house or you'd be minted. I just cannot believe that your mother didn't tell you—'

'Me neither,' said Rosie, cutting Matt off before he could exclaim once again over her mum's secrecy. 'If I owned the house, I don't think I'd sell it anyway.'

'You're kidding, right? You'd sell it for a small fortune and come back to Spain with enough money to set us up in our own business. *Carruthers and Merchant, Property Consultants.* I can see it now.'

Surely it should be *Merchant and Carruthers,* if she was the partner with all the cash? And if she actually came into a small fortune, she'd rather open a cosy B&B in the mountains than try to flog property. Rosie shook her head. There was no point in getting peeved.

'I found something weird when I was looking at the funeral flowers,' she said, keen to move the subject on from money.

'Like I said, that's a bit ghoulish, Rosie.'

'It was comforting, actually, seeing all the nice things that people have said about Mum. But there was something odd. There were some flowers and a card from someone who referred to Mum as "Saffy" and signed the card "J".'

'Saffy?' laughed Matt. 'What kind of name is Saffy?'

'It was Mum's pet name and no one, except my dad and my grandparents, ever knew it or used it.'

'The mystery deepens. Perhaps secretive Saffy had a toy boy on the go,' snorted Matt.

'It's not funny.'

'No, I know it's not, babe,' said Matt, suddenly serious. 'It's all really upsetting for you. But at least now the funeral's over, you can come home and things can go back to normal.'

Normal? That was a concept Rosie couldn't imagine right now. Only a few days had passed since she'd left Spain, but she felt like a different person already. Sadder, thinner – she couldn't be bothered to cook for one in Driftwood House's big old kitchen – and more unsettled. She'd thought that she and her mum were close, in spite of the miles between them. She'd thought her mum had told her everything important that she needed to know. But she'd thought wrong.

'Are you still there, Rosie?'

'Yeah, I'm still here.'

'I think the connection's a bit dodgy so I'll get back to work, but keep your chin up and I can't wait to see you again soon.'

'You too. I need you,' said Rosie, biting her lip the moment the words were out. Matt hated clingy women.

'I explained why I couldn't make it over for the funeral, babe.'

'Yeah, of course. That's fine. That's not what I meant. I don't know what I meant really.'

'Well, just get back over here as soon as you can. Gotta go 'cos Carmen needs my help again. Love you.'

'Love you, t— oh.' The connection had already been severed.

Rosie sat, lost in thought, as the sun climbed higher in the sky and damp seeped from the grass through her jeans. The mysterious J wasn't Jerry, but could it be Jackson Porter? The solicitor didn't seem Mum's type but he was very upset about her death. What was it he'd said in his office? *Your mother was very dear to me, Rosie.*

'Hey, are you thinking of flying?'

Rosie turned her head, to see Nessa puffing along the clifftop towards her, in grey shorts and a blue T-shirt.

'I haven't booked my flight back to Spain yet,' she called, as Nessa got closer.

'That wasn't what I meant. You're very close to the edge and the rock can be a bit crumbly. I don't want you doing a nosedive.'

'I'm sure I'll be fine,' said Rosie, but she sat up and shuffled back from the edge nonetheless. 'Are you out for a walk?'

'Just blowing away the cobwebs before another shift at Shelley's. I drop Lily off with my gran in Heaven's Brook and walk over the cliff to work as long as it's not pouring down.'

'Wouldn't it be quicker to drive?'

'Definitely, if I had a car. Jake took that when he moved out, so I take her to Gran's on the bus and then walk back.'

'Jake?'

'Lily's dad. He was a moron so I didn't much care.' Vanessa sniffed in a way that made Rosie think she did care, very much indeed. 'Anyway, how are things going for you?'

'Oh, you know.'

'Yeah, I can imagine.'

Nessa plonked herself down on the grass and turned her face towards the sky. Her nose was already sprinkled with freckles and her skin was lightly tanned, with an orange tinge.

'What do you reckon?' asked Nessa, pointing at her bare legs. 'It's out of a bottle – Saharan Chic. Not the real deal, like yours. I bet it's really hot in Spain even at this time of year.'

'It'll be nudging twenty-four degrees today.'

'Nice.'

'The heat gets a bit much in the summer, to be honest. I sometimes feel like I'm going to melt.'

'It's got to be better than a dreary English summer, though.'

'Usually, though I still sometimes dream of Devon drizzle.'

Nessa looked unconvinced, but it was true. Rosie some-times imagined standing outside Driftwood House in a damp force eight gale when the Andalusian sun was beating down in August. And when the thermometer hit the mid-thirties, she liked to picture a chill sea mist rolling in and blanketing Heaven's Cove.

'Jake and I went to Spain once, before we got married,' said Nessa, shielding her eyes against the sun. 'He got pissed and fell asleep on the beach. Looked like a lobster for days.'

'When did you and Jake…?'

Rosie stopped, not wanting to pry, but Nessa smiled, good-naturedly. 'Split up? Oh, ages ago when Lily was still a baby. He was a bit overwhelmed by the whole parenting thing. Still is.' She snorted and pushed her hands through her brown hair. 'Jake's a bit of a lightweight. My gran was right about him. Have you got a partner?'

'Yeah, my boyfriend lives in Málaga.'

'Lucky you, going out with a drop-dead gorgeous Spaniard.'

'Matt's from London, actually, but he is gorgeous.'

Rosie thought back to her mum's first and only meeting with Matt. What was it she'd said about him in that noisy continental bar? *He's very good-looking in an overly groomed kind of way.* Rosie, in the first flush of romance, had been miffed by her mum's criticism but also rather thrilled because Matt *was* extremely handsome, and he was going out with her. Over the last few months, their romance had grown into more than just a fling. He loved her and was definitely missing her.

Nessa sniffed. 'What's happening about the house, then? Are you going to move in for a while?'

'I can't.'

'Because you need to get back to exotic, faraway Andalusia?'
Nessa really was being sarcastic now.

'That, and the house is going to be demolished.'

'You can't knock down Driftwood House!' Nessa sat up
straight and squinted into the sun at Rosie. 'That house has
watched over Heaven's Cove for ages. It's like a local... sentinel,
making sure that the village is safe.'

Rosie smiled at Nessa's imagination. The thought of Driftwood House keeping a watchful eye on Heaven's Cove and its
inhabitants was strangely comforting. 'You obviously haven't
heard Belinda's latest rumour?'

'I try not to listen to all the chatter that goes round Heaven's
Cove, seeing as I'm the subject of it often enough. So what's the
gossip grapevine saying now?'

'The last thing I want is for Driftwood House to be knocked
down but talk in the village is that Charles Epping does, and
he'd like to build a hotel in its place.'

'He can't do that! Refuse to sell him the house and tell him
to get stuffed.'

'Sadly, I can't do that.'

'Why not? Someone else less horrible will buy the house, as
a home or a business venture. It's a bit dilapidated these days
but its location is amazing.'

'I can't sell the house because it doesn't belong to me. It
belongs to Charles Epping and, thanks to Belinda, you're
probably the only person within a ten-mile radius who doesn't
know that.'

Nessa's eyes opened wide. 'I thought Driftwood House belonged to your mum.'

'Yeah, me too. But it belongs to the Epping family and it goes back to them now she's no longer here.'

'Wow, that must have been a bombshell.'

'Just a bit.'

'Why didn't she tell you?'

'I have absolutely no idea… and Belinda and her village grapevine don't know she didn't tell me so please—'

'My lips are sealed.' Nessa drew an imaginary zipper across her mouth. 'So what are you going to do about the Eppings' outrageous plan?'

'I'm not sure there's much I can do. Much as I hate to admit it, their plan isn't totally outrageous because the location is probably perfect for a hotel. I suggested to Mum years ago that she ought to turn Driftwood House into a guesthouse and take in paying customers.'

'It would be amazing, with its sea views and gables and fireplaces. People go mad for that kind of retro stuff. What did your mum say?'

'She told me we were lucky to live in such an amazing house and she didn't want to share our little piece of heaven.'

'Fair enough.'

'But now her little piece of heaven is going to be destroyed.'

'Really?' Nessa put her hands on her hips. 'Surely Raging Rosie isn't going to give up without a fight?'

'Raging what?'

'Nothing.' Nessa dipped her head, her cheeks flaring pink. 'Is that what people call me?'

'No, not really. It's just how I thought of you at school. It doesn't mean anything – just stupid kids' stuff.'

Rosie wrinkled her nose in confusion. 'But why "raging"? I was far too wimpy to ever argue with anyone.'

'I don't mean that sort of raging. It was more that you seemed at odds with everything – with school, with Heaven's Cove and the rest of us. And you were full of energy and dreams. Anyway, we all had nicknames at school. I know mine – Loch Nessa Monster, wasn't it?'

'Yeah, but only because—'

'I know why – because I was rarely seen. It was quite clever really.' She sucked her bottom lip between her teeth for a moment. 'My mum was ill.'

'I know, and I'm sorry. That must have been really difficult for both of you.'

'It was a tough time.' Nessa stared at the grass for a moment, lost in thought, before shaking her head. 'Anyway, that was years ago and there's no point in raking up the past. And I'd better get to work or Scaggy will be on the warpath.'

'Mr Scaglin doesn't still run Shelley's, does he? He was getting on a fair bit when we were at school. He must be ninety by now.'

'Ninety-five at the very least. He's all right, really. Bit of a stickler for time though so I'd best get a move on. He goes mad if I turn up after nine fifteen.' Nessa got to her feet and wiped blades of grass from her backside. 'I can't believe what's planned for Driftwood House and I hope, whatever you do, that things work out for you, Rosie.'

'Don't you mean Raging Rosie?' she replied, raising an eyebrow.

'Hmm, maybe I should have kept that to myself.'

'It's fine. There are worse things I could have been called.'

Worse things she probably was being called in the village right now. Runaway Rosie sprang to mind. She glanced up at Nessa from under her eyelashes. 'Do you see much of Liam Satterley?'

'Liam?' Nessa gave her a sideways look. 'I see him round and about. Why?'

'No reason. I've bumped into him a couple of times and he seems much the same as he ever was.'

'Do you think?'

'Yeah. Still a bit full of himself. He was in the churchyard this morning and in a funny mood.'

'That's hardly surprising on today of all days.'

'Why? What's so different about today?'

Nessa glanced around and lowered her voice, even though only the seagulls circling overhead could overhear. 'As I say, I don't usually gossip but it's exactly a year ago to the day since Liam was supposed to get married. Some people were talking about it in the shop yesterday, while I was doing my best not to listen.'

'Liam Satterley was getting married?' Rosie could hardly believe what she was hearing. 'I didn't think he was the type to settle down. Far too much of a ladies' man.'

Nessa's eyebrows knitted together in a frown. 'People can change, Rosie. I get the feeling you're judging us all on how we used to be before you ran off to Spain.'

'I didn't run off. I escaped.'

'You *escaped*? From the picturesque, peaceful seaside village of Heaven's Cove?' spluttered Nessa.

'So what happened, with the wedding?' asked Rosie, ignoring the heavy sarcasm that she kind of deserved. Her interest was piqued by Liam's abandoned nuptials, in spite of herself.

'Deanna got cold feet. I always thought she was too high maintenance to be content as a farmer's wife. Anyway, she left him standing at the altar in front of everyone.'

'That's awful!'

'Yeah, and totally unnecessary. What a cow!' Nessa glanced at her watch. 'Look, I really do need to go or Scaggy will go mad. Good luck with everything and hopefully I'll see you around before you head back to Spain. Don't forget us all.'

With a smile, Nessa rushed off and started picking her way confidently down the cliff path, towards the village.

Rosie turned her face towards the sea. A fishing boat was chugging its way into harbour, followed by a bevy of gulls skimming its deck. Below her, there was a dull boom as waves hit the rock face and sprayed arcs of water into the morning air.

It really was beautiful here, and peaceful. Far more peaceful than her neighbourhood in Spain, where music drifted from open windows late into the night and there was a constant hum of conversation from people drinking at the street café beneath her first-floor flat.

She meant to picture Matt, sitting at her window with his handsome face in profile as he watched the people below, but Liam's face popped into her mind instead. The breaker of many hearts had suffered a broken heart himself. No wonder he'd been distracted and irritable this morning on such a sad anniversary.

Rosie wished she'd questioned Nessa more about what happened between him and his fiancée. She wished she'd listened when her mum told her about the goings-on in Heaven's Cove. But she'd been so obviously uninterested, so sure that life here was boring, that her mum had stopped talking much about the village at all.

Rosie sighed and got to her feet. She'd spend the rest of the day scouring Driftwood House for paperwork – anything that might cast more light on her mother's agreement with the Eppings, and the identity of the mysterious J whose flowers lay in the graveyard.

*

Three hours later, Rosie had found no paperwork of note at all – no will, nothing about her mum's move to Driftwood House, and no mention of J. In fact, all she had, after working her way through a huge pile of old bills and invoices, was a pounding head, and an aching heart from seeing her mum's instructions to herself scrawled across the paperwork: *Settle by end of the month. Query this amount. What the hell is this payment for?*

She'd laughed at that last one. Mum could never remember what she bought from one week to the next. And she was hopeless with money, unlike Rosie, who managed to stretch out her meagre wages to cover rent, nights out with friends, and food for her and Matt. Although his own much bigger apartment was nearby, and he earned more than she did, he often ate at hers, and drank her dry of white wine and sangria.

Rosie yawned and moved her shoulders up and down to ease her aching muscles. She was kneeling on the sitting room floor, in sunshine that had crept around the heavy damask curtains and pooled on the rug in front of the fireplace. The light was turning the multi-coloured rug into a bright mosaic and dust motes were dancing in sunbeams.

Although she was totally alone, Rosie felt comforted by the solidity of the house and its permanence in such a changing world. This special place had served her mother well and provided shelter and refuge over the years – when her grandparents died, when her father moved out, when she left. It had been a part of Heaven's Cove for generations, only for it now to face destruction on the whim of a greedy landowner.

Upstairs, a door banged in the breeze that was eddying through the house as Rosie came to a decision. She grabbed the letter from Charles Epping and her mother's car keys from the kitchen dresser and stepped out into the lunchtime sunshine.

Chapter Nine

The good weather had held at least. Rosie pulled her mum's battered Mini into the side of the road and peered at the wide open moorland around her.

The landscape was bathed in watery sunlight peeping from behind pillows of white cloud, and golden rays were catching a raised rocky tor in the distance. The sides of the hill were dotted with sheep, sure-footed creatures well used to the uneven ground of Dartmoor.

Rosie wound down her window and breathed in great gulps of fresh air. She'd spent many happy hours as a child tramping these moors with her mum, and hadn't realised quite how much she had missed this ancient, unspoiled land. When she thought of Spanish countryside, vivid shades of ochre flooded her mind. Dartmoor, in contrast, was a palette of soft greens and deep browns with splashes of cream and grey. It was calmer, more soothing.

Glancing at the letter in her lap, she re-read the address on the back of the envelope: *High Tor House, Granite's Edge, near Kellsteignton.*

She'd left Kellsteignton behind ten minutes ago but the sat nav stuck to the windscreen was worse than useless. It started having a hissy fit as the village disappeared in her rear-view mirror and had now given up the ghost completely. But High Tor House must be around here somewhere.

Clambering from the car, she grabbed her bag and started walking uphill to get a better view. Before long, she heard the sound of water and reached a narrow stream that sliced through the ground. A rough-hewn slab of pale stone formed an ancient clapper bridge across the rushing water, and she picked her way over it.

Darker clouds drifted onto the horizon as she kept climbing, scrambling up the last rocky parts of the tor. But the view was worth the effort, as she'd known it would be. All around her was a magnificent tree-less landscape. Sheep were grazing here and there and the rough grass was littered with huge boulders of grey granite.

In the distance, a narrow ribbon of track wound from the road, ending at a pale stone house in the middle of nowhere. That must be the Eppings' country pile – a house so remote that it would be cut off in winter when heavy snow blanketed these high parts of the moors. Who would choose to live in such isolation?

Rosie shivered, feeling nervous at what she was about to do. Charles Epping had quite a reputation in Heaven's Cove, even though he was rarely seen. He never visited the village, sending staff instead to sort out any issues, and according to rumour, he'd become increasingly reclusive and bad-tempered as he grew older.

Would he shout at her or run her off his land? Rosie jumped when a bird swooped low overhead, and gave herself a good telling off. It was ridiculous to be so on edge. She wasn't a child any more. She was a grown woman who was simply going to have an adult conversation with a rich landowner. That was the long and short of it – she would face up to Charles Epping for her mum, and for poor, condemned Driftwood House, which was increasingly taking on human characteristics in her mind. She hurried back to the car before her courage could desert her.

Five minutes later, Rosie drove through the black, wrought-iron gates of High Tor House and pulled her car to a halt on the gravel next to a white van.

The churning in her stomach only got worse as she took in the magnificent house before her. Constructed of pale grey stone, the building seemed out of place here, in the middle of vast moorland. Its mullioned windows glinted in the sunshine and a small fountain trickled in front of an arched porchway that led to a black door. The arm of the stone angel that topped the fountain had turned green in the constant stream of water.

Parked on the gravel, near a big, bright flowerbed, was a shiny, silver Range Rover that looked brand new. And Rosie glimpsed a khaki Jeep in the open double garage that had been built onto the old house. Money obviously wasn't in short supply for Mr Charles Epping and his wife.

With her heart pounding, Rosie rang the doorbell. A clang echoed inside. After a minute, a scruffy-looking man in grey chinos opened the door, rather than the *Downton Abbey*-style butler she was expecting.

'Mr Epping?'

'I should be so lucky. I'm today's hired help, here to sort out the electrics,' said the man with a rich Devonian burr. 'I'm just leaving actually. Is he expecting you?'

'Um… not exactly.'

The man stepped past her onto the driveway before she could say any more. 'Good luck, then.' He threw his bag into the back of the van before sliding into the driving seat and pulling away in a shower of gravel.

Good luck? That didn't do anything to ease her nerves. Rosie stepped into High Tor House and called out 'Hello?', her voice high-pitched and anxious. She was in a large square hallway, with a carved stone fireplace opposite her. Dark panelling lined the walls and turned-wood bannisters, worn smooth by countless hands, flanked a wide staircase carpeted in tasteful burgundy. Glass-shaded lamps on a wooden table cast a mellow glow, even though it was still early afternoon. It must be pitch-black in here during the winter months. A cold shiver went down Rosie's back.

'Hello?' she called again, more loudly this time, but no one came. The house seemed cavernous and empty. She was heading back to the front door, to try ringing the bell once more, when the faint sound of music drifted into the hallway. 'Yesterday' by The Beatles. Rosie followed Paul McCartney's voice towards the back of the house, to a panelled door that was slightly ajar.

When she gently knocked, the music was abruptly switched off.

'Who is it? Who's there?' said a deep male voice. The man sounded so cross and impatient, Rosie's courage instantly disappeared. But her impulse to flee was scuppered when the door was wrenched open.

'Who the hell are you?' The man in front of her faltered for a second, alarm sparking in his icy-blue eyes. 'What are you doing here?'

'I'm so sorry. I shouldn't have just come in but the door was open and no one was around. I did ring the bell and shout but no one came, and then I heard the music so I...' Good grief, she was burbling. Rosie took a deep breath and tried again. 'I'm very sorry to disturb you but I really need to speak to Mr Epping.'

'Who are you?' repeated the man, more urgently, pulling at the collar of his white shirt. A stranger turning up in his house in the middle of nowhere had really spooked him, which was fair enough.

She gave him a reassuring smile. 'My name's Rosie Merchant and I'm from Heaven's Cove.'

That sounded like she was about to take part in a TV game show: *survive a showdown with a scary stranger to stop a wrecking ball laying waste to your family home.*

'I see. What do you want?'

The man had recovered his composure but his bony face had set into an expression of disapproval. Rosie swallowed hard and ploughed on.

'Are you Charles Epping? I apologise for intruding but I was hoping to have a quick word with you, about my mother and Driftwood House. If that would be all right?'

The man held her gaze for a moment before breathing out loudly, as though he was deflating. 'I am indeed Charles Epping and I suppose you'd better come in, seeing as you're in my house already.' He pulled the door wide open and strode back into the room.

Rosie followed him and stood, self-consciously, next to an enormous rubber plant in a vast china pot. Sunshine was dappling on a Persian rug and casting a pale stripe across a red sofa circled by squashy armchairs. In the corner stood a mahogany desk, and oil paintings – mostly portraits of people in old-fashioned clothing – hung on the walls. It was certainly eclectic in here – a ragbag mix of old furniture, probably inherited, that was no doubt worth a fortune.

Charles, Heaven's Cove absentee landlord and recluse, now stood by the fireplace with his arm resting on the mantelpiece. He was shorter than Rosie had expected – maybe five feet ten – and younger-looking, although his hair was snow-white. His eyes, the piercing blue of arctic ice, were cold when they settled on her. He stared at her face for a moment, a slight flush rising on his cheeks, before speaking in clipped tones.

'Why have you sought me out? I'm not the easiest person to find.'

Was that for a reason? Did Charles Epping and his wife choose to stay in this remote location on purpose, to avoid other people?

Rosie tried to keep her voice steady. 'I'm here to talk about Driftwood House, which I believe belongs to you. My mother Sofia lives… lived there.'

'Yes, I was sorry to hear of your mother's death.'

His face was impassive and his tone cold, almost monotonous, as though he was merely saying what was expected in such circumstances. Rosie clasped her hands behind her back and dug her nails into her palms.

'You sent a letter via your solicitors saying that Driftwood House belongs to you, and you intend to reclaim it.'

'That's correct. But you knew that would happen.' When she grimaced, he tilted his head to one side and frowned. 'Oh, you didn't know? That's interesting.'

'Why do you think that's interesting?' Rosie couldn't keep the irritation out of her voice.

'It's interesting that your mother never told you about her arrangement with the Epping family.'

'I'm sure she meant to, in the future,' said Rosie, stung into defending her mother's incomprehensible secrecy. 'Did you know my mum?'

'I did not.' He glanced at his watch, as though Rosie was taking up his valuable time. 'Your mother was simply my tenant. A name on a rental agreement.'

'An unusual rental agreement, that let her stay in the house until her death.'

'My sister, Evelyn, always was kind-hearted.'

'What does your sister have to do with it? Did *she* know my mother?'

'They were friends.'

Rosie shook her head. The Epping family was cold, uptight and entitled, if Charles was anything to go by, and she found it hard to imagine her warm, bohemian mother having anything to do with them. Plus, Charles owned Driftwood House, so what did Evelyn have to do with any of it?

'Mum never mentioned your sister. Did they stay friends?'

Charles blinked and glanced at a large portrait hanging above the fireplace. The oil painting showed a young woman, her brown hair swept up in a bun, with the moors stretching behind her. She had the same thin, Roman nose as Charles, but her grey eyes were kinder and her mouth was turned up in one corner as though she was about to smile. A small brass plaque was fixed to the foot of the frame and etched with the words *Evelyn Amelia Epping: A flash of lightning in the darkness*.

'Sadly, my sister died some years ago. She…' Charles paused, lost in thought. Should Rosie say she was sorry? She hesitated too long and the moment was lost. 'It happened a very long time ago,' he continued. 'Your mother and Evelyn were friends at the time.'

'So did Mum move into the house because of Evelyn?'

'Your mother was always very fond of the house, according to Evelyn, and she wanted her friend to be able to live there. Evelyn asked me to set up the arrangement, and it stood until your mother died.'

'That was very kind of her. But you say you never met my mum?'

'That's correct. Look, Ms Merchant.' He strode to the French window that overlooked a large garden. 'In light of you being unaware of the house's provenance, I see that the timing of the solicitor's letter was unfortunate and I apologise for that. My wife instructed our solicitor and set wheels in motion rather more quickly than I'd envisaged. But the house does belong to my family and I understood that your mother lived there alone following the death of your father.'

'She did, and I realise that you can reclaim our home, but I'd like to know more about your intentions towards Driftwood House.' *Your intentions towards Driftwood House?* She was beginning to sound as pompous as him. 'What I mean is, what are you planning to do with it?'

Charles Epping looked up at that and held Rosie's gaze. He suddenly seemed old and tired, which wrong-footed her.

'I know it's your house and I probably sound impertinent questioning you like this, but I lived at Driftwood House for a long time and I care about what happens to it. I heard in the village that you want to knock the house down and build a hotel in its place.'

'Did you, indeed? It appears that Heaven's Cove remains a hotbed of gossip and rumour.' Charles raised a white eyebrow and set his mouth in a thin line. 'Oh, do sit down, Ms Merchant.'

That sounded more like an order than an invitation and Rosie was vaguely annoyed with herself when she complied. The fabric of the sofa was rough beneath the palms of her hands.

'Are the rumours wrong?' she asked him, aware of a spring pushing into her thigh. These family heirloom sofas were uncomfortable.

'Rather annoyingly, they're perfectly correct, but our plans are at a very early stage so I'm surprised and rather perturbed that they're common knowledge. I appear to have a spy within my ranks.'

'Please don't!' blurted out Rosie, wholly unconcerned about the Eppings' security levels, and now perched so much on the edge of the sofa she was in danger of toppling to the floor. Though if that happened, she suspected that Charles Epping would simply step over her and continue with his day.

He narrowed his eyes. 'Please don't what? I'm sorry that you haven't inherited a valuable property, as you must have imagined you would. But I'm told your mother had lived there alone for some time so you're not without a roof over your head.'

'I have a roof, abroad, where I work, and I don't care about the money. I honestly don't. But I do care about the house.'

'Why?'

'Because it's been a part of Heaven's Cove for generations, up there on the cliff. I'm sure it means a lot to the villagers and it certainly meant a lot to my mum. She loved Driftwood House and it would break her heart if it was destroyed. She's gone and I'm not sure I can bear…'

The words caught in her throat, strangling her until Rosie could hardly breathe. But she would not cry in front of this cold, unfeeling man. Charles Epping took a step towards her – was he going to throw her out? – but he stopped when the door was flung open.

'There you are! I've been looking for you.' A whippet-thin woman was framed in the doorway. She stepped into the room and peered at Rosie. 'I do apologise. I didn't realise that my husband was entertaining guests.'

'This is my wife, Cecilia,' said Charles.

Rosie got to her feet and held out her hand. Cecilia walked forward, trailed by a large grey-haired dog, and gave Rosie's hand a limp shake. Not an ash-blonde hair was out of place, and her terribly tasteful clothes – brown corduroy trousers, caramel cashmere jumper and paisley silk scarf – contrasted with Rosie's jeans and T-shirt. Her whole demeanour screamed confidence and old money.

'And who are you?' she asked, glancing at Charles.

Rosie cleared her throat. 'I'm Rosie Merchant from Heaven's Cove.'

'Are you, indeed?' Cecilia moved quickly to stand next to Charles. They made quite the couple.

'I'm from the village originally, but I'm living in Andalusia now,' Rosie told her, not wanting to seem too provincial in front of this self-assured woman.

'Heaven's Cove *and* Andalusia. How marvellous.'

Charles gave his wife a tight smile. 'Ms Merchant is here to discuss Driftwood House.'

'Is that right?' The edge to Cecilia's voice was unmistakeable.

'Her mother lived in the house until her death.'

'I'm well aware of that.' She turned to address Rosie directly. 'You must have received the letter from our solicitor by now.'

'I have, and that's why I'm here.'

'I feared as much. But I'm afraid the house does not belong to you.'

'I realise that and I'm not here to question its ownership. I came here to ask you not to demolish the house.'

'How do you—?'

'Gossip in the village,' interjected her husband, staring out of the window at the moors beyond.

'Do they know about…?' She trailed off.

'About your hotel idea? Yes, I'm afraid that also appears to be the subject of gossip.'

'I see.' Cecilia's glittery green eyes hardened. 'It's purely a business proposition, Ms Merchant. Driftwood House occupies a prime spot, overlooking the sea, and would make an excellent location for a small, tasteful hotel.'

'Have you applied for planning permission?'

Cecilia's eyes narrowed. 'Not that it's any of your concern but no, not yet. It's very much at the idea stage and quite how it's become common knowledge is beyond me. But I'm sure the local authority will be keen to have more accommodation to encourage visitors to Heaven's Cove. After all, more visitors means more footfall for local business and more income.'

More money for the Epping family coffers, thought Rosie, glancing round at the antique china vases on the mantelpiece and the grandfather clock in the corner. The furniture and ornaments in this room were probably worth more than the contents of Driftwood House and her flat combined.

'I'm quite set on this proposal,' said Cecilia, drawing in the corners of her mouth until her lips pursed. 'The elevation, and the prospect of waking to that view, would attract visitors like a magnet.'

Rosie's heart sank because she couldn't argue with Cecilia's logic. Just that morning, the sight that met her when she pulled back the bedroom curtains had taken her breath away: wisps of cloud, tinged gold by the rising sun, were drifting above a midnight-blue sea and Sorrell Head in the distance was a beacon of deep green. Cecilia could definitely make money from sharing that view. Hadn't Rosie suggested it to her mother often enough?

As she thought back to those conversations, an idea began to take shape in Rosie's mind, and was out of her mouth before she knew it. 'Why not make use of Driftwood House itself? It could be converted into a wonderful little hotel.'

'Driftwood House?' Cecilia's laugh was tinkly, as though she'd been practising it. 'I don't think so.'

'Why not?' Rosie asked, determined now to say her piece, even though she desperately needed time to think things through. This hadn't been her intention when she'd set off in her mother's rusty car this afternoon. 'Driftwood House has five bedrooms, six if you convert the attic, and all have a fantastic view of the cliffs and the sea, or across the land towards Dartmoor.'

'Why would I go to the trouble of converting a dilapidated house?'

Because its unique charm and memories would be preserved. Rosie took a deep breath and replied levelly: 'Because it would save you money.' She was wholly unsure of this fact but guessed that appealing to Cecilia's pocket might be the most effective way of persuading her. 'And visitors would clamour to stay in a house with such a history.' She remembered Nessa's words on the clifftop that morning. 'People go mad for that retro stuff.'

'The building is not particularly old and has a fairly unre-markable history,' said Cecilia sniffily, 'unless you're going to claim it housed wreckers who waved lanterns from those cliffs and lured sailors to their deaths on the rocks.'

'No, the house definitely isn't that old, but it still has its own charm, with lots of original features that people love,' said Rosie, thinking that Cecilia, so keen to knock things down, seemed rather a wrecker herself.

'Why are you so bothered about what happens to the house when you've moved to Andalusia anyway?'

'Driftwood House has been a part of Heaven's Cove for decades. And my mother loved the house and would hate for it to be demolished.' *And so would I,* she thought ruefully.

'I see.' Cecilia turned her back and ran her fingers along the carved mantelpiece. 'I've heard what you have to say and I'm sorry for your loss but I'm afraid sentiment should never get in the way of a business decision. Converting Driftwood House into a hotel would be too big a job.'

'Does it have to be a fancy hotel? What about a guesthouse?'

Cecilia turned to Rosie, her face aghast. 'A guesthouse? A seaside guesthouse?' She rolled the words around her mouth with distaste.

'An upmarket guesthouse, obviously, with magnificent views and warm and cosy when the storms roll in.'

Warm and cosy was pushing it. Rosie knew all too well how the wind whistled through the eaves, billowing the curtains through cracks in the window frames. But she was suddenly more desperate than ever to save Driftwood House from the Eppings. *It won't bring back your mum,* said a little voice in her head, but she ignored it, her breathing growing shallow and her cheeks reddening.

Cecilia shook her head but Charles was staring at Rosie. 'I haven't been near the house for years. What state is it in, and how much would it cost, in your view, to get Driftwood House up to scratch?' he asked.

'Surely you can't be giving her ridiculous idea any consideration,' huffed Cecilia, but Charles ignored her, all of his attention focused on Rosie.

'I'm not exactly sure of the cost. But it would be much less expensive than demolishing the house and building a new hotel. And transporting so many building materials up such a steep cliff would be very difficult.'

'I'm not prepared to spend any money on this outlandish notion that wouldn't work,' snapped Cecilia, standing in front of Rosie with her arms folded. 'The house has become shabby and dilapidated. You might not have seen it for years, Charles, but I visit the village occasionally.'

'What about…?' said Rosie, her mind whirling. 'What about if I start the work myself, to show you how brilliant Driftwood could be as a guesthouse?'

The look of incredulity on Cecilia's face showed she thought Rosie had taken leave of her senses. But Charles tilted his head to one side and stood so still he hardly seemed to be breathing.

'Charles?' Cecilia's voice was brittle.

'I don't suppose there's any harm…'

'Oh, for goodness' sake, it's a ridiculous idea which will only delay our project.'

'While you're finding out about planning permission and all the other things that need doing, I can spruce up the house to show you its potential,' said Rosie, feeling as if she was floating high above, listening to herself saying all this daft stuff.

She needed to get back to Spain, back to Matt and reality. She glanced out at the bleak moors surrounding the Eppings' vast lonely house, at the rapidly greying sky that pressed down like a suffocating blanket. Only that morning, Matt had sent her a photo of himself drinking coffee under an orange tree, its delicate white blossom glowing in the sun. She needed to get back to her life so it was a good job her frankly ridiculous idea was about to be dismissed.

'Four weeks.' Charles stepped in front of his wife, whose mouth snapped shut. 'We'll give you that long to make your changes at Driftwood House. The tenancy would expire in around three weeks regardless, so that's an extra week or so for you to work with.'

'You're letting your heart rule your head, and you know that's never a good idea,' snapped Cecilia, but Charles held Rosie's gaze.

'You have exactly four weeks to change our minds, Ms Merchant.'

An hour later, Rosie pulled her car into a lay-by on the crest of the hill above Heaven's Cove, rolled down her window and gazed at the village below.

Cottages were clustered around the High Street and the church where her mother was buried, and the deep-blue sea was scattered with boats. They bobbed up and down on the waves while seagulls, white dots, wheeled overhead. The pretty, old-world charm of Heaven's Cove drew in tourists like dye on litmus paper. So it was rather ironic that she, born and bred in such a beautiful place, had been so eager to leave it when she was growing up.

Why had she just agreed to spend the next month here, doing up a house that would no doubt be consigned to rubble in the end?

'What am I doing, Mum?' Rosie's words sounded dull in the empty car. 'Saving the house won't bring you back, and the longer I stay here, the more I realise that I never properly knew you at all. You never told me about the lease on the house, or the mysterious J, who knew you well enough to call you Saffy. What other secrets were you keeping?'

Rosie stopped talking to herself and turned her attention back to the view. Driftwood House was just visible from here, standing watch above the village, and she could almost imagine the house breathing in its lonely spot on the cliffs. No matter how confused she was, or nervous about what else she might uncover, its fate was in her hands.

Chapter Ten

'Liam, what time is my dental appointment? Will you drive me into town? I don't want to be late.'

Liam stopped sweeping the yard and sighed. He was getting worse. 'We talked about this earlier, Dad. Your appointment was cancelled a couple of days ago so you don't have to worry about going anywhere. Anyway, it's half past five and the day's almost over so you can relax.'

Robert Satterley, tall like his son, with wiry steel-grey hair and pale blue eyes, zipped up his padded jacket that was far too warm for spring. 'Are you sure about my appointment?'

'Quite sure. They sent us a letter, rearranging it for next week.'

'Did you show me the letter?'

'Yes, at lunchtime.'

'Ah, I don't remember.' His strong face crumpled. 'Sorry.'

'There's no need to apologise, Dad. We all forget things, don't we, Mum?'

'What's that?' His mum shook the tablecloth out of the door, scattering crumbs everywhere.

'Dad forgot his dental appointment had been postponed and was worried he'd be late.'

His mum, small, round and rosy-cheeked, patted her husband's arm. 'You've been helping me turn out the back room instead, Bob. Sorting out all those issues of *Farmers Weekly* that you've been stockpiling. Shall we do another half hour before tea?'

'If that's what you want, Pam.'

She led him inside, after a worried glance at Liam, who gave her a reassuring smile, even though he was as concerned as she was.

Everyone forgot things, so he'd convinced himself at first that his Dad's short-term memory lapses were normal for a man in his seventies. That was until he'd found his father, a few months ago, sitting in the tractor he'd driven for years, with no clue how to start it up. Since then he'd got gradually worse. Another visit to the GP was needed soon.

Liam turned to continue his sweeping and almost fell over Billy as he tried to wind between his legs.

'Billy, stop getting under my feet, for goodness' sake.'

He hadn't meant to raise his voice but this week was proving to be even more trying than he'd anticipated. When the border collie flattened his ears and mooched off into a corner of the farmyard, his belly low to the ground, Liam felt a whoosh of shame. Billy wasn't the reason for his bad temper so why should he get the backlash?

'Sorry, boy.' He fished in his pocket for a dog biscuit and knelt down in front of him. 'Am I forgiven?'

Faithful Billy – what would he do without his companionship? – licked at the biscuit before gobbling it down in one, his tail wagging. Liam had just patted him on the back when a husky voice in his ear made him jump.

'What on earth have you done that needs forgiveness? Nothing too naughty, I hope.'

Liam got to his feet while Katrina put her hands on her hips and laughed. She was very attractive when she laughed, with her big grey eyes and her dimples. Hell, she was attractive any time.

'You made me jump, Katrina. I didn't hear you approaching.'

'I'm very light on my feet.' Her scarlet toenails were poking out of her strappy sandals. Dee used to wear very similar sandals, Liam remembered, until she trod in a massive dollop of manure and complained she couldn't get rid of the smell. She threw them away in the end, presumably adding that to the list of things she hated about the farm.

'Come back to me, Liam. You're miles away.'

When Katrina pushed her beautiful face closer to his, a heady scent that spoke of spices and faraway places wafted between them. Her lips, the same colour as her toenails, were so close. He pulled back and pushed a hand through his fringe.

'I'm fine. How can I help you, Katrina?'

'I was in the area and thought I'd call in to buy half a dozen eggs and to check how you're doing.'

'I'm doing well, thanks. I'll get you those eggs.'

When he came back a few minutes later, she was still standing in the yard. Most visitors gazed towards the sea which glittered in the distance, across the fields. But Katrina was staring at the farmhouse that had been in his family for generations. It was quite a pressure, keeping the farm going now that his parents were getting older and his dad was unwell. His sister, Mel, showed no interest in farming and was happily settled in Exeter with a husband and two small children. She often advised him to let the farm go but his parents would hate living anywhere else. Plus, he'd grown to love this land. Its permanence grounded him these days.

'That was quick.' Katrina looked up at him from under her long, dark lashes.

'The hens have been laying well this week. Will these do?' Liam handed over the box and watched as Katrina inspected the brown-shelled eggs. Her mouth curved into a smile when she spotted him staring at her.

'Are you quite sure you're all right, Liam? It's been... well, it's been a difficult week for you.'

'You're telling me. But this time of year is always manic on the farm. It's a good job I've got John Harbin's lad, Tom, helping me out. He's been a godsend.'

Katrina blinked. 'No, I meant...' She rested her hand on his arm and tilted her head. '... The anniversary. Your wedding anniversary that never was,' she added for good measure, as though he hadn't thought of little else for the last twelve months.

'I'm absolutely fine, Katrina. There's no need to worry.'

'But I do worry about you, Liam. I think about you all the time, here in this big house, looking after your parents. You know that I'm here to help in any way that I can, don't you?'

Moving her hand upwards, she started gently massaging his shoulder. She was going to kiss him, that was obvious. Lean into him, put her arms around his neck and kiss him. It would be very pleasant. He was quite sure of that. And maybe, if he persuaded his parents to go out for a walk before tea, it would lead to more in his bedroom, with its white-painted furniture and floral duvet cover that Dee had left behind. He hadn't kissed anyone since Dee and it would be good to feel… something. Something positive, rather than the sadness, humiliation, anger and anxiety that had become the four horsemen of his personal apocalypse.

Katrina moved closer but her gaze suddenly shifted from his face to the lane behind him.

'Great timing,' she murmured, stepping back and dropping her hand. 'You seem to have another customer, Liam, and I do believe it's Weirdo Rosie Merchant.' A perfectly plucked eyebrow disappeared into her choppy fringe.

It *was* Rosie, in jeans and a blue T-shirt, with her mother's wicker basket over her arm. Liam breathed out slowly, unsure whether his overwhelming emotion was irritation at the interruption or relief.

'Long time no see. Come on in then,' urged Katrina, while Rosie hesitated in the farm gateway, her trainers sinking in mud from the tractor's wheels.

'I don't want to interrupt.'

'Too late for that,' said Katrina, under her breath, her face still stretched into an unnatural smile.

'You can come in. It's fine,' said Liam, uncomfortably aware that she'd no doubt seen him and Katrina about to… who knew what? 'How can I help you?'

'It doesn't matter. I can come back later.'

'No need.' Katrina pushed the eggs into the yellow tote bag she had over her shoulder. 'I was just leaving anyway so you can come in. I promise I won't bite.' When she laughed, colour flooded Rosie's face, giving her golden skin a ruby glow. And there was the tightening of her jaw again.

Liam stepped forward. 'Were you after some eggs or vegetables, Rosie? I've got cabbages and carrots in the barn.'

'Anything like that will do. Thanks.'

'Follow me and I'll show you what I've got.'

Katrina gave him her prettiest pout. 'I'll leave you to it, Liam, but promise me that I'll see you again soon.'

Everyone saw everyone all the time in Heaven's Cove so the promise was immaterial, but Liam nodded anyway. That seemed to satisfy Katrina, who leaned forward and briefly pressed her lips against his cheek. 'Bye,' she murmured huskily, her breath warming his face.

She paused as she passed Rosie. 'How are you doing? We haven't spoken for… it must be years. You look well. Have you lost a little weight? Well done, you.' Liam wasn't one for nuance but even he caught the condescension in her voice.

'I'm on the bereavement diet,' muttered Rosie, running her hand over her hips, which looked perfectly fine to Liam. She was a little bigger than stick-thin Katrina but her gentle curves suited her.

'Yes, I heard about your mum, of course. I'm sorry I couldn't get to the funeral but I had a Zoom call I just couldn't get out of. Talking of which, I'd better get home and back to work. Have you heard that I'm running my own business now?'

'I haven't.'

'Really?' Katrina flicked her shiny brown hair over her shoulder. 'I provide marketing solutions for entrepreneurial businesses.'

'That sounds interesting.'

'It is. And rather lucrative. Right, I'm off. See you soon, Liam.' With one last smouldering glance at him, she sauntered off up the lane.

'Were you expecting Katrina to be at your mum's funeral?' asked Liam when Rosie wandered over, the hem of her jeans splattered in mud. Hopefully it was nothing worse. Billy could be a little indiscriminate.

'No, not at all. She doesn't like me much and she didn't really know Mum.'

A car droned in the distance as a silence stretched between them. Liam was the first to break it. 'Did you want some veg, then?'

'That would be great, thanks.'

She followed him into the barn and studied his recently harvested crop: fat Savoy cabbages, spring greens, and carrots and parsnips still coated in red soil.

'What do you fancy?' he asked, breathing in the familiar smell of damp earth and sawdust.

'A cabbage will be fine. Look…'

When Rosie turned to him, his fingers itched to brush back the sun-streaked fringe that was flicking into her eyes. She looked tired and slightly battered this afternoon, as though life was too much for her.

'I wasn't terribly sympathetic when I saw you near the church first thing this morning, but I didn't realise it was such a difficult day for you. I found out later, though I don't want you to think I was gossiping because I wasn't. Nessa mentioned it when I said that I'd seen you. Anyway, I just wanted to say that I didn't know about the anniversary or I would have made allowances and not been so... snippy.'

Liam wasn't sure he wanted people making allowances. He'd soon tired of the pity in locals' eyes when they asked him how he was doing, and the barely disguised glee on some so-called friends' faces that he'd been taken down a peg or two. But it was kind of Rosie to care. And kinder still for her to come and apologise.

'Don't worry about it. I was slightly grumpy, to be fair.'

'Only slightly?' A slow smile lit up Rosie's face, making her eyes shine.

'OK, very grumpy. But I do have an excuse for not being on my best behaviour.'

'Me too.'

'Yeah, we make quite a sorry pair.' Liam dropped two of the largest cabbages into the basket on Rosie's arm.

'How much is that?'

'Forget it.'

'No, I want to pay.' Rosie reached for the purse in her basket.

'If you insist, fifty pence will cover it,' said Liam, vaguely registering that Katrina hadn't paid for her eggs.

He took the coin that Rosie proffered and dropped it into his jeans pocket. 'When are you going back to Spain?'

'Not for a little while.' She paused and screwed up her face, as though she was wrestling with a decision. Then she said: 'I went to see Jackson Porter, the solicitor, like you suggested. But he couldn't help me. So… I went to see Charles Epping today, at his house on Dartmoor.'

Liam stared at her. Writing to Epping about the house was one thing, but visiting him at home? No one in the village had actually spoken to the man for years – although he was discussed often enough by those adversely affected by his business decisions and rent hikes.

'You've got to be kidding me. You went to his house?'

'I did and I saw him and his wife and talked about Driftwood House and about them building a hotel in its place. Had you heard about the hotel idea?'

Liam nodded.

'From Belinda?'

'Who else? So how did your chat with the Eppings go?'

'Badly, at first. His wife looked like she wanted to kill me. But I ended up striking a kind of deal with him.'

Liam folded his arms, admiration for Rosie's chutzpah overshadowed by unease. 'What on earth have you agreed to with a man like that? You've struck a deal with the devil.'

Rosie blanched at that, and maybe it was a little strong, but she'd been away and didn't know the Eppings like he did.

'I suggested that Driftwood House didn't need to be demolished because converting it into a guesthouse could be a money-spinner instead.'

'What gave you that idea?'

'It's an idea I had ages ago and when I met Nessa she said guests would go mad for all the original features.'

'Nessa's been saying rather a lot, by the sound of it.' Liam rubbed at his eyes. He'd hardly slept last night and tiredness was beginning to catch up with him. 'So is Charles Epping going to reprieve Driftwood House and turn it into a guest-house now?'

'Not exactly. He's thinking about it and I've got four weeks to make some changes and persuade him – or rather, his wife, who's very posh and pretty scary.'

'What sort of changes?'

'I don't know. A lick of paint, some repairs, a good tidy-up.'

It would take more than a good tidy-up to bring Driftwood House up to scratch and fit for paying guests. Liam frowned.

'I can make a difference. I'm sure I can.'

'And who's going to make all these changes?'

'I am.'

'Who's paying for them?'

'I will. Paint and polish won't cost too much, and I've got some savings.'

It was a crazy notion and she was wasting both her time and her money. Epping would sweep in at the end of her efforts and knock the damn house down anyway. But Liam's retort telling her so died on his lips when he spotted Rosie's clenched fists. She was trying very hard to hold things together.

Heartbreak and grief could make people go a little crazy – he was proof of that – but keeping busy helped. For months after Dee left, he'd worked from sunrise to sundown, with no time off at weekends. So maybe a project, even a hopeless one for a no-good cheat like Charles Epping, was just what Rosie needed right now.

'Good luck with it, then,' he told her.

She nodded. 'Thanks. By the way, do you know someone around here whose name begins with J?'

Her random question took him by surprise, but he racked his brains. 'There's Jackson, you've met him. And Jimmy Collins in Field Lane. Or Joanna Johnson.'

'Jimmy's in his eighties, isn't he?'

'His nineties, I think. Why?'

'Someone left flowers on mum's grave and signed the card with a J. I'm just interested to know who J is. Maybe it *is* Jackson.'

'He was definitely at the funeral. He was really upset.'

'Which is a bit strange.'

Liam frowned. 'Not really. A lot of people get upset at funerals.'

'Is Jackson married?'

'I think so. Why?'

'Sofia!' suddenly boomed across the farmyard, and Liam cringed when he spotted his dad. He'd opened the front room window and was leaning out. 'Sofia, I haven't seen you for a while,' he called. 'Where have you been?'

'I'm sorry,' whispered Liam to Rosie. 'Dad gets a bit confused these days and you do look a lot like your mum.'

Some people would take offence or burst into tears but Rosie simply gave a wobbly smile. 'Hello, Mr Satterley. I'm Rosie, Sofia's daughter. How are you keeping these days?'

'Oh, can't grumble, though I have to go to the dentist later today.'

'That doesn't sound great but it's good to look after your teeth.'

'Definitely, even at my advanced age.' Robert laughed. 'Look after yourself, Rosie, and give my best to your mother.'

'Sorry,' said Liam again, as his dad pulled the window shut, but Rosie waved away his concern.

'It really doesn't matter, and it was good to see your dad again.'

Liam smiled at her, gratefully. 'So when does the painting, repairing and tidying start?'

'As soon as I've sorted out a bit more of Mum's paperwork, so I'd best get on. Thanks for the cabbages.'

'You're welcome.'

She gave him a small wave when she reached the gate and he watched her walk along the lane towards the village, her trainers shedding mud with every step.

Katrina was wrong, thought Liam, picking up his broom to finish sweeping the yard. Rosie Merchant wasn't weird. She was quiet, and her determination to leave Heaven's Cove made her unusual around here. But it turned out she was kind and thoughtful – and boy, was she brave. Not many villagers would have confronted Charles Epping in his own home. Liam felt bizarrely proud that she'd trusted him with the news of her deal over Driftwood House, but he still feared that her trust in Epping was misplaced. He'd never keep to his end of the bargain.

'But it's none of my business, is it,' he told Billy, stroking under the dog's chin, just where he liked it best. 'She'll find out her mistake soon enough, and then she'll be gone.'

Chapter Eleven

It took a few moments for Rosie to remember where she was when she woke up the next morning. The bed was less lumpy than hers in Spain, the light filtering through the curtains was softer, and there were no rhythmic snores from Matt.

She rolled over and stretched, suddenly acutely aware of the silence. Usually, she was woken at Driftwood House by the screech of seagulls and, if she listened carefully enough, the dull boom of waves pounding into the foot of the cliffs carried through the air. But this morning there was no sound at all.

She padded from her bed to the window and pulled back the curtains. Instead of sun-streaked sea stretching to the horizon, there was nothing. The house was cocooned in a dense blanket of sea mist that curled around the building and suffocated all noise. She laid her hand flat on the window and traced a tendril of white that pressed against the glass. Heaven's Cove may as well not exist. The world had shrunk to her, standing alone in her mother's dressing gown in a house that was on borrowed time.

Yesterday, her agreement with the Eppings had seemed rather overwhelming, and turning to Matt for comfort wasn't an option. She wasn't sure how he'd react to the news, so it was just as well he hadn't called her last night. But chatting with Liam – simply telling someone else about the whole crazy idea

– had galvanised her. She'd gone to sleep with a head full of plans, and with time running out for Driftwood House, today was the day to start putting those plans into action.

Rosie had a quick shower and forced down a slice of toast. Her appetite was still off. Then she grabbed a notebook and pen and started going from room to room, noting down what needed to be done to spruce up the house. Some things were beyond her – new furniture would be essential if the house were to welcome paying guests, along with a modern boiler for hot baths, and an updated kitchen to replace the scuffed cupboards and chipped counters.

But there was a lot that Rosie could do to freshen up Driftwood House and enable Charles Epping to see its potential. Cecilia's good opinion was already a lost cause, she feared. Mrs Epping had taken against Rosie and her guesthouse idea from the start.

After an hour, Rosie had quite a list of what she needed in order to get the tidy-up started: cleaning materials, sandpaper, paint, silicone for around the baths, and bleach for the yellowing grouting between the bathroom tiles. The front door, with its swollen timbers, was almost beyond repair, but she was determined to save it. Every Christmas, her mother would make a wreath of holly, ivy leaves, and driftwood from the beach and pin it to the storm-scoured wood. The wreath would welcome visitors and always gave Rosie a warm festive feeling, until it finally disintegrated in the wind and salt spray.

Tucking the list into her bag, Rosie stepped outside and blinked. The village was still shrouded but higher up, on the cliffs, the fog had been burned away by the sun, and Driftwood House was now an island in a sea of mist that swirled far below her. It really was beautiful up here, but she didn't have time to linger. Buttoning her jacket, Rosie walked down the cliff and was enveloped by fog.

She'd almost reached Shelley's hardware store when Katrina, in a leopard-skin coat, came out of the newsagent's, fastening her beautiful handbag that Rosie just knew was made of soft Italian leather.

Rosie ducked into the doorway of the ice-cream parlour and peered through the curls of mist blanketing the narrow lane. Having already had one run-in with Katrina, she wasn't keen on having another.

It was daft to be nervous because school was long gone and Katrina had never been a bully. Not really. But her steady drip-drip of snide comments – about Rosie's absent dad, 'spooky' Driftwood House and her inability to fit in with the 'in' crowd – had made Rosie feel that she wasn't good enough. And judging by Katrina's comments yesterday on Rosie's appearance and the brags about her own life, she hadn't changed a bit.

Now it seemed that Katrina was cosying up to Liam, the village's most eligible bachelor. Two golden people together. Who would outshine the other? Rosie wondered, before deciding that skulking in the doorway of an ice-cream parlour at the age of twenty-nine was rather pathetic. *Act like the grown-up you are!* she told herself, stepping back into the street. But she heaved a sigh of relief when Katrina glanced at her watch and wandered off towards the grocery store, her footsteps muffled by the fog.

When Rosie reached Shelley's, the sun was starting to burn through the mist. Another half an hour and the village would be bathed in bright sunshine, but for now it was cold and damp, and Rosie shivered as she looked at the store that was open for business.

It was just as she remembered: a gleaming, dark-wood shopfront, with buckets and spades in bright colours stacked outside, along with deckchairs, beach balls and, a perennial favourite on the breezy Devon coast, striped windbreaks.

When she pushed open the door, the inside was familiar too. A smell of linseed oil and polish hung heavy in the air, and wooden shelves were lined with plugs, lightbulbs, hooks, doorbells, paint and, rather incongruously, fake flowers and a glass display case of watches.

'I reckon those watches fell off the back of a lorry,' said Nessa, closing the novel she was reading and pushing it under the counter. 'Scaggy turned up with them a couple of months ago. I've no idea why 'cos no one comes into a hardware store to buy a watch, do they? Especially not knock-offs.'

Rosie smiled, genuinely pleased to see a friendly face. 'I thought you might be here.'

'I'm always here.' Nessa tugged at her Shelley's-branded apron as though she was embarrassed to be seen in it. 'So what brings you to Scaggy's hardware emporium? I thought you'd be packing up Driftwood House and heading for Spain.'

'Not yet. I need a few things.'

Rosie passed her list across the counter and Nessa read through it, wrinkling her nose. 'A few things? What are you up to? I thought you were leaving soon?'

'I am, but I want to spruce up Driftwood House first.'

'Why?' Nessa leaned against the counter and folded her arms, which Rosie noticed were a darker orange shade of Saharan Chic than before. 'I don't mean to be harsh but is there much point if the place is going to be demolished by old misery-guts Epping?'

'It might not be demolished, you never know.'

'You've changed your tune.'

'I've just had a think about it,' said Rosie, reluctant to talk about the bargain she'd struck with the Eppings. Not when Liam had made it patently clear through body language, if not words, that he thought she was barking mad. 'This is just something I have to do.'

Nessa sucked her bottom lip between her teeth. 'I get it. I went a bit nuts after my mum died too. Though that involved drinking lots and smoking spliffs rather than home improvement. But whatever helps to get you through.'

She started collecting together items on Rosie's list and piling them onto the counter. There were rather a lot and Rosie began to wish she'd brought the car with her, even though parking in the centre of Heaven's Cove, with its narrow streets, was often a nightmare.

'You'd better come and choose your paint colours,' called Nessa from the back of the store. 'What do you fancy? Daffodil Yellow? Hyacinth Blue? Epping Ebony that's as black as the old bugger's heart?'

Rosie grinned for the first time in ages and started searching through the paints. She needed light, bright colours that would make Driftwood House seem large and welcoming.

Shelley's range of shades wasn't huge but Rosie finally chose white with a hint of taupe that reminded her of bleached driftwood on the beach. That seemed appropriate.

'We don't have enough of that colour in stock but I can order more in for you,' said Nessa, piling the tins next to the sugar soap, filler, paint brushes and rollers. 'This really is a lot of effort for a house that's due to be demolished. Sorry to be a bit brutal, Rosie. But this is going to cost a shedload.'

'I know,' said Rosie, brandishing her credit card with more confidence than she felt. 'But it's something I need to do. For Mum and for all of the memories there. The thing is…'

She hesitated, wondering whether she *should* tell Nessa and risk her bargain with the Eppings being all round the village by lunchtime.

'The thing is what? Oh, don't worry. I can keep a secret. I've been the subject of gossip too often to indulge in it myself.' When Nessa shrugged, Rosie glimpsed the hurt beneath her brash exterior and decided to trust her. She'd already told Liam after all.

'There's a chance that Driftwood House *can* be saved.'

'How?'

'It's partly thanks to what we were talking about at Sorrell Head. I went to see Mr and Mrs Epping and—'

'Whoah!' said Nessa, shoving the palm of her hand towards Rosie's face. 'Stop right there! I never suggested going to see them.'

'No, but you agreed that Driftwood House would make a fabulous guesthouse.'

'I'm not sure the word "fabulous" was ever used but yeah, I did agree with you on that. But you said the house belongs to the Eppings.'

'It does. That's why I went to see them and tried to persuade them to consider converting Driftwood House into a guesthouse rather than knocking it down.'

'So what did they say?'

'They said I've got four weeks to spruce the place up in the hope they can see its potential as a guesthouse, rather than just a prime building spot.'

'Wow, that's amazing, Rosie, and just a little bit bonkers. Who's paying for this make-over?'

'Me, but it's just cosmetic stuff. Nothing too heavy-duty.'

'Hmm. I still can't believe that you actually went to see the Eppings. Did you go to their spooky house up on the moors?'

'I did.'

'That's brave. So what's it like? All *Wuthering Heights,* I bet, with mad women in the attic.'

Wasn't that *Jane Eyre?* Rosie grinned. 'It was a bit creepy and isolated and grand, but I only saw a couple of rooms. Do they live there on their own?'

'Apparently, apart from staff, I suppose. They never had kids which isn't surprising. I bet they've never had sex. I really can't imagine those two getting jiggy.' Nessa shuddered. 'What were they like?'

'Well…' Rosie thought for a second. 'He was cold and grumpy and…' She remembered his icy blue eyes. 'A bit sad, really.'

'And his wife?'

'One hundred per cent terrifying.'

Nessa snorted. 'She's mega-scary all right. Mr Epping never comes to Heaven's Cove. I've only ever seen him in photos and he was on the local news once, when one of his businesses won an award. But his wife comes to the village occasionally, swanning around in her Mercedes as though she owns the place. Which, to be fair, she pretty much does. I'm surprised she's changing her hotel plans.'

'She isn't keen on changing them at all but Charles – Mr Epping – was more open to the idea. He was the one who pushed to give me some time to change their minds about the hotel.'

'Is that right?' Nessa pushed Rosie's credit card into the machine. 'You want to be careful.'

'Why?'

'Because they'll screw you over. You'll end up doing loads of work and spending lots of cash and then they'll knock the place down anyway. Being ruthless is how rich people make their money.' Nessa winced at Rosie's expression. 'Sorry. I'm being blunt again. I just don't want to see you being taken advantage of and upset.'

'As I told my boyfriend yesterday morning, I'm upset anyway.'

'Exactly. And you don't want any more upset on top.' Nessa's smile was sympathetic. 'Why do you want to save the house anyway? I know I said it's a Heaven's Cove icon and we'll be sorry to see it go, but you'll be back in Spain, so it doesn't make sense.'

'I know. My head keeps telling me to cut my losses and get on the first flight back home. But my heart… well, that's a different matter.'

Nessa stared at Rosie for a moment and then started piling paintbrushes and rollers into a large paper bag.

'In that case, you'd better get started. Take what you can now and I'll drop the rest off to you later in Scaggy's van if I get a chance. Or, brilliant timing' – she glanced towards the shop door that had just opened – 'we can ask Liam if he's out and about later and can save us both the trouble.'

'Ask me what?' said Liam, wandering towards them.

He was looking particularly ruggedly handsome today, in tight jeans and a navy sweatshirt, with dark stubble on his chin. Rosie felt her cheeks growing hot and dipped her head. She'd never been one of the girls who blushed when Liam came into the room and she wasn't about to start feeding his ego now, even if he had listened to her ramble on yesterday about her plan to save Driftwood House.

'I was just saying to Rosie that I might not have time to drop off all these supplies at Driftwood House later, but maybe you could, if you're out in your van?'

'I'm quite busy, but I suppose I could…'

'Please don't worry about it,' said Rosie hastily. 'There must be loads to do on the farm at this time of year, and I can drive down later to collect the rest.'

Nessa leaned across the counter and put her chin in her hands. 'You'll be far too busy sploshing paint over the walls, Rosie, to come down into the village again.'

'I really won't,' said Rosie, giving Nessa the same look she often gave Matt when he opened a third bottle of wine.

'Of course you will. Big, falling-down houses don't decorate themselves.'

'I'm still sure I can spare half an hour to nip in again later.'

'But there's no need to bother if Liam can help instead, is there?'

She frowned at Rosie, clearly not sure why getting Liam involved was being met with resistance. Rosie wasn't sure either, but it felt like a really bad idea.

Before she could say anything more, Liam chimed in. 'Ladies, stop fighting over me. I need to collect a few things from Selderfield later so I can pick up Rosie's stuff and drop it at Driftwood House on the way.'

Nessa grinned. 'Great, and you could always stay and give Rosie a hand with transforming the place into the Eppings' new guesthouse…' She stopped and clamped her hand over her mouth. 'Sorry,' she mumbled.

'It's all right.' Rosie smiled. 'Liam knows about the guesthouse plan, which is just as well because you're not being very discreet.'

'Maybe not but, in my defence, buying up a load of decorating essentials in the village hardware store is a bit of a giveaway. So are you going to give Rosie a hand with the decorating while you're up there, Liam?'

Now Nessa was going too far. Rosie shook her head. 'I can manage perfectly well on my own, thank you. And I'm sure you've got better things to do, Liam.'

He held her gaze when she looked at him properly for the first time since he'd come into the shop. 'The farm is pretty busy right now, and I'm also helping out with Mum and Dad.'

'Of course. Don't let Nessa bully you.'

Nessa looked affronted at the very suggestion, but the corner of Liam's mouth lifted. 'I'm very easily bullied, to be honest.'

'Really? I find that hard to believe.'

He raised an eyebrow. 'You'd be surprised. I can be bullied into all sorts of things.'

Was he flirting? Rosie grabbed the paper bag of supplies and shoved it into her canvas bag. Of course not. Liam was simply making conversation to cover his unease at being put on the spot by Nessa. And even if he was slightly flirting, he'd probably slipped into it out of habit.

'I really can collect all of this later,' she told him.

'It's no bother.' Liam pushed his hands into the pockets of his jeans. 'I'll drop the stuff round to you later this afternoon.'

Nessa grinned, looking very pleased with herself. 'That's all sorted then. You OK with that, Rosie?'

'Yes, if you're sure, Liam. Thanks very much.'

He nodded, already looking at the batteries he'd presumably come in to buy. Nope, he definitely hadn't been flirting. Thank goodness.

Rosie swung her bag onto her shoulder and, after a brief wave to Nessa, she left Shelley's as quickly as she could.

*

Liam was as good as his word and arrived at Driftwood House mid-afternoon. Rosie, still sorting through reams of her mother's paperwork, heard the growl of an engine in the distance and went outside to watch his white van bounce up the cliff road. It threw up puffs of dust as it lurched in and out of potholes, leaving dark streaks on the paintwork.

Rosie waved as the vehicle got closer, still feeling awkward that Liam had been hounded into helping her. He seemed distracted and out of sorts when he got out of the van and stretched his long legs.

'It's a good job my van's already clapped out 'cos that road's pretty shocking,' he said, following her into the house and dumping an armful of supplies in the sitting room. 'If you want this house to take in paying guests, it'll need to be sorted out.'

'I'm sure the Eppings will fix it once they realise what a money-spinner this place could be. Anyway, whatever they finally decide – guesthouse or hotel – they'll need a decent cliff road.'

'I guess so.' He turned slowly, taking in the room's faded walls and the windows rattling in the breeze that had been whipping off the sea all afternoon. 'At the risk of sounding a bit negative, there's quite a lot that needs doing.'

'There is, but I don't have to do it all. If I can show that Driftwood House has loads of character and charm that will attract tourists, then the Eppings will step in and do the rest,' said Rosie, with more confidence than she felt.

Liam shot her a straight look. 'Hmm.'

'I'm just giving the place a facelift. It won't take long.'

Even Rosie didn't believe that, so she wasn't surprised when Liam raised an eyebrow. But he fetched in the rest of the paint and filler and brushes without a word and placed them on what was becoming a very large pile.

'Thank you so much, Liam,' said Rosie, wondering quite where to start with the facelift. It suddenly all seemed rather daunting.

'That's OK.' His shoulders dropped and he smiled for the first time since he'd arrived. 'I was already coming out this way.' He ran a finger along flaking paint on the windowsill. 'Are you sure you can do all this on your own?'

'Absolutely,' said Rosie brightly.

'And you're sure it's worth the effort?'

'Definitely.' Rosie's tone was less bright but she hoped he wouldn't notice.

'All right, then. I'd better leave you to it.'

Liam strode through the hall to the front door but hesitated on the doorstep. What was he doing? His head dropped and she heard him groan quietly before he turned to face her. 'You're never going to manage all of this on your own.'

'I will. It'll be fine.'

Liam shook his head. 'No, you won't. The farm's busy but I can spare a couple of hours tomorrow morning to help you get started.'

'God, no. You really don't have to.'

The thought of being alone with Liam for any length of time made her stomach flutter with anxiety. But he waved away her objection.

'I know I don't have to, but I will.'

'Please don't be influenced by what Nessa said this morning.'

'I'm not.'

'Then why do you want to help? You obviously think this is a lost cause and a waste of time. Driftwood House doesn't mean anything to you.'

'But it does to you.'

He held her gaze, with his pale blue eyes, as light streamed in through the open front door and dust motes danced around him. The grandfather clock in the corner began to chime the hour.

'Anyway' – Liam gave her a cursory smile – 'I need to get over to Selderfield so…'

'Yes, of course.'

Rosie followed him to his van and stood back while he did a three-point turn on the grass. Her brain was whirling. It was very kind of Liam to offer to help her tomorrow but what on earth would they talk about for a couple of hours? Years ago they'd had nothing in common, and now they had even less. It was going to be what Matt would describe as 'mega awks'.

Liam suddenly wound down his window and stuck his head out. 'By the way, Nessa asked me to say, seeing as I'm here, that some people you know will be in The Smugglers Haunt tomorrow night, and you should join them. I'm supposed to persuade you.'

'Um…'

'Seven thirty-ish, and they'll be eating pub grub. Fred does a passable fish and chips on Saturday nights but I'd give the pasta a miss. Nessa said she really hoped to see you there.'

Maybe she'd go, maybe not, thought Rosie, watching Liam's van lurch back down the track. But when the dusty van reached the edge of the village and was hidden from view, a sudden wave of loneliness took her by surprise.

She'd been lonely before – in unfamiliar European towns before she found her feet; gazing at the endless Namibian desert with no one to share the experience; and recovering from flu in a Greek hostel with only bed bugs for company. But that loneliness had been eased by the excitement of being somewhere different and laying down memories. This loneliness was intensified by sorrow and a nagging, familiar sense of not fitting in that dragged her back to years gone by.

Talk of the get-together in The Smugglers had unsettled her, she decided, vowing not to go. What was the point when she'd be faraway soon enough, under the Spanish sun and in the arms of Matt – who hadn't been in touch at all since yesterday morning, actually.

She checked her phone. There were the two messages she'd sent him earlier, both with ticks to show he'd read them, but neither had a reply. That was strange. His phone had started ringing one thousand miles away by the time she changed her mind and jabbed at the screen to end the call. Mid-afternoon in Málaga, he was probably at work, mentoring Carmen, and too busy to talk. Or maybe he was still enjoying a siesta. Perhaps he was enjoying a siesta *with* Carmen.

Rosie pushed the thought from her mind. Carmen was gorgeous, with her long black hair and eyes the colour of coal, but she trusted Matt. Plus, she hadn't broken the news yet that she was stuck in Heaven's Cove for a while longer. And that conversation was best tackled when Matt was home and slightly sozzled after a glass or three of rosé.

She turned her attention back to the paint and supplies, now piled in the middle of Driftwood House. Was all of this a waste of time? Nessa was probably right and the Eppings would screw her over, but she couldn't just give up. Not when she could almost hear her mother's voice, urging her on. What was it her mum used to say to her all the time, when she was growing up? *You never know what you can do, Rosie, until you try.*

Chapter Twelve

Rosie straightened up with a groan and pushed the heel of her hand into the aching small of her back.

The armchair she'd just dragged into the middle of the sitting room was heavier than it looked. The squashy cushions on the chair still had a dent where her mum used to sit. Though it was always Dad's chair when she was growing up. He'd drop into it after work and eat his tea in front of the telly. But Mum claimed it after he left.

Rosie was devastated when he as good as disappeared from her life when she was ten, following his affair with a work colleague. Although she and her dad shared few interests and often clashed, she loved him and regular phone calls and the occasional get-together didn't make up for his absence. But after a while, she began to appreciate the calm he left behind. It was good not to be roused from sleep by the sound of raised voices and banging doors.

She brushed her hand across the cushions where her mum would sit, curled up with her feet underneath her, watching American shoot 'em up detective shows. They were her favourite, even though she was the least confrontational or aggressive person ever. Rosie could picture her sitting there, elbow on the arm of the chair, chin in her hands, eyes on the flickering screen.

Rosie shook her head to dislodge the image. This was no time to be sad and distracted when there was so much work to be done. Yesterday, she'd washed down all the walls on the ground floor, and today the painting would begin. She started rooting through the paint pots and brushes, looking for the dustsheets she was sure she'd bought. The furniture in here was old, but it was solid – her aching back was testament to that – and it would do for now, with a few new cushions here and there.

She rooted through the pile again. She'd meant to buy dustsheets. She was sure they'd been on the list but they weren't included in the supplies that Liam had delivered yesterday.

Rosie stood with her hands on her hips in the midst of the muddle. Maybe she could drape sheets from the airing cupboard over the huddle of furniture, like Dad used to do. She could remember her bed, dressing table and books covered in paint-splattered white sheets when Dad had decorated her bedroom.

Twenty years on, the walls of her old room were still a deep purple – she'd never been a pastel-pink kind of child. The purple was going to need at least two coats of white paint to cover it, she realised. And the furniture in there would definitely need protecting from her lack of decorating finesse. Maybe the old dustsheets were stored in the attic? It was worth a look.

Rosie climbed the last rung of the loft ladder and stepped gingerly into the gloomy space. She hadn't been up here for years, not since she'd helped search for her mum's old foot spa and had come across an enormous spider instead. Mum had stood up so quickly when Rosie screamed, she'd cracked her head on the sloping roof. Understandably, she hadn't been best pleased and Rosie had avoided the attic ever since. Being yelled at by a parent and terrorised by a massive arachnid had drilled avoidance into her soul. But now Mum was gone and it was time to brave the terrors of the attic like the grown-up she was.

The floor was boarded over and safe to walk on, but the single lightbulb hanging from the apex of the roof cast dark shadows. It really was quite creepy up here, especially with the wind whistling and moaning through loose roof tiles.

Taking a deep, dusty breath – did that musty smell mean there were mice? – Rosie switched on her torch and started sweeping its beam ahead of her.

It was pretty much a dumping ground up here. Cardboard boxes overflowing with books, and transparent plastic cases packed with old blankets and duvets vied for space with a box of Dad's old DIY tools, Grandma's old Singer sewing machine, an ancient gramophone with a wind-up handle, several boxes of vinyl records, and Rosie's old scooter – the one she'd fallen from on the quay when she was seven years old and broken her arm. Memories came flooding back as Rosie stood amid the detritus of her family life. A life that had once been so safe and secure, but now had so many people missing from it. She gulped and brushed away a tear that plopped onto the grimy floorboard. Where were the dustsheets, so she could leave this attic and its painful memories behind?

Rosie picked her way forward, trying to ignore the huge cobwebs that shone like delicate, silver filaments. She wasn't a frightened child any longer. She was an adult. A seasoned traveller. An orphan.

But there was far too much junk up here to search through and no sign of the dustsheets. Rosie had turned back towards the loft ladder when she spotted a pile of old tablecloths on top of a cardboard box: a blue spotted cloth she remembered from her childhood, a Christmas one covered in sprigs of holly, and a plain white one that had yellowed with age. They'd be perfect for protecting Driftwood House's furniture.

She gave them a shake to dislodge any spiders and shoved them under her arm. It was only then that she spotted *Sofia's Stuff* scrawled across the top of the closed box underneath in black marker pen.

The box was sealed with plenty of brown parcel tape but the tape had lost its stickiness over the years and Rosie was able to peel it back easily. Inside there was a jumble of clothing – skirts, dresses and cardigans that smelled of moth balls. Why had her mum bothered keeping all of this stuff? It could have gone to a charity shop rather than sitting up here mouldering for decades. In fact, it was about time it did.

Rosie pushed the box across the floor and, with only the slightest hesitation, shoved it through the open loft hatch. It bumped down the stairs and came to rest on the landing, on its side. She threw the bundle of tablecloths after it before carefully making her way down the ladder and stepping over the mess.

Then, she sat cross-legged on the landing carpet and started emptying out *Sofia's Stuff*. None of the clothing was familiar and it all looked pretty old. When Rosie hugged one of the jumpers tight and sniffed it for her mother's scent, she could smell only the slight tang of damp. The clothes would need washing before they could go to a charity shop.

Underneath the jumble of clothing, Rosie's fingers hit something cold and hard. She pushed her other hand beneath the clothes and brought out a metal box that glinted copper in the light. The sides of the box were smooth and unremarkable, save for a few dents and scratches, but the lid was beautiful. Strips of different metals – copper, silver and gold – were woven together in a pattern that reminded Rosie of making willow baskets in primary school. She ran her fingertips across the colourful strands and tried to open the box, but it was locked.

She stared at it for a moment, as though force of will might make the box spring open, and when – surprise, surprise – that didn't work, she started shaking out clothes in search of a dropped key. But there was nothing, other than a couple of lost buttons.

Rosie wasn't the type of person to listen in to private conversations or read people's diaries. She'd always thought that people who did were idiots, and likely to find out things they'd rather not know. But her mother had deliberately kept her in the dark about the Eppings owning her childhood home, and the mysterious J who must have known her so well. What other secrets had she been keeping? Suddenly, finding out what was in the box became the most important thing in the world.

Where would her mum keep a key to a copper box that she'd hidden away in the attic? Taking her find with her, Rosie went to the sitting room and started rummaging through the oak bureau. There was so much old tat in here – ancient bills, brass radiator keys, tags for Christmas presents, endless half-used rolls of sticky tape – but nothing that would fit the small lock in front of her.

The box might even be empty, thought Rosie. It wasn't particularly heavy and nothing rattled when it was shaken. But why would her mother have locked and buried an empty box in a muddle of old clothing in the attic?

Rosie picked up the box again and studied its small lock before fetching the tool box from under the stairs. Many of the ancient tools inside were rusty, but a small screwdriver caught her eye. That might do the trick. Inserting it into the lock, she jiggled it up and down. This kind of thing looked easy on TV detective shows – how tricky could picking a lock be? Very tricky, she soon realised, abandoning the screwdriver for a larger one that she forced under the lid. It was a shame because the box was beautiful, but brute force was the only option.

Sitting back on her heels, she started levering the screwdriver upwards as carefully as she could and the side of the box began to warp and bend. At last, with one final push, the lock gave way and the lid sprang open.

Rosie exhaled loudly – she hadn't realised she was holding her breath – and peeked inside. For one mad moment, she wondered if the hidden box might be full of stolen cash or counterfeit notes. But the box contained nothing more than a few folded sheets of paper and a letter inside a ripped open envelope.

The letter was addressed to her mother at *Cove Cottage, Smuggler's Lane, Heaven's Cove.* That was the tiny, damp house where Sofia had lived when she first moved to Heaven's Cove, eighteen months before Rosie was born. As a child, Rosie would stand outside the cottage and imagine her mum living there as a young woman, before she was married to her dad; before Rosie even existed. But the thought of not being in the world was too much to get her childish head around. Now, it was her mother who was no longer in the world, and some days that was too much for her adult self to take in.

Rosie pulled the letter from its envelope and, feeling like a thief stealing secrets from the dead, began to read the black writing that sloped across the single sheet:

My darling Saffy,

You are in my heart for as long as the world turns. Before you, my life was empty and cold, and your love has brought me more happiness than I deserve. The thought of our wedding day, and spending the rest of my life with you, fills me with joy.

Rosie stopped reading. She'd been so keen to discover what lay inside the box, but reading such an intimate letter felt wrong – especially as the handwriting was different from the scrawled messages inside the Christmas and birthday cards she'd received from her father. This was a love letter to her mother from another man; a man whom Rosie knew nothing about.

She sat quietly for a while, with the letter in her lap, wondering what to do next. Her mother had hidden it away for a reason, but how could this secret hurt Sofia now she was gone? And Rosie had to know… Taking a deep breath, she scanned through the letter again and her eyes strayed to the final two lines:

Know that you are always loved.

J

Rosie's hands shook as she smoothed out the letter and grabbed her phone. She flicked through her photos to the card that was tied to the lilies on her mother's grave. The writing was the same: the 'a' not closed, as though written in haste, and the loop-less lower stroke of the 'g'. The mysterious J from the card was her mother's secret suitor, declaring his undying love in this letter, and a part of Sofia's life to the very end. How could Rosie not know who he was?

Tipping out the remaining contents of the box, she found a yellowing copy of the house lease that had come as such a bombshell, her birth certificate, and a pair of white knitted bootees with pink edges. There was also a faded photo of her as a tiny baby, being held in bed by her mother with another older woman standing next to them.

On the back of the photo, carefully printed in her mother's handwriting, were the words: *Me with Rose Emily (born 4.10 am, 8 June 1989) and Morag MacIntyre.*

Driftwood House creaked and groaned while Rosie turned the photo over and over in her hands. She'd never seen it before, but very few old photos were on display in the house. Her mother had always been one for looking ahead and keeping the past in the past.

Overwhelmed by a feeling of nostalgia, for precious things lost, Rosie went to the large oak cupboard in the hall, got on her knees and started rooting through it. At the back, her fingers closed around her mum and dad's wedding album. She hadn't looked at it in years.

She opened it and flicked through the small number of photos. Her mum said she and Dad hadn't bothered with a proper photographer because they'd decided suddenly to get married. So the only photos were snaps taken by the strangers they'd pulled in off the street to witness the ceremony.

Rosie had thought it wonderfully romantic when she was growing up – her parents loved each other so much, they couldn't wait to be wed, so took themselves off to the register office in Exeter on a whim.

She looked at the first photo of her parents standing hand in hand on the steps of the office. Her mum with long fair hair, staring at the camera, and Dad next to her. They were both smiling but looked uncomfortable, as though they were nervous. Her father was in smart trousers, an open-neck shirt and dark jacket, and her mother was wearing a flowing green maxi-dress that matched her eyes. Rosie was pretty sure that dress was still in the back of her mum's wardrobe.

She studied the picture more closely. The letter from J must have been sent to Cove Cottage not that long before this wedding photo was taken. But no one in the village had ever mentioned Sofia having a fiancé before Rosie's dad, and Belinda would be all over any hint of long-lost romance like a rash. It would be gossip gold in Heaven's Cove, even after all these years.

Rosie sat back on her heels, feeling confused. Rather than uncovering her mother's secrets at Driftwood House, she was only adding to them day by day.

She ran her fingers across the faces of her parents in their wedding clothes. Did her dad know about J when he stood in the register office and said 'I do'? Did he know that Sofia had presumably loved another man enough to promise to marry him?

'I hope not,' she said into the empty hallway, feeling close to tears. Though maybe her dad had been well aware of J and had stolen Sofia away from him. Rosie sighed. Dealing with bereavement was hard enough without the secrets her mother had left behind, like landmines littering her way forward. Secrets that were making her doubt the close relationship she'd thought she had with her mum.

'What the…?'

Someone was hammering on the front door, the noise echoing through the empty house. Rosie jumped up and her parents' photo album slid facedown onto the tiles.

Chapter Thirteen

The front door was in a terrible state. Anyone could break in if they were even slightly determined, and Rosie was up here on her own at night. No one in Heaven's Cove would stoop to burglary, but who knew about the tourists that were starting to flood into the village now the weather was improving?

Liam blew air through his pursed lips and ran his hand across the warped wood. The splits in the grain were like wounds under his fingers. Stormy weather had battered this house and, though it was still standing, the fabric of it was damaged. He knew how it felt.

Good grief, he was identifying with a dilapidated old house now. He really needed to pull himself together and get back out there. *Get yourself back on the horse* was how Alex put it, as though Dee was a race that he'd lost, rather than the woman who'd ripped out his heart.

It wasn't like no one was interested. Katrina had texted him only this morning to check if he was going to the dance in the village hall in a few weeks' time. She'd definitely be up for some no-strings fun if her boyfriend's back was turned.

'Shall I go to the dance, boy?' He bent and patted faithful Billy, who was nuzzling at his feet. 'Maybe Alex is right and it's time to get back to who I was. I mean, it's over a year since—'

The words died on his lips when the door, with a nails-down-blackboard shudder, was dragged across the tiles, and Rosie poked her head around it.

'Oh, it's you.'

She seemed surprised to see him. Actually, she seemed distressed. The dark circles under her eyes were purple shadows against her flushed cheeks.

'Did you forget that I said I'd help for a while this morning?'

'I remembered first thing but then I got distracted and forgot. Sorry. Come in.'

With more scraping of wood on tile, she pulled the door fully open and he could see her properly. Her blue T-shirt had grubby streaks, her jeans were faded and ripped, and was that a cobweb in her hair? When he reached out and brushed his hand across her head, she stepped back in alarm.

'What are you doing?'

'Getting this.' He held up his fingers, now covered in sticky filaments. 'It looks like a spider's web.'

'I've been up in the attic.' Rubbing her hands across her head, she turned slowly on the spot. 'Please tell me the web didn't come with its own spider.'

He laughed. 'I can't see one. But surely living in a hot country means you're used to spiders. Don't they have huge ones over there?'

'Yeah, all sorts of scarily massive wildlife, but they don't tend to live in my hair.'

When she giggled, Liam caught a glimpse of what Rosie must be like in Spain, far from the sorrows of Heaven's Cove: happier, less vulnerable, more carefree.

'Would you still like me to give you a hand this morning?' he asked, hoping she wouldn't send him away. He'd grumbled to himself on the walk here because there was so much work to do on the farm, but now, seeing her, he wanted to stay.

Rosie hesitated, before stepping aside and beckoning him into the hall. 'If you don't mind. I think I can do with all the help I can get.'

She padded across the tiles in her bare feet, bending on the way to pick up an open photo album and place it on the hall table.

'Old photos of Mum and Dad,' she explained, before leading him into the sitting room.

This must have been a grand room once, thought Liam, with its picture rails, large fireplace and sash windows overlooking the sea, but not now. His eye was drawn to cracks in the coving, tired paintwork and window frames in desperate need of repair. In fact, seeing the room again only confirmed what he'd feared yesterday: that Rosie had her work cut out if she was going to impress the stuck-up Eppings. Since his last visit, furniture had been pushed together into the middle of the room, and paperwork was scattered across the floorboards.

'Sorry,' said Rosie, though why she was apologising, he wasn't sure. When she gathered up the paperwork and shoved it into the bureau, he noticed a tremor in her hands. She was still upset.

'Is everything all right?'

'Have you ever been in here – apart from when you delivered the stuff from Shelley's?' she asked, waving her arm around the room and ignoring his question.

'No, I've been in the kitchen a couple of times while I was delivering post but that's all. Your mum was friendly in the village but kept herself to herself up here.'

'So what do you honestly think of this room?'

'I think… it has potential.'

'That bad?'

'Not really.'

Rosie shook her head. 'You used to lie much more efficiently. Oh…' She closed her eyes. 'Sorry, if that sounds rude.'

If that sounds rude? How else could it sound? But he knew what she meant. Not so long ago, he'd been a master of the white lie. *I'll ring you tomorrow. You look amazing in that dress.*

But that was before the only woman he'd ever truly loved deceived him with the biggest lie of all: *Of course I love you.*

Rosie was staring at him, biting her lip.

'It's fine,' he told her. 'So what are you planning to do in here first?'

'I thought I'd paint the walls – I've already washed them down. A coat of paint should freshen things up straight away, don't you think?'

She sounded desperate, surrounded by piles of furniture and pots of paint. She sounded like someone who'd bitten off more than she could chew, which meant the Eppings would win. Like they always did when money was involved. Affluent Charles and Cecilia Epping got richer by pushing up rents on local homes and business premises until people couldn't cope. They didn't care about the ordinary villagers of Heaven's Cove at all.

'What do you want me to do first?' asked Liam, trying not to think about the rent rise on the fields that he leased from the Eppings. If his worries spiralled, he would only end up imagining his mum and dad having to sell up and move from Meadowsweet Farm.

Rosie wrinkled her nose. 'Can you wave a magic wand and make this place into a perfect little guesthouse?'

'I'm afraid magic is outside my remit, but if you've got any fields that need planting or courtyards that need hosing down, I'm your man. And I'm sure I can slap on some paint.'

Rosie's face relaxed into a smile. 'Are you sure you can spare the time?'

'I can spare an hour or so. Tom's helping out this morning and he's brought his younger brother with him. Dad might give them a hand too if Mum can spare him.'

'How are your parents these days?'

'Fine.'

'Really?'

Liam breathed out slowly. 'Kind of fine. Dad's getting more and more forgetful which can be… difficult at times.'

'How's your mum coping?'

'She's worried, like me, but OK. They get on pretty well, considering, and she likes that he's home more these days, rather than being in the pub. Dad was a bit of a lad when he was younger.'

Rosie narrowed her eyes. She looked like she was about to say something but, instead, she thrust a paintbrush into his hand.

*

One hour helping out at Driftwood House soon became two. Not that Liam minded. The rhythmic strokes of the paintbrush were soothing and it was peaceful here, high above Heaven's Cove, with only Rosie for company, although she hardly spoke.

She'd been painting the opposite wall for a while, but seemed distracted and kept abandoning her paint and switching to other tasks. A couple of times she opened the bureau and looked at the paperwork that she'd gathered up from the floor and shoved inside. When she did it for a third time, Liam paused from slapping on paint and wiped his mouth with the back of his hand. She was never going to get Driftwood House up to scratch if she couldn't concentrate.

'Something interesting?' he asked.

'No. Not really.' She turned over a photo she was holding. 'Have you heard of someone called Morag MacIntyre?'

'Sounds like a good Devon name.'

Rosie's smile was half-hearted. 'I just thought you might know her.'

'Afraid not. Why?'

'Nothing important. She's in this photo that I found in the attic.'

He squinted at the picture she was waving at him. 'Is that a baby?'

'Yes, it's me. Look!'

The baby was wrapped in a white knitted shawl and clasped to a woman's chest. 'Is that you and your mum?'

'Yeah, that's right.'

'You were tiny.'

'I was premature, around six weeks, I think.'

'Did you find that other paperwork in the attic too?'

He was prying but she was acting very oddly – staring into space while paint dripped from her brush onto the floorboards, or abandoning her painting all together to pace up and down. She stared at him with her big, troubled eyes: an intense gaze that sliced right through him.

'I found the photo in a box in the attic, along with a copy of the legal agreement about this house,' she said, at last. 'The one that the Eppings sent me.'

'Was there any explanation with that? Anything to explain why your mum kept it from you?'

She shook her head.

'Did you find anything else with the lease and photo?'

'A few bits and pieces – my birth certificate and an old letter to my mum. A love letter.'

'From your dad?'

Their conversation was interrupted by the shrill ring of a phone. Rosie snatched up her mobile and winced when she looked at the screen.

'Hey, Matt,' she said, her voice over-bright and high-pitched.

'Hey, there.' Matt's voice was tinny but Liam could just make out the words.

'How are you?' asked Rosie.

'I'm missing you.'

'Me too.'

'Yeah but I'm missing you big time, babe.'

Liam might have been mistaken but Rosie recoiled slightly at the word 'babe'. It made Matt, whoever he was, sound slightly sleazy, thought Liam, fully aware of his own hypocrisy. He was pretty sure he'd called girlfriends 'babe' in the past.

'I'll be back soon, Matt.' Rosie was hunched over the mobile, trying to keep her conversation private.

'When, though? The sun's out and interest in our properties is soaring. We could do with you in the office,' said Matt's tinny voice.

Liam raised an eyebrow. One minute Matt was missing Rosie and the next he was moaning that she wasn't at work. What a charmer!

Rosie lowered the phone. 'I'll take this outside. Back in a minute.' As she grabbed a cardigan and slipped through the front door, he heard her say: 'Oh, no one. Just a local who's giving me a hand.'

No one.

Liam's brush hit the wall rather too hard and paint splattered over his jeans. Not that it mattered, when they were just for working on the farm. He dabbed at the white specks with a cloth and watched Rosie out of the window.

Standing in the biting sea breeze, she pulled what looked like her mum's old cardi tightly around her and burrowed her shoeless feet into the grass as she continued her conversation. Liam was no body-language expert but the chat wasn't going well if her furrowed forehead was anything to go by.

When the call ended, she pushed her phone into her jeans pocket and stood for a moment, face into the wind. Liam pulled back from the window as she came indoors.

'Everything OK?' he asked casually.

'Yeah, well no. Not really. I just broke the news to Matt that I need to stay on here for a few more weeks. I've been avoiding telling him.'

'Ah. How long have you two been together?'

'A few months. He joined the property agency I work for, though he's got ambitions to set up one of his own. He sees himself as an entrepreneur.'

'That's nice. He didn't sound Spanish.'

Damn, that gave away that he'd been listening in to the call, but Rosie didn't seem to notice.

'Matt's not Spanish. He comes from London, St John's Wood, but he's lived abroad like me for a few years.'

'It's a shame he couldn't come back with you for your mum's funeral.'

Rosie's face clouded over. 'It's pretty busy at work at the moment. I'll see him when I get back.'

'I take it he wasn't best pleased with your extended stay?'

'No. He can't understand why I'm trying to save a house that's probably doomed anyway. I sometimes ask myself the same question. It doesn't make much sense.'

She pushed her painty hands through her hair, leaving a white streak across her fringe. Liam balanced his brush on the paint pot and leaned against the wide stone windowsill.

'Things don't always make sense when you've had a big shock. People don't always behave logically when strong emotions, like grief, are involved.'

'What about anger?'

'Yep.'

'And guilt?'

Liam nodded. 'That too.'

'I feel so guilty, about everything,' blurted Rosie, her bottom lip trembling.

'Your mum wouldn't blame you for not saving Driftwood House, you know.'

'Logically I know you're right, but I can't shake the feeling that she'll haunt me forever if this house, the home she loved, is destroyed by the Eppings. I'll have visitations in the night.'

'Lucky you.'

Though Rosie laughed briefly, she still seemed close to tears.

'I didn't see her as much as I should have,' she said, stroking the wool of her borrowed cardi. 'I couldn't be bothered to come back to Heaven's Cove. I thought this place was boring and a bit… beneath me.'

'But I'm sure you were still close,' answered Liam, starting to feel out of his depth as a tear trickled down Rosie's cheek.

'I'm beginning to think I didn't know my mum very well at all. I keep finding out things about her. Secrets.' She stopped and bit down hard on her lower lip.

'What sort of secrets?'

'Nothing really. Just the lease,' said Rosie, though her glance at the bureau made Liam wonder if she was telling the truth. 'I just wish I'd taken the time to know her better.'

'I don't think we ever really know anyone. I didn't know Dee as well as I thought I did.'

Why on earth had he mentioned Dee? He never mentioned her these days and neither did his friends. It was as though she'd been expunged from his life.

'What happened with the wedding?' asked Rosie quietly.

Liam stared through the window. Grey billows of cloud were casting patterns on dark water, and bright wild flowers were pushing through the grass. Everything was uncomplicated and beautiful. He brushed dust from his jeans and tried to keep his voice light. 'I'm surprised you haven't heard the whole sorry tale from Belinda or your mother.'

'I try not to spend too much time with Belinda, and Mum gave up telling me stuff about Heaven's Cove. She hated gossip, anyway. Sorry, I shouldn't have asked.'

'No, it's all right.' Usually, Liam kept what happened to himself – every detail a heavy weight that dragged him down. But here with Rosie, in Driftwood House, keeping secrets felt toxic. 'I met Dee two years ago, in a night club, and she moved into the farmhouse with us six months later.'

'Local lothario Liam Satterley was in love.'

Was she taking the mick? Liam's sideways look was returned with a gentle smile. 'So what happened next?' she asked, taking a step towards him.

'On the day of the wedding she realised she couldn't marry me after all. Terrible timing, huh?'

'Why did she change her mind?'

'It was the age-old story,' he said, still keeping his tone bright, jokey even. 'She'd fallen in love with someone else. Hard to believe, isn't it?'

He gave his Jack-the-Lad laugh, the one everyone expected. But it came out all wrong because his chest was so tight.

'Impossible to believe! I mean, how could she possibly do better than you?' asked Rosie with a smile.

'I know, right?'

'Is she still with… the other man?'

I'm so over her I have no idea what she's doing now. That's what he should have said. But instead he pulled his phone from his pocket, clicked onto Facebook and searched for Deanna's name. The sight of her familiar, beautiful face made his stomach lurch, even after all these months. He pushed the phone at Rosie. 'Take a look.'

Rosie scrolled through Deanna's timeline, through endless photos of her in the arms of another man, before handing the phone back. 'I hope you don't often look at her Facebook.'

'Hardly ever,' he lied.

When Rosie glanced up at him, he noticed for the first time the freckles scattered across her nose.

'Well, Deanna's pretty, but her new boyfriend is pug-ugly.'

Liam's snort of laughter echoed through the stripped room and Rosie's beaming smile lit up the gloomy morning. She looked like an oil painting, thought Liam, standing amid chaos with her hair all over the place, paint on her nose and streaks of red soil from the clifftop between her toes. A sudden beam of sunlight had caught her sideways on and she was glowing.

A ringing phone – Liam's this time – broke the spell. His mum was calling.

'Is everything all right?' he asked as he answered it, his eyes back on Rosie.

'Yes, love. No need to panic. Are you still up at Driftwood House helping Sofia's girl?'

'Yes, but I'll be back soon.'

'That's fine. I wasn't chasing you. I was ringing to speak to Rosie, actually.'

'Rosie?'

'That's right. If you could pass me over.'

'Um… OK.' Liam held out the phone, puzzled. 'My mum would like a word, if that's all right.'

Rosie frowned but took the phone and wandered into the hall. She came back a couple of minutes later and handed the phone back.

'What was that all about?'

Rosie smiled. 'Your mum's invited me to yours for a Sunday roast tomorrow. She thinks I'm wasting away up here on my own. I did say not to worry, but she was quite insistent.'

'Tell me about it.' Liam pushed the phone into his pocket. He wasn't sure how he felt about Rosie coming round and wished his mother had cleared it with him first. But it was done now. 'Well, she's a great cook so you'll get a good meal, and the third degree, probably. She likes to know everything about her guests.'

'That's mums for you.' Rosie's smile faltered. 'I suppose I'd better get on with the painting.'

'And I'd better get back to the farm because there's lots to do.'

'Of course. Thanks for giving me a hand with my guilt-trip venture and for all the painting you've done. The room looks better already.'

She was right. A coat of light, bright paint had worked wonders. Liam wiped paint splatters from his hands and carefully placed his brush on a wodge of kitchen towel. 'You're welcome. Oh, and you know who might have more information about Morag Macinwhatsit? Belinda.'

'Belinda, who knows everything about every person in the area?'

'That's the one.'

'I asked your mum about Morag and she didn't know her, so Belinda is probably my best bet.'

'She might be in the pub tonight, if you're going to take up Nessa's invitation.'

'I'm not sure. I might be too knackered after working on the house all afternoon.'

'Nessa will probably march up the cliff and drag you out if you're a no-show.' Liam grinned. 'I'll see you in the pub, if you make it, and if not, I guess I'll see you tomorrow.'

'Yep, half past one for eating at two o'clock.'

After a quick goodbye, Liam left her to her decorating and hurried down the cliff path. He'd been at Driftwood House longer than he'd intended and the afternoon was going to be crazily busy.

Earlier this morning, the thought of spending time alone with Rosie, even though he'd been the one daft enough to offer, hadn't filled him with joy. They hadn't particularly got on at school so being together for hours was bound to be awkward. But it had been all right, he realised, as his feet dislodged small stones which tumbled over the cliff edge.

At school, Rosie had been a nerd. There was no other word for it. He remembered her watching from the sidelines, never keen to join in, with her head constantly in a book, and always making it clear that Heaven's Cove wasn't enough for her.

She was still different from the confident, polished women he was used to, but he didn't see that as a bad thing any more – he no longer felt like running with the crowd himself. He grinned to himself as he reached the edge of the village. Maybe local lothario Liam Satterley and nerdy Rosie Merchant would end up friends after all. Especially if his mum had anything to do with it.

Chapter Fourteen

Liam was right. If anyone in Heaven's Cove knew of Morag MacIntyre it would be Belinda. And she was currently in The Smugglers Haunt, sitting at the bar with her husband.

Rosie stopped peering through the window, smoothed down her simple cotton dress, and pushed open the pub door. A wave of sound hit her and she hesitated, unable to put one foot in front of the other.

'This is ridiculous,' she murmured, as butterflies fluttered in her stomach. She'd moved across continents to reinvent herself in far-flung places, struck up conversation with total strangers, and built a new life for herself in Spain. Yet here she was, in her home village, too scared to face the people she'd grown up with. Perhaps it was the realisation that her reinvention wouldn't wash here.

'Get a grip,' she said to herself, more loudly, crossing the pub threshold and plastering a smile on her face.

The place was packed and, with its low, beamed ceiling, absolutely roasting. For the first time since arriving in Heaven's Cove, Rosie felt comfortably warm in her summer dress that she'd picked up for a song in a Spanish market.

Belinda, perched on a bar stool, glanced at Rosie before putting her hand over her mouth and murmuring to her husband. The back of Rosie's neck prickled, as it always did when she suspected she was being talked about.

'Hey, Rosie!' Nessa was waving from a table in the corner, near the stone fireplace. 'Rosie, we're over here,' she yelled again. 'Come and join us.'

Rosie waved back and wandered over. She was mostly here for Belinda, but maybe it would do her good to mix with other people for a while.

Nessa was sitting in a huddle of people Rosie recognised, including Katrina, who was wearing a leather jacket and huge, sparkly diamond earrings. Rosie scanned the pub for Liam, but he was nowhere to be seen.

'You came!' said Nessa when Rosie reached her. 'That's great. We're just dissing Larry the Lech and his wandering hands.'

Their old PE teacher did have a disconcerting reputation among his students for being rather too hands-on. He'd resigned abruptly one spring term and was never mentioned by the teaching staff again.

'Come on, sit down,' said Nessa, shifting along the wooden bench to make room for her.

Rosie sat down and smiled, though her heart was hammering. 'Hello, everyone.'

'Well, look at you, Rosie Merchant, all grown up,' said the man next to Nessa. 'Excellent tan, and sorry about your mum. Shame you weren't here when it happened. You know everyone, don't you? I'm John, you know Nessa, obviously, and that's Heather, Phil and Katrina.'

'Of course. It's nice to see you all after so much time.'

The group nodded while Rosie checked them out. John was heavier than she remembered with a thicker neck and less hair, but otherwise he looked full of mischief and much the same as he had at school. Heather, who gave Rosie a shy smile, must have ditched her glasses with their pebble lenses for contacts and her amazing amber eyes were now on full show. Phil's wedding ring glinted when he raised his pint and took a slurp. And Katrina, now minus her jacket, sat at the head of the table like a queen bee, looking even more fabulous than when she'd been flirting with Liam in the farmyard.

Her flimsy halter-neck top, a scrap of midnight-blue silk, revealed toned arms and shoulders, and her glossy dark hair, streaked with chestnut highlights, shone under the fairy lights strung above the bar. The scarlet nails she was drumming on the table were either false or she had a live-in maid. Those were not hands accustomed to housework. Rosie moved her own paint-splashed hands off the table and placed them in her lap.

John bought a round of drinks and after necking a glass of red wine with indecent haste, Rosie began to feel more at ease amongst her old school friends.

It was interesting to hear how life was treating them, and she didn't have to say much. John and Phil seemed happy to keep the conversation going with their tales of skinny-dipping on the beach in their teens, and climbing the cliffs while drunk.

But Katrina wasn't about to let her relax.

'What about you, Rosie, sitting there all quiet as usual, like a little mouse?' She leaned forward, cutting across Phil's anecdote. 'You must be going back to Spain quite soon.'

'Yes, I am, in a couple of weeks or so.'

'Not until then?' said Katrina, raising an eyebrow. 'I thought you'd be desperate to top up your fading tan.'

'There are a few things I need to do at the house first.'

'Before it's knocked down to make way for a hotel.' She gave a faux pout of sympathy. 'That's such a shame. You won't have anywhere to come back to.'

'We'll see.'

'I didn't realise that the house didn't belong to your mum. Nobody did.' Katrina twirled a diamond ring on her right hand and gave a perfect pearly-white smile. She'd definitely had work done on her teeth. 'Did you know I'm living in Bellesfield now?'

'I didn't.'

'I have a rather gorgeous new-build on the edge of Bellesfield Park, right near the river.'

'That sounds great,' said Rosie, not envious in the slightest.

'It is. My ex got the boat and I got the house in our divorce. I definitely got the better deal. And now Stephen's moved in. He's a very successful chartered surveyor.'

'Oh, you live with your boyfriend?'

'Yes. What's so surprising about that?'

You were flirting with Liam the other day like there was no tomorrow.

Having seen the heartache caused by her dad's affair, Rosie hated cheating with a passion. She could cope with bad moods in boyfriends, the occasional white lie, even dodgy personal hygiene. But cheating was her red line in the sand. However, what Katrina got up to was none of her business.

'No reason,' said Rosie. 'I just didn't know.'

'Really? Like I said when we met the other day, my business is going very well too. Everything's brilliant, actually. Really brilliant.'

'Wish I lived in bloody Bellesfield,' said Nessa, checking her mobile phone. 'Sorry, got to keep an eye on it in case I'm needed. Lily's getting over chickenpox and her sleep pattern's gone to pot.'

'God, you're not infectious, are you?' Katrina moved her pert backside as far away from Nessa as she could.

'Yeah, probably,' said Nessa, with a wink at Rosie. 'But don't worry, Kat. The pox doesn't leave too many scars. Hey, Rosie,' she added with a sideways glance at Katrina. 'Why don't you tell us about your amazing life abroad so we can all be horribly jealous?'

Katrina sniffed and carried on twirling her diamond ring.

'Yeah, what's it like?' asked John.

'Well, it's good.' Rosie stopped but everyone waited, expecting her to go on. 'I live in Andalusia and I'm working in a B&B and also for a property company at the moment.'

'I hope you're not fleecing Brits,' interjected Katrina, with another sniff. 'My ex and I were going to buy a holiday place in Tuscany, a little villa in the hills, with an infinity pool and grounds. But it turned out the property people were running a scam. We could have lost thousands.'

'That sounds awful but I'm not involved in any scams. Our properties are all bona fide and really nice, with views of the Med.' *If you don't mind hanging over the balcony, that is.*

Katrina's reply was drowned out by John yelling and waving over Rosie's shoulder. 'Hey, mate! We're over here, in the corner.'

Even with her back to him, Rosie knew John was waving at
Liam by the way Katrina pouted and patted the bench next to
her. Liam, carrying a pint, squeezed into the space. She hadn't
left much room for him, Rosie noticed. His thighs were wedged
against hers.

'Hi, all,' said Liam, putting his pint down. He nodded at
Rosie. 'You made it, then.'

'I thought I might have a quick word with Belinda.'

'Good idea. I bet she knows.'

Katrina looked at the two of them and blinked. 'Knows
what?'

'Just some information I need. Nothing important.'

'Hmm.' Katrina started twirling her dark curls around her
middle finger. 'So I assume there's no Spanish husband yet
then, Rosie?'

'No, my boyfriend, Matt, is English actually.'

'Your boyfriend?'

'Yep, that's right. I've got a boyfriend too.'

Nessa giggled into her vodka and lime.

'Has he come over to Heaven's Cove with you, to help you
sort out your mum's stuff?'

'He had to work.'

Katrina's sympathetic tilt of the head was accompanied by
an exaggerated frown. 'Really? That's a shame he couldn't come
and support you.'

Liam wiped foam from his upper lip with the back of his
hand. 'He's been ringing Rosie, begging her to go back to
Spain.'

'Wow, that's so romantic,' squeaked Nessa, before being silenced by a look from Katrina, a look that Rosie remembered from school – sharp, cold, intimidating.

'Perhaps you'd better head back as quickly as you can, then, Rosie.'

'I will before too long, don't you worry. I miss the wonderful weather, and Heaven's Cove seems pretty boring compared to southern Spain.'

Katrina looked sour, which was what Rosie was aiming for. But she regretted point-scoring when she spotted Nessa's downcast face. Liam was staring into his pint.

'Though there's a lot I've missed about this place,' she added quickly.

'What, exactly?' asked Nessa. 'The rain, the smell of fish and the total lack of privacy maybe?'

'Of course, all that goes without saying. I've missed the view from Sorrell Head too, and the change in seasons, and people who've known me for a long time.'

She was only saying it to be polite and make Nessa feel better, but there was some truth in it. In Spain, surrounded by people who barely knew her, Rosie was a blank canvas on which she could project anything she wished. Over there, she was confident, bold, funny – sexy, according to Matt. In short, nothing like the timid Rosie of her school days. But sometimes she missed parts of who she was back then and what she had in Heaven's Cove: security, permanence, family.

Her thoughts were interrupted by the sound of a smashing glass at the bar, and a huge cheer from everyone in the pub –

everyone save for Belinda, whose floral dress was now drenched in spilt beer.

'I think she might be leaving,' shouted Liam, nodding at Belinda, who was gathering up her coat and bag.

Rosie stood up quickly, almost knocking over John's pint and prompting another cheer from the people around her.

'Sorry. I'm still as clumsy as ever. I really must have a word with Belinda, and then I'll head back to Driftwood House because there's a lot to do. But it was lovely seeing you all again.'

'See you tomorrow,' said Liam, eliciting a jaw drop from Katrina.

Rosie pushed her way through the throng and caught up with Belinda outside, as she was pushing her arms into the coat being held up by her husband.

'Hello, Belinda and Jim, how are you? I hope you didn't get too wet in there.'

Jim! Rosie had just realised something, but she shook her head. Just because Belinda's husband had a name that began with J, that didn't mean he was her mum's secret love.

'If Fred drank less and served his customers more efficiently, fewer accidents would happen,' said Belinda tartly, mopping at her dress with the handkerchief produced from Jim's pocket. 'This dress is dry clean only.' She stopped mopping and stared at Rosie. 'And how are you doing in that big house all on your own? I hear you ordered supplies from Shelley's. Paint and the like.'

'I'm giving the place a bit of a facelift before I leave.'

'For what reason?' asked Belinda, waving her husband away when he tried to mop the beer that was dripping off the hem of her dress onto the cobbles.

Should she lie? Tell Belinda… what, though? However you looked at it, decorating a house that was earmarked for demolition was not the most sensible of actions. If she told Belinda the truth, it would be all round the village like a shot – but people would find out soon enough, anyway.

'I've suggested to the Eppings that, rather than building a new hotel, Driftwood House would make a wonderful guesthouse. They've given me a few weeks to spruce the place up and show them its potential.'

Belinda gasped, her mouth gaping open. If Rosie had thrown off her clothes and danced naked around the quay, Belinda could not have looked more surprised.

'You've been in touch with Charles and Cecilia Epping?'

'I went to see them.'

Belinda's jaw dropped further. 'You *went to see* Charles and Cecilia Epping? Where?'

'At their house on Dartmoor.'

'Were you invited?'

'No, I turned up on the off-chance that they were in.'

Belinda grabbed hold of the low wall next to her for support. 'You went, uninvited and unannounced, to High Tor House and demanded that they turn Driftwood House into a guesthouse, rather than demolishing it and building a hotel?'

'That's right. Though "demanded" is a bit strong. I requested.'

'And they did what you asked?'

'Kind of. Cecilia is still keen on her hotel idea but Charles gave me a chance to show Driftwood House's potential.'

'Unbelievable!' Belinda was now sitting on the wall, with silent Jim beside her. 'I have been trying for weeks to elicit their financial support regarding the village hall which is in need of more repair. But all of my efforts – letters, emails, phone calls – have been ignored. Not that I was ever confident the Eppings would help. She's rarely seen in the village and I don't believe he's set foot in Heaven's Cove for years.'

'Yet they're still very influential.'

'They're rich and they own local land and property, including Driftwood House, as I've only recently discovered.' She tutted as though her lack of knowledge about the house's provenance was Rosie's fault. 'Mind you, I've heard from my source that they don't seem as flash with the cash as they used to be. Though rich people can be quite tight, I've found. Do you think they'll agree to your guesthouse plan?'

Not if Cecilia had her way. Rosie shrugged. 'Maybe. Probably not, but it's worth a try.'

'Personally, I'd rather have Driftwood House up there on the cliff than a hotel. But the parish council, which I head, is far too busy to get involved in another project. Especially one that, no offence, has so little prospect of success.' Lowering her voice, she leaned forward. 'You didn't hear it from me, but the Eppings are not always to be trusted. They have a very bad reputation around here. They show very little interest in the village and, as landlords, they've proved themselves to be hard-headed and intransigent.' Belinda rubbed her finger across her mouth. 'But my lips are sealed on the matter.'

Well, that was a first. Jim caught Rosie's eye and the corner of his mouth twitched upwards.

'But tell me,' said Belinda, unsealing her lips pretty sharpish, 'why are you bothering to try and save Driftwood House when you'll be back in Spain before long? You've certainly made your dislike of Heaven's Cove clear.'

'I've realised that the house is full of memories and means a lot to me. And just because I choose to live somewhere else, that doesn't mean I dislike the village.'

'Hmm.'

Belinda looked unconvinced and Rosie suddenly felt ashamed. This close-knit community in a beautiful part of England meant the world to the people who lived here.

'I suppose it's that I don't always feel a part of Heaven's Cove, that's all.'

Belinda's sour expression softened as she moved closer and took hold of Rosie's hands. A strong smell of lager wafted between them. 'Of course you're a part of Heaven's Cove, you silly girl. You're one of us. Always have been.'

Rosie gulped, her eyes suddenly prickling with tears. 'Thanks. I appreciate that.'

'Yes, well.' Belinda dropped Rosie's hands and stepped away. 'Jim and I had best be getting home so I can get out of this wet dress.'

'Before you go,' said Rosie, remembering why she'd followed Belinda outside in the first place. 'Do you happen to know someone called Morag MacIntyre?'

'Midwife Morag? Yes, of course. She lives in Callowfield, next to the grocery store, I think. She's not a midwife now, of course. She must be well into her eighties. But she used to be…' Belinda trailed off, her eyes narrowing. 'Why do you ask?'

'No particular reason. She was in a photo that I found at the house. Her name was on the back of the picture and I wasn't sure who she was.'

'Hmm.' Belinda still looked far from convinced but she'd started shivering in the stiff breeze blowing off the sea, so made no fuss when Jim linked his arm through hers and led her off towards their cottage.

A midwife. That would explain why Morag was pictured with Rosie so soon after she was born. But why had her mother kept the photo in her box of secrets?

The breeze was strengthening, rustling through the leaves of the ash trees that flanked the pub, and scudding dark clouds across the navy sky. A smell of rain hung in the air, but Rosie walked to the quayside and sat on the cold stone, with her legs over the edge of the harbour wall.

A lone seagull, ghostly white, flew above her head while she drummed her heels against the stone and checked her phone. Matt hadn't been in touch since their conversation this morning which meant he was still annoyed with her for not heading home immediately. She could call him now but, as it was ten thirty on a Saturday night in Málaga, he was probably in a bar and not in the mood for a chat.

Pushing her phone back into her bag, Rosie listened to the soft suck and whoosh of the waves and thought about her next move. The list of jobs to be done at Driftwood House was ridiculously long and time was running out. But she could spare a couple of hours tomorrow morning for a trip to Callowfield. And perhaps Morag could shed some light on the secrets her mother had taken to the grave.

Chapter Fifteen

It was a very modest house, right next to a Spar store and opposite a meandering stream lined by trees in full leaf. But the small garden leading to Morag MacIntyre's front door was pristine, with rows of pink and purple hyacinths.

Rosie pushed open the wooden gate and walked along the path, breathing in the sweet scent of the flowers. Their perfume was delicate, unlike the powerful smells of citrus and baked earth that she'd grown used to abroad. It was funny but she wasn't missing those brasher scents at all.

Rosie rapped on the door with its gleaming brass knocker and waited. Midwife Morag appeared middle-aged and weighed down by life in the photo Rosie had found, so she wasn't prepared for the sprightly white-haired woman who answered the door.

'Hello, are you Mrs MacIntyre?'

'Yes, that's me. Can I help you?'

'I hope so. My name's Rosie Merchant and I live at Driftwood House in Heaven's Cove.'

'Driftwood House, up on the cliffs?' There was the faintest hint of a Scottish accent.

'That's the one. I think you might have delivered me twenty-nine years ago.'

'Rosie Merchant, you say.' She hesitated and wrinkled her nose before her face broke into a huge beaming smile. 'Rosie! After all this time. My, you're all grown up.'

Before Rosie could reply, she was pulled into a hug, and it was so unexpected, so comforting, she relaxed and let herself be held for a few seconds.

'How marvellous to see you after all these years,' breathed Mrs MacIntyre in her ear. 'I do so love meeting my babies. Come in, and please call me Morag. We're both adults now.'

She released Rosie and beckoned for her to step inside, straight into a stuffy living room. A gas fire was pumping out heat in the corner, even though the day was overcast and mild.

'Take a seat, won't you, and I'll get you a cup of tea.'

'That's very kind of you, Mrs... Morag. I wasn't sure that you'd remember me. I really am who I say I am. I brought my passport in case you need proof.'

'Oh, I rarely forget a baby,' said the elderly lady, gesturing at Rosie to put her passport away. 'I remember your delivery well, and your mother too. How is she?'

'I'm afraid she died recently.'

'But that's terrible news! She can't have been very old.'

'She had a stroke. It was very sudden.'

'I'm very sorry to hear that. I moved away from Heaven's Cove many years ago, so I'm not very up to date with village news.' She pushed her gold-rimmed glasses further up her nose and gazed at Rosie, her brow furrowed. 'So what brings you to my door so soon after the death of your poor mother? No, don't answer that! Let me get you a cup of tea first and then we can chat.'

While Morag disappeared into the kitchen, Rosie took a proper look around the room. It was cluttered and cosy with a sofa, a squashy armchair, side tables covered in crocheted cloths, and china knick-knacks on every available surface. Not a speck of dust could be seen.

A small sideboard was covered in silver-framed photos of Morag in her younger days, holding a succession of tiny babies. She must have delivered them all. Was Rosie among them? She scanned the pictures but wasn't sure she'd recognise herself anyway. All babies looked much the same to her.

'Here you go, my dear,' said Morag, walking back into the room carrying a tray. She placed it carefully on a table and gestured for Rosie to sit on the sofa, before taking a seat in the armchair opposite. 'Tell me, do you still live at Driftwood House? It's such an interesting house and in such a marvellous location.'

'I'm staying at Driftwood House at the moment but I live abroad most of the time.'

'How exciting.' Morag poured a dash of milk into a china cup before adding tar-dark tea from a pretty teapot. 'Do you take sugar?'

'No, thank you.'

'So why don't you tell me why you've come to see me after all this time?'

Rosie took the cup, wondering where to start. She'd planned to move into this slowly, via a little chit-chat about the old days and Morag's work as a midwife. But it seemed that the woman who delivered her preferred the direct approach.

Rosie took a deep breath. 'Since Mum died, I've discovered that she hadn't always been completely… truthful with me. I don't mean that she lied, just that she didn't always tell me everything. She kept secrets from me and I don't understand why.'

'You know, people often keep things secret for a good reason,' said Morag, with a definite Scottish lilt.

'I realise that. But now my mum's no longer here, I need to make sense of what's been going on.'

Morag slowly stirred sugar into her tea. 'I can understand that. But how can I help you?'

'I found an old photo, taken shortly after I was born, of you, Mum and me – your name was on the back of it. Mum had hidden the photo away with an old letter she'd received, and I wondered if you could shed any light on why she might have done that?'

'What sort of letter are we talking about?'

'A love letter.'

'From your father?'

Rosie hesitated before shaking her head.

'Can't you ask the person who wrote the letter?'

'It's not properly signed so there's no one I can ask apart from you.'

'I see.'

A carriage clock on the mantelpiece ticked loudly as Morag sipped her tea and Rosie waited. Morag seemed in no hurry to tell her anything.

After the fourth sip, Rosie asked gently: 'Can you tell me anything about my birth? You probably don't remember very much about it because you've delivered so many babies.'

Morag stopped sipping and stirred another lump of sugar into her tea.

'Actually, I'll never forget it! I received a call from your father in the middle of a fierce storm. Sofia's waters had broken so I drove up that blessed cliff in the wind and rain because she wanted a home birth. I had to abandon my car in the mud halfway up and walk the rest of the way. I wasn't sure I'd make it but I was determined, and far younger then, of course, so my legs worked properly.' She chuckled quietly and massaged her knees. 'Happy days.'

'It sounds like quite a night.'

'It was memorable.'

'Were there any complications with my birth?'

'I don't think so. Not that I remember. You were a bonny baby.'

'Was I premature?'

Morag's hesitation was slight but it jarred with Rosie, whose nerve endings felt exposed. 'That I don't remember. Why do you ask?'

'Mum told me years ago that I was a honeymoon baby and very small, so I assumed that I came early. She and Dad were married seven months before I was born.'

'That must be right, then. Would you like a biscuit? I've got chocolate digestives here, or pink wafers. The wafers are my favourite.'

'No, thank you.'

Morag was keeping something back. Rosie was sure of it, but what could she do? Thumbscrews weren't allowed and she wasn't a thumbscrews sort of person anyway. She was suddenly overwhelmed by a longing for everything to go back to the way it was, when her mum was alive and Rosie knew nothing about the secrets she'd kept.

Rosie rested her head in her hands for a few moments and, when she looked up, Morag was staring at her intently.

'Sometimes it's best to let things lie, especially after a bereavement when everything is up in the air. Couldn't you speak to your father about this?'

'Mum and Dad got divorced when I was a child and he died a few years ago. He'd moved away by then and I only saw him every now and again.'

'Ah, I see. Don't you have other family who might have known your mother well? I'm not sure I'm the best person to speak to about things that happened so long ago.'

'There's no one else.'

'No one at all?'

When Rosie shook her head, Morag frowned. 'That puts me in a rather difficult position. Are you sure you want to pursue this, Rosie?'

'Absolutely sure,' said Rosie, with more conviction than she felt.

'Very well.' Morag carefully placed her cup and saucer back on the tray. 'You weren't premature. If anything, you were a week or two overdue. It's true that you were fairly small, but so was your mother and there had been some stresses during the pregnancy.'

'So I was conceived a couple of months before Mum and Dad got married. So what? It was the late 1980s.'

'Indeed. The stigma about sex before marriage was long gone, and not before time. Are you quite sure I can't get you a biscuit?'

'I'm quite sure.' Rosie's stomach flipped. She was treading a dangerous path but couldn't turn back. Not now. She held the older woman's gaze. 'There's more, Morag, isn't there?' When no reply was forthcoming, Rosie leaned forward, hands on her knees. 'The letter I found is very confusing. I need to know the truth and I think you're the only person who can help me.'

'Oh dear.' Morag picked at a piece of fluff on her lilac jumper and dropped it into the wastepaper basket next to her chair. 'This is so very awkward, but you're an adult and, as such, you have a right... everyone has the right...'

She swallowed and placed her hands in her lap, the thin wedding band on her finger catching the light from the window. Her speech was slow and measured, as if she was weighing every word.

'Your mother came to me during her pregnancy, Rosie. Sofia and her husband... Donald? Daniel?'

'David.'

'That's it, David. They'd just moved into Driftwood House and I was living nearby and working as a community midwife. Your mum was fairly new to the village and was the sort of woman who kept herself to herself. She was a loner, if you like. But over the months that she was my patient, we became friends. I think she needed someone to talk to.

'At first Sofia was adamant that she'd fallen pregnant on her honeymoon, just like she told you. I heard in the village that she and David had split up and only got back together shortly before they decided to marry. But I could tell that she was further ahead in her pregnancy than she claimed and, just before you were born, she finally told me… are you sure, Rosie, that you want to hear this?'

How could she possibly be sure until Morag told her? And then it would be too late to take anything back. You couldn't un-know something. Rosie nodded slowly.

'Very well. I'm so very sorry that you have to hear it from me, but what your mother told me was that David wasn't your biological father.'

How am I supposed to react? wondered Rosie, as Morag's words sank in. *Is this fizzy feeling in my chest due to shock, or is it resignation because, deep down, I've had my suspicions since finding the letter and photo hidden together?*

When Rosie stayed silent, Morag looked at her with concern. 'Are you all right, my dear?'

'I–I've seen my birth certificate and David's listed as my dad.'

Morag gave the slightest of shrugs. 'People hide the truth, for all sorts of reasons.'

Another heavy silence spread through the small room. A pregnant silence, thought Rosie, while a totally inappropriate urge to laugh bubbled up inside her.

This was all so surreal, so far from how her life was just a few weeks ago. Back then, she was selling pricey apartments to tourists, helping to run a B&B by the beach, and lying next to Matt at night, listening to cicadas in olive trees. She was blissfully oblivious to the secrets that underpinned her family life.

'It must be such a shock,' said Morag, moving from her chair and squeezing Rosie's shoulder.

Not so much a shock, thought Rosie, as a deep shift within her of what she'd believed from childhood. She'd painted her dad the villain of the family, blaming him for having an affair and leaving. But he *had* kept in touch afterwards, albeit intermittently, and he'd always called her his daughter, in spite of knowing the two of them had no biological links whatsoever – if, indeed, he did know. Her mother had taken on the role of blameless victim in Rosie's mind, but she'd been less than truthful about so many things – Driftwood House, the mysterious J, and how her daughter had been conceived. Had she known her mother at all?

'Did David know that I wasn't his baby?' she asked.

'I believe so. Are you sure you're all right?' Morag's bony fingers pressed into her flesh. 'I shouldn't have told you. I'm sorry.'

Rosie gulped in a deep breath of stuffy air. 'No, you were right to tell me. I asked you to, and I should know the truth.'

'Now that you do, I hope it won't change the way you think about your dad – about David – too much. He was the man who brought you up, after all.'

'Until I was ten. Until he left.'

At the time, Rosie was convinced he'd gone partly because of her. *Of course he didn't, Rosie Posie. Your dad leaving had absolutely nothing to do with you.* But now she feared that her mother had been lying, again.

'Have more tea.' A curl of steam wafted into the air when Morag pressed the refilled cup into Rosie's hands. 'And a biscuit too. You must have a biscuit.'

Rosie picked up the chocolate digestive placed on her lap and took a bite. The sweetness fizzed on her tongue. 'I have another question, please, Morag.'

'Oh dear.' Morag demolished half a pink wafer in one bite.

'Do you know who my father is, my biological father?'

'I don't, I'm afraid.'

'Does his name begin with J?'

'I truly don't know, Rosie. Your mother never told me and I didn't pry. It was her business.'

'And now it's my business.'

Morag sighed. 'Your mother had her reasons for not telling you. She wanted you to have a good relationship with the man you thought of as your dad and, as he said nothing to you about it, he was presumably keen that you should never know. That no one knew, in fact.'

'But why didn't she tell me the truth after Dad left, or when I grew up? I don't understand.'

'Sometimes secrets can take on a life of their own until there's no way out.' Morag gazed into the distance, far away in her thoughts. Then she gave her head the slightest of shakes. 'I'm sure your mother would have told you one day, but she passed away far sooner than she expected.'

That would have been quite a chat over her mum's favourite caramel lattes at Driftwood House. *You know the man you've called Dad for almost thirty years, Rosie? The man who left us, the man whose death you mourned? As it happens, he wasn't your real dad at all.*

Rosie brought her attention back to the stifling room. 'Did you and Mum stay friends, Morag?'

'For a while but our lives moved on, and I moved away. I was surprised your mother didn't keep in touch, but perhaps I knew too much to have around. I'm sure I was soon forgotten.'

'I don't think so. She kept your photo hidden away for almost thirty years with the love letter.'

Morag smiled. 'That's very touching. Perhaps it was meant as a back-up if she wasn't around to tell you the truth when the time was right. She meant for you to find it and to come and find me.'

'Perhaps. Is there anything else at all you can remember from back then?'

'Nothing, except that Rose was your mother's choice of name. She was most insistent about it, which I've always remembered because it's my sister's name.' Morag settled back in her chair and picked up a chocolate digestive. 'But that's enough talk of the past. Why don't you tell me more about you, Rosie, and about your life abroad? It's been a while since I've travelled and I'm not averse to living vicariously through your adventures.'

An hour later, Rosie left Morag's cosy home and walked to the outskirts of the town which edged Dartmoor. A vast landscape, black under the shadow of dark clouds, stretched out before her. It rose to the peaks of rocky tors and dipped into shallow valleys all the way to the horizon.

This morning had been intense, but rather than feeling shocked or upset following Morag's bombshell, Rosie felt eerily calm. It was as if pieces of a puzzle had slotted into place, and things made more sense now – why her mum never wanted to talk about her birth; why her dad sometimes looked at her as though he didn't know her at all.

She and her dad had clashed frequently. They were different in so many ways: colouring, temperament and interests. But he was a good man to take on another man's child and raise her as his own. Even if it had become too much for him eventually.

It was almost a decade since he'd died, but Rosie sat at the edge of the moors and cried for her dad all over again.

Chapter Sixteen

Rosie pulled into the yard at Meadowsweet Farm, turned off her engine and checked her watch. Five to two – she was late, but at least her eyes weren't so puffy and red. Stopping at Driftwood House on her way back from Morag's to splash cold water on her face had helped, sort of.

She twisted the rear-view mirror towards her and winced. Her face was still a bit blotchy in places but it would have to do, and hopefully the dark-blue floaty dress she'd put on would tone down her colouring. Mum always said that navy could hide a multitude of sins. But then her mum had said a lot of things and not all of them were true.

Rosie traced her fingers across her high cheekbones and oval jawline. She looked a lot like her mum. Everyone said so. But did she bear any resemblance to her biological father who was, presumably, letter-writer J? Maybe he'd found out a child was on the way and had done a runner. And now she'd never know because her mother had taken those secrets to the grave.

'Hello, there!' Pam Satterley, in a green spotted apron, was waving at her from the front door. 'The potatoes have this minute come out of the oven, so you're just in time.'

You can do this, thought Rosie, plastering on a smile. *Pretend your life hasn't just been turned upside down, eat food and make*

polite conversation until you can escape back to Driftwood House.
She got out of the car and waved back.

'You've been inside Meadowsweet Farmhouse before, haven't
you?' asked Pam, ushering her into a narrow tiled hallway.

'No, never.'

'Really? That's surprising. Didn't Liam invite you to the
teenage parties he threw when his dad and I went to visit my
parents in Ireland? The parties he thought we didn't know about?'
Pam laughed and rolled her eyes.

'I was never on his guest list.'

'Never mind, it's good to have you here now, although I'm
sorry it's in such sad circumstances, after what happened to
your mum. Come on through to the kitchen.'

The large kitchen, at the back of the house, was just as Rosie
had imagined. Steaming saucepans sat on a black Aga, close to a
huge table that was covered in trays of golden potatoes and roast
parsnips, and four large dinner plates, waiting to be filled. Shelves
on one wall held a chaotic muddle of books and magazines, and
there were muddy boot marks across the flagstone floor. A large
joint was waiting to be carved on the wooden worktop and Rosie's
stomach growled as smells of rosemary and lamb wafted under her
nose. It had been days since she'd cooked herself a decent meal.

Robert Satterley glanced up at her from his seat at the table.
'You're not one of those vegetarians, are you?'

'For goodness' sake, Bob, let the poor girl get through the
door before you start quizzing her,' scolded Pam, before turning
to Rosie with a frown. 'You're not vegetarian, are you?'

'No, I eat pretty much everything.'

'Thank goodness for that.' Pam brushed her fingers through her short grey hair. 'Liam, do you want to take Rosie through to the dining room? Lunch will be ready in a couple of minutes.'

She hadn't noticed him there, standing almost behind the open back door. He stepped forward, looking smarter than usual. He'd swapped his sweatshirt for a white open-necked shirt, and his jeans for black cord chinos. His dark hair, newly washed, flopped across his forehead.

Was this in her honour or did he always dress up for Sunday lunch? Rosie was glad she'd put on the dress that Matt said made her look sophisticated.

Matt! She'd meant to call him from Driftwood House but time had run away with her, and the clifftop signal was often dodgy anyway. She made a mental note to try and call him later, to tell him what she'd discovered. But for now, she had to pretend all was well.

Rosie smiled at Liam and followed him into a small room which overlooked the fields that led down to the sea. Light streaming in through the window bounced off glass ornaments grouped together on an oak dresser.

'This is a lovely, bright room.'

Liam gestured for her to take a seat at a polished table laid with glasses and cutlery. 'We don't use it much. We usually eat in the kitchen but Mum's rolling out the red carpet today. She thinks you're very exotic because you live abroad.' Was he mocking her? Liam shifted from foot to foot. He seemed to be on edge rather than taking the mickey. 'Why don't you take a seat and I'll get your food.'

He reappeared a couple of minutes later with a plate piled high with lamb, potatoes and vegetables.

'Thank you. It looks amazing, though I'm not sure I can eat so much.'

Liam gave an understanding nod. 'Just do the best you can. Mum likes to feed people up.'

He went to collect his own plate and took the seat the farthest from her as his parents came in with their lunch.

'Mint sauce?' asked Pam, passing Rosie a small silver jug. 'Do you know, you're the first visitor we've had to Sunday lunch since... well...'

She glanced at Liam, who finished her sentence. '...since Dee.'

That was why he was on edge, thought Rosie. This must be bringing up bad memories for him.

'Do you have a boyfriend?' asked Pam, spearing one of her roast potatoes with a fork and dropping it onto her husband's plate.

'I do. He's called Matt and he lives near me in Spain.'

'Did he buy you that pretty ring?'

Rosie turned the silver ring on her middle finger. 'The ring was a Christmas present from Mum, but Matt bought me this dress.'

'And very lovely you look in it, too. Doesn't she, Liam?'

Much to Rosie's relief, Robert piped up before his son had a chance to answer.

'Why isn't your young man here?' he asked, making the table shake as he cut his meat. 'A young girl like you could do with a bit of support.'

'Especially with all the work you're doing at Driftwood House,' added Pam. 'I know Liam's given you a hand but it's not the same, is it.'

'Matt would love to be here but I'm afraid work got in the way. He supports me with his phone calls and texts.'

Rosie noticed that she seemed to spend a lot of time justifying her boyfriend's absence. Work didn't sound crazy busy whenever they spoke and, truth was, she'd started wondering herself if he could have managed a quick trip to Heaven's Cove, if he'd really wanted to.

'How's the farm doing?' she asked, keen to move the subject on from missing boyfriends.

'Liam is doing a grand job.' Pam gave her son a warm smile. 'We don't know what we'd do without him, especially now Bob can't do so much. But it's hard work and we'll never be rich. What about your exciting life in Spain? What's that like?'

'It's hot and busy and fun, most of the time.'

'I haven't been to Spain for years but I remember it as very beautiful.'

'I live in a built-up area but the countryside is gorgeous.'

'I'm sure it is. Though not as picturesque as Heaven's Cove, surely?'

'It's a different kind of beauty – more awesome than pretty. I'm planning on heading back as soon as I find out what's happening to Driftwood House.'

'Why not stay here?' asked Robert. 'You and your mum can live together up on the cliff.'

Sorry, mouthed Pam, patting her husband's hand. 'Do you remember what I told you about Sofia, Bob?'

'That's OK. My life's not here any more, Mr Satterley. My boyfriend and my friends are in Spain.'

Liam looked up from his lunch and caught Rosie's eye. 'You have friends here too – Nessa, Katrina, me.'

Nessa was definitely a friend, Katrina definitely wasn't, and as for Liam… well, he'd helped her with the house and she was sitting at his lunch table. She and Liam Satterley were friends! Her geeky teenaged self would never have believed it.

She smiled at him while Pam dished yet more potatoes onto her plate.

Much to Rosie's surprise, she managed to eat all of her lunch, plus a bowl of homemade apple crumble and custard. The rest of the conversation was light – with no mention of her mum, Driftwood House or the Eppings – and, after the morning's revelations, Rosie relaxed and enjoyed being part of a proper family for a little while. Liam seemed more relaxed too, and thoughts of missing dads and mystery lovers vanished from her head.

'That was delicious, Pam, and I can't believe how much I've eaten!' Rosie sat back in her chair and patted her stomach, which seemed to have grown. 'Thank you so much for inviting me. You must let me help you with the washing up.'

But when she stood up, Pam took her dirty bowl from her and shooed her towards the door. 'Bob and I will do the clearing up and Liam can take you on a tour of the estate.'

'Estate?' Liam laughed. 'It's a small farm that Rosie has seen before. But I can show you around if you'd like.' He frowned at her strappy sandals. 'Mum's wellies will probably fit you.'

Liam strode across the fields, with Rosie slapping along beside him in wellies that were far too big. He talked to her about the crops he'd recently harvested and the financial challenge of running the business, and it was all far more interesting than she'd ever imagined.

After a while, he stopped at a five-barred gate and checked it was fastened shut.

'This is where I like to sit and survey my estate.' He grinned before climbing up the gate and sitting on top of it. 'Would you care to join me?' He held out his hand. 'Can you manage in that dress?'

Rosie hesitated for a second before grasping his hand and clambering up the gate to sit beside him. 'It's a bit wobbly up here.'

'It's fine when you get used to it. I didn't want to ask over lunch, but now we're on our own... did you manage to track down your elusive Morag MacIntyre?'

'I did, thanks to Belinda. I paid her a visit earlier this morning, actually, before I came round.'

'Why exactly did you want to see her?'

'To find out more about my mum, when she was young and I was a baby.'

'Was it helpful?'

'Kind of.'

Liam nodded, encouraging her to go on.

Rosie gnawed at her bottom lip. Should she tell him, or might it get back to Katrina – who'd love the fact that she didn't know who her father was?

'Morag didn't know much,' she said, making a snap decision. 'But we had a good chat about Mum in her younger days.'

'Are you glad you went to see her?'

'Yeah. She was a nice woman.'

'That's good. How's the decorating going at Driftwood House?'

'The sitting room's looking much better already and I've filled and sanded every window frame in the house, ready for painting. My life is nothing but glamour and excitement.'

Liam grinned. 'Sounds like it. Do you think these cosmetic changes will do the trick?'

'Maybe. I hope they'll be enough to show the Eppings what an amazing guesthouse Driftwood House could be.'

'Hmm. I could nip up this week and sort out your front door?'

'You really don't have to.'

'I know, but it's not very secure, and it won't give a good first impression of the house when the Eppings turn up. I'm busy tomorrow but I can come up on Tuesday morning. It's a date.' He paused. 'I mean—'

'I know what you mean.'

Liam nodded and pointed to the land that sloped towards the beach. 'Those fields over there are the ones we rent from

Charles Epping at an extortionate price. I'm hoping we get a good crop from them this year. It'll make all the difference.'

'Then I hope so too.'

Rosie held on tightly to the gate, the hem of her dress wafting in the breeze. A skylark swooped and trilled over her head and there was a faint wash of waves against rock in the distance. Everything was perfectly peaceful.

'I used to think that staying in Heaven's Cove and becoming a farmer would be boring, but I can see the appeal,' she said quietly.

'I can too, now. I resented the farm madly when I was a teenager and my future was all mapped out. I envied you.'

'You envied me?' When Rosie wobbled alarmingly, Liam put out a hand to steady her.

'I did. You had big dreams that could come true. You weren't tied like I was.'

'I didn't think you minded, and I envied you because, unlike me, you were popular and un-nerdy.'

'Is un-nerdy even a word?' He laughed. 'You were different from the other girls, Rosie, but that's not necessarily a bad thing.'

'Katrina thought so.'

'Katrina is very mainstream.' He turned carefully on the gate until he was looking directly at her, his eyes cornflower-blue against his white shirt. 'I admire you for doing your own thing and moving away from Heaven's Cove.'

'And I admire you for staying.'

She smiled, holding his gaze, and neither of them moved for what seemed like ages.

Liam suddenly looked away and jumped down from the gate. 'I'd best be getting you back to the house. I expect Mum will try to fill you up with cake before you head for home.'

'Cake? I couldn't eat another morsel.'

Rosie stumbled when she jumped down and Liam caught her in his arms. Her cheek rested against the soft cotton of his shirt.

'Careful,' he murmured, standing her upright and stepping back. 'You don't want to get your dress muddy. Matt wouldn't approve.'

The atmosphere had shifted and they walked back to the house, across the fields, almost in silence.

Chapter Seventeen

Liam didn't mean to snoop. He'd done some questionable things in the past – telling fibs, letting people down, being careless with people's hearts. Things that made him go hot and cold when he thought of them these days. But he'd never been a sneak.

However, it was hard to miss the list that was lying on the kitchen counter at Driftwood House: a list of men, many of whom he knew.

Jackson Porter

Jim Kellscroft

Jason Fulton

James Garraway

Jeremy Brockman

Jacob Dawe

Justin Maunder

The common denominator was a first name beginning with J. Rosie seemed determined to track down her mother's mystery flower-giver, though Liam wasn't sure why she was bothering. Not when her mum was gone, and she'd be leaving for Spain in a couple of weeks' time.

'Liam, is that you?' shouted Rosie from upstairs.

'Yep,' called Liam, stepping back from the list with a guilty start. 'I'll be up in a minute.'

First, he placed a homemade gammon pie in the fridge and dropped a handful of carrots into the vegetable rack. His mum insisted on sending food parcels, convinced Rosie was wasting away. She probably was, if the empty shelves in her fridge were anything to go by. That's what came of spending every waking minute sprucing up Driftwood House for the Eppings.

The thought of them walking through the place as if they owned it – even though they did – made him shudder, and he just hoped they'd appreciate the hard work Rosie had put in to improve the house over the last two and a half weeks. Even he, with all of his initial misgivings, had started to picture Driftwood House as a cosy bolthole for paying guests.

The kitchen, in particular, was looking miles better now he and Rosie had painted the walls and back door, polished all the surfaces and scrubbed the table. And the sitting room was transformed from a gloomy, shabby space to a light, bright room with yellow cushions, bought online, that seemed to draw sunshine right into the house.

'I'm working in the bathroom,' shouted Rosie, swearing as something heavy fell to the floor and thudded above his head. 'I'm not sure what I'm doing.'

Liam grinned and climbed the stairs to the main bathroom, which was opposite Sofia's old bedroom where Rosie now slept.

'There you are.' She smiled and stood up from where she'd been crouching barefoot in the bath tub. 'I left the back door open in case I didn't hear you arrive. What do you reckon?' She brandished the toothbrush that she was using to scrub the discoloured grouting. 'It's starting to look better, isn't it?'

'Definitely.'

She turned to survey her handiwork. 'This place will look polished before you know it.'

Rosie didn't look polished. Her old jeans were covered in paint and there were splodges on the big white shirt, probably an old one of her mum's, that she'd tied at the waist. Her hair was tumbling down from its hairband, and she wasn't wearing a scrap of make-up. Katrina would be horrified at Rosie's lack of glamour, but actually she looked amazing: healthy, natural, radiant.

'Oh, no. Have I got paint on my face again?'

She started scrubbing at her cheeks, turning them pink.

'Not that I can see.'

'Good. I thought you were staring at me.'

'I was admiring your fabulous grouting. Mum sent more provisions, by the way.'

'Good grief, I'm going to be the size of a house. It's kind of her though. Can you tell her thank you? And do you fancy a cup of tea? I was about to take a break.'

'I've only got a couple of hours free to give you a hand.'

'Five minutes won't matter, if we have a cuppa.'

She clambered out of the bath tub and padded downstairs, with Liam following.

He'd only intended to fix her front door – smooth the warps in the wood, stop it making such a racket when it scraped across the tiles, and protect it with some paint. But there was so much to do in the house, he hadn't felt he could abandon her once the door was done. So he'd started nipping in when he could spare an hour or two.

Now he'd been calling in for a fortnight, and their initial awkwardness with each other had eased into a quiet companion-ship. Rosie seemed distracted a lot of the time, grieving for her mum and missing her life in Spain, so they didn't really talk much. When they did speak, it was always about the house or the farm or her work abroad. And when her boyfriend rang, she never mentioned that Liam was there.

In the kitchen, Rosie filled the kettle at the sink and switched it on. 'Nessa came in yesterday after work and helped me paint the conservatory, which was…' She spotted the list on the worktop near the fridge and turned it face down. 'It was kind of her.'

She stood with her back to Liam for a few moments before turning with the list in her hand. 'Did you see this when you came in?'

'I didn't mean to but it was hard to miss. I didn't realise you were still trying to track down the mysterious J.'

'I'm interested to know who he is so I've been through Mum's address book for everyone whose first name begins with J, and I've started trawling through recent mentions of local people online.'

'It seems like a lot of effort to find someone who brought flowers to a funeral.'

'Mmm.' Rosie stared into the distance. 'How well do you get on with your dad?'

'My dad?' That was a bit left field, but Rosie nodded, with the same anxious expression Liam remembered from school. 'I get on fine with him, I guess, considering he's so much older than me. He didn't settle down with my mum until he was well into his forties. Before that, he was quite the ladies' man, apparently.'

'That's where you get it from.' Rosie's cheeks flushed pink. 'Sorry. I just meant—'

'I know what you meant.' Liam shrugged, resigned to his reputation and the fact that people weren't allowed to change in Heaven's Cove – even if heartbreak ripped you apart and you weren't the same person at all once you came back together.

'Can you keep a secret from everyone, but especially from Belinda?' Rosie's eyes looked huge, and when Liam nodded she carried on staring at him as though she was trying to read his mind. 'OK,' she said at last, ignoring the kettle belching steam at the ceiling. 'Keeping this to myself is driving me crazy. When I went to see Morag a couple of weeks ago, the midwife who delivered me, she said that my mum told her that' – she swallowed, before blurting out in a rush – 'my dad who brought me up isn't my real dad.'

That wasn't the secret Liam was expecting, not at all. He'd anticipated a stash of cash in the attic, a handy windfall to fund Rosie's globetrotting life. Not a secret, long-lost father.

'Do you know who he is?'

Rosie shook her head. 'Morag didn't know and Mum never told me. She never told me anything, it seems.' Sliding the teapot towards her, she started shovelling in spoon after spoon of tea leaves. 'It makes me so angry with her. Is it all right to be angry with someone you love? Someone who's died?'

'I'd be furious.'

She paused from filling up the teapot. 'Would you, honestly?'

'I would. I'd feel let down and kind of duped.'

'That's it, exactly.'

'But your mum was a good person and must have had her reasons for keeping you in the dark. Do you want to find your father? Is that what the list is about?'

'I think I do, though it feels disloyal to my dad – the man who I always called Dad, even though he left us.'

'He brought you up, he *was* your dad. But he's not here any more so you can't hurt him.'

'I know.' Rosie swallowed, close to tears.

'What does Matt think about all this?'

'He's trying to be supportive but he's not that interested. He thinks I should let sleeping dogs lie and go back to Spain.'

'He might have a point,' said Liam, though it stuck in his throat to agree with her boyfriend.

'Probably, but I'd like to know where I come from and why Mum was so secretive. Can you imagine finding out that everything you thought about your parents was built on a lie?'

He couldn't imagine it. His mum and dad drove him mad at times. Living in the same house as your parents at the age of thirty was always going to throw up challenges. But he never doubted that they told him the truth.

Liam shook his head. 'What makes you think that the mysterious J who put flowers on your mother's grave might be your real dad?'

'It all fits together. Wait here.'

Rosie disappeared into the sitting room while he emptied the tealeaf mountain from the teapot and spooned in the requisite amount. They were both going to need a drink after this. When she returned, she thrust a letter into his hands. 'Read that. It's a letter to my mum that I found in a locked box in the attic.'

It was quite a letter. Liam scanned through it and then read it again, more slowly. It was the sort of lovey-dovey letter that would prompt Alex to put his fingers in his mouth and gag. Liam too, a while back, before he'd been properly in love. But now, although it struck him as a bit flowery, he found the letter heartfelt, and sad if J never did get to marry Sofia. Maybe she'd left him standing at the altar, too. Poor bugger.

'What do you think?' asked Rosie, standing close and looking over his shoulder.

'I think it's a very heartfelt love letter.'

'And J is still around and cares enough to leave flowers and an anonymous message on Mum's grave.'

'Was this letter hidden away with the photo of you and Morag?'

'They were both in the locked box.'

'Like a fail-safe, in case anything happened to your mum before she had a chance to tell you about your father.'

'That's what Morag suggested. She reckoned the photo was like a breadcrumb, leading me to her so I could choose whether or not to find out the truth.'

'Are you going to approach the men on your list?'

'And say what? Did you have an affair with my mum thirty years ago, because I think I might be your daughter? It would be all round the village like a shot, and Belinda would self-combust.'

'She really would, especially if her husband turned out to be your dad.'

'I don't know why I put him on the list. I know it's not him.'

'Do you think, though, that Belinda might know who your mum was going to marry before she married David?'

'Absolutely not. There's no way she'd have kept that quiet all these years.'

'That's true. Perhaps it was a secret affair and your mum and J were going to elope.'

'Who knows? That's the point, I don't know and I need to, Liam. So for now I'll keep digging quietly about the men on my list and see what that turns up.' She took the letter from him and folded it. 'Anyway, talking about this just makes me sad, so let's have our tea and get on with the decorating. You won't say anything about this to anyone, will you?'

'Of course not,' said Liam, disappointed that she felt she had to ask.

'Thanks. You *are* a friend.'

When she smiled at him, her eyes still shiny with tears, he walked quickly to the door. The room was suddenly hot and stuffy, and he was finding it quite hard to breathe. 'I'll carry on with the grouting if you can bring my tea up.'

He took the stairs two at a time, rather like he was running away from Rosie. Liam had never run from a woman before.

They usually ran towards him. But intense, emotional Rosie made his locked-down heart feel unsteady, and that was a feeling he couldn't afford for two good reasons: one, she already had a boyfriend, and two, she'd soon be gone from his life for good.

Chapter Eighteen

Liam finished piling up the Savoy cabbages and stood back to make sure they weren't going to topple over. They seemed secure enough. He smiled at the sight of his stall, which was a rainbow of colour – carrots, parsnips, spring greens and spinach, many of the vegetables still sporting a thin coating of rich, red Devon soil.

Around him, other stallholders were setting up, ready to sell produce to the tourists and locals who flocked into Heaven's Cove for the monthly Farmers' Market. Though 'farmers' was a broad church these days. Stalls selling face creams and massage oils jostled for space with potters and jewellery makers.

'Morning, Liam. Nice day for it.' Peter tipped his hat and continued on his way down to the sea. He'd be ferrying tourists around the bay for hours – mid-week market day was always busy, especially when the sea was like a millpond. There wasn't even a hint of a breeze this morning to ruffle the waves.

'My, my. That's looking good, Liam.' Belinda stopped to run her hand across the display of cabbages, which wobbled alarmingly. 'We're blessed with the weather so let's pray for a good turnout. What do you think of the sash?'

She turned slowly on the spot, so Liam could better see the shiny blue sash that draped from one shoulder to the opposite hip. *Support Your Village Hall!* was picked out across the fabric in large gold letters. A collecting tin was hanging from her arm. 'We're raising funds to buy a new hot water boiler in the kitchen.'

'The sash looks great. I'm sure a lot of people will donate.'

'No one will escape me,' muttered Belinda, in a tone that made Liam think she was probably right. She stepped a little closer and her shoulders slumped. Oh no, the blessed head tilt was on its way. Liam moved quickly behind his stall as Belinda's head dropped to one side.

'And how are you doing now the first anniversary is well behind you, Liam, honestly?'

Honestly? He was still lonely, heartbroken and humiliated. He'd always been confident around women, cocky even, so maybe he'd had it coming. But no one around here was ever going to let him forget what happened. He'd hoped that the sympathy brigade would have moved on by now to other poor unfortunates, but the anniversary seemed to have galvanised them all over again.

'I'm absolutely fine, thank you, Belinda. There's no need to worry about me.' Liam gave her one of his sunniest smiles. The one that used to make Deanna's heart miss a beat, or so she'd led him to believe.

'If you're sure. Isn't Tom helping you out today?'

'He's busy on the farm. There's a lot to do and we're rather behind.'

'Then I'd better leave you to get on with things because the hordes are about to descend.'

She wandered off to harangue some other stallholder, much to Liam's relief. He *was* going to be busy without Tom to give him a hand, but at least that meant none of the locals could linger for a sympathetic chat and head tilt.

Two hours later, Liam was desperate for a coffee. A rich, aromatic scent was wafting through the market from the coffee stall near the quay and driving him crazy. But there was no way he could abandon his stall when so many people were milling around. He couldn't afford to lose any sales.

'I'd better buy you out of carrots to thank you for your help at Driftwood House.'

When he looked up, Rosie was standing there in jeans and a baggy jumper, even though the sun was high in the sky and he'd stripped down to his T-shirt an hour ago. She looked tired because she'd been working all hours on the house for almost four weeks now, and the Eppings were due to visit the day after tomorrow and give their verdict.

Liam had continued to help her out when he could, and the hours spent together had made him value her company all the more. She was peaceful to be around and, painting barefoot and fresh-faced in her jeans, much less high maintenance than most women he knew. He'd even told her a little more about his relationship with Dee, and she'd confided in him how out of place she'd often felt in Heaven's Cove, which made him sad. His heart still felt unsteady at times, when she gave him her slow smile or giggled, but he'd given himself a good talking to and had got a grip. They were simply friends.

Behind Rosie, tourists were milling about and several were getting out their purses. Today was going to be a bumper day for selling produce, which was great, but he needed a break. When she smiled again, he started untying the canvas apron he was wearing.

'You could buy carrots or you could do me a favour and watch the stall for five minutes while I get a coffee. What do you reckon?'

'OK.' She looked taken aback, but pleased, as she pushed her sunglasses further into her hair. 'What do I need to do?'

'It's pretty simple. Here are the scales, the prices are displayed, and the cash box is here. Thanks. I'll be as quick as I can.'

There was a huddle of people around the stall when he hurried back, ten minutes later, revived with coffee. He would have been back sooner but the market was buzzing, and moving quickly through the crowds was impossible. Hopefully, Rosie hadn't been overwhelmed. She seemed to be doing just fine.

He paused by the organic herbs stall and watched while she shovelled parsnips into a brown paper bag and gave a tourist his change. She'd put on the apron and twisted her hair into a ponytail. Having her hair up suited her, and she looked relaxed and happy as she chatted with customers.

She spotted him as he weaved his way back to the stall and raised her hand to give him a wave.

'Thank you, and sorry that was a long five minutes. The queue for the coffee stall was mad. Here, I got you a drink to show my appreciation.'

'Thanks. It's quietened down a bit now but it's been really busy. You need two of you on here, really.'

'Tom usually lends me a hand on market day but we're flat out on the farm at the moment.'

Rosie sipped from her cardboard cup and squinted at him through the steam. 'You're flat out because you've been taking time out to help me. Let me return the favour and give you a hand for a change.'

Liam hesitated. 'You don't have to. I've been happy to help at the house.'

'And I'm happy to help you, too. I've got tomorrow to give Driftwood its final touches before the Eppings descend, and it'll be nice to see a few people, to be honest. It gets a bit lonely up there on my own.'

Liam nodded because he knew all about being lonely. 'How's the search for J going?'

Rosie's smile faltered. 'I've done a bit more discreet digging and have eliminated a few men from the list. They're either too young, too old, or only moved to Heaven's Cove recently. The rest don't look that promising, to be honest, but I don't have time to pursue it.'

'I've made a couple of discreet enquiries myself, but couldn't Matt give you a hand? He could do a bit of searching online.'

'He's quite supportive when we talk on the phone but he's too busy to spend time sorting out my business.'

Matt was a self-centred idiot, thought Liam, trying to keep his expression neutral. If Deanna had been so upset and in need of help, he'd have given it. He'd also have moved heaven and earth to be with her, rather than whining from a thousand miles away.

'Anyway.' Rosie smiled. 'Would you like me to stay and help for a while?'

She'd already started pushing purple sprouting broccoli into a bag for a new customer so it seemed churlish to turn down her offer.

Liam nodded. 'That would be helpful. Thanks.'

At first it was awkward, having Rosie with him behind the stall. There wasn't much room and they performed a peculiar dance to avoid bumping into each other. But after a while she seemed to relax – he supposed he did too – and the occasional arm brush as they served customers went unremarked.

When the sun climbed in the sky, it grew warmer and even Rosie ditched her jumper as the stream of shoppers continued.

'Phew, it's quite full-on, isn't it?' remarked Rosie during a brief lull.

'It's not always this manic. The good weather has brought everyone out, so it's fortunate you're here to help.'

'It's good for me, too, to think about something else for a while.'

'Something other than the house and your mum.'

'Yeah, and my dad. The man I've always thought of as my dad. I've been thinking a lot about him these past few days. I wish I'd known the truth so I could have thanked him for kind of adopting me. After he cheated on my mum and left us, I was furious and not very nice to him for ages, but he didn't let on even then that I wasn't his.'

When Rosie pushed hair from her eyes, Liam noticed dark shadows along the underside of her arm.

'What's that?'

He caught her hand and turned her arm over. Ugly purple bruises were blooming from her inner elbow almost to her shoulder.

'It's nothing.' She tried to snatch her hand away but Liam held on tight. 'I fell off the ladder yesterday while I was painting the coving in the hall.'

'Hell, Rosie, you've got to be careful. I bet that hurt.'

'It's fine, though it smarted a bit.'

She was trying to sound upbeat but her voice caught and something twisted in Liam's heart. Rosie stared at his hand while he traced his fingers gently across her soft, bruised skin. And when she lifted her eyes to his face, Liam glimpsed a vulnerability he hadn't seen before. The hubbub of the market, the wash of the waves and the screech of seagulls faded away as his fingers rested on her skin.

'I do hope I'm not interrupting anything.'

Liam dropped his hand to find Katrina staring at him with one perfectly arched eyebrow raised. She picked up a cabbage and held it out, across the stall. 'These look lovely, Liam. I'll have some of the spinach as well. I'm into smoothies right now. They do wonders for my complexion. Talking of which, look at your freckles, Rosie! You really need to keep slathering on the sun cream or you'll have skin like leather by the time you're forty.'

Liam knew he was often oblivious to subtext. He'd never really bothered with it in the past. He was an upfront, in your face kind of person. But only an idiot would be unaware that

Katrina was being unkind, and Rosie was certainly aware of the weight behind her words.

When she pulled down her ponytail and let her hair swing in front of her face, annoyance lodged in Liam's chest. Katrina was absolutely beautiful, well-off – thanks to her divorce settlement – and clearly had the hots for him, if her flirting was anything to go by. But she could be bitchy at times.

'I'd better get going,' said Rosie, taking off her apron and folding it before passing it back.

'Are you short-handed, Liam?' Katrina leaned across the vegetables in her low-cut top. 'No worries 'cos I'll help you out for a while.'

'Thanks but there's no need. It's not so busy now.'

'Nonsense. It's no trouble at all, and I've been so tied up with work, I haven't seen you properly for ages.'

Crikey, she was keen. Before Rosie had managed to slip out from behind the stall, Katrina had shimmied into the small space and she pressed against him while Rosie squeezed past. There were lots of men around Heaven's Cove who would welcome Katrina pressing her pneumatic body against them, and Liam was surprised that all he felt was vague irritation.

'Rosie!' Belinda's panicked voice cut across the market hubbub. 'Rosie, where are you?'

'She's here,' called Liam, waving his arm in the air to attract Belinda's attention. She pushed her way through the crowds and stood, panting, in front of them. 'What on earth's the matter?'

'Guess who I just saw driving along the High Street?' she puffed, before pausing expectantly. Were they expected to guess?

'Lady Gaga?' said Katrina, sounding bored.

'Lady who?'

'Gaga, she's a singer and... oh, never mind.' Katrina sat down heavily on the stool behind the cash box.

'It was Charles and Cecilia Epping,' declared Belinda. 'In a big car, driving through Heaven's Cove as clear as day, though I swear that man hasn't set foot in the village for a decade. Oh, dear. I should have jumped in front of them with my sash on. They might have contributed to the village hall fund, though I doubt it.'

'Which way were they heading?' asked Rosie.

'Towards Driftwood House, of course. That's why I had to tell you. I think Charles and Cecilia Epping are on their way to your house... their house... your house.'

'But they can't. They're not supposed to visit until Friday.'

Belinda held her palms up to the china-blue sky. 'What did I tell you? The Eppings are a law unto themselves.'

Without another word, Rosie turned and started weaving her way through the crowds.

'Do you want me to come with you? I don't mind,' yelled Belinda, but Rosie was already gone.

Katrina got to her feet and peered after Rosie. 'Why is she in such a panic? And what did she mean, that the house isn't ready for them yet? Tell me, Liam.'

But Liam was too busy thinking to answer, even though Katrina gave him her prettiest pout and blinked her big grey eyes at him.

'Haven't you heard?' said Belinda. 'Rosie is trying to persuade the Eppings to turn Driftwood House into a guesthouse.'

'A guesthouse? Is that why there's paint in her hair? And how the hell does someone like Rosie know Charles and Cecilia Epping anyway?'

The two women bent their heads together and carried on gossiping as Liam ran the apron that Rosie had just given him through his fingers. Belinda was right about the Eppings doing what they wanted, when they wanted. They wouldn't care how much work Rosie had put into the house. As he'd warned her, she'd made a deal with the devil.

Chapter Nineteen

Rosie pushed her way through the throng of people, inwardly groaning at the tourists for descending on Heaven's Cove on today of all days. The day that Charles and Cecilia Epping decided to pay an early visit to Driftwood House before Driftwood House was properly ready. Cecilia would never agree to the guesthouse plan now.

Rosie rushed on, past Colin's fish stall where she'd planned to buy a shiny silver mackerel for her tea. Fish was good for the skin, wasn't it? She mentally kicked herself for being stung by Katrina's comment, which had taken her back to their school days.

And what was that moment when Liam stroked her arm? Even though they'd grown closer over the last few weeks, his kindness and concern were disorientating. Nessa's admonition at Sorrell Head suddenly sounded in her head: *You're judging us all on how we used to be before you ran off to Spain.* Nessa was right – they'd all changed, and maybe Liam even liked her as more than a friend these days.

Rosie hurdled an empty box left behind one of the stalls and berated herself for being an idiot. Liam would hardly be interested in her when Katrina was around. However much he might or might not have changed, she was surely much more his type – bold, poised, beautiful, and living just up the road rather than a thousand miles away.

With random thoughts still pinging around her brain, Rosie raced on, along the High Street to the end of the village. *Maybe Belinda got the wrong end of the stick,* she told herself as she puffed up the cliff. *It probably wasn't the Eppings she saw at all.*

But when she got higher, there was a silver Range Rover in the distance, parked outside Driftwood House, and two figures standing near the edge of the cliff.

They didn't turn when she reached the house so she let herself in and threw her jumper into the under stairs cupboard. Clearing up the kitchen took only a few minutes thanks to the dishwasher, and the sitting room, with its newly painted walls, was tidy. The cream curtains were freshly laundered, a vase of wild flowers she'd picked that morning was on the windowsill, and the room smelled of polish.

The faded rug still needed a good vacuum and the wide, cream skirting boards needed washing down. They were on Rosie's to-do list, along with other last-minute tweaks to the house. But the Eppings' premature arrival meant things would just have to do.

Rosie glanced out of the window. The Eppings had seen enough of the sea and were walking back towards the house, Cecilia taking two steps for every one of her husband's loping strides. With a last look around the sunny room, Rosie went outside and stood on the grass.

It was rather like waiting for a royal visit, Rosie decided, as the couple got closer – Cecilia in black trousers with a beige silk blouse, and Charles wearing a navy linen jacket with a thin, blue scarf around his neck. She shivered, although the sun was warm on her shoulders, and resisted a sudden urge to curtsey when they reached her.

'Hello, Miss Merchant. You're home, I see,' said Cecilia, pursing her lips. 'We knocked on the door but there was no reply.'

'I was in the village. I wasn't expecting you until Friday.'

'We were out for a drive nearby and a diversion here made sense. It will save us making another trip later in the week.' She glanced at Charles, who was shielding his eyes with his hand and staring up at the roof. 'So,' she said briskly, 'I get to see infamous Driftwood House at last.'

'Haven't you seen it before?'

'Only from a distance. I've never wanted to brave that bone-rattling track before.'

'It is a bit potholed but I'm sure it could be improved quite easily,' said Rosie, biting down annoyance that Cecilia appeared to have condemned her family home without ever properly seeing it.

'Perhaps.' She inspected her polished nails. 'Can you show us around? We need to get to another appointment and only have ten minutes to spare.'

Just ten minutes to save Driftwood House from the wrecking ball. Neither combative Cecilia nor her silent husband were going to make this easy.

'I didn't have very long to make changes so they're only cosmetic but I hope you can still see Driftwood House's potential as a guesthouse.'

'You've had long enough, I'm sure. Come on,' barked Cecilia to her husband, who was staring at the house with a faraway expression. He wasn't even concentrating, thought Rosie with a pang of disappointment. Maybe Liam was right and she had made a deal with the devil – but she wasn't about to give up on the house without a fight.

'As you can see, the house is solid and attractive with many original features that are local to Devon. And its weathered appearance only adds to its appeal.' That last bit was pushing it, but Driftwood House had far more character than some brand new hotel. 'Why don't you come inside?'

Cecilia's intake of breath when the front door slammed behind them in the breeze wasn't the best of starts. And 'quite small' was her only comment when Rosie showed her the sitting room and pointed out its fabulous view of the sea and how cosy it would be for guests in winter, with its thick walls and the log burner blazing.

In the kitchen, she wrinkled her nose when Rosie talked about how spacious the room was, and she seemed wholly unimpressed with the vast original sink and the black Aga that, fortunately, Rosie had polished yesterday until it shone.

While Cecilia paced around the kitchen, rapping on the worktops as though they might break, Charles ran his hand across the large oak table. 'Did your mother do a lot of cooking in here?' They were the first words he'd spoken since entering the house.

'Mum didn't much enjoy day-to-day cooking. She found it boring, but she loved making cakes. Her speciality was a triple-layer Victoria sponge with fresh cream and strawberries on the top. She always made one for my birthday when I was growing up.'

Too much information. Rosie stopped speaking, acutely aware that no one cared.

But Charles smiled. 'Sofia always did have a sweet tooth, or so Evelyn told us.'

'We don't have time to chat. Let's get on,' snapped Cecilia, giving the kitchen garden a cursory glance through the window before marching into the hall and up the stairs, followed by Charles.

Damn, Rosie hadn't checked the bedrooms. The duvet on her bed was turned back, and yesterday's knickers were very possibly on the bathroom floor. She took the stairs two at a time, while Cecilia, on the landing, communicated her impatience by tapping her long fingernails on the bannister rail.

Tap-tap-tap. She was certainly desperate to get out of this house. The sound of her impatience echoing through the house was both agitating and infuriating.

At the top of the stairs, Rosie hurtled past the Eppings into the main bathroom and kicked her underwear behind the basin before they followed her in.

'I suppose this is a decent-sized room at least,' said Cecilia, frowning at the stain on the bath enamel that wouldn't come off, however much Rosie scrubbed. She ran her hand across the shower curtain before pulling her hand back as though she was burned. 'Is that mould?'

It *was* mould – a spot of black fungus the size of a five pence piece where the curtain rested against the tub. Rosie forced herself to smile.

'This room would certainly benefit from a new suite, including a walk-in shower, but that could be installed fairly inexpensively. The main thing is this room is a fabulous size and would make a wonderful master bathroom for the main bedroom that overlooks the sea. You could charge a premium for that sort of accommodation.'

'The main bedroom is where?' asked Cecilia, already bored with the bathroom and Rosie's ideas.

The bedroom caught her attention a little more, and she spent a couple of minutes looking around, before wandering off along the landing to investigate the other rooms by herself. Charles stayed put, gazing through the window across the cliffs to the sea. The wind that had sprung up was whipping at the waves and there were white horses as far as the eye could see.

'The view from this room is rather magnificent,' he said, after a few moments.

'It really is,' Rosie enthused. 'Whatever the weather, sun or cloud. Watching a storm front roll in across the sea is amazing.'

'I can imagine.' He pushed a hand through his snow-white hair. 'I also imagine that your mother liked living here.'

'She loved it.'

'But you didn't.' It was a statement, rather than a question.

'Just because I live elsewhere, it doesn't mean that I don't love this house.'

Charles raised an eyebrow. 'I suppose not, otherwise why would you be trying so hard to save it?' He picked up a silver-framed photo of Rosie from the chest of drawers. 'Was this your mother's bedroom?'

'Why?'

Now that did sound rude, but Rosie's patience with her inconveniently early visitors was wearing thin. They owned the house, but it was still her home for the next few days. She took the photo from Charles and carefully placed it back exactly where it had been before.

'I was merely interested to know what became of your mother, after Evelyn's death.'

'Didn't you ever try to contact her yourself?'

Charles regarded Rosie for a moment before turning his attention back to the ever-moving water. 'I don't deal directly with tenants.'

'Even a tenant who was great friends with your sister? A tenant who you remembered had a sweet tooth?'

Colour flooded Charles's face and he opened his mouth to speak, but his wife beat him to it.

'What are you two muttering about in here?' she called from the doorway. When neither of them answered, she marched across the room and hooked her arm through her husband's. She seemed pale under her carefully applied make-up, and jittery, as though she'd seen a ghost.

Rosie's antipathy towards this cold woman softened slightly. Living in the middle of Dartmoor, with the snow piling up in winter, must be rather lonely, however much money you had.

'Can I get you a cup of tea?' she asked. Cecilia hesitated, suspicion etched across her face. 'I promise it's not a bribe to save the house. I think I'd have to do rather better than a cup of Earl Grey. You just look like you could do with catching your breath.'

'We don't have the time.' Cecilia paused again and her voice was softer when she added: 'But thank you.' She glanced at her husband. 'Perhaps you'd be good enough to show us the other bedrooms and then we can leave you in peace.'

Once Rosie had shown them the bedrooms – and suggested that the attic could be converted into an additional bedroom with en suite facilities at a relatively low cost – Cecilia declared she'd seen enough.

'What's your verdict on Driftwood House?' asked Rosie nervously, as the couple stood at the open front door. The weather had turned and clouds bunching over the sea promised showers by tea time.

'My husband and I will discuss it and we'll be in touch. Thank you for your time.'

Rosie wasn't an idiot. Cecilia clearly hated Driftwood House and would be pushing for it to be demolished. And Charles would agree, if his apparent indifference to the house was anything to go by. He'd hardly said a word since their tetchy exchange in the bedroom.

Cecilia walked towards the Range Rover but Charles hesitated in the doorway. 'Was your mother happy here at Driftwood House?'

Rosie frowned, caught out by such an unexpected question. 'Yes, I think so.'

'I understand she was divorced.'

'That's right.'

'Is your father still alive?'

'He died a few years ago.'

'I see. I'm sorry.' He paused. 'Whatever we decide, there are obviously still things here in the house that need to be resolved. Your mother's possessions will have to be moved elsewhere for a start. So you can ignore when you were expected to vacate the property and stay until your flight back to Spain, as long as we're only talking about an additional few days.'

'That would be helpful. Thank you.' The tension in Rosie's shoulders eased slightly because at least she wouldn't be homeless before heading back to Málaga.

Cecilia suddenly leaned out of the car window. 'For goodness' sake, Jay, do hurry up or we'll be late.'

Rosie's breath caught in her throat, as Charles put his hands to his neck. 'I do believe I've left my scarf upstairs. Do you mind?'

Rosie stepped back silently, to allow him back into the house, and the moment he started climbing the stairs she hurried to the car.

'Yes?' said Cecilia, making no effort to disguise her irritation. 'When will you make a decision about Driftwood House?'

'As I said, my husband and I will discuss the situation.'

'Thank you.' Rosie glanced through the open front door. Charles was coming down the stairs with his scarf around his neck, so it was now or never. 'Sorry for asking, but did you just call your husband Jay? I thought his name was Charles.'

Cecilia frowned. She must think that Rosie was mad. 'I don't see that it's any of your business but my husband's middle name is James and close friends and family often call him Jay. Is that all right with you?'

'Yes, that's perfectly fine. Thank you,' said Rosie brightly, as Charles arrived at the car and slid into the driving seat. 'Thank you for coming, have a good day and I hope you won't be late, wherever you're going.'

Rosie sat down heavily on the grass and watched the car pick its bumpy way down the potholed track. She'd just burbled at the end there and couldn't even remember what she'd said.

There was no way Cecilia was going to give up her plan to demolish Driftwood House, but that wasn't uppermost in Rosie's mind right now. Charles Epping was known to those close to him as Jay, and though he claimed he'd never known her mother, people lied – the last month had taught her that if nothing else. Could he be the author of the hidden love letter?

Cold, unfeeling Charles Epping and her warm vibrant mother. That was hard enough to get her head around but the next notion almost blew her mind. If he was Saffy's long-lost lover, could he also be her father?

Chapter Twenty

This is not a good idea, insisted Rosie's inner voice as she pushed open the door to the café. But she ignored it, as she usually did, sat at a table next to the window with her laptop and logged on to the free Wi-Fi. The signal in here was far more reliable than at Driftwood House, and better for snooping on the Eppings.

The past was often best left in the past. Her mother had obviously thought so. Why else would she have guarded her secrets so zealously? But then she went and died and her secrets were now floating to the surface, like flotsam on the beach after a storm. And Rosie was feeling rather storm-battered.

Grief felt flat. It had settled on her like a suffocating blanket, draining her energy and dulling her thoughts. But this latest shock was different. It fizzed and made her fingers tingle. She'd hardly slept last night and, when she did at last fall into an exhausted slumber, her dreams were full of her mother embracing Charles Epping in a clifftop hotel while Belinda took notes.

Rosie looked through the window, past the striped bunting, at the shops and whitewashed cottages lining the cobbled High Street. Front doors opened directly onto the street, with doorsteps worn down by centuries of footsteps, and the blue sea sparkled nearby. Villagers had enjoyed the same view for hundreds of years. Everything in Heaven's Cove was solid and permanent. But her own history, her roots, were shaky and unclear.

'Can I get you something?' Pauline, owner of the Heavenly Tea Shop for donkey's years, was standing by the table. She was wearing a pretty floral apron and smelled of vanilla and coffee beans. 'It's good to see you in here. How are you doing after what happened to your mother? Such a terrible tragedy.'

Pauline had a foghorn voice and a couple of tourists on the next table gave Rosie a sympathetic smile.

'I'm OK, thanks, Pauline.'

'What's happening at Driftwood House?'

'I'm not sure yet.'

'Those Eppings are a nightmare.' Pauline glanced nervously over her shoulder and dropped her voice to a loud whisper. 'None of us around here can stand them. They're absolutely loaded but I bet they won't contribute to the village hall fund at all. They don't give a monkey's about Heaven's Cove.' She straightened up and took a small spiral notebook from her pocket. 'Anyway, enough about those two. What can I get you?'

'I'll have a coffee please, an espresso.'

'Nothing else? I've got carrot cake and eclairs and home-baked scones. You could have a lovely cream tea. Your mum always enjoyed one of those.'

'I'm not very hungry at the moment so just a coffee, please.'

Pauline snapped her notebook shut. 'Coming up.'

Rosie went back to her laptop and typed in a search for *Charles Epping, Dartmoor*. Dozens of entries scrolled up on the screen, including a link to Wikipedia. She clicked and started reading.

> *Charles Epping is a businessman and landowner. His ancestor George Epping was knighted by King Henry VII for providing support during The Wars of the Roses and granted several hundreds of acres of land in the county of Devon.*

His family was given the land. They didn't even have to work for it. Rosie frowned and continued reading the brief entry. There was an Epping family tree which stretched back to William the Conqueror.

High Tor House had its own section, which told her that it was built in the late fifteenth century and had been extended during the centuries that followed. It was reputedly haunted by the ghost of a white lady who walked the building. Rosie shivered, remembering the chill she'd felt in the hallway when she first went inside.

She scrolled to the end of the entry for personal information. Charles and Cecilia were married in London on 5 May 1989, a month before she was born. There was no mention of Charles Epping having any children, and a separate Google search brought up nothing relevant. What was Rosie expecting? An entry about his missing love child?

'Here you go.' Pauline placed a steaming coffee on the table and a plate next to it. 'I know you said you weren't hungry but you're looking a bit peaky so this is on the house. With you living in Spain and all, I chose the most exotic European item we have on the menu.'

She nodded at the golden pain au chocolat on the plate and Rosie's stomach growled when its sweet smell hit her nose. She hadn't been able to face breakfast after such a disturbed night but she was hungrier than she'd thought.

'Thanks, Pauline. That's really kind of you.'

'You're most welcome. Are you still trying to persuade the Eppings not to knock down Driftwood House?'

Rosie nonchalantly nudged her laptop screen out of Pauline's line of sight. 'Kind of. I've spruced up the house in the hope that he'll change his mind about the hotel.'

'Hmm. He doesn't come across as the kind of man who changes his mind, and his wife's a piece of work by all accounts. They don't let anything stand in their way – what the Eppings want, the Eppings get.' Pauline sniffed. 'But good luck with it.'

Pauline really wasn't a fan. No one in Heaven's Cove seemed to be, so what would they think of her if it turned out that she and Charles Epping were so closely related? Rosie shook her head. It was a crazy idea. There was no way that her mum would have taken up with such a cold fish.

When Pauline went off to serve a young woman who'd just come in with her baby, Rosie went back to her screen. She nibbled at the soft pastry and scrolled through more information about Charles Epping's life, pausing when she got to his sister.

Evelyn Amelia Epping, Charles's younger sister, died at the age of 27 in August 1988 after being involved in a traffic collision near Bayeux in Normandy. She was engaged to Viscount Pelham at the time and due to marry before the end

of the year. Before her death, she was patron of a number
of charities in Devon.

What a terrible tragedy for Charles and his whole family. It showed that however rich and grand your family might be, death still cast its shadow. Rosie felt a sudden stab of sympathy for cold, austere Charles Epping in his haunted house on the wild moors.

She was about to close down the computer when a link to the Epping family crest caught her eye. She double-clicked and leaned in closer to the screen. The crest was an intricate mixture of green and blue curlicues, with golden lions on either side of a large shield. And at the centre of the shield, picked out in bright red and dominating the crest, was a flower – a rose.

What was it that Morag had told her? *Rose was your mother's choice of name. She was most insistent about it.*

Rosie slammed the laptop lid shut and smiled shakily at the tourist couple who glanced up in alarm. It had to be a coincidence. Her mother had called her child Rose because she liked the name, that was all, not to drop another breadcrumb that would one day lead that child to her father.

'Is everything all right over there, Rosie?' called Pauline across the café. 'You've gone awful pale under that tan of yours.'

'Yes, thanks, Pauline. I've left money under the cup.'

Then, she stuffed her laptop into her bag and fled the café, leaving her half-eaten pastry on the table.

*

'Pick up, pick up,' Rosie pleaded, rushing along the High Street towards home with her mobile pressed to her ear.

Matt was never parted from his phone. It was virtually welded to his hand – he even took it into the toilet. But getting him to answer his phone these days was another matter. When she'd called him last night, he hadn't answered at all, though he'd texted later to say he was working late.

She rang off when her call again clicked through to Matt's voicemail and hit the redial button for the third time because she really needed to speak to him right now.

Her breathing was too short, too shallow, and her fingers had started to prickle with pins and needles. Rosie deliberately slowed everything down but kept walking as Matt's phone started ringing once more. Finally, he picked up.

'Can't speak. It's ridiculously manic here for a Thursday. I'll ring you back later, babe.'

'No, please wait, Matt. I really need to speak to you.'

'Can't it wait?' He lowered his voice. 'A couple from Manchester are about to sign on the dotted line for that dodgy apartment near the car wash. The one with the broken air-conditioning system.'

She paused, confused. 'I thought we'd agreed that one shouldn't be on the market?'

'What can I say?' He raised his voice again. 'Mr Jimson absolutely loves it, don't you, sir?'

'Can you spare me two minutes? I need to talk because I think' – Rosie looked around to make sure Belinda wasn't about to leap out from a side alley – 'I think that Charles Epping might be my biological father.'

'What, that bloke who owns your old house?'

'The very same.'

'And you think he's your dad because…?'

'I found out yesterday that people close to him call him Jay. Remember the love letter to Mum that I told you about?'

'Of course I do. The letter and the house are all you talk about these days.'

'Well, it was signed with a J so he might have written it.' She stopped speaking but Matt said nothing. 'Are you still there?'

'Yeah, I'm thinking. Why didn't you ring and tell me?'

'I tried but you didn't pick up and I didn't want to explain it over text.'

'You should have told me straight away.'

'You should have answered my calls.'

'I'm a busy man, Rosie.'

Urgh, this wasn't the time to rehash old disagreements. Rosie ploughed on.

'So his family call him Jay and he let my mum live at Driftwood House for years. He claims it was because she was friends with his sister but she died ages ago and he doesn't seem the sort of man to honour an old agreement. Plus, my mum was insistent that I be called Rose and I've just found out that his family crest has a rose at its centre. He and Mum obviously had a falling-out, and she never told me about him because everyone around here hates him. It all makes sense.'

Or it had until she'd said it out loud. Matt's silence down the line spoke volumes. It was all circumstantial evidence that would never stand up in the police procedural documentaries that her mum loved to watch.

'Sorry, Matt, I'm leaping to conclusions.'

'Maybe, maybe not. Hold on, I'm going outside.'

Rosie heard muffled voices, a door closing and then the sound of traffic zooming past. She could picture the busy street, lined with palm trees, and Matt sheltering in the shade.

'Do you really think this Epping bloke could be your dad?'

'Possibly, maybe, probably. I don't know.'

'Have you spoken to him about it?'

'God, no, and I'm not planning to. You should see him, Matt. He's cold and unfeeling and I'm not sure I want him to be my dad anyway. I already had a dad.'

'One who left you and your mum when you were a kid.'

'I don't need you to remind me of that.'

'Sorry. I don't mean to be blunt. This is just a lot to take in.'

'I know. It's all too much on top of everything else.'

What Rosie needed right now was to talk to her mum. She'd wrap her arms around her and explain and make everything all right. But that could never, ever happen. Nothing would ever be the same again.

'I want to come back to Spain.' Rosie was crying now, as she reached the cliff path. 'You were right, Matt. I was stupid to stay here and to try and save Driftwood House. It doesn't matter. None of it does. Mum's gone.'

'Well, yeah, but you were trying to do right by your mum. That's understandable.'

'Understandable but still crazy. Charles Epping and his horrible wife will do exactly what they wanted to do in the first place. It's hopeless. I'll get the first flight back to Málaga.'

'Now, don't be hasty, Rosie. There's no point in rushing back while you're not thinking straight. Why don't you take a day or two to collect your thoughts and pack things up at the house, and I'll be waiting for you when you get back? I've got to head indoors to the Jimsons before they change their minds, but promise me you'll take the time to get your head together before you do anything else.'

Rosie stopped on the cliff path and let the breeze cool her hot face. She could see that bolting from Heaven's Cove would cause its own problems. Many of her mum's possessions were still scattered around the house and needed to be boxed up. 'OK, I promise, though I can't wait to get back. I miss you, Matt.'

'I miss you too, babe. Gotta go.'

Rosie dropped the phone into her jacket pocket and gazed across Heaven's Cove. The village looked beautiful from up here. At its centre, the church tower rose above huddled cottages and narrow streets. Boats bobbed at the quay, and close to the bright strip of sand at the cove, she spotted the fields that made up Meadowsweet Farm. Liam would be there right now, working hard, and paying rent for his fields to a man he couldn't stand. The man who might be her father.

When Liam had rung her yesterday, to ask about the Eppings' visit, she'd said nothing about Charles also being known as Jay. She didn't want to say anything before finding out more. That's what she'd told herself. But the truth was she didn't want Liam to think badly of her, as he surely would if she turned out to be an Epping herself.

With a deep sigh, Rosie trudged on for home. Her head had started to ache after talking to Matt, and Driftwood House seemed musty and full of old secrets when the front door banged shut behind her. She paced from room to room, unable to settle, and spent the rest of the day packing up precious possessions of her mum's that she wanted to keep. Another restless night followed, filled with dreams of perfect red roses turning to ash in her hands.

Chapter Twenty-One

Liam dropped the axe he'd been wielding and pulled up his T-shirt to mop his face.

Dee used to watch him chopping wood because she said he looked sexy. Today, all he looked was hot and miserable, and Billy, his only audience, was staring at him with a bored expression.

'Are you fed up too? Would you like a walk, boy?' The dog's excited barking at the 'w' word gave him his answer. 'Come on then. A quick run on the beach will do us both good.'

Was he talking too much to his dog? Probably, but Billy was good company who gave out far more than he expected back. Last night, Liam had been to the pub with Alex, but knocking back pints and flirting with any woman who came close had lost its sheen. At least with Billy he didn't have to pretend he was the person he no longer seemed to be.

Shutting the yard gate firmly behind him, Liam started walking towards the beach with Billy trotting obediently at his heels. The lane was empty of traffic this afternoon and the only sounds were the chirping of birds nestling in the high hedges on either side of the road, and the dull boom of waves crashing into the headland.

The sun on his face was cheering and made him feel calmer. He'd had a busy morning but, however hard he worked, there was only so much income the farm could make. And he was still worried about the rent rise on his fields. Charles Epping really had no clue how normal, un-rich people lived. And he wouldn't give a damn about Driftwood House. Liam wondered again how Epping's visit to the house had gone two days ago. Rosie had been distant and unforthcoming when he'd rung her to find out, so he hadn't called again.

'No cars so you can come off the lead, Billy.' Liam unclipped it but the dog stayed by his side.

Ahead of him, a woman in a flowing lilac sundress had just reached the beach. A canvas tote bag was slung over her shoulder and her hair was shining gold in the sun. It was only when she stopped and stooped down to take off her sandals that he realised it was Rosie.

Liam's first instinct was to turn around and head back to the farm. Not because he didn't want to see her – he really did, but that was the problem. Every time he saw Rosie, he felt closer to her and that just wouldn't do. What was the point of getting closer if it meant he'd miss her more when she was gone?

He stopped walking, ready to retrace his steps, but the stupid dog ruined everything by suddenly running ahead. His barking alarmed a flock of birds who rose from the hedgerow as one.

Rosie shielded her eyes to see what was causing the ruckus and stood up slowly, holding her shoes.

'Hey,' said Liam, when he reached her. 'How are you doing?'

'All right, thanks. And you?'

'Yeah, OK.'

'Good.'

Rosie squidged her toes into the sand while Liam tried not to think of the last time he'd seen Rosie, when he'd run his fingers along the soft skin of her arm.

'Have you been busy today?' she asked.

'Yeah, very.'

'Spring must be a busy time of year.'

'It is.'

'How are your mum and dad?'

'Fine.'

This was quite pathetic. How many women's arms had he stroked over the years? Absolutely loads, without turning into a monosyllabic idiot. Alex would tell him to get a grip.

Liam pulled himself together and gave Rosie his best twinkly smile. 'I was about to take Billy for a walk on the beach. Why don't you join us?'

'Why not?' Rosie gazed out to sea and smiled. 'Wow, the beach is looking good today. I needed some fresh air and knew it would cheer me up.'

She put her hands on her hips and turned her face to the sun while Liam bent to pat Billy's flank.

'Off you go, boy. Have fun.'

The dog needed no further encouragement. He sped away, barking joyfully as he weaved among the tourists who had spread their towels out across the warm sand.

Liam straightened up. 'I'm sure you have good beaches in Spain.'

'We have fabulous beaches. But the ones near me tend to be busier. They're absolutely rammed in the summer with sun loungers. This one is very… unspoiled.'

Liam visited this beach almost every day. Every inch of it was familiar to him, but now he saw it through fresh eyes. It *was* very unspoiled and beautiful. The sun was shining in a cloudless sky – the first really hot day of the year – and children in swimsuits were running in and out of the retreating tide and splashing in rock pools. An expanse of washed sand glittered like it was scattered with diamonds and huge boulders that had tumbled from the cliffs cast welcome shade at the back of the beach.

'Shall we walk then?' asked Rosie, swinging her strappy sandals between her fingers. 'Aren't you going to take off your boots?'

He didn't usually bother, for a quick walk with Billy. But he unlaced his boots, took off his socks and sank his toes into the warm sand. That felt good.

Together, the two of them started walking just above the tide line on the cooler, more solid sand, while Billy splashed in the water.

'Any more news from the Eppings?'

Rosie stiffened beside him. 'Nothing as yet.'

'How were they when they visited Driftwood House? You didn't say much about it.'

'They were… odd. Neither of them seemed to like the house very much, and Cecilia hates me.'

'Are you sure?' He laughed. 'No one could hate you, Rosie.'

'You'd be surprised.'

When she grinned and turned her face towards him, he noticed the freckles scattered across her nose and the glow from her bare, tanned skin. He quickly looked away, across the waves to a yellow boat on the horizon.

'So when will they tell you what they've decided about the house?'

'It doesn't matter because they're not going to go for the guesthouse idea anyway.'

'Are you sure?'

When she side-stepped a wave, her hand brushed against his. 'One hundred per cent. Cecilia's torturing me by stringing it out, that's all.'

'I see. That's a shame. Driftwood House will disappear and the Eppings will win again.'

'They always win, don't they?'

'Seems that way.'

Rosie stopped and squinted into the sun. 'You don't like anything about them, do you?'

'Why would I? They care about no one but themselves and don't give a monkey's about Heaven's Cove. So what happens to you now?'

'Now I finish packing up Mum's things and I go back to Spain in a few days' time. There's nothing to keep me in Heaven's Cove any longer.'

'Not even the rain or the cream teas or the fabulous people?'

Fabulous people? Why did he say that? It made him sound full of himself, like when he was at school. Rosie gave him a straight stare. 'And what about the search for your dad?' he asked quickly.

'I've given up on that.'

'Why?'

She brushed away a fly that landed on her bare shoulder. 'The only dad I ever knew is gone and that's that. I don't need another one.'

There was something else. The way she bit down hard on her bottom lip gave her away, but before Liam could say anything more Billy ran out of the waves and started leaping around them. He was barking loudly and getting totally over-excited. Oh, he wouldn't. Not again.

'Billy, no! Oh, for f—'

Water droplets flew through the air, splitting the light into mini rainbows, as the really, *really* stupid dog decided to shake himself. Good grief, the water was absolutely freezing. When Rosie squealed, Liam pushed her behind him, trying to save her from the worst of it, and took the full force.

'I can only apologise. Again.' Liam licked his wet lips and tasted salt. 'I don't know what's wrong with the daft dog. He never normally misbehaves like this. I think you bring out the worst in him.'

'Don't worry about it.' Rosie looked at Liam's sopping wet T-shirt and started to laugh. He'd never heard her properly laugh before and the sound of it lifted his spirits. 'You'd better stretch out on the sand to dry off. You're absolutely soaked.'

Liam sank down onto the warm sand and leaned back on his elbows. Rosie sat down next to him, pulled up her knees and locked her arms around them. 'Billy is quite a character.'

'That's one word for him,' said Liam, tutting at his ridiculous dog. Billy was now rolling around on the beach and his fur was stiff with sand. 'I'll be hosing him down in the yard when I get back.'

'He won't much like that.'

'I don't suppose he will.'

Rosie lowered her cheek onto her knees, with her face towards the sea. Liam watched her hair dance in the breeze for a moment. She seemed so worn out, so bowed down by life and its secrets.

'So you'll still be here tomorrow, then,' he said.

'I will. Why?'

'There's an eighties disco in the village hall tomorrow night. Belinda and her committee put on dances there quite regularly. Why don't you come and switch off for a couple of hours?'

Rosie raised her head. 'Do you go?'

'Always.' That was a lie. He hadn't been to one in ages.

'I bet you're a good dancer on the quiet.'

'You saw me dance at school discos so you know full well that *Strictly*'s got nothing on my moves.'

When Rosie turned her head towards him, he realised that his mouth was very close to hers. She really did have the most beautiful skin and her teeth were so white against her golden tan. A fair curl of hair had tumbled onto her shoulder and, without properly thinking it through, he pushed it back behind her ear, his hand brushing against her cheek.

Rosie stared at him, her eyes the colour of the autumn leaves that blew across his farm. Neither of them moved as seagulls wheeled overhead and children ran past them to the sea.

Liam, the ladies' man, would have rested his hand on the back of her neck and gently pulled her towards him until their lips met. But that wasn't who he was any more. Globetrotting Rosie already had a boyfriend and wasn't interested in a failing farmer from Heaven's Cove anyway.

He'd just dropped his hand when a long, dark shadow loomed over them. Shielding his eyes, he looked up into the sun.

'Oh!' Rosie was scrambling to her feet, shaking sand all over him. 'You came! You didn't tell me.'

She threw her arms around the neck of the man standing in front of them while Liam got to his feet and wiped away the sand sticking to his damp T-shirt.

'Been for a swim?' asked the man, staring at Liam over Rosie's shoulder. He was sporting a tidy moustache and goatee, and his arm around her waist was the same colour as Rosie's skin.

'We were walking and Billy, Liam's dog, shook water everywhere.' Rosie grinned. 'I can't believe you're here, Matt.'

'You didn't think I'd be happy letting you cope with all this on your own, did you?'

Matt hugged Rosie tightly to him while Liam raised an eyebrow. It seemed to him that Matt had been perfectly content to let Rosie cope with 'all this' on her own up until now.

'Let me introduce you properly.' Rosie disentangled herself from his embrace. 'This is Liam, who I've known for ages. He's the person who's been helping me with the painting.'

'I'm Matt, the boyfriend. It's kind of you to help Rosie out, Liam.' Matt's beady grey eyes bored into Liam's. He didn't smile.

'It's not a problem.'

'So how do you two know each other?'

'We went to school together.'

'Really? Rosie's never mentioned you before. Mind you, she rarely mentions Heaven's Cove. She's far too busy with our life in Spain.' He grabbed her hand and pushed his fingers between hers.

She folded her fingers over his. 'How come you're in Heaven's Cove, Matt, and how did you know I was on the beach?'

'I was worried about you so I decided to ditch work and jump on a plane. Juan said he and Carmen can manage until we get back. This place really is in the middle of nowhere, isn't it? It took me ages to get here from the airport, and then a strange woman called Linda or something noticed my suitcase and started chatting to me. She said she knew you and she'd seen you heading this way. So I took a chance and spotted you on the beach. Both of you.'

'I went for a walk and bumped into Liam – he runs a farm nearby.'

'So, you're a farmer, are you, Liam?'

'Uh-huh.' Every time Matt said his name, it put Liam's teeth on edge.

Matt pushed a hand through his short, brown hair and smiled, his teeth as dazzling white as a toothpaste ad. 'You have my gratitude. The world needs more farmers. Farmers rock, though I could never do it – be stuck in one place, year in, year out. I need more adventure in my life. That's why Rosie and I gelled so quickly and became soulmates. We're made for each other, aren't we, babe?'

Was Liam mistaken or did Rosie wince slightly?

She hooked her arm through Matt's. 'Come on, I'd better get you home to Driftwood House so you can unpack. I still can't believe you're here. Liam, thanks for the walk and I'll see you again sometime.'

'Sure. You get your boyfriend settled in and Billy and I will finish our walk.'

'Good to meet you, Liam.'

He clearly didn't mean it and Liam felt himself bristle. 'Yeah, you too.'

Matt picked up his shiny black suitcase and hooked his other arm around Rosie's waist. Together, the two of them walked off across the sand.

'Well, Billy, what do you think of Matt, then?' Liam bent down and pushed his fingers through the dog's matted fur. 'What's that you say? *Matt seems like a total dick?* Yeah, that was my first impression too.'

Chapter Twenty-Two

'You didn't mention the mountaineering,' huffed Matt, hauling his suitcase to the top of the track. Dust puffed up around him when he dropped his case and stood, hands on hips, staring at Driftwood House.

'What do you think?'

Rosie wasn't sure why she felt nervous. It really didn't much matter what Matt thought of her childhood home. It would soon be rubble anyway. But she was still pleased he was seeing it at its best. Sunlight sparkled on the windows facing the clifftop, which was sprinkled with bright spring flowers. A light aircraft hummed overhead, adding to the faint rhythmic boom of waves hitting rock.

'You weren't joking when you said it needed some work.' Matt whistled softly. 'What a dump.'

'It's hardly a dump. It just needs some tender loving care.'

'A bit like you, babe.'

Matt swept her up into his arms and Rosie relaxed into his embrace. It was good that he was here, to support her and help her pack up what she needed to in the house.

'Did you miss me?' he whispered in her ear.

'Of course.' She had. Quite a lot. And she'd have missed him even more if she hadn't been so focused on her grief and saving this house and unravelling secrets. She hugged him tight. 'Thank you for coming. Were you getting lonely in Spain without me?'

'Lonely and overworked, though Carmen is showing a great deal of promise. We've all been working overtime since you left at a moment's notice.'

Rosie stiffened in his arms. 'I didn't have much choice. My mother died.'

'I know,' murmured Matt, stroking her hair. 'Everyone understands and you need to stay until you've seen things through. It's a bit of a bombshell, this dad thing.'

'It certainly is.' Rosie pulled away, not keen to talk about it so soon after Matt's arrival. She picked up his suitcase. What on earth had he packed? It weighed a ton. 'Come inside and I'll show you around.'

Matt banged the front door shut and gazed around him, squinting as his eyes adjusted to the gloom.

'The place could do with a new front door, but this entrance hall is a decent size and the original tiles and coving would be catnip to a buyer. Is that damp?'

'Afraid so. The walls are a bit porous in places, though Liam says it's easy enough to fix where the water's getting in.'

Rosie suddenly remembered Liam's gentle touch when he pushed her hair behind her ear. For a moment, she'd thought he was coming on to her, like the Liam of old, especially after that weird moment on market day. Teenaged Rosie would have been appalled, and just a tiny bit thrilled. But then he'd dropped his hand anyway. Of course he had. And Matt had arrived – a man who truly wanted her for herself.

'I'm so glad you're here, Matt,' she said, launching herself into his arms. 'Everything feels right now you're here.'

'Of course it does, babe. Of course it does,' he murmured. 'Come on. You can give me the Driftwood House tour later. Why don't you show me the bedroom first?'

An hour later, Rosie lay with her head on Matt's chest while he snored softly. Pale light filtered through her childhood bedroom, settling on dust in corners and Matt's grey underpants on the floor. She hadn't slept in here since arriving back at Driftwood House, but Matt sleeping in her mother's bed wouldn't have felt right.

Quietly, Rosie got up, slipped on her dressing gown and sat by the open window. A gentle breeze billowed the curtains while she studied Matt lying spread-eagled under the duvet.

She'd told him downstairs that everything felt right because he was here. But right now she felt more unsettled than ever. It was wonderful of Matt to – eventually – make the journey to support her, but he seemed out of place in Heaven's Cove, as though he'd washed up by mistake in sleepy Devon.

Somewhere in the house, a door slammed as a draught snaked through an ill-fitting window. What was she doing here when her life was now a thousand miles away? She was settled there, kind of. She had an apartment, a boyfriend, two jobs, friends to drink with in the local bar, and the weather was amazing. She looked through the window at the dark clouds massing on the horizon.

But sometimes she missed the passing seasons, the unpredictable weather and the sense of being rooted. She and Heaven's Cove hadn't always seen eye to eye, but this village, this view, had anchored her recently while grief and secrets swirled around her. Most of all, she missed her mum, whose presence could almost be felt within these walls.

'You all right, babe?' Matt yawned and stretched his arms above his head.

'Fine, thanks. I was getting some air.'

'What were you thinking?'

Rosie tensed. She hated that question. 'This and that. Mostly, I was thinking about Heaven's Cove and about Mum.'

'I am sorry about your mum.' He raised himself up on one elbow. 'She was quite a one for secrets, wasn't she? Lying about this house *and* not saying a word about your mysterious father. What a woman! Do you really think that Epping man is your dad?'

'I don't know. I think it's likely but I don't have any proof.'

'You could get it.' When Matt sat up, the duvet slipped down his hairy chest. 'You could force him to do a DNA test.'

'I don't think anyone could force Charles Epping to do anything.'

'I bet you could. There must be some legal way of forcing the issue.'

'I don't want to force anything, and Mum obviously didn't want me to know him.'

'Yeah, but your mum's dead.'

Wow, that was blunt. Rosie winced but Matt was too busy getting out of bed and pushing his legs into his pants and trousers to notice. 'I don't understand why you're so reluctant to pursue this.'

'I don't know. Everyone in Heaven's Cove hates the Eppings so it won't do much for my popularity round here if they think we might be related.'

'What do you care? You'll be back in Spain in a few days' time. Have you said anything to him about it?'

For one moment, Rosie thought he meant Liam, before realising Matt was talking about Charles. She shook her head.

'Well, you have to tell him that you might be his daughter.'

'Why?'

Because if he's your dad, Rosie, he might want to know. Because you deserve to know who your real father is. Because you must have a million questions about how he and your mum got together and why they parted.

Please say something like that. Rosie stared at Matt, willing him to say the right thing.

Matt pushed his arms into his *I love Málaga* T-shirt. 'Because if he's as rich as you say he is, you need to make sure you're in his will. In the meantime, you can get him to gift you this place so you can sell it to a property developer and make some serious money. He owes you that much.'

Cold disappointment flooded through Rosie. Did Matt understand her at all? When she stayed silent, he padded over in his bare feet and put his arms around her. 'I realise how difficult this all is, Rosie, and I want you to know that I'm here to support you. Always. Oops, I'd better get that.'

Matt pulled his ringing phone from his trouser pocket and glanced at the screen. 'It's work. Speak to you in a bit.'

In the doorway, he paused to blow her a kiss before wandering along the landing and padding down the stairs.

Rosie pulled her dressing gown more tightly around her and drew her feet up onto the wide windowsill. She used to sit here as a child with her fingers in her ears when her mum and dad were arguing downstairs. The man she thought of as her dad.

Rosie blinked to clear the tears that were blurring her view of the sea and the sky. She knew exactly why she was reluctant to say anything to Charles Epping about her suspicions. His appalling reputation in Heaven's Cove was a part of it, but mostly she was scared – scared that having been rejected by one father at the age of ten she would be rejected by another at almost thirty.

Lots of people lose one father, said the little voice in her head. *But two? What would that say about you, Rosie?*

Chapter Twenty-Three

Matt stood on the quayside, still as a statue, peering out across the water.

'Where did you say it was?' he asked.

'Over there, on the right.'

'I can't see it. Mind you, I can't see anything much in this weather.'

'It juts out into the water in a kind of heart shape. That's why the locals call it Lovers' Link.' Rosie stopped pointing. 'It's really pretty,' she added for his benefit, because there was no way Matt could glimpse it through the misty haze hugging the waves. 'It's a prime, unspoiled location that would sell for a fortune to a property developer.'

Matt perked up at that, as Rosie knew he would, and started squinting into the distance, a deep furrow between his eyes.

Damn it. Rosie wanted to show off Heaven's Cove at its best: quaint whitewashed cottages pretty against a china-blue sky, narrow cobbled lanes filled with happy people in shorts, and excited children with buckets and spades heading for the beach.

Instead, a sea fret was rolling in, the sky was steel grey, and any tourist daft enough to visit the village today looked miserable as sin.

'Nope, I definitely can't see it.' Matt turned to her and shivered. 'Is it always so dreadfully cold here? No wonder you'll be so happy to come home.' He pulled Rosie into a bear hug.

'Now what else did you want to show me before we head back to the relative warmth of your draughty childhood home?'

'Maybe the church?'

'The church?' She may as well have suggested a visit to a local abattoir from the look on his face.

'It's a gorgeous little church: fifteenth century with beautiful stained glass and... buttresses.'

Did it have buttresses? She wasn't quite sure what a buttress was, but old churches probably had them.

'That sounds totally riveting, babe.'

Rosie did not appreciate his sarcasm. 'Come on, it won't take long, and I can show you where Mum is buried.'

'All right. The church it is,' huffed Matt, making Rosie feel that she was using her mother as a bargaining chip.

It really was hopeless trying to get Matt to like Heaven's Cove, and she wasn't even sure why she was bothering. She'd moaned about the village often enough, but the last few weeks had opened her eyes to its beauty. What was the old saying: *You don't appreciate what you've got until it's gone?* Soon Driftwood House would be gone and she'd be gone from Heaven's Cove too, with little reason to return.

'I think my toes have got frostbite,' whined Matt, stamping his feet on the pale, wide stones of the quay. He didn't half moan a lot, but Rosie knew when she was beaten.

'How about we give the church a miss and have a hot chocolate instead? I know a nice little café on the High Street.'

'Now you're talking.' Matt smelled of menthol when he bent to kiss her nose. 'Lead the way.'

The Heavenly Tea Shop was heaving and Pauline hardly acknowledged them when they stepped inside.

'Find yourself a table,' she shouted from the counter, raising her fleshy arm to her hot, red face. 'If you can.'

'The whole of Heaven's Cove is in here,' moaned Matt, squeezing past a pushchair to sit at a tiny table near the back of the café.

'Most of the people in here are tourists,' replied Rosie, disappointed that the table was too far from the window to take advantage of the fab view of the High Street, down to the sea. Though little was visible today because the plate-glass window was opaque with condensation.

Matt picked up the menu. 'Right, let's get those hot chocolates down us.' He glanced across the café. 'Isn't that the woman who nabbed me when I first arrived in this godforsaken place?'

'Where?'

By the time Rosie had swivelled in her seat, Belinda was upon them, crumbs of cake scattered across her ample bosom.

'What good fortune! I'm so glad I bumped into you and your young man. We're taking five minutes to have a cup of tea before we start rearranging the village hall, ready for this evening.'

Rosie waved at Jim, who gave her a rueful smile back.

'Now, Rosie,' said Belinda, frowning when the child behind her started squealing. 'I've been bursting to find out how it went with the Eppings the other day.'

'I don't know for sure, Belinda. They had a look around Driftwood House and then left.'

'Did they make any decision about the house's future?'

'Nothing official, but I'm not very hopeful, to be honest.'

'That's a shame. Have you been in touch with them since their visit?'

'Not yet.'

'Don't tell anyone but apparently I was right to suspect they're not quite as well off as they used to be. Bad business decisions, according to my mole.' She winced as the child's squeals reached a crescendo. 'Frankly, I'm amazed that you've been able to establish any sort of rapport with the Eppings. It's very surprising.'

'Not really,' interrupted Matt. 'Rosie and Charles Epping probably have more in common than you realise.'

Rosie's foot connected with Matt's shin under the table. Was he about to spill her secret, to Belinda of all people, in a busy café?

'Is that right?' There was a zealous glint in Belinda's eyes. She licked specks of glazed sugar from her lips. 'Tell me more.'

'There's nothing to tell,' said Rosie loudly, giving Matt's leg another kick for good measure. 'We have Driftwood House in common but its fate lies in Charles and Cecilia Epping's hands. It's lovely to see you, Belinda, but we don't want to keep you from your work at the village hall.'

Belinda glanced between Rosie and Matt, her eyes narrowing. 'There is rather a lot to do. I suppose I'd better leave you to your refreshments, but maybe I'll see you at the dance this evening?'

'Maybe,' said Rosie, running her finger down the menu. 'I think I might go for a cream tea, Matt. What about you?' She dropped the menu and leaned across the table when Belinda scurried off, back to long-suffering Jim. 'What the hell do you think you're doing?'

'What do you mean?'

'Don't come over all innocent, Matt. You were hinting big time about me and Charles Epping. That's why I had to get rid of her. Belinda is the biggest gossip in town. If she ever gets the slightest wind of my suspicions, it will blow her mind – and then it will be all round the village in no time.'

'Would that be so bad?'

'Of course it would. Everyone would know that… he might be…' She couldn't say the words out loud. Not here.

'Indeed,' said Matt smugly, 'and that would force Charles Epping's hand, which would be good.'

'No, not good. Bad, very bad. And what hand would it force? There is no hand because I haven't spoken to him about it.'

'Exactly. But if he heard the rumours, he'd have to speak to you about it and confront his past.'

'Which I'm in no hurry for him to do.'

'I know, and I don't understand why when he should make reparation for what he's done.'

Because I'm frightened of opening yet another can of worms. Because my normal life has become a swirling soup of secrets. Because my mum must have had a good reason to lie to me for so long.

Why couldn't she say any of that to the man she was supposedly in love with? Rosie sighed. 'It's my secret which means it's mine to keep. Please, Matt.'

He stared at her through the hot fug of the café for a few moments before giving a curt nod and returning to his menu.

*

One cream tea later and Matt was in a much better mood. He even started humming under his breath when the two of them walked, arm in arm, towards the church.

This is nice, thought Rosie, as the sun finally burned through the mist and lit up the old buildings around her. This was how she'd hoped it might be when Matt had arrived out of the blue – the two of them, together, enjoying time in one another's company. She had missed him.

'Thanks again for flying over to support me.'

'You're welcome. You know, I—' Matt paused, distracted by his phone, which had been ringing almost constantly since he'd arrived in Heaven's Cove. And usually – yep, Rosie glanced at the screen before he answered – the calls were from Carmen.

'Do you need to answer it? I'm sure Carmen could ask someone else in the office for advice.'

'I know, babe, but she looks up to me as a mentor.' He shrugged in an 'I can't help being fabulous' kind of way. 'And it's her birthday today so I can't give her the brush-off.'

'Hey, Rosie. Wait up!'

Out of the corner of her eye, Rosie caught a flash of bright pink and spotted Nessa approaching in a fuchsia T-shirt dress, with Lily's hand grasped in hers.

Matt had seen Nessa too and gestured that he'd take his call elsewhere before retreating into the doorway of Maria's Rock Shop which, in addition to selling striped sticks of sticky Devon candy, sold every sweet you could feasibly think of.

'Is that your boyfriend?' asked Nessa, puffing to a halt in front of Rosie. 'Very nice.'

'He won't be a minute. He's taking a work call.'

'Good-looking, flies across the continent to support you *and* he's in demand. Sounds like a very sexy combination to me.'

'Behave! Hey, Lily, how come you're not on your bike today?'

Rosie grinned at the young girl, who sucked her thumb and eyed her warily.

'Jake was supposed to be picking her up this morning to take her out for lunch but he's bailed on me at the last minute so Lily's disappointed, aren't you, love? We're on an outing to Maria's to cheer her up. There's no heartache that a pineapple chunk can't ease, and I speak from experience.'

'I'll bear that in mind. Shouldn't you be at work?'

'Scaggy has given me an actual Saturday off, which is a miracle. He'll use it against me and make me go in every single summer Sunday, but whatever. I had a pampering day planned, to get ready for the dance tonight, but Lily can help me get myself tarted up. We might even fit in a trip to the beach if the sun ever properly comes out. What about you?'

Rosie didn't reply because she'd just had a thought. If today was Carmen's birthday, she wasn't likely to be at work. It was her twenty-fifth – she'd been going on about getting 'old' for months – and she'd told anyone who'd listen about the fabulous day she had planned at a water park with friends. Rosie glanced at her boyfriend, who was laughing into his phone, more animated than he'd been all morning.

'Earth to Rosie! Is anyone there?'

'Sorry, Nessa. What were you saying?'

'I asked how the visit from the Eppings went. I heard from Belinda that they'd called round unannounced, which sounds just the kind of thing they'd do – turn up early and take their prey by surprise.'

'I'm hardly prey, but I was surprised, all right.'

'So how did it go?'

'Not great and I'm sure the house will be demolished.' Rosie glanced again at Matt, who had turned so all she could see was his back. 'Charles Epping said almost nothing, and Cecilia Epping hates me.'

'She hates everyone, by all accounts. She's a right sour-faced bi—' Nessa glanced at Lily's upturned face and clamped her lips tightly together. 'So where does that leave you?'

'I'll be heading back to Spain next Wednesday. There's only so long I can take unpaid leave from my jobs without losing them both.'

'That's a shame. It's been good having you around again. Me, Katrina, Belinda, and Liam... we'll all miss you.'

'I don't think Katrina will even notice that I've gone.'

Nessa gave her a grin. 'Well, maybe not Katrina... Oh, it looks like your boyfriend's finished his call. Hi, I'm Nessa.'

Matt wandered over and shook the hand that Nessa proffered.

'Rosie said you were on a work call. You can't escape the office, even in the depths of Devon.'

'I sometimes think the office would collapse without me,' laughed Matt.

'You said it was Carmen's birthday today,' interrupted Rosie.
He hesitated. 'That's right.'

'I thought, 'cos it's her twenty-fifth, she was going to the
water park to celebrate with friends.'

'She is. She's there now but she's got a tricky viewing booked
tomorrow and needed some advice.'

'On her day off?'

'That's right.'

'On her birthday?'

'That's how keen she is to get on. Carmen wants to do well
and knows I can show her the ropes.'

Did he sound defensive or was Rosie overreacting? The
latter, probably. Her brain was frazzled with everything that
had happened recently. And Matt wanted to be with her or he'd
never have flown a thousand miles to help her with Driftwood
House. She put her hand on his arm and squeezed. 'Then she's
lucky to have a mentor like you.'

'Are you two coming to the dance later?' asked Nessa, being
pulled by Lily towards the sweet shop.

'What is this dance that everyone's going on about?'

'Hang on, Lily! It's an eighties disco this evening in the village
hall. You should both come. It'll be a laugh,' she shouted, before
Lily dragged her through the shop door.

'Do you know everyone around here?' asked Matt as the
door shut behind her.

'Pretty much.'

'Where do you know Nessa from?'

'We were at school together.'

'Like that farmer I met on the beach. I expect we'll bump into him next.'

'I doubt it. Liam will be busy working.'

'I don't know how he can bear to stay here and run a farm. It's boring and lacking in ambition, if you ask me.'

'It's nothing of the sort. Liam cares for the land, like his family's done for generations. He nurtures new life.'

'Nurtures new life? There's no need to get evangelical about it when all he's doing is growing a few carrots.' Matt sniffed. 'So what about the disco? Do you fancy it?'

'Maybe. I'm not sure.'

'We might as well. There's nothing else to do around here.'

'Nothing apart from watching dolphins swim in the bay, enjoying awesome views from the cliffs, walking through beautiful countryside, and scoffing cream teas in cosy cafés.'

'It's still not Málaga, though, is it? Where did you say this old church was?'

He wandered off, kicking at an empty drink can that someone had dropped in the street.

Rosie watched him scuffing along, with his hands in his pockets. Heaven's Cove certainly wasn't southern Spain with its vibrant culture and endless hot sandy beaches. But this village had its own charm, and bigging it up to Matt was helping her to recognise and appreciate that more and more.

Chapter Twenty-Four

Liam groaned as music thudded through his skull, colliding with the headache that had been brewing all afternoon. Now he remembered why he'd stopped coming to these village dances. He'd avoided several over the last year and, according to Alex, was fast turning into an old fart.

Sipping at his warm beer, he stepped back, but not before Michaela had stomped on his toes in her silver ankle boots. For someone who ran a weekly keep-fit class in this hall, she was surprisingly sturdy.

'Sorry,' she yelled, before being whirled away by her husband to some eighties classic whose name Liam couldn't recall. Belinda had booked the disco, and probably stipulated the music choices too.

This evening was a throwback, rather like Heaven's Cove itself, which often felt like a living museum, with its historic buildings and fishermen setting off from the quay, as they had done for centuries.

Liam contemplated his love-hate relationship with the village while the music got faster and the dancing more frantic. He was no longer happy in Heaven's Cove, but there was nowhere else he'd rather be. It was quite a conundrum.

He stood on tiptoe and scoured the crowd bobbing up and down under the strobing lights. Alex was chatting up Coral's daughter, Ella, and Nessa was throwing some moves on the edge of the dance floor. But Rosie wasn't here.

'You made it, then.' When Liam turned, Katrina was standing very close to him. Her glossy dark hair brushed his shoulder when she tilted her head. 'Actually, a little bird told me that you might be braving Belinda's disco.'

'Who was that?'

'Morris, when I bumped into him in the bakery.'

'Ah.' Liam vaguely remembered mentioning to Morris that he might give the dance a go, and nothing remained a secret in Heaven's Cove for long. Though Rosie's bombshell about her dad not being her real father seemed to have slipped under people's radar.

What a secret for Rosie to uncover so soon after losing her mother. And she'd trusted him with it. For a moment, the pounding beat faded and he was on the beach again, his hand brushing the soft skin of her cheek.

'Liam, I do believe you're not listening to me,' scolded Katrina, moving even closer. 'I said that I was worried you'd totally given up on these sorts of dances.'

'There's nothing much else to do around here on Saturday nights.'

'I'm sure I could think of something. Did I mention that Stephen is away at some boring conference in New York? He's not back until Monday so I have the whole weekend to myself. What do you think of that?'

The touch on Liam's arm was light, but it spoke of heated kisses and company. They could slip back to her place and make out on the very expensive designer rug she'd told them all about. She looked amazing in her tight, shimmery blue dress and would no doubt look even more amazing out of it.

'Well, look who's here.' Katrina was craning her perfect long neck towards the door. 'And she's brought an attractive man with her. Wonders will never cease. Hey, Rosie,' she called, waving. 'Over here.'

Rosie weaved her way through the dancers, her fair hair falling loose to her shoulders. She smiled at Katrina but didn't catch Liam's eye.

'Who's this you've brought with you, Rosie?'

'This is Matt, my boyfriend.'

'Gosh, she's kept you well hidden.'

Matt, in tight jeans and black T-shirt, looked rather taken aback by the full Katrina dazzle. He took hold of her hand, raised it to his mouth and brushed his lips across her skin, right in front of Rosie. God, what a creep.

'I live in Spain with Rosie,' shouted Matt above the music, which seemed to be getting louder. 'Well, we're not actually living together.'

Maybe not, but they were definitely sleeping together. Not that it was any of his business. Liam took a large gulp of his warm beer and wished he'd stayed at home with Billy.

'What kind of dance is this?' laughed Matt, eyeing up the locals strutting their stuff.

'Matt's never been to a village disco before,' said Rosie, smoothing down her shirt that was white as snow next to her golden skin. 'He grew up in London.'

'Very cosmopolitan,' purred Katrina.

Matt leaned closer to Rosie as 'Thriller' started playing. 'Shall we give it a go?'

'I don't know. It feels weird being here so soon after Mum's death.'

'I know, babe. But she wouldn't want you to be unhappy, would she? Come on.'

Before Rosie could say anything more, Matt put his hand into the small of her back and propelled her into the gyrating crowd. He put his arms around her waist and started whirling her around the floor, almost bumping into Nessa.

'Who knew that little mouse Rosie would land such a fit boyfriend?' Katrina glanced up at Liam from under her long black lashes. 'Aren't you going to ask *me* to dance, Mr Satterley?'

'Yeah, sure.' Liam held out his hand. He was here after all, so there was no point in behaving like a boorish idiot.

An hour and a half later, Liam leaned against the bar and stole a glance at his watch. He'd head for home soon and only Katrina would notice he'd gone.

Rosie's perfume, the delicate scent of an English country garden, suddenly mingled with the hall aroma of beer and sweat. She was behind him. He moved along a little, giving her enough space to reach the bar.

'Hi, Liam.' Her thin gold bracelet glittered in the light when she waved her hand, trying to attract barman Jim's attention. Belinda never hesitated to volunteer her husband for a raft of different jobs.

'Hi.'

Rosie smiled and moved her head closer so he could hear her properly. 'This disco is like a throwback to our school days. I keep expecting to fall over Year Twelves snogging in the corner.'

'Did you come to the school discos?'

'Sometimes. I stood on the sidelines, hoping someone would ask me to dance, but no one ever did.'

'Not even me?'

'Especially not you. You were far too busy getting off with all the cool girls.'

'What can I say? I was irresistible.'

'Yeah, you've always been the local heart-throb.'

'That's me.' He swirled the remains of his pint around his plastic glass. 'Where's your boyfriend?'

'He's been dancing with Katrina. She ambushed him, though he didn't look too upset about it. But he's just had a phone call from a work colleague and has gone outside to answer it.'

Pinpricks of light from the disco danced across her pretty face when she turned to the crowd and started tapping her foot. The years fell away and Liam could imagine her watching and waiting for an invitation that never came.

'Would you like to dance?' He held out his hand.

'What did you say?'

He put his mouth closer to her ear. 'I said, would you like to have a dance?'

She looked round at that. 'Why? To make up for all the times you never asked me?'

'Sort of.' Liam grinned. 'Not really. I just thought you might like to dance. With me. Though it's fine if you're waiting for Matt to come back and—'

'All right.' She placed her hand in his. Her skin was cool despite the stifling heat in the packed hall.

After putting down his beer, he led her into the middle of the dance floor and began to move to the beat. A few years ago, he would have danced unselfconsciously, knowing that he looked good and people were watching him admiringly. What was it Alex once told him disconsolately after a few too many beers? *All the women want to cop off with you and the men want to be you.* Or rather more Anglo-Saxon words to that effect.

But more recently his confidence had done a runner. He wasn't the catch he used to be – before the farm began to fail, before his cheeks reddened from working outdoors in all weathers, before he was dumped and became, to use another of Alex's phrases, *no feckin' fun at all.*

'This is great,' shouted Rosie, her hips swaying in time to the music. She closed her eyes and the stress etched across her face fell away as the beat pounded through their bodies.

'That was Madonna's "Material Girl",' said the DJ with an American accent, even though it was Clive who drove delivery vans by day and had probably never been farther than France in his life. 'Now, let's slow it down with some romantic vibes from eighties classic "Time After Time" by Cyndi Lauper. This is for all you Heaven's Cove lovers out there.'

'Cheesy, or what?' groaned Rosie.

'Mega cheesy.' Liam laughed. 'Clive's an eighties throwback himself.'

All around them, couples, bodies entwined, started swaying to the beat while he and Rosie stood stock still in the middle of the dance floor. This was getting awkward. Rosie, cheeks flaming, turned to go but Liam put his hand on her waist and pulled her towards him.

'To make up for all those times I never asked you,' he said into her ear, feeling the soft brush of her hair against his skin.

'You old charmer,' laughed Rosie, against his chest.

At first, they moved to the music woodenly, his hands on her waist and her hands on his shoulders. Acquaintances from years back. Old friends, or maybe new ones. But as more dancers packed in around them, his hands moved across her back and she slid her arms around his neck until their bodies met. He tightened his arms around her and their bodies moved in sync to the music as she rested her cheek against his shoulder.

Tears prickled Liam's eyes and he blinked furiously. What on earth was the matter with him? Slow dancing with women was what he did. Everyone expected Liam Satterley to get off with someone by the end of the evening. But Deanna had changed him when she arrived in his life. And she'd changed him even more when she'd left him at the altar.

After that, he believed he'd never trust his heart to anyone ever again. But with Rosie, it felt safe. Right, somehow, and he *was* attracted to her. That was the truth, however much he tried to ignore it. But she was going to disappear too: back to her life in Spain, with Matt.

At least he had this moment of comfort. Liam closed his eyes and enjoyed the feel of Rosie in his arms, her forehead nestling against his neck.

All too soon, the song came to an end and the beat picked up. Rosie pulled away and smiled up at him.

'Thank you,' she shouted into his ear. 'You are now absolved of all guilt for leaving me snivelling on the sidelines at the school disco.'

'Happy to oblige.'

Jeez, did he just give a mock salute? What an idiot he was. No wonder Rosie frowned before heading off the dance floor. He followed her back to the bar.

'What have you two been up to?' asked Matt, walking towards them and shoving his phone into his jeans pocket.

'Dancing, for old times' sake. Was that Carmen on the phone?'

'Yeah.'

Did Liam imagine it or was Matt looking shifty?

Rosie picked at the pearl buttons on her shirt. 'She must be really spooked about her viewing tomorrow if she's ringing you at this time of night, on her birthday.'

'She is. Don't forget that everyone's feeling the strain because neither of us are in the office at the moment.'

Clever, thought Liam, putting Rosie on the back foot by making her feel guilty for being away.

'Do you fancy another dance?' asked Matt, taking hold of Rosie's hand.

She shook her head. 'Do you mind if we head back to Driftwood House? I'm tired and it still feels a bit odd being here.'

'Of course, if that's what you want. We could both do with an early night.'

Liam definitely didn't imagine the look of triumph that Matt gave him.

After Rosie and her annoying boyfriend had gone, Liam downed the dregs of his pint and wiped the back of his mouth with his hand. He retrieved his jacket from the back of a chair and stepped out of the village hall into a still evening. There was no point in saying goodbye to Alex because he was snogging Ella in the corner.

At the junction of Church Lane, where the church tower rose above the trees, he heard footsteps behind him on the cobbled path.

'Are you going so soon, Liam? You didn't say goodbye to me.'

Liam turned, groaning inside. 'I couldn't see you, Katrina.'

'Am I that easy to miss?' She tossed her hair over her shoulder and gave Liam her best smouldering smile.

'You're not the kind of woman who can be overlooked.'

'The disco won't go on for too much longer. Aren't you going to stay for the last few dances?'

Liam shook his head. 'Sorry to be boring but I've got to be up early tomorrow morning. Every morning, in fact.'

He couldn't remember the last time he'd had a lie-in. There was always a long list of tasks to be done, and Billy howled as though his heart would break if he wasn't let out into the yard soon after sunrise.

'That's a shame.' Katrina stepped closer, breathing out gin fumes. 'Are you all right, Liam?'

'Of course. I'm always all right.'

'Hmm. Has Rosie skittered off too?'

'She and Matt have gone back to Driftwood House to get an early night.'

'I dare say they'll be heading back to Spain soon.'

'Next Wednesday, I think.'

'That's a shame. I'm sure we'll all miss her.' Katrina's mouth settled into a thin line. 'Are you quite sure you're all right, Liam?' Draping her arms around his neck, she pulled herself tightly against him. 'You can tell me if you're lonely. I get lonely sometimes.'

Standing on tiptoe, she pushed her face towards him until their lips met and she kissed him. It was a long, deep kiss and, after a few seconds, he began to kiss her back, pushing his fingers through her long hair. The distant beat of the disco faded and his world shrank to her lips that tasted of gin and her body moulding to his. This was all right. This was what he'd been missing all these months.

Katrina was the first to pull away. 'Come with me.' She linked her fingers through his and started leading him towards the car park. 'We can go back to mine.'

'You can't drive.'

'Of course I can. I haven't had that much to drink.'

'What about Stephen?' Liam stopped so suddenly, her hand slipped from his.

'What about him? He's in New York, I told you.'

Liam shook his head. 'I can't.'

'You don't have to worry about Stephen. He's away doing who knows what. We have a very open relationship, if you know what I mean.'

'I still can't. I'm sorry, Katrina.'

'We can go back to yours if you're going to be all weird about my place.' There was a petulant tone to her voice as she traced her finger down his arm. 'Anyway, he'd never know, Liam. He'd never, ever know about us.'

It was so tempting. They could be discreet and the warmth of another person in his bed would be so welcome. Who cared if he was doing the same to Stephen that Deanna had done to him? He never used to care if the women he bedded were already in relationships.

But his heart was different now and, anyway, it wasn't Katrina he wanted.

He put his hands into his pockets and stepped back. 'You're beautiful, Katrina, and most men would kill to spend the night with you, but I can't start something that could never continue. There's too much at stake.' He shook his head when she opened her mouth to speak. 'I'm sorry. That's just the way I feel. And it's not you…' Oh no, he was spouting a stupid cliché, but on this occasion it was the truth. 'It's really not you, it's me.'

Katrina stood and watched him, an expression of disbelief on her face as he walked away. She'd probably start spreading rumours that he was impotent, and Alex would never let him hear the last of it if he found out. But it was done now and another lonely night with no one but Billy for company beckoned.

Chapter Twenty-Five

'How come you haven't got a hangover?'

Matt massaged his temples and stared blearily at Rosie over his Weetabix. She paused from wrapping her mother's crockery in newspaper and gave him a proper once-over. He'd fallen into a deep sleep the minute they'd got home last night, and he did look a bit rough this morning.

'I didn't drink much. I was mostly on orange juice and lemonades.'

'Very wise. That horrible beer was stronger than it looked.'

'Did you enjoy the evening?'

'Yeah, it was amusing.'

'Amusing? What do you mean?'

'It was a laugh seeing all the local yokels jigging about to Spandau Ballet and Duran Duran. Honestly, a disco in the village that time forgot! You were so right about this tin-pot little place.' He glanced through the window at the leaden grey sky. 'And the weather is freaking awful.'

Rosie sat back on her heels and brushed hair from her face. 'I don't think I've ever described Heaven's Cove as tin-pot, and loads of places run eighties discos. It's fashionably retro.'

'Moronic, more like,' grumbled Matt, prodding his spoon into his congealing cereal.

'I'm quite fond of these people,' actually,' she told him, wondering if Matt classed Liam as a local yokel. Had she once done the same? What a terrible snob she'd been.

Matt ignored her and jabbed at his phone on the worktop, which had just beeped with yet another message. He read it and smiled.

'Anything important?'

'Just work stuff. Nothing for you to worry about. Any chance of a cup of tea seeing as we've been working so hard?'

Rosie wiped newsprint from her hands onto her jeans and pushed the half-filled cardboard box to one side. Actually, she'd been working hard but Matt not so much. Since getting up, he'd spent most of the time on his phone, complaining about the intermittent signal. But a cup of tea would go down well and she could do with a break.

Matt watched her closely while she filled the kettle and retrieved the teapot from a box. She'd been thinking too much about last night and had packed it by mistake.

'It must have been awful growing up here in the middle of nowhere,' said Matt, drumming his fingers on the worktop.

'Not really. I thought it was the most boring place on earth sometimes but I had loads of space to run around in, and fresh sea air to breathe, and people in the village who looked out for me.'

Matt sniffed. 'Well, I'm glad I was brought up in exciting London. Get yourself into that Epping bloke's will and you can buy property there, somewhere like Chelsea or Kensington.'

'Neither of which have any coastline, and I love the sea.'

'Blue sea in Spain, sure. Not the freezing cold, grey sea around here.'

'It can be bracing at times. But we have blue sparkling seas too, you know. And green waves, the colour of moss, that roll into shore. Sometimes the sea looks black when storm clouds are banking on the horizon, or calm and pale as milk. It's always changing and always beautiful.'

'If you say so.'

'I do. Life doesn't begin and end in London or Spain, Matt. And I don't want to get myself into Charles Epping's will. If I do go to see that man, it's because I'm looking for answers, not a meal ticket.'

'Chill out, Rosie. Of course getting answers is far more important than any inheritance. Honestly, you're no fun any more.'

She felt a sharp stab of irritation. She didn't usually stand up to Matt but he was being a complete arse this morning. 'Sorry if I'm not the life and soul of the party. My mother's just died, my childhood home is about to be demolished, and I've discovered that my real father isn't who I thought he was.'

'I know, babe. It's all dreadful, but at least I'm here to support you. Come here.' Matt pulled her into his arms and she rested her head against his chest. 'Why don't you sit down and I'll make you that cup of tea instead?' He led Rosie to the stool he'd just vacated and moved his bowl out of the way, though not into the dishwasher, she noticed. 'While you're drinking your tea, I'll have a shower and perhaps a little lie-down first because my head is absolutely banging.'

The tea helped. Rosie sipped it slowly and picked up Matt's spoon, which had dripped milk across the counter. Her distorted reflection in the shiny metal showed up the pale streak of paint in her fringe, as though the secrets swirling around Driftwood House had turned her prematurely grey.

Matt's vibrating phone made her jump and the spoon clattered onto the worktop. His mobile was driving her mad this morning with its incessant beeping. A quick glance revealed yet another text from Carmen, who was certainly working hard this morning, probably with a hangover too, after her birthday celebrations. *Matt, you are always…* That was all the preview on the screen revealed.

Rosie hesitated, listening for movement upstairs, before typing in Matt's code and bringing up Carmen's text in full.

Matt, you are always such a naughty boy.

What the hell? English was Carmen's second language and she didn't always get it right, but even so… Rosie scrolled through Carmen's text exchange with Matt that morning. The first text had arrived shortly after seven o'clock from Carmen:

Buenos días, Matt. How do you do today?

Matt had replied within two minutes: *Muchos bored in Devon and missing España.*

Missing only España? was Carmen's immediate reply.

España, the sunshine, el vino and you of course.

I am horribly missing you too. When do you come back to Málaga?

As soon as possible. This place is doing my head in.

Poor Matt. I will make you feel much better again when you return.

Is that a promise?

Matt, you are always such a naughty boy.

Rosie carefully placed the phone back on the worktop and sipped her tea with shaking hands. Matt was flirting or worse with confident, beautiful Carmen, who could wrap men around her little finger. Basically, he was cheating on her with the continental version of Katrina.

She should feel angry. She should march upstairs and confront him with the texts, and maybe throw him out of the house. She should at the very least cry. But she continued sipping her tea, too numb to do anything else. Matt had betrayed her, but it was just one more loss in a steady stream of them. Her mother, her childhood home, her beliefs about her parents, and now the boyfriend she thought she knew were all gone, or soon would be. And in three days' time, she'd be back in Spain and Heaven's Cove would be gone, too.

Heavy footsteps sounded on the floorboards in the room above. Matt was taking his hangover back to bed. Rosie grabbed her jacket and went out into the gloomy morning, banging the kitchen door behind her.

She walked to the edge of the cliff and stood with her hands on her hips, hair blowing in the breeze. Far below, a curve of sand had almost disappeared under the tide, and waves were churning against the rocks. The sea and sky were slate-grey, mirroring her mood.

It was such a familiar view and one that usually soothed her. But today all she could see were Matt and Carmen kissing in dark corners of the office, in empty apartments for sale, maybe even in Matt's bed while she was away, the secrecy of it all heightening their excitement. Secrets were everywhere, building like a high tide, and she was drowning in them.

A sudden shaft of sunlight painted a bright stripe across the water, like a path out of Heaven's Cove. Getting away from here was a good idea. She could carry on selling apartments in the sunshine, find herself a new boyfriend, and put this village and its complications behind her. No family. No Driftwood House. Nothing to hold her back. Nothing to anchor her down.

She *could* do that, but those secrets would be lead weights around her neck. Rosie looked back at the house, still in shadow, and felt it was watching her in turn, wondering what she was going to do next.

'I don't know,' she shouted, before looking round to make sure no one had heard her. Not content with talking to her dead mother, she was now yelling at condemned bricks and mortar. But the clifftop was empty and the window of her bedroom, where drunken Matt was sleeping off his hangover, was closed.

Drunken, cheating Matt who seemed very interested in even the sniff of an inheritance. Rosie turned her face to the sun and stroked her fingers across the car key nestled in her jacket pocket. She was upset about him and Carmen. Of course she was, and angry that they'd gone behind her back. But it was hard to take the moral high ground when she had a guilty secret of her own.

She closed her eyes, remembering the rush of emotion she'd felt when Liam had pulled her into his arms last night. It had taken her by surprise, as had the vulnerability in his pale blue eyes. The dance had been magical – she hadn't wanted it to end – and when Matt had drunkenly kissed her, back at Driftwood House, she'd wished it was Liam's lips on hers instead.

There, that was her confession. One that Matt didn't deserve to hear and Liam wouldn't want to hear, especially if he ever found out that Charles Epping might be her father. Like mother, like daughter – Rosie was turning into a keeper of secrets herself.

She took the car key from her pocket and turned it over in her hands, keen to be away from Driftwood House when Matt emerged from his drunken slumber. She'd drive out into the Devon countryside and enjoy its verdant beauty before leaving the county for who knew how long in just a few days' time.

Deciding she was going to drive into the countryside was one thing, but getting there any time soon was quite another. The tourist season was ramping up and roads through Heaven's Cove were clogged with overheated families scowling at one another inside saloon cars.

Rosie was in a jam that stretched from the quay to the castle ruins and was going nowhere fast. She was drumming her fingers on the steering wheel in frustration when a frantic banging on the passenger window made her jump.

'You OK?' asked Nessa, pushing her face through the half-open window. 'Where are you off to?'

Rosie tried to smile. 'Nowhere. Just out for a drive.'

'You don't fancy giving me a lift to my gran's, do you? Save me going by bus.'

'Yeah, that's fine. Get in.'

The first thing Nessa did after sliding into the passenger seat was fully open the window. A good job too, because she stank of turpentine.

'Sorry. One of Sam Fuller's boys managed to knock a bottle of turps off the shelf and it went everywhere. Don't put a match near me or I'll go up like a firework. On the plus side, Scaggy sent me home early to get changed, so swings and roundabouts.'

Rosie rolled her window down and grinned in spite of her low mood. Nessa was like a tonic. She'd miss her when she left Heaven's Cove.

'Ooh, it's chilly in here now.' Nessa shivered and started doing up her denim jacket. 'You must be longing to get back to the sun. Talking of which, I've been meaning to ask if there's any chance of me coming over for a long weekend when you're back in Spain? I won't be a nuisance.'

'You're never a nuisance, and that would be really nice, actually.'

'Thanks.' Nessa grinned and wriggled back into her seat, sending turpentine wafts Rosie's way.

At last the queue began to move and Nessa fiddled with the radio as the car left the village behind. She gave up after being met with nothing but static, and folded her arms.

'So what's going on then, Rosie?'

'What do you mean? I told you, I'm out for a drive.'

'But why are you out for a drive on your own?'

'Matt's having a lie-down so I thought I'd come out for some air.'

'That's a good idea 'cos there's not much air up there on top of the cliffs. Personally, I'd have opted for a lie-down next to Matt. So are you going to tell me what's really going on?'

Rosie gave Nessa a sideways glance. 'Absolutely nothing.'

'Don't tell me, then, but you look upset and I don't think you could grip the steering wheel any harder.'

Rosie made a conscious effort to relax her shoulders.

'Have you fallen out with your brooding boyfriend?'

'You could say that.'

'Why? What's happened?'

Rosie groaned because it was obvious Nessa wasn't going to let this drop. 'I found some flirty texts between him and Carmen.'

'And Carmen is…?'

'A Spanish woman we work with.'

'What's she like, this Carmen? Aesthetically challenged, fifty-something, whiffs of garlic?'

'Beautiful, twenty-something, smells delightful.'

'Ah.' Nessa started picking at her nails. 'Do you think there's something going on between them?'

'Yes. He's hardly been off the phone to her since he arrived.'

'What a cheating swine when you've been through so much recently. I thought he had a look of Jake about him. How are you feeling about it?'

'How do you think?' Rosie gripped the steering wheel even harder. 'I feel angry, upset and betrayed.'

'I bet, though you're keeping it together better than I did. When I found out Jake had been cheating, I had a mega meltdown, which wasn't pretty. You're really calm, considering.'

'On the outside maybe, but inside everything's a huge muddle and I don't know how I feel about anything or anyone.'

'Does that include Liam?'

The car swerved as Rosie turned to stare at Nessa. 'What do you mean by that?'

'Bloody hell, watch where you're going! What I mean is that I saw you and Liam slow-dancing last night.'

'It was just a dance for old times' sake,' said Rosie, keeping her eyes straight ahead and trying to ignore the heat rising in her face.

'Really? I don't remember Liam dancing with you like that back in the sixth form. I don't remember him dancing with the likes of you and me at all.'

'We weren't his type.'

'Which was surprising because most females were, back then. But he seems to like you well enough now.'

'Liam Satterley is not interested in someone like me, Nessa. I doubt I could even ruffle his feathers.'

'He honestly isn't the same person he was at school, you know. That cow Deanna really screwed him over. Jake leaving me was gutting but at least he didn't humiliate me by doing it in front of everyone.'

Rosie's heart suddenly ached for Liam, waiting at the altar for a bride who never arrived.

'What she did was awful but he seems to be OK now.'

'Like you're OK?'

Nessa had a point. Rosie was putting a brave face on everything but she still felt rubbish inside. When she didn't reply, Nessa looked out of the window at the trees lining the road, their branches swishing in the breeze.

'Though he seems to be getting back on the horse, if you'll excuse the expression.'

'What horse?'

'Katrina, though never, *ever* tell her I called her that. The last time I saw Liam he was all over Katrina. I spotted her leaving the disco last night and was going to beg a lift home but by the time I caught up with her, she and Liam were snogging in the street and wandering off hand in hand so I left them to it.'

When the car swerved up the grass verge, Nessa gripped the sides of her seat.

'Are you sure you saw Liam kissing Katrina in the street?'

'Yep, full on, tongues and everything. Um, slow down. It's thirty miles an hour on this road.'

Rosie eased her foot off the accelerator and tried to catch her breath. Liam was a free agent so why did this feel like yet another betrayal?

'What about Katrina's boyfriend?' she asked, keeping her voice level.

'He's at some conference abroad, apparently.'

'So she and Liam slept together behind his back? I thought you said Liam was different from how he was at school.'

'He is, but she's been throwing herself at him shamelessly. You must have noticed.'

'Not really,' lied Rosie, trying to focus on the road, her concentration shot to pieces. She'd thought Liam was different these days. She'd even imagined she might have feelings for him. But he was still the sort of man who cheated and deceived people.

'Hey, you're going to miss Gran's house. Turn left here, into the lane.'

Rosie's bag shot across the back seat and dropped onto the floor when she screeched around the corner on two wheels.

Nessa, still gripping the sides of her seat, nodded at a small cottage. 'That's the one.'

'It's very pretty,' said Rosie, slamming her foot on the brake and juddering to a halt.

'Outside, it's all thatched roof and roses round the door. Inside, it's full of draughts and wall-to-wall spiders, but Lily loves it. Anyway, thanks for the lift, Rosie.'

'Would you and Lily like a lift home?'

'Nope. We're good, thanks.'

Nessa couldn't get out of the car fast enough. She raced up the garden path as Lily flung open the front door and ran outside. The young girl threw herself at Nessa's legs and clung on like a limpet until Nessa stooped down to give her a hug.

Seeing them together made Rosie's eyes prickle and she sat motionless in the car after they'd disappeared into the cottage. Being tied down by family responsibilities was best avoided. That was what she'd told herself for the last decade. Yet here she was getting all upset over a mother and child sharing a hug.

Was it because she'd never hug her own mum again? Or because, although Jake was absent much of the time, at least Lily knew exactly who her mum and dad were? She wouldn't grow up with secrets that ambushed her when she was least expecting it. Secrets that would retain their power until they were out in the open.

Hardly able to see through her tears, Rosie pulled away and started heading for Dartmoor. It was time to find out the truth about her parents.

Chapter Twenty-Six

'Clapped-out' was the only way to describe her mum's Mini when it was parked next to a gleaming black Mercedes at High Tor House. A tall woman with red hair opened the door and Rosie wasn't sure whether the look of horror on her face was due to seeing her or the heap of rust in the driveway.

'My name's Rosie Merchant. Would it be possible to see Mr Epping please?'

'I don't know.' The woman shifted as though she felt uncomfortable. 'I'm Caroline, the housekeeper.'

'Hello, Caroline. Is Mr Epping in?'

'He's busy in the garden and I'm afraid that Mrs Epping is out.'

Phew, Rosie was glad about that. She plastered on her best smile. 'I'm sure Mr Epping wouldn't mind being interrupted.'

Caroline shook her head. 'Mrs Epping was most insistent that he have no visitors. Is it important?'

You could say that, Caroline. I want to ask Mr Epping if he might happen to be my father.

Rosie smiled again. 'I'd like to see him if possible. I've driven quite a long way and I'm willing to wait.'

Caroline stared at Rosie who stared right back. It was a good job Cecilia wasn't at home, thought Rosie, or she'd have set the dogs on her at this point. But Caroline blinked first.

'I suppose I can ask if he'd like to see you. Follow me, please.'

Rosie followed Caroline through the hall and into the sitting room where she and Charles had first met. Rosie took more notice this time of the portraits hanging on the walls. They were ancestors, she supposed. The great and good in the Epping lineage. Did any of the men in their old-fashioned clothing or the women in their best jewels look like her?

'Excuse me, Mr Epping,' shouted Caroline through the open French windows. 'You have an unexpected visitor.'

Somewhere in the house, an animal was howling. Caroline turned to Rosie. 'If you'll excuse me, I was in the middle of feeding the dogs and they won't wait.'

As she swept from the room, Rosie gazed out at the garden that stretched towards a tor in the distance. Her mum, a keen gardener, would have loved it. Much of the garden was given over to grass but there were tall plants in huge terracotta pots at the edges of the lawn, and near the house was a wide stone patio. On it, clustered in groups, were dozens of pots in colours from scarlet and bronze to the cerulean blue of the Spanish sky. Bright spring flowers overflowed from each of them and Rosie itched to get her fingers into the soil.

She walked closer to the window, past a small writing desk with an inlaid blotter. A half-finished letter, written in thick black strokes, was lying on it, next to a silver Montblanc fountain pen. Pulling out her phone, she scrolled through the pictures until she got to the card left on her mother's grave and compared the two. The writing did look very similar. She picked up the letter to study it more closely but hastily put it back when Charles came into sight, striding across the lawn. With the sun behind him and the lines on his face in shadow, he looked younger. Thirty years ago, with dark hair, he must have been rather dashing.

Rosie swallowed hard. Maybe she'd been too hasty coming here with secrets and accusations whirling around her brain. Suddenly, she wasn't sure she wanted to know the truth at all. But it was too late to flee.

Charles slipped off his muddy shoes on the patio and stepped into the room.

'Miss Merchant, what are you doing here? I'm afraid if you've come about Driftwood House, it's too late. My wife has decided – *we* have decided – to push ahead with the hotel plan. I'm sorry, after you put some effort into improving the house, and I'm sorry because I know the house means a good deal to you. But it's for the best and you'll soon forget it when you're abroad. Our solicitor was about to contact you.'

So Driftwood House was definitely doomed. Rosie had suspected as much, but hearing Charles say it out loud left her feeling cast adrift.

'Is there anything I can say or do to change your minds?'

'Nothing.' He started fiddling with the buttons on the cuff of his pale blue shirt. 'There are… business reasons why the hotel plan has to go ahead. I'm sorry, and it's a shame you had to travel here to find out this information.'

Rosie shook her head. 'I didn't really come here about Driftwood House. There was something else I was hoping to discuss. When I was sorting through Mum's things, I came across a letter which was signed by someone with the initial J.'

'Did you now?' Unease flickered across Charles's face.

'I didn't know who this mysterious J was but then…' Rosie took a deep breath. 'Then, I heard your wife call you Jay while you were at Driftwood House.'

'My middle name is James.'

'Yes, she told me.'

'I see.' He closed the French windows with a bang before turning back to Rosie. 'What did this letter say?'

'It said that J loved her and couldn't wait to be with her.'

Charles stared at Rosie, a muscle twitching beneath his left eye. 'Why are you telling me this?'

'You told me that you didn't know my mother but I think you were…' She hesitated, unsure about using the word 'lying' and accusing him so bluntly of being untruthful. 'I think you were mistaken.'

'What would it matter if the letter were from me?'

'It mattered to my mother at the time and it matters to me now. I found the letter hidden away and want to know the truth. Please.'

Charles walked across the room in his socks and sank heavily onto the sofa. His next words were so quiet, Rosie could hardly hear them. 'I can't believe she kept the letter all this time.'

'So the letter *was* from you?'

'I could deny it but there seems little point now your mother's gone and you've turned detective. If I answer your questions, will you keep the information to yourself?'

'Of course, I have no intention of gossiping about my mum,' said Rosie, reeling at the revelation that he *had* lied. What else wasn't he telling her?

'Good.' Charles settled back on the sofa and clasped his hands together in his lap. 'What do you want to know?'

'Did you love her?'

Charles raised his eyebrows at that. 'You're very direct, aren't you? Just like Sofia. That was one of the qualities I admired in her the most – the way she saw the world as a place to be conquered. She wasn't afraid of anything.'

'So did you love her?' demanded Rosie, holding his gaze although her insides had turned to jelly.

'What is the point in raking all of this up? It's ancient history.'

'Not for me. My mum's not here and I've realised there's so much I never knew about her. I'm asking you to help me fill in some of the blanks.'

Charles rubbed his eyes and stared out of the window for so long, Rosie thought she'd blown it. But then he sighed. 'Perhaps this is better out in the open, as long as it stays in this room. Yes, I do believe I loved your mother. We had a relationship a long time ago, when she was about your age. You look so like her, it gave me quite a shock the first time I saw you. The years fell away.' He continued staring into the garden, lost in thought.

'How did the two of you meet?'

'Through my younger sister, Evelyn. I was telling the truth when I said that Evelyn and your mother became friends. My sister was the patron of a local charity and your mother was a volunteer. They both had good hearts.'

'So you began a relationship?' Rosie raked her hands through her hair. 'It's hard for me to take in because you and Mum seem so different.'

'Don't people say opposites attract? I always thought that was rubbish until I met Sofia. I'd led a rather sheltered life – nannies, public school, top drawer university – and I'd never met anyone quite like her. She was a free spirit, brave, and full of life, but I don't need to tell you that. She was dating your father when we met but she broke off the relationship when she and I' – he hesitated – 'grew fond of one another.'

'I didn't realise she was going out with Dad at the time.'

Charles nodded. 'We didn't mean to hurt him.'

'But you did.'

'Your mother dealt with the situation as kindly as she could.'

Rosie thought back to how disgusted she'd been with her dad for cheating on her mother twenty years ago. She'd thought there was no excuse, no good reason. But perhaps it was partly payback for what had happened to him a decade earlier.

'We never expected to become so close because we came from such different backgrounds, and I was almost ten years older and supposed to marry Cecilia.'

'Did Cecilia know about Sofia?'

'She did, later.'

'Poor Cecilia,' muttered Rosie, wondering if that was when the woman's softer edges had hardened.

'Poor Cecilia indeed.'

'Were you engaged to her at the time?'

'No, but our families had an understanding.'

'An understanding?' spluttered Rosie. 'We're talking about the late 1980s, not the 1800s.'

'My family did things differently. They followed a different code and I was brought up to do the right thing within it.'

'And falling in love with my mum didn't fit into their plans.'

'Certainly not. That's why we kept our relationship as secret as possible. We met clandestinely and planned our future but it all went wrong when Evelyn died in the car accident. My parents were completely destroyed with grief. We all were, and I couldn't be selfish and add to the damage.'

'And you viewed being in a relationship with my mother as damage?'

'I didn't, but my family would have.' He closed his eyes briefly. 'To be brutally honest, your mother was strong enough to cope with the inevitable fall-out but I wasn't.'

'Would the inevitable fall-out have included being disinherited? You might have been happy to live at Driftwood House, but only until this place became available to you.'

That was something she hadn't meant to say and it elicited a sharp intake of breath from Charles.

'My family affairs are not your business, and you know very well what happened next. I broke off my relationship with your mother.'

'You broke off your engagement. You'd promised to marry her: *"The thought of our wedding day, and spending the rest of my life with you, fills me with joy."* That's what you said in the letter.'

Charles went pale at that and Rosie was glad. Her mother must have been devastated by her fiancé's betrayal, and it wasn't only her mother he'd deceived. 'When did Cecilia know about my mum?'

'Not at the time, but I told her later when she needed to understand the agreement regarding Driftwood House.'

'The house that was my mum's consolation prize.'

'It was never that. I cared about your mother and wanted to make sure she always had a roof over her head. I wanted to—'

'—do the right thing?' Did that sound sarcastic? Rosie certainly hoped so. No wonder Cecilia was so keen to see Driftwood House reduced to rubble.

'I wanted to do the right thing, yes. We used to meet on the cliffs and your mother loved that house, so I bought it when it came up for sale. It was going to be a surprise. I imagined the two of us living there, but then Evelyn died and everything changed.'

'And now you're taking the house back because Mum is dead and you don't have to pretend to care any more.'

Charles flinched at that. 'I'm not proud of my behaviour back then. But I didn't pretend to care about your mother.'

'Did you stay in touch?'

'That wouldn't have been fair on any of us. Your mother resumed her relationship with your father and married him almost immediately. And Cecilia and I moved to be near her parents in Northumberland after our wedding and only returned to Devon ten years ago when my father died.'

'When you inherited this amazing house.'

'That is correct.' Charles's mouth drew into a tight line. 'I think we've said all that needs to be said. I truly am sorry about your mother but Cecilia is right that it's time to draw a line under all of this and proceed with our hotel plan. The link has been broken.'

'For you, maybe.'

'What do you mean by that?'

'I mean…' Rosie hesitated. Once the words were out, she couldn't take them back, and she wasn't sure she wanted this cold man in her life.

'Meaning what exactly?' repeated Charles.

A clock chimed in the far reaches of the house, its tone deep and melancholic.

'I think you might be my father.'

It was said. Silence stretched between Rosie and Charles, sticky as treacle. A sudden gust of wind swirled through the potted plants beyond the French windows, and Rosie thought of Liam. What would he think of her being so closely related to this man?

Charles suddenly jumped to his feet. He shook his head, breathing heavily. 'Why would you say such a thing? Are you so desperate to save a dilapidated house?'

'This has nothing to do with Driftwood House,' said Rosie, . blood pounding in her ears.

'Your father is David Merchant.' Charles sounded so arrogant, so sure. What had her mother ever seen in this man?

'Do you know the date of my birthday?'

'Obviously not. Why would I?'

'It's the eighth of June, 1989. That's seven months after my mum and David were married, and apparently I wasn't a honeymoon baby.'

Charles blanched, his face as pale as the chalk-white vase behind him. 'You must have been premature.'

'That's what my mum implied. But I've spoken recently to the midwife who delivered me and I was full-term.'

'That can't be.'

'And Mum told the midwife that—'

'What can't be?' Cecilia had slipped into the room unnoticed. She stood by the door, tapping her foot on the polished parquet. 'What the hell is she doing here?'

Colour flooded Charles's cheeks. 'I didn't realise you'd be back so early, Cecilia.'

'I said, what the hell is she doing here? I left instructions that you weren't to be disturbed.'

Cecilia almost spat out the words and Rosie stood up to go. Now that she'd confronted Charles and found out the truth about his relationship with her mother, what was the point in carrying on? She wasn't going to beg him to admit they were related, or waste her time persuading him she was telling the truth. But Charles spoke, his voice now low and calm.

'Miss Merchant is claiming that I'm her father.'

'That's preposterous! This gold-digging ploy won't save your home, Miss Merchant.'

'Gold-digging?' Rosie stood in front of the fireplace, drawing in shallow breaths. 'I don't want your money and if you're determined to destroy Driftwood House, so be it. I thought your husband might want to know that he might have a daughter, but I was wrong.'

'Charles?' barked Cecilia. But Charles said nothing. He was looking at Rosie as though he'd seen a ghost. He sank back slowly onto the sofa, his hand on his chest. Oh God, he'd have a heart attack if this continued. Pushing past Cecilia, Rosie hurried through the hall to the front door.

'Your ploy will come to nothing,' shouted Cecilia after her. 'There will be no DNA tests, no more meetings, and no rumours about parentage or you'll be hearing from our solicitor. Fly back to where you came from and leave us all in peace.'

Rosie fumbled opening the door, almost fell through it and rushed to the Mini, her feet crunching on the gravel. Dark clouds had blotted out the sun and drops of rain were splattering on her dusty car. What had she done? Sharp stones pinged against the Mercedes as she slammed the Mini into reverse, did the worst three-point turn of her life and zoomed between the stone pillars that marked the entrance to High Tor House.

The long track back to the road was pitted with potholes but she didn't slow down. The car bounced and scraped while she put distance between herself and Charles. The man had broken her mother's heart in a cavalier fashion so what had she been expecting – a touching reunion?

'Stupid! Stupid!' she spat out, hitting the steering wheel and trying to see the road through her tears. She'd lost her mother and Driftwood House, and the man she felt more certain than ever was her father was cold and heartless. She would never see him or have anything to do with him again. Cecilia was right. It was time for her to go back to Spain because, even though Matt had betrayed her too, there were no more secrets or lies waiting for her there.

Chapter Twenty-Seven

Rosie turned her key in the lock at Driftwood House and pushed open the front door. As the wood scraped across the flagstones, she vaguely registered that the timber was swelling again and needed to be sanded down a little more. Though that thought was swiftly followed by the realisation that it didn't matter. The house was condemned.

'I'm so sorry,' said Rosie to the empty hallway. Though whether she was apologising to the house or to her mother for what she'd just done, she wasn't quite sure.

'Sorry for what?' mumbled Matt, coming out of the kitchen, clutching a piece of toast. Heaven knew how long he'd been asleep. He still had bed-head hair and he yawned, showing his wide white smile.

'I don't know. Sorry for disappearing?' answered Rosie, too emotionally wrung out to face another confrontation.

'Did you?' He rubbed a hand across his bleary eyes. 'Did you go for a walk?'

'I went for a drive, to Dartmoor to see Charles Epping.'

'Wow, well done!' Matt was fully awake now. 'So what did the old dog have to say for himself?'

'Nothing.'

Matt's toast, slathered in butter, began to bend and drip onto the tiles.

'What do you mean, nothing? You did tell him that he's your father, didn't you?'

'I said that I strongly suspected he was.'

'And he said nothing?'

'Not a lot. He didn't believe me and his wife accused me of being a gold-digger.'

'That is outrageous, Rosie. It must have been very upsetting. So what happened next?' he asked, stepping towards her.

'I left.' Rosie moved away from him and wiped splattered butter from her jeans with shaking hands.

'You left? Is that it?' Matt ushered her into the kitchen and gestured for her to sit on a stool. 'I'll make you a cup of tea and you can tell me all about it.'

She wasn't going to tell him all about it. She wasn't planning on telling him much at all, but the words came tumbling out because she needed to get it off her chest.

Matt listened attentively as he made the tea and then sat down next to her. 'So what's your next move?'

'My next move about Driftwood House?'

'Who gives a monkey's about this old place, Rosie? I'm talking about Epping. What's your next move with him?'

'There is no next move. I go back to Spain and forget him.'

'Don't be daft. There must be a next move. You can confront him again, demand a DNA test and, if that fails, threaten to go to the press and sell your story. A man like that will value his reputation.'

'Why would I do that? He wants nothing more to do with me and the feeling is mutual. And I have no desire to humiliate his wife, even though she's awful. She must have been hurt enough at the time.'

'Oh Rosie.' Matt took her hands in his. 'You can't let Charles Epping win. He owes you, and what's he worth? Five million? Ten? Maybe more, with all the land and property he owns. As his flesh and blood, you deserve a big chunk of that.'

'I don't want his money, Matt. I'm not a gold-digger, whatever Cecilia thinks.'

'Of course you aren't, babe. But isn't it selfish to give up on money like that?'

'Selfish? How can it be selfish?'

'Just think what you could do with a huge injection of cash. Think what we could do. You could finance me to set up my entrepreneurial property business, which would clean up in the area.'

'And that's what all this is about. I thought as much.' Rosie stood up so quickly, she spilled tea all down her sweatshirt. Jeez, it was hot. She pulled the sodden fabric away from her skin.

'What are you talking about?' asked Matt, his eyes narrowing as he handed her a wodge of kitchen roll.

'I wondered why you were so keen for me to tell Charles Epping he's my father. You've got your eye on his money to kickstart your business. I hoped you were being empathetic, but I'm starting to realise that's not your style, is it?'

'Bit harsh, babe. I'm only trying to help you.'

'Help me or help yourself? And please do stop calling me babe.'

Matt's face darkened. 'I get that your mum has just died and you're upset about everything. That's why you're so obsessed with this shabby old house that rattles in the wind that never ever stops. But you might as well get everything you can out of a man who abandoned you and your mother. And I'm not going to apologise for being ambitious. You had ambitions and dreams before you came back to this crappy cove in the middle of nowhere.'

'Dreams change.'

Matt shook his head. 'You need to get back to Spain pronto, Rosie, because you're in danger of becoming weird and boring, just like the people around here.'

'Do you really want me to come back?'

'I'm here, aren't I?' answered Matt sulkily.

'You only came after I told you that a very rich man might be my father, and you've been pushing me to claim my so-called inheritance ever since. Someone less charitable than me might think you were after my money, Matt.'

'That's crap, Rosie. But do we just miss out on all that money, on that chance of financing our future? Don't you see that it *is* rather selfish?'

Anger bubbled up inside Rosie, like red-hot lava. 'Let me get this straight. You want me to beg a man who has just sent me packing to recognise me as his daughter so that you can set up a business that's economical with the truth in pursuit of a good sale.'

'It's short-term pain for long-term gain, ba… sweetheart. You and me, we're in this together for the long haul.'

Rosie gasped at his ability to barefaced lie. 'Really? What about you and Carmen?'

'What about her?'

'I know everything,' fibbed Rosie.

Matt puffed up his chest, before deflating like a balloon. 'Have you been talking to Juan? What did he tell you?'

'Every detail.'

'He's such a bloody telltale! It was only a couple of kisses, to start with.'

'To start with? So, there was a lot more after that.'

'Don't twist my words, Rosie. I'm not proud of myself but you were away and, when Carmen practically threw herself at me, one thing led to another. I was flattered.'

And there was the problem. Matt, like the dad she grew up with and like Liam, took flirtation too far and ended up deceiving and betraying people. Charles Epping, too, was no stranger to betrayal, though his had been in the name of 'doing the right thing'.

'This doesn't have to change anything between us,' Matt whined, giving her his best puppy-dog eyes. 'I'm sorry, Rosie. I'll tell Carmen to back off because I'm all yours.'

'Will you still be mine when temptation keeps on coming and Epping's money doesn't?'

'That's below the belt, Rosie.'

'Which is rather ironic, coming from you.'

Matt bit his lip, his expression sour. 'I probably deserved that, but I don't want us to be over. Please forgive me, Rosie, because I love you. Come back to Spain and we can go back to the way we were. Say something!' he demanded, when she remained silent, though what did he expect her to say?

Of course I forgive you, Matt, and it's all Carmen's fault, maybe?
It wasn't, though Rosie would be having a stiff word with her
about female solidarity when she got back to Spain. *You're a
selfish pain in the arse?* That kind of went without saying. *You've
broken my heart?* He hadn't, much to her surprise. He'd bruised
it, undoubtedly, but her heart felt too battered right now to
fully register any extra hits.

Rosie spoke calmly and clearly. 'I'm coming back to Spain,
but I'm not having anything more to do with Charles Epping,
not ever.'

'Even for me?'

'Even for you, because, hard though it may be to take in,
none of this is actually about you, Matt.'

'That's true, I suppose. It's all about this past-it house, and
this awful village and people like Nessa and Belinda and local
idiot, Liam, and his bloody biceps.'

'He's not an idiot.'

Matt shook his head. 'I'm going home, Rosie. I'll pack and
be out of here in an hour or two. Are you coming with me?'

Rosie looked at him, standing in the doorway, blocking
the light. She could swallow her pride and forgive him, forget
Charles Epping and Driftwood House, and go back to Spain
right now. That would simplify her complicated life.

'Well?' urged Matt.

Rosie looked around the newly painted kitchen, where she'd
learned to bake fairy cakes with her mum. 'I'm not coming
with you. I think we both know that our relationship is over.'

'You're totally overreacting,' spluttered Matt, his face turning red.

'No, I'm not. You've been seeing Carmen behind my back, and I deserve better. Can you tell Juan I'll be back in the office on Thursday, as we arranged?'

'It's not over, Rosie. I won't accept it. We can continue this conversation when you're back in Spain and talking more sense.'

Rosie shook her head. 'We won't be continuing the conversation, Matt. We're definitely over,' she said firmly to his retreating back as he stomped up the stairs.

Chapter Twenty-Eight

Liam shielded his eyes from the low-lying sun. The sky was blazing orange and gold over a silver sea and seagulls wheeling above the cliffs were dark silhouettes. And there, perched high above the village and his farm, he could make out Driftwood House. The building belonged to Heaven's Cove and was an integral part of the village but it was set apart, rather like Rosie herself.

He scuffed his feet into the soil, wondering why his thoughts kept returning to Rosie Merchant. She and her unpleasant boyfriend would be gone soon enough and life in Heaven's Cove would return to normal. No more fighting to save Driftwood House. No more slow dances at village discos.

Deliberately, he turned his attention back to the view which never failed to soothe him these days. Not so long ago, the wide open sea and acres of land had bored him, and the responsibility of taking over the struggling family farm had felt stifling. The more he felt trapped, the more he'd caroused with his friends – drinking too much, kissing too many women.

But he'd grown into the landscape and now he appreciated the quiet moments when nature engulfed him and he could breathe.

'All right, Billy. Give it a rest, mate.' The dog's sharp barks were shattering his peace.

'I think he's barking at me.'

Rosie was standing next to him. The air around him shifted and, for a moment, he thought his mind had conjured her up. But this figment of his imagination was solid enough when her hand brushed against his arm. 'I don't want to disturb you.'

'You're not. I was only looking at the view.'

Rosie tilted her chin to the sky and took a deep breath. 'It's beautiful here, isn't it? I didn't appreciate how magnificent the views are from Heaven's Cove.'

'Me neither. I rather took it all for granted.'

'You don't know what you've got until it's gone, until you move away.'

'As you know, that was never an option for me, and most days I'm glad.' He turned and looked at her properly for the first time – jeans, grey sweatshirt, hair pulled into a ponytail, dark circles beneath her big eyes. 'What are you doing here? Are you and your boyfriend all out of eggs for Sunday tea?'

'I wanted to tell you face to face, before I leave, that I've heard from Epping's solicitor that Driftwood House can't be saved.' A spasm of pain passed across her face. 'Let's be honest. It was pie in the sky to think it could be. Mum's gone and the house will go with her. Perhaps that's the way it should be. But I thought you deserved to know first, after your work on the place, and I'm sorry it turned out to be a waste of your time.'

She sounded business-like, distant.

'I was happy to help but I'm not surprised. Charles Epping is a bastard who screws people into the ground. Money is king as far as he's concerned. I can't stand him or his family.' He took a deep breath. 'So you got a phone call, did you? I thought you went to see the Eppings earlier today.'

Rosie scuffed her feet across the ground. 'No, what made you think that?'

'Someone thought they saw you out that way.'

'Not me.'

She was lying. The pink spots in her cheeks were telltale signs – she'd be absolutely rubbish at poker. And Alex was adamant that he'd passed her car this afternoon, just a mile or two from the turning to High Tor House.

Rosie stared at her hands with their long tanned fingers. Why didn't she want to tell him? he wondered.

'It's such a shame about the house,' she said. 'I know it's just bricks and mortar but losing Driftwood House feels like another small death.' She dipped her head. 'Stupid, isn't it?'

'Not at all. It's been your home since you were born. So what happens next?'

'I finish packing up the house and head for Spain.'

'You and Matt.'

'He went earlier today. Matt and I… well, it's all got a bit complicated.'

She flushed again and Liam fought the urge to put his arm around her shoulders. It would be fine as a friendly gesture but, after the feelings stirred up by their slow dance, he wouldn't mean it as a friend. He'd end up wanting to kiss her and what was the point of all these emotions? He'd only just put a lid on them. He turned his face again towards the sea.

'Complicated how?' he asked levelly.

'We've broken up and he's flying back to Spain right now, probably to see Carmen.'

'Who's Carmen?'

'The workmate I discovered he's been having an affair with.'

'You're kidding me! The man's a complete dick! Are you OK?'

When he looked at Rosie, she was staring at the glowing sky, her face in profile. 'I am, actually. I thought I loved Matt and he loved me, but I think I was only kidding myself.' Her hand flew to her mouth. 'Sorry, was that insensitive after Deanna decided that she didn't…? I don't mean…'

'It's fine. I've heard far worse and it was a year ago now. Life goes on.'

That was the platitude he often spouted with no weight behind it but Liam suddenly found it hard to picture Deanna's face. She'd meant the world to him and yet now he'd started to forget her and, for the first time since being jilted, he could imagine being with someone else.

He stole a look at Rosie, who had closed her eyes with her face towards the dying sun. Golden beams of light danced across her hair, making it shine. At last he'd found someone he was willing to let his guard down for and she was about to fly off into the distance. Typical.

'Actually,' said Rosie, eyes still closed. 'I know life goes on but it's been a bit of a shit day all round. The sort that you know has been seared into your brain, even though you'd rather forget it completely.'

'Do you want to talk about it?'

Rosie hesitated. 'No, but thanks.'

'You'll forget it eventually, I expect. Well, not so much forget as let it go.'

Rosie opened her eyes and fixed her gaze on him. 'You're pretty wise, Liam Satterley, for a heartbreaker.'

'That's what all the girls say.'

Why had he said that? It was the kind of glib remark that old Liam might have made.

Rosie's smile never reached her eyes. 'I can imagine. How is Katrina?'

'She was fine the last time I saw her. Why?'

'No reason. She seemed a bit worse for drink by the time we left the disco, that's all.'

'I think she'd had a fair bit. So when are you leaving Heaven's Cove?' asked Liam, keen to move the conversation on from Katrina, who would never forgive him for turning her down. She was the type to bear a grudge.

'I'm finishing packing up the things I want to keep and I've found a company that will collect and sell the furniture that I don't. And my flight's still booked for Wednesday afternoon. What else can I do?'

'You could stay.' Liam folded his arms and kept his eyes on the sunset. The sky had turned a blazing red as the sun slipped below the horizon.

'Stay where? Driftwood House will be gone.'

'There's always Josie's B&B while you find somewhere else locally. Or you could sleep here, with me. I mean' – he tripped over his words – 'with me and Billy.'

Mentioning the dog in no way made the offer sound less sleazy and he knew he hadn't quite shaken off his old reputation in Rosie's eyes. 'What I mean is, I wouldn't mind putting you up in the spare room while you sort out your next move. My parents would be fine with it. In fact they'd probably love it.'

'Why would you do that?'

'I quite like you.'

Billy's ears pricked up. He was lying near the back door, watching the two of them. Rosie crouched down and stroked his back, then she glanced up at Liam. She looked upset. He hadn't meant to upset her.

'That's kind of you.' Her voice was wobbly. 'But with Driftwood House gone, my life is in Spain.'

'Yeah, sure. It was just a thought, trying to help you out.'

'Thank you. It was a kind thought.'

'I have my moments.'

She straightened up and smoothed her hands down her jeans. 'I guess this is goodbye then. I probably won't see you before I leave.'

'Will you be back?' Did that sound too desperate?

When she shook her head, hair came loose from her ponytail. 'Probably not, now there's no Mum and no Driftwood House to come back to.'

'Maybe you'll come back to see Nessa?' Now he was sounding desperate.

'I doubt it. She's angling to visit me for a few days in the sun instead.'

'Ah. Then I wish you luck in the rest of your life, Rosie Merchant.'

'You too. And thanks again for your help.'

'Think nothing of it.'

'Say goodbye from me to Katrina.'

'Yeah,' said Liam, no longer properly listening as he leaned in to kiss Rosie's cheek. When she turned her face, his lips brushed against hers. The lightest of touches that sent shivers through him. 'I was going for the continental goodbye, the double-cheek kiss, even though we don't have such exotic things in these parts. Belinda wouldn't allow it.'

He sounded uber jolly and ridiculous. She must notice. Rosie wrapped her arms around her waist and gave him the serious look he remembered from school. 'See you around, Liam.'

'See you around, Rosie. And you were never a nerd. Not really.'

'See? You *are* kind.'

Rosie spun on her heel and walked to the gate. She only looked back once, before she was hidden behind the high hedge that separated the farm from the lane.

That was that, then.

'It's just you and me, boy. Maybe it's better that way.' Billy lay on his back and stared at his master, his eyes huge and sad. 'Don't look at me like that. We'll be fine. Who needs women anyway?'

With one last glance at the darkening sky, Liam went into the farmhouse and closed the door.

*

Rosie could hardly see one foot in front of the other. Her sandal slipped on the cliff path and she stumbled and almost fell. This was ridiculous.

She stopped and roughly wiped her eyes with the backs of her hands, like she used to when she was a child. She'd never been a crier but right now she couldn't stop.

She could have cried about the mum she'd never see again, the boyfriend she'd lost, the childhood home that was doomed, or the cold man who didn't care that he might be her father.

But this time she cried with disappointment that Liam was still the kind of man who spent the night with women when their boyfriends' backs were turned. She was far from perfect herself, but she'd never cheat, not knowing the heartache and pain it caused, which could ripple through families for years.

And yet, in spite of all that, in spite of knowing that Liam was the kind of man who didn't mind causing that pain, she'd still desperately wanted him to kiss her properly. Not an accidental brush of the lips and a stilted 'continental kiss' on both cheeks; a full mouth-on-mouth kiss with her arms around his neck, his hands in her hair, and her body pressed up against his.

If she'd kissed him instead, he might have gone along with it, and she'd have enjoyed it. He was probably a fabulous kisser – he'd had a lot of practice. But afterwards, the disappointment she already felt in herself – for being an inattentive daughter, the failed saviour of Driftwood House, and a snob about Heaven's Cove – would only have got worse.

How could she kiss Liam, anyway, when he'd run for the hills if he knew her father could be the man making his life a misery? That would amount to kissing under false pretences. Plus, she'd literally just lied to him about seeing the Eppings that afternoon.

With hindsight, she should have said she'd visited them to discover Driftwood House's fate, but instead she'd panicked and lied. Like a complete idiot.

Rosie fished a tissue from her pocket, blew her nose, and continued walking up the cliff path. A full moon was rising in the navy sky, casting silver beams across the waves and lighting her way forward.

So much had happened during the short time she'd been back in Heaven's Cove, much of it either traumatic or downright confusing. But there were some positives. At least she understood, now, why her mother sometimes found it hard to trust people, and kept herself to herself so much. And the resentment she'd harboured towards her dad had lessened and been replaced with gratitude to him for taking on another man's child. If only she'd known while he was still alive, she could have thanked him.

She'd also grown to, if not *love* Heaven's Cove, at least like it a whole lot more, and the people in it. She could feel the tug of the place. *You could stay.* Liam's words sounded in her head, like a siren call dragging her home. But what was there to stay for with her mum and Driftwood House gone? Her home was now far from here.

Rosie had reached Driftwood House. She ran her fingers across the old front door before going inside and turning on the hall light. The wind had dropped and everywhere there was silence. No creaking timbers, no rattling window panes, no mum calling out a welcome, no Matt waiting to greet her. Nothing at all and no one.

Chapter Twenty-Nine

Over the next two days, doors began to creak at Driftwood House and the wind moaned through the eaves as though the building was anticipating its fate.

Rosie kept herself busy, packing up final precious mementos, arranging to store the small pieces of furniture she wanted to keep, and finalising the house clearance once she'd left for Spain. The proceeds would go to charity, the children's trust that she believed her mother and Evelyn were volunteering for when they first met.

The fridge was filled with enough food for her and Matt so there was no need to venture into Heaven's Cove, and she was glad to stay away. The village had wheedled its way into her heart more than she'd thought possible and she didn't want to make leaving any more difficult.

Matt had sent her just one text after heading to the airport. It was short and to the point: *Rosie, let me know when you're back in Spain and we can talk about us. I still think you're making a big mistake with Charles Epping. You need to think of your future. Matt.*

Her future or his? Rosie would let him know when she was back but she knew for certain that their relationship was over. She doubted he'd be too heartbroken – Carmen would see to that.

Sighing, she folded a pair of jeans and placed them in her suitcase. At least in Spain she could soak up the sun, throw herself into her work and put all of this behind her. Or maybe she'd move on to somewhere new. Another country, where she could reinvent herself and live another life. The prospect, once so exciting, now made her feel apprehensive and exhausted.

She glanced at her watch. Just time for a quick walk to the cliff edge to look over the view for the last time before leaving for the airport with Nessa. Rosie had promised her Sofia's car and, in return, Nessa was insisting on driving her to catch her flight.

Rosie had closed the front door behind her for the final time when she heard a vehicle labouring up the cliff track. Had Nessa got someone to drop her off? If so, her friend had a very posh car. The gleaming black Audi, now streaked with mud, pulled to a halt in front of her and the tinted window slid down.

'Ms Rose Merchant?'

'That's me.'

The bald, unsmiling man in the driving seat reached across and took a letter from the passenger seat which he passed through the window. 'I've been asked to deliver this to you.'

With that, he closed his window, executed a careful turn and lurched slowly back down the track.

Rosie turned the typed envelope over in her hands. It was addressed to her, and the cream paper inside bore the embossing of the Eppings' solicitor.

Dear Ms Merchant,

I am writing on behalf of my clients Charles and Cecilia Epping to inform you that the possibility of constructing a

small hotel in Heaven's Cove is now being pursued on an
alternative site. Plans to demolish Driftwood House have
therefore been shelved indefinitely.

Yours sincerely,
Ellis Buck

Rosie read the two sentences over and over, hardly able to
believe what she was seeing.

'Hey, Rosie, are you all set for Spain?'

'Hi, Nessa, I didn't hear you arrive.'

'I walked and almost got run over by some idiot in a posh
car. Who was that?'

'Someone delivering a letter.'

'Haven't they heard of Royal Mail?' grumbled Nessa,
picking up Rosie's suitcase to test its weight, and grimacing.
'Is it important?'

'You could say that.'

Rosie handed the letter over and watched as Nessa's face
broke into a huge grin.

'But that's great, isn't it? It seems the hideous Eppings do
have hearts after all.'

'Hmm.' Rosie wasn't sure that any hearts were involved.
Either Cecilia was trying to keep Rosie sweet so she wouldn't
make a fuss, or Charles Epping was salving his conscience, just
as he'd done with her mum.

'So what happens now? Do you still want to go to the airport,
now the house has a reprieve? Do you think the Eppings will

go for your guesthouse idea? Ooh, you could stay and run it. Didn't you say you help out at a B&B already? There you go, you've got experience and you love the place, so you're the perfect person to get it off the ground.'

'That was never the plan, and I've already got jobs that I need to get back to before my bosses give me the boot. I can't give up everything because the Eppings have deigned to change their minds.'

Nessa's face fell. 'But you must be happy that the house has been saved.'

'Of course I am. Wow. I really am.'

It had only just properly sunk in that Driftwood House, her anchor, would not be reduced to rubble. Whether the Eppings made it into a guesthouse or sold it on as a family home, it would remain here on top of the cliffs, keeping watch on the village below.

'No one wants you to go, Rosie. I bumped into Belinda by the castle ruins on the way here and she said she wished you were staying – eventually, after giving me all the goss on Fiona's recent tummy tuck. John feels the same, and Katrina gave me a regal wave from her posh car when my bus went past her earlier. She probably knew I was coming here.'

'That's kind of Belinda and John, but I doubt that Katrina will miss me. She'll be too busy getting it on with Liam behind Stephen's back to even notice I've gone.'

'Ooh, no, she won't be happy with Liam right now. He gave her the old heave-ho.'

'After sleeping with her?'

Rosie wasn't sure which was worse – sleeping with a woman behind her boyfriend's back, or discarding her immediately afterwards. Both were pretty awful.

'No, *before* sleeping with her,' said Nessa, scanning through the letter again.

'But you saw them getting into Katrina's car on Saturday night.'

'I saw them heading for her car but Liam thought better of it. I told you he'd changed.'

'Are you quite sure?'

'Absolutely sure. Siobhan Jones – you know her, wears loads of red lipstick. She spotted them from her bedroom window. Katrina had a face like thunder when Liam walked off, apparently. Anyway, she told Belinda, who told Martin, who told Lucas, who told John, who told me.'

Heaven's Cove really was gossip central, but this was gossip that made Rosie's heart glad. 'So Liam definitely didn't sleep with Katrina while her boyfriend was in New York?'

'No, he didn't.' Nessa narrowed her eyes. 'Why? Does that make you more likely to stay?'

'Why would it?'

'Why, indeed.' Nessa was smirking. She suddenly shielded her eyes with her hands. 'Who's that? Well.' She gave Rosie a hefty nudge in the ribs with her elbow. 'I do believe it's Liam and Billy. Hey, Liam! We were just talking about you.' She started waving, huge arcs of her arm in the air. 'You're just in time for the celebrations. Guess what's happened? It's such good news.'

'What news?' Liam strode up while Rosie tried to steady her breathing. She hadn't expected to see him again, ever.

'Rosie's just found out that Driftwood House is saved. Isn't that fantastic?' Nessa swooped in for a hug with Rosie. 'Apparently the Eppings are thinking of building a hotel somewhere else instead.'

'I wonder what changed their minds.'

Liam didn't look happy about Driftwood House's reprieve, and ever affable Billy, picking up his master's mood, started growling softly.

'It's absolutely brilliant news, isn't it?' said Nessa, not sounding so sure now. She glanced at Liam's face, which was set like stone, and grabbed the dog's collar. 'Billy could probably do with stretching his legs a bit more. I'll walk him out towards Sorrell Head. See you two in a minute.'

She scuttled off, dragging a very reluctant Billy with her.

'Are you all right?' asked Rosie, but Liam paced up and down in front of her, not catching her eye.

'You tell me. This letter was just delivered to the farm by a man who asked for directions to Driftwood House.'

He thrust an envelope at Rosie, who pulled out the paper inside with trembling hands. Cold dread was seeping through her.

Dear Mr Satterley,

I am writing on behalf of my clients, Charles and Cecilia Epping, regarding the land south-east of your property which is rented from the aforementioned clients. The rental agreement comes to an end later this year and they are giving you notice that it will not be renewed.

The letter continued with lots of legal language but Rosie had got the drift. 'How much land is it?' she asked, her heart sinking into her boots.

'Enough to make all the difference between Meadowsweet Farm surviving or failing. I couldn't work out why the agreement would be cancelled just like that and came here to find out why the delivery man was coming here too, but now I know. The Eppings aren't thinking of a hotel up here any more. My farm is now the potential site for their business venture.'

'I'm so sorry, Liam.'

He shook off the hand she placed on his arm. 'You did go to see Charles Epping the other day, didn't you?'

Rosie nodded, her happiness about Driftwood House's reprieve turning to ashes in her mouth.

'Did you beg him to save Driftwood House, at whatever cost?'

'No, of course not. I wouldn't do that.'

'Then why did you lie when I asked if you'd been to see him?'

'I panicked.'

'Why would you panic unless you'd just sold my livelihood down the river?'

'That wasn't why I went to High Tor House.'

'Then tell me why you'd go to see such a dreadful man who doesn't care at all about anyone or the lives he wrecks? Why that would make you panic, rather than tell me the truth?' He pushed both hands through his hair, totally bewildered. 'Why, Rosie? Make me understand. I thought we were getting on well. I thought… oh, it doesn't matter what I thought.'

'I'm pretty sure that Charles Epping is my father.'

Rosie didn't know she was going to say the words until they were out of her mouth. Liam stepped back as though she'd hit him.

'Don't be so ridiculous.'

'It's true. He's the person who sent Mum the love letter. They had a relationship just before I was born, and there are other things that make me think he's—'

'Your dad?'

Rosie nodded miserably.

'So you went to High Tor House for a cosy family reunion, I suppose.'

'No, it wasn't like that.'

'How was it then, Rosie? It must have been quite a reunion for him to then turn round and save Driftwood House for you.' He shook his head, disgust on his face. 'Were you ever going to tell me?'

'I'm sorry. I should have said but…'

Before she could finish her sentence, Liam strode off towards Nessa. 'Billy!' he yelled. 'Here, boy, now!'

The dog gambolled up and followed as Liam hurried down the cliff path, almost falling in his haste to get as far away from Rosie as possible.

'What was that all about?' asked Nessa, hurrying over. 'Liam can be a bit moody at times but he looks well upset. You too. Lovers' tiff, was it?'

'Charles Epping is ending the rental agreement on Liam's land.'

'Why?' Nessa's hand flew to her mouth. 'No, he's not thinking of building his stupid hotel there instead, is he?' Her shoulders dropped. 'But Liam will never keep his farm going without that land.'

'I know.' Rosie's voice wobbled.

'It's not your fault.' Nessa put her arm around Rosie's shoulders and squeezed. 'It was Charles Epping's decision and he doesn't care about anyone.'

'But it *is* my fault,' Rosie whispered, guilt clutching at her insides.

'How on earth can it be?'

'Can you keep a secret?'

It seemed a little late to be asking that now Liam knew and was angry enough with her and the Eppings to head straight for Belinda's house.

'Of course I can,' said Nessa, wrinkling her forehead. 'Working in Shelley's, you wouldn't believe all the things I hear about people in this village and keep quiet about. For example, Seth had a fling years ago with a woman in Bailey's Ford, Felicia in Dolphin Cottage likes to do her housework totally naked, and newsagent Colin wears a hairpiece, and I've never told anyone.'

The fact that Nessa was telling her right now was disconcerting but Rosie felt too wretched to care. Cecilia had threatened to sue if her husband's reputation was tarnished – whether she could or not, Rosie wasn't sure. But his reputation was pretty much shot to pieces around here anyway. And it would take a huge hit when locals discovered he was about to destroy Liam's farm.

'Don't tell me if you don't want to,' said Nessa.

'I do want to.' Rosie took a deep breath. 'Liam thinks I deliberately sacrificed his farm to save Driftwood House.'

'But that's mad. It was Epping's decision. Why would he listen to you?'

'Because I'm pretty sure I'm his daughter.'

'Yeah, of course you are, and Daddy always does what his darling daughter wants.' Nessa's laugh died when she caught sight of Rosie's face. 'Good grief, you really are his daughter.'

'I'm afraid so.'

'When did you find... I mean, how did you... what the actual...?'

'I found information in the attic at Driftwood House while I was clearing things out.'

'Didn't your mother ever say anything about it?'

'No. All my life I thought that David was my dad. He *was* my dad, as far as I was concerned, and I don't suppose she knew how to tell me otherwise.'

'She must have thought she'd have the time to work it out.'

'Then time ran out.'

Nessa shook her head. 'Sofia and Charles Epping, getting it on – that is, like, blowing my freakin' mind.'

'Tell me about it,' said Rosie glumly.

'So have you told him that he's the daddy?'

Rosie nodded.

'And?'

'He's not interested in finding out for sure, and his wife almost ran me off the premises. But that's fine. I don't want to see either of them ever again.'

'That's rough.' Nessa patted Rosie's arm. 'Did he mention anything about Meadowsweet Farm?'

'Nothing, and I never meant for this to happen.'

'I know that, but what a mess!' Nessa continued patting Rosie's arm as though she was a child. Her eyes widened when she caught sight of her watch. 'Look at the time! We'd better get a move on if you're still planning on catching that flight. What are you going to do?'

Rosie closed her eyes. That was the big question.

For goodness' sake, he was going to fall if he didn't watch out. His body would hurtle through space and plunge into the sea that was pounding the rocks below. Right now, he didn't much care. But faithful Billy might jump into the waves to try to save him.

Liam slowed his pace and tried to slow his breathing. His lungs felt as though they might explode. Or was it his heart?

'I'm an idiot!' he said out loud. Such an idiot to drop his guard and trust someone again. He was such a terrible judge of character. Deanna had fooled him, and Rosie had done the same. When her guesthouse plan had failed, she'd sold him down the river to Charles Epping and sacrificed his farm for Driftwood House – a house she'd never live in because she'd be hundreds of miles away in a different country.

He stopped completely and drew in a deep breath of fresh salty air. The sea stretched out before him and there, to his right, he could make out Meadowsweet Farm near the cove, and the land that would soon no longer be his to work.

In the end, all of his sacrifices had been for nothing. He'd appeal to the Eppings of course, but he couldn't possibly compete with their own flesh and blood. Like father, like daughter.

It was hard to reconcile that Rosie was so closely related to such a cold, uncaring man, and he wondered how long she'd suspected that Charles could be her father. How long she'd lied to him by acting as if everything was normal when it was anything but.

Chapter Thirty

The plane would be taking off about now and heading to Mál-aga. She should be on it, flying back to her uncomplicated life in Spain – sun, sea, lazy afternoons under the palm trees, and two jobs that she could do in her sleep. Two jobs that she was due to start again tomorrow.

Instead, she was driving through a rain storm across Dart-moor to confront a man she'd hoped never to see again. And her sunny, simple life abroad was going tits up.

Here, out on the moor, the clouds were so low they'd settled like mist on the high ground ahead of her. At least she wasn't far now from High Tor House. It would be good to get this over with. But was the road moving? She suddenly realised the tarmac ahead was covered with swirling black water. A stream had burst its banks in the downpour and was blocking the way forward.

'Not now,' she groaned, slamming on her brakes and pulling the car onto the sodden grass. The road was impassable.

Pulling her jacket from the backseat, Rosie got out of the car and held out her hand. The rain had stopped for the moment but the glowering grey sky was threatening more downpours. In the distance, she could just make out the high chimneys of the Eppings' mansion. There was nothing for it – she'd have to walk, and she'd be quicker going in a straight line over the moor rather than following the curve of the road.

The landscape stretched around her, vast and deserted, as she picked her way across the rough ground. Weathered boulders littered the earth, ready to trip her if she lost concentration, and the carcass of a sheep, picked bare by scavenging insects, only added to her low mood. Life and death were all around her.

The stream currently flowing across the road blocked her way again on higher ground, but here the rushing water was still within its banks. Someone centuries ago had bridged the stream with huge, flat slabs of stone and she gingerly made her way across, trying not to look at the torrent beneath her feet. The chimneys of High Tor House were still visible above a ridge of ground that didn't seem to be getting any closer.

Cresting the ridge at last, Rosie spotted sheep scattered across the landscape and between her and the back of the Eppings' magnificent house stood an ancient circle of pitted stones.

When she reached them, she brushed her hand over one of the lichen-stained stones and felt a tingling across her shoulders. Ancient magic, or the chill that was seeping deeper into her bones with every passing minute? The chill, she decided, ever pragmatic. But she stopped for a moment in the centre of the circle. If her mum were here, she'd start swaying to the beat of 'unseen forces' and channelling the stories of the men and women who once walked this land. She always reckoned that stone circles were mystical places for communing with the long gone.

It was a load of rubbish and yet... with only two bored sheep to observe her, Rosie began to spin with her arms outstretched.

Rain dripped off her nose as she turned and let out a loud yell. Her mum would have called it a primal scream, and boy, it did feel good to let out some of the emotion that was churning inside her.

Liam's fraught face loomed in her mind, his expression when he had told her that his farm was doomed and accused her of betraying him. Did he really think she would stoop so low as to save Driftwood House at the expense of his home and livelihood? Did he think so little of her? Tears stung her eyes as she spun and spun and yelled some more into the cold, damp air.

She stopped, feeling dizzy and ridiculous, which was when she spotted two figures in the distance. Standing together, with black clouds bunched behind them, they were watching her.

'Wonderful!' muttered Rosie, as tall yellow grasses swayed in the wind and a bird screeched overhead. The Eppings, out taking a stroll, had just seen her behaving like a total loon. Though what people in their right minds would choose to walk in such filthy weather?

No one moved while Rosie deliberated between fight or flight. Fleeing back to the car was tempting, but Liam's farm was doomed unless the Eppings changed their minds. Rosie put her head down and started walking towards the couple.

They watched her approaching, Charles in a blue waterproof jacket and Cecilia, like a crow, in black from her boots to her hat. She was the first to speak.

'Why are you here again? I thought we'd made it clear that you weren't welcome.'

She seemed more wary than angry, thought Rosie, feeling her feet sink into the muddy ground. 'I need to speak to you, please. Just for a few minutes, then I'll be out of your lives forever.'

'Are we supposed to take your word on that? You seem adept at turning up out of the blue.'

'I promise you I'm leaving for Spain as soon as I can book a flight.'

'I thought you were leaving today.'

'Who told you that?'

'I have my sources. You're not the only person with spies in this county.'

'I don't have spies anywhere.'

'Yet you knew about our hotel plan and now you're stalking us.'

Rosie laughed because the accusation was so ridiculous, but Cecilia stared, her face pallid next to the black of her jacket. She looked hostile and a little bit scared.

'I want you to go,' she said, her voice harsh and shrill. But Charles put a hand on his wife's arm.

'Let the girl speak, Cecilia.'

'You don't have to listen to what she has to say.'

'I think I do.' He turned to her. 'Why are you here, Rosie?' It was the first time he'd called her by her first name and a shiver went down Rosie's back. 'You should have received word that Driftwood House is no longer being demolished. My wife has been persuaded to change our plans.'

A good deal of persuasion had been required if Cecilia's sullen expression was anything to go by.

Drops of rain had started falling again and Rosie pulled up her hood. 'I'm grateful that Driftwood House is saved, I truly am, but the land you're considering instead is a part of Meadowsweet Farm, and taking that land back will destroy a man's livelihood.'

Charles regarded her coolly. 'It's a sound economic decision and nothing personal.'

'It's very personal. Don't you care about the people whose lives your decisions affect?'

'No one lives on the land we're now considering for the hotel. No homes will be demolished.'

'A livelihood will be wrecked. Liam Satterley and his parents rent the land from you and their farm will probably go under without it.'

A muscle twitched below Charles's left eye. 'That's unfortunate.'

'Unfortunate? Surely it's more than that if a farm that's been run by the same family for generations has to fold and a man – a good man – will have no income to keep a roof over their heads. The people in Heaven's Cove matter.'

'As I say, it's an unfortunate consequence of business, and it's best not to become over emotional about these matters.'

The heavens had opened but Rosie – cold, tired and over-whelmed – hardly noticed the rain driving against her face.

'Was it also an unfortunate consequence when my mum became pregnant with me? Is that why you abandoned her? You stick rigidly to your rule of always *doing the right thing* but it seems to me that you end up doing the wrong thing instead.

And you're so hard-hearted you don't care anything for Heaven's Cove. I'm glad my mum married David. He was a better dad than you would ever have been. So I don't care if you think I'm a chancer who's making everything up. I don't care if you're sure that I'm not your daughter.'

'Oh, I'm not sure about that at all.' His words were so quiet, Rosie almost missed them. But Cecilia didn't.

She grabbed his arm. 'Be quiet, Charles. What are you saying?'

'I'm merely acknowledging that it's not beyond the realms of possibility that this young woman is my daughter.'

'She doesn't look like you.'

'Not particularly, but, I've been thinking…' He paused, rain dripping from the hood of his jacket and down his nose. 'Come with me.'

Neither Rosie nor Cecilia could keep up as Charles rushed towards the house, taking one loping stride for every two of theirs. He led them through the back gate, past a huge herb garden, and through a door into a large, modern kitchen.

A woman kneading bread on the worktop looked up in alarm when they all bundled inside, and wiped her forehead with the back of her hand. A smudge of flour settled above her dark eyebrows. 'Is everything all right, Mr Epping?'

'Yes, thank you, Maria.'

The air was full of the sweet smell of cakes baking in the huge range oven and steam was rising from a pot bubbling on the hob. The Eppings were so rich and posh they had a housekeeper *and* a cook.

Rosie stood in the doorway like a statue. What was the point of being here? Charles was easing his conscience by saving Driftwood House and didn't care about Liam's farm. He would throw a family farm and a good man to the wolves purely for the sake of profit.

But Cecilia hissed, 'Not here,' in her ear and, grabbing her arm, propelled her through the kitchen. Charles was marching along a corridor, past a dark drawing room with deep green wallpaper and shelves of books. Finally, he flung open the door to the sitting room that Rosie had been in during her last visit. Rain was battering at the French windows and the garden outside looked wet and grey.

'Stand there,' Charles ordered Rosie.

When she didn't move, he took her arm and positioned her in front of the fireplace, touching her face to gently turn her chin towards the garden.

'Jay, what are you doing?' Cecilia really did seem scared now.

'Tell me what you see.'

Cecilia looked at Rosie and then stared at the huge portrait above her head. 'I don't know.'

'Look again,' said Charles, sounding unutterably tired. 'The set of the chin, the shape of the mouth, the fire in the eyes. They're the same.'

'I know you still miss Evelyn but this isn't the way to get her back.'

'Don't you think I know that, Cecilia? Maybe I'm only seeing what I want to see. That's why I've tried to ignore this nagging feeling and not revisit the past, but what would Evelyn think of me?'

'What you *want* to see?' Cecilia crumpled at the knees and sat down heavily on the sofa. 'Do you want this girl to be your daughter?' Rain dripped from her jacket and left a dark stain that seeped into the fabric. 'You've always told me you didn't want children.'

'Of course I told you that. It was kinder when we had no choice in the matter,' said Charles gently.

'I thought you'd come to terms with us not having children years ago.'

'I had, Cece.' Charles sat on the sofa next to his wife and stroked her hand. 'At least I thought I had, but Rosie stood right there when she was last here, just before she left, and I could see the resemblance. She's the spitting image of her mother, but there's something of Evelyn about her too.'

'Why didn't you say something to me about it?'

'What could I say that wouldn't break your heart? How could I suddenly become a parent when it's all you've ever wanted?'

'I've always felt second best compared to Sofia, Jay, and when I couldn't have children…'

Rosie watched in horror as Cecilia's face collapsed and she began to sob. *Stop!* Rosie wanted to shout, *women like you aren't supposed to cry,* but Cecilia's glacial façade had splintered. She put her head in her hands and her shoulders shook as she cried.

'Shush,' murmured Charles, taking his wife in his arms and rocking her gently.

As Cecilia's sobs subsided, he looked up at Evelyn, forever immortalised in oil. 'What you said was right, Rosie. I'm not a good man. I've betrayed people who love me and I make cold, calculated decisions that affect people's lives, all while telling myself I'm doing the right thing. Meanwhile, it's people such as you and my wife who bear the fall-out.'

He kissed the top of Cecilia's head. 'I didn't know Sofia was pregnant but I did abandon her. Then, I eased my conscience by giving her Driftwood House. I thought she'd throw the offer back in my face but neither she nor David had much money, and she must have known by then that you were on the way. I can't believe she didn't tell me.'

Rosie blinked, close to tears herself. 'Perhaps she was scared of being rejected for a second time.'

Still holding his wife, Charles slumped back against the sofa. 'So what happens next? Driftwood House is safe – that was something I *could* do for you – but I suppose now you'd like me to take a DNA test, to confirm that we are related?'

When Cecilia stirred in his arms, he spoke quietly into her ear. 'It'll make no difference to you and me, Cece. I love you dearly and you're a far better person than me.'

'But I'm not,' said Cecilia, pulling away and wiping her nose roughly with the back of her hand. 'I denied you a child.'

'No,' said Rosie loudly. 'I'm truly sorry, Cecilia, if I've raked up old distress. Of course it's no one's fault that you weren't able to have children.'

She shouldn't have said that. Poking her nose into a personal conversation was a terrible idea. But rather than telling her to mind her own business, Cecilia stared at her, biting her lip.

'She's right.' Charles reached out and stroked his wife's hair with such tenderness, Rosie's throat tightened. But Cecilia shook off his hand and got to her feet. Without another word, she hurried from the room and the door banged behind her.

Charles leaned forward with his elbows on his knees, his face as pale as a ghost.

'I rather fear you've seen us not at our best.'

'It's good to see you have…' Rosie tailed off, still shaken by what she'd witnessed.

'Good to see I have a heart?' Charles shook his head. 'Oh, you have no idea.' He looked round to make sure that the door had slammed shut. 'I was in love with your mother, properly in love. As I told you, no one except my sister knew about us. Maybe that was part of the headiness of it all – clandestine meetings, secret kisses, forbidden love. I was expected to marry well and your mother didn't make the grade. That didn't matter at first when I met her through Evelyn, who was far less of a snob than I was.'

He frowned. 'Than I am. We were going to elope and tell my parents when it was a fait accompli so they'd have to accept her eventually. We were going to live simply at Driftwood House.'

'But none of that happened.'

'Evelyn died and my parents were devastated. They found out through letters Evelyn had kept that I was engaged to Sofia and begged me to change my mind. The truth is that my sister was the brave one of the family and her courage had rubbed off on me. But that disappeared after she died. We were all in shock and I couldn't bear to inflict more distress, so I did what was expected of me.'

'You did the *right thing*?'

'Yes. I broke off my relationship with Sofia and married Cecilia shortly afterwards. I heard that Sofia had got back together with David and I was glad that she was with someone else. It helped my conscience.' A spasm of pain swept across his face.

'I told you the date of my birth. Could I be your daughter?'

'Timings-wise? Yes, it's very possible. The last time your mother and I met, well… I wasn't proud of myself but, in my mind, we were saying goodbye. I told her afterwards that I was marrying Cecilia and I'll never forget the way she looked at me. I think she hated me in that moment. But there's one thing I can't get past. However much I'd hurt her, I still think Sofia would have told me about you, if you were mine.'

'She did tell you, Jay.'

Cecilia, still tear-stained but more in control, had slipped back into the room. She held out an envelope to her husband. 'This arrived before we were married and I opened it. I couldn't bring myself to throw it away. That seemed too hard-hearted, even for me.' She gave Rosie a straight stare. 'But I hid it from you.'

Charles's hands were shaking as he pulled a single sheet of paper from the envelope and, after reading the words on it, he buried his head in his hands.

'What? What does it say?' Rosie snatched up the letter and read aloud.

Jay – I'm contacting you to make you aware that I'm pregnant with your child. I don't expect anything from you. I certainly don't expect you to disappoint your family and leave Cecilia. David still loves me and, even though he knows about the baby, he wants to marry me – he's a decent man who will give me and my child the stability we need. You and I didn't part on good terms but you deserve the chance to be a part of your child's life. If you want to know your child, reply to this note. If not, David will become the child's father and he or she will never hear about you from me. Sofia.'

Rosie ran her fingers across her mother's handwriting. The rain had ceased and the wind had dropped. Everywhere was silent. Charles stood up slowly, as though it took every ounce of strength he possessed, and, without a word, walked from the room, closing the door quietly behind him.

Cecilia watched him go before taking the letter from Rosie and placing it back in its envelope.

'My husband can no longer bear to be in the same room as me. And I imagine that you hate me, as much as he now does.' She stared through the window at the grey, wet world outside. 'You'll have plenty to tell the inhabitants of Heaven's Cove when you get back. *Cecilia Epping was so terrified of losing the fiancé she loved, she did something quite dreadful.*'

Rosie couldn't speak. She was smothered in secrets that had wrapped their corrosive tendrils around people's hearts and changed lives forever. What would have happened, thirty years ago, if Charles had seen that letter? Her heart ached for her mother, waiting for a message from the father of her child that never came.

Cecilia turned on the lamp on the writing desk, flooding the room with an amber glow.

'Driftwood House has haunted me since Charles and I were married. Every day I thought of you growing up there, without a father.'

'I had a father,' murmured Rosie, suddenly feeling fiercely protective of the man who had helped to raise her.

'Of course. I meant without your biological father.' Cecilia paused. 'I thought reducing the house to rubble would finally lay our ghosts to rest and discourage you from ever coming back to Heaven's Cove. But instead it brought you to our door.' She raised an eyebrow. 'How ironic.'

'I don't know how you've lived with such a huge secret for all of these years,' said Rosie, shaking her head.

Cecilia laced her fingers together as though she was praying. 'When we found out there would be no babies, I thought it was punishment, divine retribution, for keeping you from my husband. But I was too embroiled in the whole situation and he'd missed too much by then for me to show him the letter and confess what I'd done.'

Her sigh sounded more like a sob and, in spite of everything, Rosie felt a stab of sympathy for this woman who'd trapped herself in a web of lies.

'Being unable to have your own child was coincidence, not punishment.'

'Are you sure?' Cecilia rubbed her eyes like a tired toddler. 'Do you know, I was frightened of you when you first turned up at our door? I was scared you'd blow my secret sky high and turn my husband against me. I *was* his second choice. It's stupid to think otherwise, but we've grown together over the years and I didn't want that to end.'

'I'm sure it won't. He'll understand when he's had the time to take it all in. It's not easy.'

'Not for him and not for you.' Cecilia closed her eyes and let out a long, slow breath. Then she looked at Rosie and gave a sad smile. 'There's a kindness in you that's hidden deeper in Charles.'

'I'm not always kind, and I think what you did was dreadful. But I don't hate you, whatever you think, and I won't be telling anyone in Heaven's Cove.'

'Why on earth not?'

'Because I don't want my mother's memory tainted with gossip, and nothing would be gained from telling people. It wouldn't change what's happened and, whatever you think, I'm not looking for money or vengeance. That's not the sort of person I am.'

'Then your mother brought you up well.'

'She did, and my dad too.'

'David sounds like a thoroughly decent man.'

Rosie swallowed. 'He was, far more decent than I ever realised.'

Cecilia walked to the fireplace and stood beneath Evelyn's portrait. 'So what happens next? Will you go back to Spain?'

'I'm not sure. My life has been there for the last few years but...' Rosie shrugged.

'Life doesn't always work out the way you expect.'

Cecilia traced her hand across the Epping family crest carved into the stone fireplace, her fingers coming to rest on the rose at its centre. 'Should you decide to remain in Heaven's Cove, I'm sure you can continue living at Driftwood House now we plan to build our hotel on the outskirts of the village instead.'

Rosie's heart sank. After all this, the Eppings still planned to take back Liam's fields and ruin Meadowsweet Farm. 'Will you still go ahead with that? I assumed your hotel idea was an excuse for you to knock down Driftwood House.'

Cecilia shook her head. 'It was a way to kill two birds with one stone, but we do need to increase our income.'

'Why? Look where you live.' Rosie waved her arm at the old paintings and the antique furniture and what looked like a stable block in the distance. It all amounted to more than most people could ever hope to accumulate in a lifetime.

'Old houses like this cost a fortune to run and our business investments have been disappointing recently.'

'You could always downsize.'

Cecilia raised an eyebrow. 'You may have seen a softer side to me this afternoon, but I don't see me giving up the family seat and living anywhere less grand. Do you?'

An image of Cecilia living in a two-up, two-down cottage in the middle of Heaven's Cove flitted into Rosie's mind, and swiftly flitted out again. 'So what happens to Meadowsweet Farm?'

'You came here to plead for the man who runs it.'

'That's right.'

'It must have been difficult for you to come back after the way I spoke to you the last time you were here. This man must mean a great deal to you.'

Rosie hesitated, picturing Liam's eyes, his smile, the vulnerability behind his brash façade. 'He does,' she said, fully realising the truth of it.

Cecilia sniffed, and snapped back into business mode. 'We can't simply abandon the plan. We need to generate some kind of income. I'm afraid your friend will have to forfeit the land at Meadowsweet Farm.'

Rosie was finding it hard to think straight, but there had to be a solution. 'What about...?' She tried to marshal her thoughts into some sort of order. 'What about if Driftwood House *is* turned into a guesthouse and I stay and run it for you and my...' She couldn't say it. Not yet. '... your husband.'

Cecilia raised a perfectly plucked eyebrow. 'Would you give up your life abroad for this farm?'

Rosie held her breath. Would she? Images of Spain cascaded through her mind – dusty landscapes, hot sunshine on her back, itinerant travelling friends who came and went, homesickness that she never allowed herself to acknowledge. If she went back, Liam's farm would likely fold. If she stayed, at least Meadowsweet Farm would have a fighting chance.

She made up her mind. 'I'd give it up for roots and permanence, and for Liam, yes.'

Cecilia stared at her. 'So it's not simply the land. It's the man. Does he know how you feel?'

'No, it's not like that, we're just friends.'

'I see.' She thought for a moment. 'I suppose after what I did thirty years ago, some people might say that I owe you a favour. If you're quite sure you want to stay and run Driftwood

House as a guesthouse, you can tell your friend that his rental agreement on the land will be renewed.'

Thank you was on the tip of Rosie's tongue, but she didn't say it. Three decades of a lost relationship couldn't be swept away by a grand gesture. It would take time. But she smiled and nodded at Cecilia, who nodded back.

'Now, I must go and find my husband because we have a great deal to discuss.' She blinked and swallowed hard. 'You can stay if you wish and speak to him later.'

Rosie shook her head, suddenly desperate to escape the confines of High Tor House and clear her mind. 'I need to get home, but please tell him I said goodbye.'

By the time Rosie had yomped back to her car, the sky was clearing and the sun was peeping from behind grey cloud. The road ahead was still slick with water but the torrent had slowed.

Rosie stood for a while, watching a lone Dartmoor pony standing on a rise of ground. The black and white piebald horse, with its distinctive fat belly and short legs, stopped munching grass and stared back at her, before returning to its meal.

She'd be able to visit Dartmoor for pleasure now she was staying at Driftwood House. Rosie slid into the driving seat and rested her head on the steering wheel. Since arriving back in Heaven's Cove, her life had been a whirlwind of emotion and revelation, but today had topped everything that had gone before.

'Charles Epping is definitely my father. He's my dad.'

Nope, however much she said it out loud, it would take a while to sink in. And she wouldn't be saying it out loud to anyone for a while, maybe not ever. It was a secret she was happy to keep, as long as Liam hadn't already spilled the beans. At least Nessa, having professed her hatred of gossip, would stay quiet.

Rosie turned the key in the ignition and decided she would go to see Liam later and tell him that his land was safe, but nothing about the deal she'd made. Staying at Driftwood House was her decision and she didn't want him feeling that he owed her anything. She was staying to help Liam; that was true. But an unexpected feeling of relief had washed over her from the moment she agreed to remain in Heaven's Cove. She was also staying for herself.

Chapter Thirty-One

Green shoots were pushing their way through the rich soil. The land was producing another harvest, as it had done on Meadowsweet Farm for generations. But it would all soon come to an end. And, although it wasn't Liam's fault – the Eppings had the final say – he felt a failure.

He knew how he'd be remembered in Heaven's Cove, long after he'd been forced to move on in search of work. *Started off a right cocky Jack the Lad but turns out he couldn't keep a fiancée and couldn't keep a farm.*

Telling his parents was going to be awful. They were still blissfully unaware of the changes ahead and he didn't have the heart to unsettle them. But he couldn't keep the news to himself forever.

Liam would usually turn to Billy for comfort, tickle behind his ears and soak up his uncomplicated adoration. But even his dog had given up on him today. Billy couldn't be roused from his bed – he'd rather sleep the afternoon away than spend another minute with such a misery.

Get a grip, Liam told himself, looking out over the fields that would soon be lost. *No one's died and Mum, Dad and I can move on and do something else if need be.* Quite what, he wasn't sure. Katrina had marketing skills, Alex was a whizz on computers and Rosie could sell property on the Costa del Sol. His skills were limited to coaxing new life from the earth but maybe he could find work on another farm somewhere, or in a garden. He'd make a living somehow for himself and his parents. His material needs would be met, but when it came to his heart…

Liam rubbed a hand across his face, wondering where Rosie was now. Probably a thousand miles away, making up with that chancer Matt, who must love the fact that her new-found father happened to be one of the richest men in Devon.

He closed his eyes and remembered the Rosie he knew at school, serious and studious with long plaits and a watchful gaze. Then he pictured her now – gentle, sun-kissed, full of life, and sporting an expression he often couldn't read. Did she want to kiss him or punch him?

Punch him, he guessed, after he'd accused her of sacrificing his farm for Driftwood House. She'd never have done that. He'd realised as much once his flash of temper had faded, because Rosie wasn't devious – not like he used to be. His farm was simply collateral damage.

But he was still upset she hadn't confided in him that Charles Epping might be her father. How could she keep that a secret after he'd tried to help her find her dad? She clearly didn't trust him.

Liam sat down on the old wall that marked the eastern boundary of Meadowsweet Farm and drummed his heels against the stone. Tomorrow he would have to pick himself up and start all over again.

Someone was walking around the edge of the field towards him. Liam shielded his eyes from the glare of the late afternoon sun and hoped against hope it wasn't his dad. He loved his father, and the anecdotes he told about the old days were interesting, the first time you heard them. Even the fifth or sixth time. But his dad repeated himself endlessly these days and Liam just wasn't in the mood.

He squinted as the figure got closer. The person was slight, and wearing a dress which meant it wasn't his dad unless he was even more confused than Liam thought.

Please don't let it be Katrina, here to have a go at me for giving her the brush-off, thought Liam. He'd managed to avoid her for the last few days but it was only a matter of time before she caught up with him.

The woman was getting closer, and blood started pounding in his ears as he recognised Rosie, in a simple green sundress with her hair in a ponytail. He stood up, though he had no idea why, and sat straight back down again.

'Hey, Liam. Are you busy?' asked Rosie, standing in front of him with her hands on her hips.

'Not really, no.'

'What are you doing?'

'Honestly? I'm having a bit of a pity party.'

He could see her cheekbones when she smiled. 'Can anyone join in?'

'Feel free.'

He gestured at the wall next to him and tiny chips of stone cascaded onto the soil when she sat down.

'Don't you have Billy with you?'

'He didn't fancy coming because he's fed up with me moping about.'

'Are your mum and dad OK?'

'They're fine, thanks.'

'We're lucky with the weather. It's much nicer here on the coast than inland.'

'Yeah, that's often the way.' That was enough small talk. 'I thought you'd left Heaven's Cove for good and gone to Spain,' he said, gazing straight ahead and being careful not to move in case his arm brushed against hers.

'I thought about it but decided to go and see Charles Epping instead.'

'Is he really your father?'

'Yeah, I'm afraid so.'

'How long have you known?'

'Not long. When he and Cecilia inspected Driftwood House, she called him Jay. His middle name is James and people in the family call him Jay. It's like a nickname, I suppose.'

'Did you confront him about it?'

'Not then, but I did later.'

'And did he admit that he's your father?'

'He did, in the end.'

Liam took a breath. This sounded too much like an interrogation.

'That must have been hard to hear. Why didn't you say anything to your friends?'

'Would you, if you found out that the most disliked man in Heaven's Cove was your father?'

'Probably not. But you could have told me.'

Rosie bit her bottom lip, like a child trying to be brave. 'I could have, and I almost did. But I didn't want you to hate me.'

Liam shifted round and looked at Rosie for the first time since she'd sat beside him on the wall. The vulnerability written all over her face made his heart ache.

'For goodness' sake, Rosie, I could never hate you. Is that what you thought?'

She nodded. 'You hate the Epping family and now I'm a part of it.'

'But you're not like them. You're like your mum, who brought you up. Did you tell Matt about it?'

'Yes,' said Rosie, her voice flat. 'But he was only interested in the Eppings' money. That's why he came over from Spain.'

Liam nodded, too angry to speak.

'That's why we've definitely split up for good,' added Rosie miserably. 'That and him kissing Carmen.'

Liam's anger suddenly shifted into irrational, inappropriate elation that he pushed down. 'The man's a moron.'

'He is, a bit.' She tried to giggle but it came out all strangled and strange, and Liam's mood shifted again as a strong desire to throttle Matt overwhelmed him. He stood up once more, shook out his legs and sat back down.

'It must have been so difficult, finding out that man's your father.'

'It's been…'

When Rosie faltered, Liam put out his hand and covered hers. 'I can see why your mum didn't tell you.'

'She thought I was better off without him. She wrote to him, to tell him that she was pregnant.'

'So what happened?'

Rosie paused. 'The letter never arrived.'

'So he knew nothing about you? That's tragic.'

'Not really. I had a dad who I loved and who loved me in his own way, even though I wasn't his, and Mum and I got to live at Driftwood House my whole life. It wasn't so bad. But I want you to know that I honestly never mentioned your farm when I was talking to the Eppings about saving Driftwood House. I'd never do that. Not to you. Not to anyone.'

'I know.' Liam moved his hand from Rosie's and pushed his fingers through his fringe. 'I realised that when I'd calmed down. Also, Nessa rang and told me I was being – I think her words were *a total arse* to even suspect you of any wrong-doing.'

'That sounds like Ness.' She gave a shaky grin. 'There is one advantage to being related to the cold, heartless family who want to build a hotel on your fields.'

'Which is?'

'I find out before anyone else that they've gone off their hotel idea so your agreement with them will be renewed as normal.'

Liam's insides did a strange lurch. 'Are you saying there won't be a hotel at Meadowsweet Farm?'

'That's right. In fact, probably no hotel at all, anywhere.'

'Rosie, you're a bloody miracle worker!'

Liam leapt to his feet, pulling Rosie with him, threw his arms around her waist and whirled her around. She squealed and grabbed hold of his shoulders as they turned together in the sunshine.

They were both laughing when he stopped spinning and put her feet back on solid ground. She tilted her face towards him, her cheeks flushed and her hands still holding on tight to his shoulders.

He wanted to kiss her. He wanted to kiss her so much, and from the look in her eyes she felt the same. But she was leaving and, for the sake of his heart, it was better not to start something that would finish almost before it began.

When he dropped his hands and sat back on the wall, Rosie sat down beside him but further away than before.

'I guess people round here will discover my secret soon enough,' she said, quietly, after a while.

'Not from me.'

'I did wonder if you'd rush round and tell Belinda because you were so angry.'

'Can you imagine her face?' said Liam, keeping his voice light to disguise the catch in his throat. 'She'd collapse from the excitement of the juiciest bit of gossip ever, and also from the shame that your secret had gone un-gossiped about for years. But no, I haven't told her or anyone else and I won't. Nessa won't either.'

'Thank you. I'm not sure my local reputation as a weird, stand-offish snob could take the hit.'

'I'll trade you your reputation for mine as an arrogant ladies' man who got his comeuppance.'

Rosie laughed at that, proper laughter that made her eyes sparkle and her cheeks glow pink in the sunshine.

'That's not how I see you. At least not now.'

'Ouch.' Liam swallowed, knowing he was on dangerous ground but unable to resist. 'How do you see me, Rosie?'

She stared at him as though she was sizing him up. 'I used to see someone who joked his way through life and was arrogantly careless of people's feelings. But now, I see someone who's been horribly hurt and has lost his confidence and trust in others, but someone who's become a kinder and gentler man in the process.'

Liam blinked, bent his head and re-tied the perfectly tied shoelace in his trainer.

'How do you see me, Liam?' asked Rosie.

He sat up and took a deep breath. 'I used to see someone weird, a loner who didn't fit in and thought she was above anything to do with Heaven's Cove.'

'And now? Please don't tell me I'm exactly the same, not after the few weeks I've just had.'

He laughed at that, noticing the strands of hair that had fallen from her ponytail and were framing her lovely face. 'Now, I see someone kind and empathetic who's strong enough to deal with surprises that would have felled other people; someone who likes her own company but is still one of us.'

'Even though it turns out that my father is Charles Epping?'

'I don't give a damn who your dad is,' said Liam, sliding his arm around Rosie's waist and bending his head towards her.

'And I don't care that you're leaving. I mean I do, but if I don't kiss you, Rosie Merchant, I'll go freakin' insane.' The words were out of his mouth before he knew what was happening. His heart would have to take its chances.

Rosie didn't move. Did she really want to kiss him or had he horribly misjudged the situation?

She looped her arms around his neck so suddenly, the two of them overbalanced and fell into the grass that edged the field.

'Oops,' she laughed, her arms still around his neck, and her body on top of his. And that was when he realised he'd been careless with his heart already and it belonged to her. It would hurt like hell when she left Heaven's Cove, but at least he had this moment.

'Hey,' said Rosie, 'before you kiss me, I have news.'

'I don't care.'

She arched her head back as he began to kiss the soft skin at the nape of her neck.

'You will care,' she gasped. 'Driftwood House is being turned into a guesthouse, and I'm staying to run it.'

'What?' He rolled over, on top of her, and pushed his hands into the grass to lift himself up.

'You heard,' she said softly, raising her hand and brushing a finger across his lips. 'It's all agreed with the Eppings.'

Liam frowned. 'Did you do that for me?'

'Wow, you are still just a tiny bit arrogant, aren't you?' laughed Rosie. She cupped his face in her hands and pulled him back down towards her. 'I did it for me, Liam Satterley.'

Chapter Thirty-Two

The battered Mini bounced the last few metres up the pitted cliff road and Rosie parked it at an angle, in a strange kind of homage to her mother. She'd promised the car to Nessa but offering to be her friend's unpaid taxi service for the foreseeable would, hopefully, soften the blow of her hanging onto it.

She got out of the car and brushed at the grass stains on her dress. Her lips were still tingling from Liam's kisses and, for the first time in ages, the fluttering in her stomach was because of excitement rather than sorrow. Her cheeks glowed at the thought of her and Liam, entwined in a field at Meadowsweet Farm. Rosie Merchant and Liam Satterley, whoever would have thought it? Neither of them, that was for sure.

She smiled to herself as she walked towards Driftwood House, now bathed in the setting sun. But the smile died on her lips when a figure stepped out of the shadows.

'You weren't in, so I waited. I hope that was all right.'

'Of course,' said Rosie, her heart pounding. 'Where's your car?'

'I left it in the village and walked. I thought the fresh air would do me good.' He sounded stilted and unsure. 'I know I've behaved badly, to you and to your mother, but can we talk? Then I'll leave you in peace, if that's what you want.'

Rosie gave the front door a hefty shove with her shoulder and stood back for Charles to walk past her. 'You'd better come in.'

The house was gloomy in the dusk and Rosie flicked on the hall light. They both stood still, the lightshade swinging back and forth in the draught from the closing door.

'Let's go and sit in the conservatory.'

She always found the view across the Devon landscape soothing, and her nerves were on edge. Charles followed her without a word and took a seat on the rickety sofa, next to the huge cheese plant Rosie's mum had grown almost from seed. Suave, sophisticated Charles Epping was gone, replaced by a man who tapped his foot incessantly on the quarry tiles.

'I don't quite know how to start.' He swallowed. 'I don't know what to say to the daughter I never knew I had.'

'Would it have made a difference if you had known? If Cecilia hadn't hidden the letter from my mum?'

When Charles closed his eyes briefly and frowned, deep lines scored his face. 'The honest answer is I like to think so but I don't know for sure. I'd already treated your mother appallingly so who's to say I wouldn't have continued to do so?'

'You treated Cecilia appallingly, as well. She loves you.'

'I know, and I love her, too.'

'Are you angry with her for hiding the letter?'

'Of course, she should never have done that. But I'm more angry with myself for ever putting her in that position. As I told you, Rosie, I'm not a good man.'

'That's no excuse.'

'I agree, however it's an explanation. I was weak when your mother needed me the most. I never forgot her and you might be pleased to know that I hated myself for a very long time.'

'That gives me no pleasure.'

Charles tilted his head and fixed his piercing blue gaze on Rosie. 'Then you are very like Saffy.'

Hearing him use her mother's pet name sent shivers down Rosie's spine. 'After all these years, why did you leave flowers on Mum's grave?'

'I was notified that the tenant at Driftwood House had died. Your mum's death hit me harder than I would have expected after so long and I felt I should mark it in some way, and then, soon afterwards, I find out about you.' He breathed out slowly. Behind him, lights in scattered farmsteads and houses were starting to come on. They glittered like stars in the darkening landscape. 'I'm sorry I wasn't around when you were growing up.'

How different her life might have been, thought Rosie, if Charles had been a part of her childhood. If he'd read her mother's letter and decided that 'doing the right thing' meant marrying the mother of his child, rather than poor, frightened Cecilia.

He'd soon have tired of living in shabby Driftwood House, so she'd probably have been brought up in his spooky house in the middle of Dartmoor. She'd have gone to a private school. No Heaven's Cove Primary, or the high school in the next town. No gossipy villagers. No Nessa. No Liam. The thought of never having met Liam made her catch her breath.

'I had a brilliant childhood, here with Mum and Dad in this house on top of the world. Or that's how it felt when I was little.'

Charles smiled at that. 'I'm glad.'

He looked around the conservatory, his eyes falling on a framed photo of Sofia, taken on a Spanish beach. The camera had caught her, in her blue swimming costume and tortoiseshell sunglasses, as she laughed at something Rosie said. She looked so beautiful and happy, Rosie had given her the framed picture as part of her present two Christmases ago.

'Didn't your mother ever tell you anything about me?'

'No, not even after my dad died. She never even told me that you owned this house.'

'Sofia completely cut me out of your lives.'

'She thought you'd done the same.'

Charles nodded and hung his head, weighed down by memories. And in spite of her antipathy towards this man, Rosie felt a pang of compassion.

'You weren't mentioned but she never forgot you. I only found out about you because of the mementos she kept.'

'That's kind of you to say in the circumstances. What do you think Sofia would make of me being here now?'

Rosie swallowed, close to tears. 'I think she'd be glad that the secret's out at last.'

'I truly hope so. Look, Rosie, I have no right to expect anything, but what happens next?'

'What would you like to happen?'

Charles rubbed his eyes, his face grey with exhaustion. 'I have no experience of being a father and I don't wish to take the place of the father you had. I know I never can and I don't deserve to. But I'd like to get to know you, at your own pace, if that would be acceptable.'

When Rosie nodded, Charles visibly relaxed and sank into the sofa. 'Cecilia told me that you've agreed to run Driftwood House as a guesthouse. I'm glad you're not going back to Spain, and I'd like to give you the house as a gift. It's not a bribe,' he added quickly, as Rosie started to speak. 'Driftwood House is mine to give away now I'm the head of the family and, whether you want to see me or not, Driftwood House is yours.'

'I can't possibly accept it.'

'Please. You must.'

'What would Cecilia think of that?'

'It was actually her idea, while we were discussing the future. I'm beginning to realise that I don't deserve her either.'

He pulled a handkerchief from his trouser pocket and blew his nose loudly while Rosie tried to stay calm.

'Thank you for your offer, but there's no way I can accept Driftwood House.'

'Why not?'

'Cecilia told me about your financial challenges and said income was needed from this house.'

'We might have to sell a painting or two. but you're my daughter and it's time I started acting like a father. I insist that you have Driftwood House. My solicitor is already drawing up the paperwork so I'll hear no more about it.'

Somewhere in the house, a door banged as Rosie took in the news. Not only was Driftwood House saved, it was also hers. A sense of peace wrapped itself around her heart as Sofia beamed from the photograph.

'Of course, with Driftwood House in your possession, you can sell it and move on if you'd rather. I don't think Heaven's Cove has always been to your liking.'

'You could say that.' Rosie smiled, thinking of all the plans she'd made in this very room to escape from the village. 'But I think I'll stay here and open my own guesthouse, if that's all right. This place will make a wonderful retreat for tourists, and it'll give me something to throw myself into.'

'Would your decision to stay have anything to do with the young man whose case you championed this afternoon?'

'Partly, but also I've been travelling for long enough and now it's time to come back home, where I belong.'

After Charles had left, Rosie walked through the gathering dusk to the cliff edge, spread out her jacket and sat down on it.

Tomorrow, she would tell Liam her news. She touched her mouth, still able to feel his lips on hers. He would be pleased she had even more reasons to stay.

Her mum too, even though it was too late for them to spend time together. The wave of grief that washed over Rosie was tempered by the knowledge her mother could finally rest in peace, now that her secrets had lost their power.

Her mum would have been so happy to see Rosie in love. *Fancy you hooking up with Liam Satterley. He'd better treat you right or he'll have me to answer to.*

Rosie laughed and looked back at Driftwood House. Light was spilling from the open front door and she could almost imagine her mother standing in the doorway, waving.

She turned her attention back to the dark sea. The sandy beach wasn't visible; only the white tips of the waves were flashes of brightness in the gloom. But Heaven's Cove was lighting up like a beacon. White light from the shopfronts of stores now closed, the colourful fairy lights outside The Smugglers Haunt, and there, on the edge of the village, a golden glow from Meadowsweet Farmhouse. She was home.

Epilogue

Three Months Later

'I didn't realise this many people lived in Heaven's Cove,' said Rosie, pressing up against Liam in the kitchen doorway so that Alex and Ella could squeeze past. The house was absolutely rammed with villagers.

Liam took the opportunity to slide his hands around Rosie's waist, as she'd known he would, and kiss her on the nose. 'Everyone's curious about what's been happening to Driftwood House. They're keen to see what magical transformation you've brought about.'

Rosie grinned. It wasn't so much a transformation as an upgrade. Driftwood House had kept what helped to make it so special. All the original features – from the pretty tiles in the hall to the stone fireplaces and picture rails – were intact, as were the cosy rooms overlooking the sea. But the house now had an updated kitchen, refurbished bathrooms, and a new bedroom with an en suite in what used to be the attic.

The attic that had once housed clues to Rosie's past would now host guests at Driftwood House. The spiders and the mysteries had been banished.

It had been a hectic few months. A team of workmen had worked flat out for most of the summer, with Rosie's help and

Liam's too when he could get away from the farm. His mum and dad had also given a hand with the painting, when Robert wasn't wandering off or worrying about some non-existent appointment.

He seemed happy enough today, though, in his role as waiter. Dishing out drinks to people as soon as they came through the front door was keeping him busy.

'Get a room, you two,' laughed Nessa, wandering past with Lily in her best sparkly party dress. 'This place looks brilliant. You've worked wonders and I hear you've got your first guests booked in for next week?'

'That's right. A young couple from Birmingham booked online and are arriving on Tuesday. I'm really excited.'

Rosie ruffled Lily's hair. Never one to coo over babies or young children, she'd grown very fond of Lily over the last few weeks. She was even starting to understand the appeal of motherhood, however much Nessa tried to put her off with tales of broken nights and collapsed pelvic floors.

'Hey up, batten down the hatches 'cos Katrina's here,' murmured Nessa.

Liam gave Rosie's waist an extra squeeze. 'I know I'm irresistible but try not to fight over me.'

'She can have you,' laughed Rosie. 'Why don't you go and dish out some beers in the kitchen and I'll go and say hello to her?'

'Do you need a bodyguard?' asked Nessa.

'Thanks, but I think I can manage.'

Rosie took a deep breath and walked purposefully towards Katrina, who was standing at the open front door, as though she couldn't bring herself to step inside. They'd only met properly twice since she and Liam had become an item, and Katrina had been very off on both occasions. It was daft and it couldn't continue in such a small community. Rosie plastered on her best welcoming smile.

'Hi there, Katrina, I'm really glad you could make it to our opening party. Can I get you a drink?'

'Fizz or orange juice?' asked Robert, popping up seemingly out of nowhere.

'Is it champagne?' Katrina took a flute glass from Robert's tray and gave the bubbly liquid inside it a sniff.

'I'm afraid I couldn't run to the real stuff but it's nice all the same. What do you think of Driftwood House?'

Katrina looked around the hall, which was festooned with balloons and streamers. 'Old houses aren't really my thing. But it doesn't look awful.'

High praise indeed from the queen of mean. Nessa, eavesdropping in the corner, began to snigger and Rosie shot her a stern look.

'I hear that your very modern house at Bellesfield is lovely, Katrina, and I'm told you're very talented at interior design.'

Katrina stopped bristling and flicked her hair over her shoulder. 'I do have a natural flair for colours and furnishings.'

'Then perhaps you'd do me a favour and have a look around? I could do with suggestions for any last-minute improvements I could make.'

'Are we just talking about the house?'

When she gave Rosie's pretty jumpsuit a once-over, Rosie resisted the urge to inform her that it was a present from Liam.

She would be the bigger person here because she was happy and in love.

'Just the house would be great, thank you.'

'So let me get this straight, you're asking for my help?'

Hhmm, Katrina was really pushing it. Rosie's smile grew even wider.

'If you don't mind.'

Katrina nodded and pulled a small notepad from her Gucci bag. 'I don't mind at all. I'll make a few notes as an aide memoire. You could paint that wall over there an accent colour, for a start.'

Nessa sidled up when Katrina, already scribbling furiously, wandered into the sitting room.

'Are you going to do what she suggests?'

'Probably not, but it's good to get her on side, and she'll be so busy dissing the house she'll forget to have a go at me and Liam.'

'Crafty. You're good at getting people on side, aren't you? Talking of which, is your… is Charles really going to put in an appearance?'

'He and Cecilia said they'd call in if they got a chance, and I hope they will.'

It hadn't been plain sailing over the last few months since finding out that Charles was her father. Keen to make up for lost time, he wanted to spend hours with her, whereas Rosie, still mourning her mother, wasn't so sure.

But the two of them had met up a few times and Rosie had discovered they had some traits in common. On the negative side, they were both impatient, with a tendency to be judgemental – though Rosie's days of being judgemental about

Heaven's Cove and the people in it were over. But they also shared a sense of humour that Charles usually kept well hidden.

Cecilia mostly kept out of the way, but she'd become warmer to Rosie when their paths did cross. Rosie had definitely gone up in her estimation when she'd turned down the money Charles offered to do up the house and had arranged her own bank loan instead.

'Oh, my goodness! Look who's arrived,' yelled Belinda, rushing into the hall from the kitchen. The wine in her hand sploshed over the side of her glass and dribbled onto the floor. 'Charles and Cecilia Epping have just pulled up outside. How on earth did you manage to get them here?'

Rosie smiled. 'They've taken an interest in the house and the work that's been done.'

'Even though it turned out that the house didn't belong to them?'

'That's right.'

Rosie tried very hard not to let her face give anything away. Belinda wasn't daft, and she didn't quite believe Rosie's story that additional paperwork had been found which showed Sofia and David had bought the house some years before.

The Eppings don't make mistakes like that, she'd told Rosie. But she'd been assured that, on this occasion, they had, and they'd both be willing to tell her so should she need further corroboration.

'Are you ever going to tell her the truth?' asked Nessa, watching Belinda rush to the open front door.

'Maybe one day.'

'You do realise that finding out you're Charles Epping's secret love child will cause her head to explode?'

'Shhh, keep your voice down because I imagine a lot of people around here would have the same reaction.'

'Does he-who-shall-be-nameless want you to tell people the truth?' she whispered.

'I think so, though Cecilia's not so sure. Anyway, they've both said it's up to me.'

'That's good, so you can wait until you're ready.'

Rosie nodded, though she was still getting used to the whole idea and wasn't certain she'd ever be ready. She wasn't sure that her mum would want the village to know about her affair with Charles, and it felt disloyal to her dad. So it would remain a secret between them for the moment. A secret she was happy to keep.

So much had changed for Rosie over the last few months. Her mum was gone, she'd moved back home, and Matt had disappeared from her life completely, apart from a recent text saying he was fed up with Carmen and asking if their relationship could be rekindled. She hadn't replied. And then there was Liam.

Rosie caught his eye across the room and smiled. He winked back.

'Mr Epping and Mrs Epping, too,' boomed Belinda, suddenly, almost curtseying at the front door. 'What an honour that you're gracing us with your presence.'

Charles and Cecilia stepped into the hall, and Cecilia shot Belinda one of her best haughty glances – the ones that no longer made Rosie quake.

'Thank you for coming,' said Rosie, hurrying over. Charles had put on a smart grey suit in honour of the occasion, and Cecilia was wearing her best pearls. 'You've probably met Belinda in the past. She's a stalwart of the village and I doubt that Heaven's Cove could run without her.'

Belinda blushed and dipped her head as Charles and Cecilia shook her hand.

'Well,' said Cecilia, gazing around her. 'This place is looking very special, Rosie. Well done.'

'I'm sure that your business is going to be a great success,' added Charles.

Belinda narrowed her eyes when he bent and kissed Rosie on the cheek. She definitely knew something was up, but she wouldn't find out what from them.

'Hello,' said Liam gruffly, wandering over and standing so close to Rosie she could feel the heat from his arm against hers.

'Liam, it's good to see you.'

Charles held out his hand and Liam, with only the slightest of hesitations, shook it. The two had reached a kind of truce since Charles, with no fanfare, had reduced the rent on the fields at Meadowsweet Farm to the old level before the rent rise.

'I need to take Rosie away for a minute if you'll excuse us. My dad will get you a drink.'

As Robert plied the couple with fizz and orange juice, Liam linked his arm through Rosie's and pulled her through the crowd to the back door.

'What's going on?'

'You'll see.' He led her into the back garden and around the side of the house. 'Now close your eyes.'

'Why?'

'Just do it. You trust me, don't you?'

'Of course I do.'

She closed her eyes as he led her forward. She could feel the sunshine on her back and taste salt in the sea breeze.

Liam put his hands on her shoulders and manoeuvred her into position before saying gently, 'Right, open your eyes.'

She was in front of Driftwood House. Lily was standing by the door, holding a large picture she'd drawn. There was a big house with smoke drifting from its chimney and a stick figure with yellow hair, that Rosie took to be her. *Driftwood Guesthouse is open!* was painted across the top in big red letters.

'Mummy did the spelling,' she lisped.

Rosie laughed. 'It's wonderful, Lily. You're going to be a brilliant artist.'

Behind Lily stood Nessa and Alex, holding a piece of red ribbon across the doorway of Driftwood House.

'Here you go,' said Liam, thrusting a pair of scissors into her hands. 'We thought you should officially declare Driftwood Guesthouse open.'

'Wouldn't the Eppings as VIPs be better suited…?' began Belinda, but she was drowned out by Nessa shouting 'Speech!'

People crowded into the hall behind her to see what was going on.

'I don't know what to say.' Rosie looked at the faces turned expectantly towards her. If only one of them could be her mum.

She blinked away the tears that were threatening. 'Um, thank you for coming, and thank you to everyone who's helped to get Driftwood ready for its first paying guests who are arriving next week.'

'Hooray,' shouted Peter, one of the team that had carried out all the work. The other team members were in the kitchen enjoying the beer, the last time Rosie looked.

She took a deep breath. 'I came back to Heaven's Cove a few months ago not under the best of circumstances, and I didn't think I would stay. I was determined not to stay, in fact. But that was before I realised there was a lot to stay for.'

Rosie glanced at Charles Epping, who gave a slight nod, before she turned and smiled up at Liam. 'So thanks all of you for welcoming me back to Heaven's Cove, and I hope that Driftwood Guesthouse will bring in lots of tourists to enjoy our wonderful village, and to spend loads of money in our local shops.'

That elicited another cheer.

'I lost such a lot when my mum died.' Rosie swallowed. 'But I've gained a great deal too, and I know she'd be so happy to see her beloved Driftwood House survive and thrive.' She brandished the scissors. 'So I guess there's nothing more to do except cut the ribbon.' She caught the ribbon in the teeth of the scissors and snipped. 'I now declare Driftwood Guesthouse well and truly open for business.'

Liam scooped her up into his arms as everyone cheered and clapped. And for the first time ever, Rose felt she truly belonged in this special village. That was her mum's legacy to her.

'I'm so proud of you,' Liam whispered, stepping with her in his arms over the threshold of Driftwood House. 'Welcome back home, my darling Rosie.'

A Letter from Liz

You've reached the end of *Secrets at the Last House Before the Sea* – thanks so much for reading it. I've loved creating a close-knit community on the beautiful Devon coast and rather wish I could move to Heaven's Cove myself. Writing this book has helped get me through the pandemic lockdown, and I hope, in turn, that it's given you a few hours of enjoyment and escapism.

My next book, which I'm writing now, is also set in Heaven's Cove, at the height of summer. I'm introducing lots of new characters to the village, but a few old favourites will be popping in too. You can find out when that book will be published by signing up at the following link. We won't ever share your email address and you can unsubscribe any time you like.

www.bookouture.com/liz-eeles

I'll be posting updates on how the writing of the next Heaven's Cove book is going on social media, along with other writing stuff and lots of photos. So do stop by and say hello if you get a chance. The links to my Facebook page, Twitter/X and Instagram are all at the end of this letter.

Finally, before signing off, can I ask a quick favour? If you did enjoy *Secrets at the Last House Before the Sea*, it would be great if you could post a review, which might encourage new readers to visit Heaven's Cove. It doesn't need to take up a lot of your time. Just a few words would do, and I'd really appreciate it. Thank you.

Until next time, take care and happy reading!
Liz x

lizeelesauthor

@lizeelesauthor

lizeelesauthor

www.lizeeles.com

Acknowledgements

Thank you to everyone who's helped along the way to wrestle this book out of my head, onto the page and into the world. In particular, a heartfelt thank you to: my publisher Bookouture – it was my lucky day when our paths crossed four years ago; my wonderful editor, Ellen Gleeson, who has championed this book from the start and been endlessly insightful and encouraging; and my family and friends for being supportive about my books and so many other things besides.

Publishing Team

Turning a manuscript into a book requires the efforts of many people. The publishing team at Bookouture would like to acknowledge everyone who contributed to this publication.

Commercial
Lauren Morrissette
Hannah Richmond
Imogen Allport

Cover design
Eileen Carey

Data and analysis
Mark Alder
Mohamed Bussuri

Editorial
Ellen Gleeson
Nadia Michael

Copyeditor
Jennie Ayres

Proofreader
Becca Allen

Marketing
Alex Crow
Melanie Price
Occy Carr
Cíara Rosney
Martyna Młynarska

Operations and distribution
Marina Valles
Stephanie Straub

Production
Hannah Snetsinger
Mandy Kullar
Jen Shannon

Publicity
Kim Nash
Noelle Holten
Jess Readett
Sarah Hardy

Rights and contracts
Peta Nightingale
Richard King
Saidah Graham

Sales
David Murphy
Jess Harvey

Typesetting
Ramesh Kumar Pitchai